A DOG
FOR
THE JOB

AUSTRALIAN
BARKERS AND BITERS

BY

ROBERT KALESKI

With Illustrations by Hugh Maclean

SYDNEY

THE N.S.W. BOOKSTALL CO. LTD

1914.

Fully set up and printed in Australia by John Sands Limited, Sydney

Inscription in a copy of Kaleski's *Barkers and Biters*.

A DOG FOR THE JOB

Australia's Cattle Dogs, their colonial and later history

Noreen R Clark

Publisher: Inspiring Publishers,
P.O. Box 159, Calwell, ACT Australia 2905
Email: publishaspg@gmail.com
http://www.inspiringpublishers.com

 A catalogue record for this book is available from the National Library of Australia

National Library of Australia The Prepublication Data Service

Author: Noreen R Clark
Title: A DOG FOR THE JOB
          Australia's Cattle Dogs, their colonial and later history
Genre: Non-fiction
ISBN: 978-1-922792-43-3
1. Australian Cattle Dog - Australia - History
2. Australian Stumpy Tail Cattle Dog - Australia - History

FOREWORD

Nearly 20 years on from the release of A Dog Called Blue, Noreen Clark has again demonstrated why she is the premier historian of Australia's cattle dogs and their forebears. A Dog for the Job picks up where A Dog Called Blue left off in 2003. Noreen humbly acknowledges the misguided deductions of both herself and others in earlier publications.

Noreen's depth of breed knowledge as a former long time breeder of Australian Cattle Dogs, alongside her professionally developed skills both as scientist and librarian, has allowed her to access, interpret and verify information with a thoroughness not previously achieved. She has dispelled some entrenched myths and provided a much clearer overall picture of the development of Australian Cattle Dogs and Australian Stumpy Tail Cattle Dogs. Further, by considering the societal structure and lifestyle of the colonial period, Noreen has been able to give insight into the evolution of the ancestors of the modern Australian Cattle Dog and Australian Stumpy Tail Cattle Dog.

Noreen's analysis of the writings of Robert Kaleski and the comparison of his earlier works to those of his latter years (post 1920s) is overdue. She disproves unlikely assertions, such as the Dalmatian infusion in the breed foundation, along with the mistaken belief that the Australian Cattle Dog and Australian Stumpy Tail Cattle Dog do not share a common ancestry. Her summation chapter "Gathering the threads" is essential reading.

I remain in awe of the effort that Noreen has devoted to rectifying the questionable and out of date. *"When you have eliminated the impossible, whatever remains, however improbable, must be the truth."* A Dog for the Job proves this.

Connie Redhead
Landmaster Australian Cattle Dog Kennels

CONTENTS

ACKNOWLEDGEMENTS

A Dog for the Job grew from *A Dog Called Blue*. At first, not a particularly robust plant, but it gained strength and vigour as time went on from the generous support and encouragement given it by:

Stella Carpenter	Gitte Johannessen
Barbara Coder	Graham Rigby
Margaret Davis	Sue Sommerlad
Sue Dickerson	Kath Williamson (Scholtes)

and particularly by Helen Hewson-Fruend (1938-2007) and A. J. (Bert) Howard (1927-2022).

IMAGE CREDITS

Photos

Sue Dickerson: *Tirlta Peace of Mind*; *Tirlta Dartbrook*.

C. B. George: *Tisiphone, Eurydice*; *Minos*.

David Hancock: Blue working dog of a type found in Britain c.1990.

Iris Heale: *Gibson Lady Blue*; *Hillview Brighton Boy*; *Sunny Boy*; *Glen Iris Red Ember*; *Glen Iris Stumpy*.

Helen Hewson-Fruend: Repeat matings from dogs with different percentages of "blood" and the outcomes.

A. J. Howard: Halls Heeler, born c.1890; Working cattle dogs of probable Halls Heeler descent, c. 1940; Thomas Simpson Hall (1808-1870).

Peter Kaleski: Inscription in a copy of Kaleski's *Barkers and Biters* 1914.

Bernadette Merchant: *Woodglen Fire Tail*; *Ambajaye High Tail It*.

Graham Rigby: Tasmanian Smithfields.

Monica Shifflet: Cover of *Australian Barkers and Biters* 1914.

Hilton Sinclair: *Berrilyn Nettle* with foster kids; *Berrilyn Happy*; *Berrilyn Breton*.

Betty Southall: *Geraldmine Ugy Bear.*

Leila Watson: *Neangah Royal Mitzi*.

Kath Williamson (Scholtes): *Tirlta Wasting Light*.

Halls Heeler born c.1890 on Blairmore, a former Hall property. (A. J. Howard)

Publications

Calthorpe (formerly Dartbrook) House c. 1890. (Warner, R. M. 1990. *Over-Halling the Colony* plate 19)

Robert Kaleski (1877-1961). (Kaleski, R. L. 1933. *Australian Barkers and Biters*)

Jack (*Sydney Mail* 16 April 1898)

Rowdy and *Blue Fly*. (*RAS Annual* 1908)

Nipper (Sir Bedivere 1903. The Australian Cattle Dog. *The Town and Country Journal*. 9 September 1903, p. 34)

Floss (Sir Bedivere 1903. The Australian Cattle Dog. *The Town and Country Journal.* 9 September 1903, p. 34)

Danger (Rose, J. H. 1908. The Australian Cattle Dog, *RAS Annual 1908* p. 233-237)

Nugget (Kaleski, R. L. 1933. *Australian Barkers and Biters*, p. 81)

Silent Jack. (*Sydney Mail* 23 August 1922 p. 17)

Working cattle dog with possible Smithfield ancestry. (*Sydney Mail* 5 January 1927 p. 5)

Robert Kaleski's *Thornhill Tiger* (Kaleski, R.L *Australian Barkers and Biters* 1933 p. 79)

Some Rock. (*Sydney Mail* 18 April 1938 p. 30)

Nebo Rock. (*Sydney Mail* 22 April 1936 p. 38)

Nebo Rock. (Edwards, C. A. 1995. *Old Timers* 1995, p. 64)

Mrs W. W. Campbell. (*Sydney Mail* Wednesday 15 October 1930 p. 33)

Stumpy Tail Cattle Dog. (*Courier Mail* Dog Book, p. 8. Brisbane, Queensland Newspapers, 1938)

Little Gem. (*American Kennel Gazette* 1 September 1930)

Little Logic. (Kennel Control Council 1973. Dogs of Australia)

Oatley Peter. (Edwards, C. A. 1995. *Old Timers*, p. 239)

Young Autocrat. (Edwards, C. A. 1995. *Old Timers*, p. 238)

Bobby Blue. (Edwards, C. A. 1995. *Old Timers*, p. 240)

Logic Return. (Edwards, C. A. 1995. *Old Timers*, p. 64)

Trueblue Patches. (Edwards, C. A. 1995. Old Timers, p. 135)

Broombees Bobby. (Edwards, C. A. 1995. *Old Timers*, p. 201)

Wooleston Blue Jack. (Harling, D. & D. 1986. *Australian Cattle Dogs*, p. 69)

Wooleston Blue Jock. (Harling, D. & D. 1986. *Australian Cattle Dogs*, p. 65)

Wooleston Blue Jenny. (Kennel Control Council, 1973. *Dogs of Australia*)

Tallawong Blue Jenny (Hewart, T. 1973. *The Champions* p. 26)

Dustyroad Toby. (*National Dog Annual* 1983 p. 4)

Taits Glen Bonita. (Edwards, C. A. 1995. *Old Timers* p.186)

Taits Glen Susy. (Edwards, C. A. 1995. *Old Timers* p.186)

The Cur dog. (Bewick, T. A. 1807. *A General History of the Quadrupeds.* p. 329)

ILLUSTRATIONS

Ch *Nugget* [1908]

Silent Jack [1919]

Working cattle dog with possible Australian Smithfield ancestry

Robert Kaleski's *Thornhill Tiger* [192-]

Gd Ch *Some Rock* [1927]

Interstate Gd Ch *Nebo Rock* [1929]

Gibson Lady Blue [1929]

Gd Ch *Tisiphone* [1929], Gd Ch *Eurydice* [1933] and Gd Ch *Minos* [1929]

Mrs W. W. Campbell and Gd Ch *Miss Valentine* [1925]

Stumpy Tail Cattle Dog, illustration by Ian McBain

Gd Ch *Little Gem* [1926]

Ch *Little Logic* [1939]

Judge/breeder, Arch Bevis, with Ch *Bonnie Blue* [1942] and Ch *Kenwyn Tiger* [1942]

Ch *Oatley Peter* [1942]

KC & KCC Ch *Young Autocrat* [1942]

Qld Gd Ch *Bobby Blue* [1944]

RAS & CCC Ch *Logic Return* [1949]

Ch *Kalamunda Rex Regis* [1949]

KCC Ch *Neangah Royal Mitzi* [1949]

KC & KCC Ch *Trueblue Patches* [1951]

Ch *Hillview Brighton Boy* [1953]

Broombees Bobby [1953]

RAS Ch *Wooleston Blue Jack* [1954]

Berrilyn Nettle [1955]

Berrilyn Happy [1959]

Ch *Wooleston Blue Jock* [1965]

Ch *Wooleston Blue Jenny* [1967]

Berrilyn Breton [1970]

Ch *Tallawong Blue Jenny* [1973]

Ch *Dustyroad Toby* [1979]

Taits Glen Susy [1965]

Taits Glen Bonita [1962]

Working cattle dogs of probable Halls Heeler descent, c. 1940

Sunny Boy [1944]

Ch *Glen Iris Red Ember* [1973]

The Cur Dog, 1807
The Shepherd's Dog, 1807
A Scotch Bob-tailed Sheep Dog, 1807
Old English Sheepdog, 1897
Early engraving of the dingo, 1807
Halls Heeler born c.1890 on Blairmore, a former Hall property.

Coloured photos   **pages 116-121**

Thomas Simpson Hall (1808-1870)
Ch *Glen Iris Stumpy* [1990]
Gd Ch *Woodglen Fire Tail* [1995]
Gd Ch *Ambajaye High Tail It* [1999]
Blue working dog of a type found in Britain c.1990
Working cattle dog, Cunnamulla area, Qld. 2015
Ch *Geraldmine Ugy Bear* [1994]
Tasmanian Smithfields
T Ch & O Ch *Tirlta Peace of Mind* UDX, left, and Ch & O Ch *Tirlta
      Dartbrook* UDX
Tirlta Gem of the South
Tirlta Wasting Light
Rock painting of a dingo and ancestral figure
The Shepherds Dog and the Cur
The Dingo, or the Dog of New South Wales
Cover of *Australian Barkers and Biters*, 1914

PREFACE

A Dog for the Job draws on its predecessor, *A Dog Called Blue* (2003), but only for the period after c.1870. Discussion of the earlier period is substantially incorrect. This is how it came about.

During the early 1990s I collected Robert Kaleski's writings on Cattle Dogs, Sydney and Brisbane Royal catalogues, and Queensland stud books. I also had the ANKC pedigree database forAustralian Cattle Dogs, running under the Breedmate© pedigree application, to which I had added earlier litter registrations from Queensland, Melbourne and Sydney. (My database forms the basis of the database, Australian Cattle Dog Pedigree, https://www.acdpedigree.com/.) Beyond noting inconsistencies between Kaleski's early publications and his later ones, I didn't know how to address the Cattle Dogs' early development. Then a chain of curious coincidences led me to A. J. (Bert) Howard.

Bert, I was told by Hall family members, was expert on the history of the Halls Heeler, ancestor of the Australian Cattle Dog. He was also, as I discovered during many enjoyable visits, happy to share his knowledge with me for inclusion in *A Dog Called Blue*. But Bert took most of his information about Australian Cattle Dogs from the *Notes from the breed seminar* 1978(Australian Cattle Dog Society of NSW)[1] and Sanderson's *Complete Book of Australian Dogs*[2]. Neither drew on primary sources.

Fifteen years after *A Dog Called Blue*, I revisited Bert's Kaleski-based assumptions – soon to discover that the Halls could not have imported the Halls Heeler's British ancestors as Kaleski insisted, Bert's assumptions now crumbled but his advice to me was, however, excellent: "If you want to know how the dogs came about, you must find out what the people were doing," he insisted. Except that they existed and that the Halls depended on them, we know nothing about the Halls Heeler. We don't know much about the Halls, either. Although active in local public affairs, they did not seek prominence in the larger colonial society of which they were a part. They did not seek a place among the power brokers and the colonial gentry of the day but were satisfied with building a vast cattle empire. Unknowingly, they left behind them a unique legacy: a working dog that made a lasting contribution to Australia's rural economy, the Halls Heeler.

The Halls Heeler: the name was coined by Robert Kaleski and Kaleski became the authority on Cattle Dogs in 1903 when his breed standard was published. His authority was recognised when he was invited to contribute to *The Australian Encyclopaedia*. After the late 1920s, however, his writings displayed a lack of cohesion. Unsubstantiated facts and unexplained contradictions appeared, leading one to suspect a possible health concern causing this decline in mental capacity. There are, however, no relevant records so I have offered comparisons of his early and later writings in support. Although Kaleski's credibility wavered he was endlessly faithful to the Cattle Dog breed. Admiration and respect for his unflagging allegiance to Australia's working dogs is his entitlement.

The story is a complicated one with many interweaving threads. Chapter 17 "Gathering the Threads" summarises and collects the threads.

Noreen Clark
Inglewood
Michelago N. S. W.

"When you have eliminated the impossible, whatever remains, however improbable, must be the truth," said Sherlock Holmes.

(Sir Arthur Conan Doyle: *The Sign of the Four*)

INTRODUCTION

Dogs arrived in New South Wales with the First Fleet in 1788 and with other shipments of immigrants, both free and convict, in the years that followed. The early canine immigrants included working dogs – stock dogs – of one kind or another but not clearly identifiable with modern breeds. The concept of "breed" as we now understand it, did not emerge until after the 1850s when dog shows were invented. For the most part dogs were identified by their use and selected for their suitability to the job asked of them. Among the workers of stock were herd guardians and drovers dogs. Herd guardians were large, robust, aggressive dogs, capable of protecting cattle and sheep from marauders. As large, wild predators disappeared from Britain the need for herd guardians also disappeared but the Old English Sheepdog may be a descendant of such dogs.[1] Droving needed, not only a herd protector but a dog with considerable stamina. In his *British Dogs* (1888) Hugh Dalziel wrote, of the drover's dog:

> In all parts of England and Scotland I have seen drovers, and narrowly scanned their dogs, and I have come to the conclusion that no distinct breed can be justly described as the Drover's Dog ... the drover utilising for his purpose the kind of dog that comes most readily to hand.[2]

The New South Wales colonists, like the British herdsman and drovers of the time, also used whatever dogs came to hand and could do the jobs asked of them. The jobs were similar: control and protection of stock in small areas and droving, and protection of cultivated areas from wandering stock. Dingoes, aboriginal hunters and feral domestic dogs preyed on the colonists' stock, and wandering mobs of cattle trampled cultivated areas. The problem became extreme after Governor Macquarie began selling off government stock in the 1810s, on easy credit, to colonists. Until fencing became widespread, in the later 1820s, grazing stock were followed by herdsmen during the day and confined in yards at night.[3] Almost certainly the herdsmen used dogs to control the stock in their care as well as watchdogs, to warn them of approaching aboriginal hunters, escapee convicts and other dangers.

The early colonial working dogs included coarse-haired dogs similar in type to the present day Tasmanian Smithfield as well as the smooth coated, speckled or mottled ancestors of the two Australian Cattle Dog breeds. Ancestors of the Tasmanian Smithfield, a working breed with a strong present day following in Tasmania, may well have been one of the first stock dogs, or even the first, used in the New South Wales colony. The Smithie, as he is commonly known in Tasmania, may share ancestry with the Old English Sheepdog .

The Australian Cattle Dog is the dog breed that Australians most closely identify with – together with his cousin the Australian Stumpy Tail Cattle Dog. Not the Australian Shepherd Dog, an American breed except in name. Not the Australian Kelpie; he came later and more or less ready-made from Scotland. The Australian Cattle Dogs are ours. The Australian Cattle Dog and the Australian Stumpy Tail Cattle Dog share ancestors and early history. The two did not begin to separate into separate breeds until the pressures of the show ring forced recognition of two types: long-tail and short-tail.

The Cattle Dog story is bound up with the story of George Hall and his family, free immigrants to New South Wales who arrived in 1802. The first Cattle Dog breed historian, Robert Kaleski, even named the Cattle Dog's colonial ancestor after the family: the Halls Heeler. The Halls Heeler's European ancestors arrived in the same ships that brought the convicts their civilian and military minders, and the early free settlers to the colony. The dingo was already very much at home in Australia with some 6,000 years or more residence behind him but his ancestors and origins were very different from those of the newly arrived European domestic dogs. He was essentially a predator: a hunter, not a herdsman's or drover's dog.

The First Fleet sailed from Portsmouth, on England's south coast, on 13 May 1787, under the command of Captain Arthur Phillip, governor elect of the future colony. The public agenda was that the colony would reduce the overcrowding in Britain's prisons. A hidden agenda was that the colony might eventually facilitate British trade in the Pacific and there was also an humanitarian view: that the colony would offer felons a chance to rehabilitate themselves and become worthwhile citizens.[4] The storm-battered convoy straggled in to Botany Bay on 17/20 January 1788. Phillip considered the sandy, arid foreshores of Botany Bay unsuitable for settlement and, after exploring Port Jackson (Sydney Harbour) further north, established settlement there on 26 January. As well as offering magnificent harbourage, Port Jackson had a permanent water supply, the Tank Stream, and arable land. The Colony of New South Wales was formally proclaimed on 7 February 1788. The official ceremony was performed by Judge-Advocate David Collins and marked the formal beginning of the British colony with Phillip as its Governor. Collins gave thanks:

> Thus, under the blessing of God, was happily completed, in eight months and one week, a voyage which, before it was undertaken, the mind hardly dared venture to contemplate, and on which it was impossible to reflect without some apprehensions as to its termination.[5]

The route taken, via Rio de Janeiro and the Cape of Good Hope, was determined primarily by the prevailing winds and currents in the Atlantic Ocean. Eleven ships made up the First Fleet. They took animal cargo on board at the Cape, both as food supplies for the rest of the voyage and as foundation for future government herds:

> 1 bull, 1 bull-calf, 7 cows, 1 stallion, 3 mares and 3 colts, together with as great a number of rams, ewes, goats and boars and breeding sows as room could be provided for were loaded.[6]

Few of the First Fleet sheep survived but pigs, goats and poultry throve. The cattle escaped during the early weeks of the colony and were not seen again until 1797. By then there were several hundred of them and they were described as "ferocious" and "not to be easily approached".[7] The loss of Second Fleet cattle was high but, in 1795,

131 head of cattle were imported from India to form the basis of the government herd. During the following five years 296 cows were brought in from the Cape Colony and by 1804 the government herd officially numbered 2,000 head.[8] By 1818, the Rev. Samuel Marsden's herds were the largest in the colony and included cattle from recognised British breeds. Sheep remained in short supply and an embargo on the export of British sheep remained in place until 1824. Nevertheless some British sheep arrived earlier, either as gifts to individuals or as residual food livestock on various ships, uneaten during the voyage.

The low death rate among convicts on the First Fleet attests to the care given to the planning of the expedition in much of which Phillip was closely involved. Some 1,420 persons embarked of whom about 1,373 survived the voyage. In hideous contrast was the infamy of the Second Fleet two years later. Of the 939 male convicts and 78 females embarked only 692 males and 67 females completed the journey. More than 500 of those who survived the voyage, itself, were sick or dying on arrival. The mortality rate on this fleet was the highest in the history of transportation to Australia: a third of the convict complement on some of the transport vessels. The Third Fleet, in 1791, was less of a disaster but the cumulative effect of two shipments of convicts, with a large proportion of them in ill health, stretched the colony's limited food supplies. Governor Phillip complained to Lord Grenville, Secretary of State for Foreign Affairs, as strongly as he dared:

> Of the convicts mentioned by your Lordship to be sent out, 1,695 males and 168 females have been landed, with six free women and ten children. It appears by the returns from the Transports that 194 males, 4 females and 1 child died on the passage; and, although the convicts landed from these ships were not so sickly as those brought out last year, the greatest part of them are so emaciated, so worn away by long confinement, or want of food, or from both these causes, that it will be long before they recover their strength, and which many of them never will recover. Your Lordship will readily conceive that this addition to our numbers will for many months be a deadweight on the stores.

> The surgeon's returns of this day are: 'Under medical treatment and incapable of labour, 626 ... 576 of whom are those landed from the last ships.[9]

The Fourth Fleet is an informal term that collects the various convict transports after 1791 and includes the *Coromandel* that brought George and Mary Hall and their four children to New South Wales in 1802.

Phillip asked repeatedly to be sent immigrants with farming and trades experience. The first of them came in 1793 – five single men and two families. A later government offer, of free land in New South Wales to qualified settlers, was made in 1798. George Hall, and others from the congregation of the Wells Street Presbyterian Church in London, were among those who responded. It seems that intending settlers had to bring only themselves and their families, clothing and some of their personal possessions.[10] This group, later known as the *Coromandel* free settlers, had much to offer the colony but it was not until 1802 that the transport ship, *Coromandel*, dropped anchor in Sydney. On board, some with wives and children, were:

George Hall: carpenter/joiner, agricultural machinery.

Andrew Johnston: carpenter/joiner.

John Johnston: agricultural machinery.

James Davidson: carpenter/joiner.

John Howe: a grocer, from a rural background; "would wish to be employed in the Colony as a Teacher of Youth".

James Mein: carpenter/joiner.

Andrew Mein: carpenter/joiner; died during the voyage.

William Stubbs: trade unknown.

John Turnbull: tailor.

George Hall kept a diary during the voyage. Accounts of weather conditions, from dead calm to squalls, were enlivened by references to passenger and crew misbehaviour. Mrs Selby preferred the bed of Mr Donald to her own and her continuing activities provoked righteous indignation, not to say entertainment, for much of the voyage. Less amusing were recurrent quarrels (mostly petty) between members of the *Coromandel* group and insubordination among the crew. Tragedy, too, was there. George noted two deaths during the voyage, both from the *Coromandel* group, and he also remarked on the deaths of pet animals. A cat and a dog, belonging to *Coromandel* passengers, were thrown overboard during the voyage – probably out of spite – but this is a rare mention of what was certainly commonplace. Domestic pets were among the early immigrants to the colony and their presence taken for granted.[11] After his arrival in New South Wales George was too busy to maintain a diary beyond notes on daily tasks. He felled timber, probably as a building material, and built a hut for himself and his wife and children. Busy though he was, he still had time to help his *Coromandel* friends. The earliest entries are from Whittingham Farm, George's grant in Toongabbie. (Whittingham Farm was named for a village near Lorbottle where George was born.)

> Monday July 5th 1802
>
> Came out to Whittingham Farm with my 2 Men Fall some timber and build a Tent hut ...
>
> Monday 12 began Falling Timber ...
>
> Monday 19 Falling Timber by day and building Johnsons Hut ...[12]

The agricultural land at Toongabbie had been farmed to exhaustion by the time of George Hall's Whittingham Farm grant. In its place George was given a grant in the Hawkesbury Valley to which he soon added. By the time of his death, in 1840, George owned land in the Hunter Valley as well as in the Hawkesbury Valley and closer to Sydney, and after 1840 George's sons acquired more property in the name of the George Hall Estate. By the 1850s Hall lands extended from the Hawkesbury Valley in New South Wales to Surat in Queensland. Their full extent is not known but their area exceeded 4,000 km^2.

The end of convict transportation in the late 1840s and the gold rushes of the 1850s made the Halls increasingly reliant on their own family members for labour. Even more so the Halls were dependent on the working dogs that they had developed for their own use: dogs for the job of working stock on the George Hall Estate lands. Without the Halls Heeler (its development is credited to Thomas Hall, one of George Hall's most able sons) the Halls would have been unable to manage the enormous area under their control. The Halls Heelers seem largely to have remained in Hall ownership until the 1870s when the George Hall Estate properties, with the stock on them, were sold.

Dog shows were introduced in England in the 1850s and interest in them soon spread to the Australian colonies. Towards the end of the nineteenth century the descendants of the Halls Heeler – by then known as Cattle Dogs – appeared in the show rings of Sydney, Melbourne, and Brisbane, together with miscellaneous dogs whose only distinction was that they worked cattle. In the absence of a breed standard show judging was at the whim of the judge. Referring to a show in 1897 a columnist described the cattle dog entries:

> ... probably useful in working stock, the exhibits are out of place on the show bench as there is no standard to guide a judge in making awards in what are termed, in New South Wales, cattle and sheep dog classes. The animals comprising them are usually of a nondescript character ... It is only where working trials are provided and the particular merits of the dogs tested, according to the cleverness displayed by them in their work, that intelligent awards can be made. The points which the dogs may possess as show dogs cannot count, for they have none by which a judge can be guided in arriving at a decision.[13]

A few years later, in 1903, Sir Bedivere, a regular contributor to *The Town and Country Journal*, echoed these sentiments in an article entitled "The Australian Cattle Dog".

> Classes have been provided for cattle-dogs [but] there has been no definite standard of type, judges using entirely their own discretion in selecting those dogs for prizes which from their general outward appearance seem best qualified for working cattle. As a natural consequence, decisions are so varied, particularly at

country shows, that the only deduction which can be made from them is that any dog is a cattle-dog which can heel and drop, has the quality of silence, endurance for a hard day's work, coat that will resist grass seeds, well-built body, good legs, and small compact feet, with good pads ... Obviously it must be impossible to satisfactorily judge for all of these qualities, unless a trial is given, which is seldom the case. There are now, however, a few breeders whom this description would not entirely satisfy, and, thanks to their efforts, a definite type and considerable uniformity of colour is being evolved.[14]

Foreshadowed by Sir Bedivere an enthusiastic young Cattle Dog breeder and exhibitor, Robert Kaleski, published the first breed standard for Cattle Dogs later in 1903. Kaleski's identification of the Cattle Dogs' original "maker" accompanied the standard. He was the first, and only, Cattle Dog fancier to associate Thomas Hall with the dog breed that became so much a part of his own life.

This breed was first made, as far as I can ascertain, by a Mr. Hall or Wall, of Muswellbrook, about forty years ago. He imported the blue-gray Welsh merle for working cattle ... but crossed them with the dingo, and founded the present variety, which, by selection and careful breeding, became a distinct breed and throws true to type ...[15]

From this point on, the ancestry of the Halls Heeler was engraved in granite and not to be questioned. Nor were any of Kaleski's other statements about Cattle Dogs to be questioned, regardless of how absurd they were.

Kaleski was a prolific writer, and a very skilled and fluent one. His publications span some fifty-five years although he wrote very little after the late 1920s. He should always be remembered for his devotion to Australia's working dogs; it was unsurpassed. His scholarship, his knowledge of nineteenth century books on dogs, was also exceptionally thorough. After the late 1920s, however, Kaleski's writings on Cattle Dogs are so contradictory that they should be ignored. For reasons unknown (but possibly medical) Kaleski's memory and grasp of subject deserted him. This becomes evident if comparison is made between his early and later publications. Kaleski's article on Cattle Dogs in *The Australian Encyclopaedia* in 1958 is particularly misleading and contradictory but, regrettably, this article is one of those most commonly used as an authoritative source.

The distinctive speckle of exhibited Cattle Dogs such as *Nipper*, bred in 1899, set Kaleski to "burrowing" (his word) in British books on dogs, in the hope of recognising in them a speckled British ancestor for the speckled Cattle Dogs that he so admired. His burrowing was rewarded in publications such as Dalziel's *British Dogs* and Vero Shaw's *Illustrated Book of the Dog*. "Stonehenge" added to the story, in his *Dogs of the British Islands*. The several descriptions of a mottled or marbled "heeler" persuaded Kaleski that Thomas Hall had "imported the blue-gray Welsh merle" to breed from but Kaleski's perspective of dog breeding was that of the late nineteenth century with its emphasis on type and appearance as laid down in breed standards. In Hall's time, dogs, particularly working dogs, were bred to carry out a particular job, essentially for their working aptitude. Their appearance was unimportant. Convinced that the Welsh merle was a distinct breed as he understood breeds, Kaleski proposed it as the British ancestor of the Halls' dogs. He was equally convinced that the Halls Heeler was developed from a deliberate mating between the "blue-gray Welsh merle" and dingo but neither conviction can be sustained. A much more realistic scenario suggests that Thomas Hall found potentially useful working dogs among the strays that infested the colony and bred on with them. The dingo may have been a coincidental ancestor of the Halls Heeler but he did not contribute the Halls Heeler's heeling characteristics as Kaleski insisted. The Halls Heeler's European ancestors were nip-and-drop heelers: blue or red mottled dogs, some of which were naturally bob-tailed. They handed down to the Halls Heeler their nip-and-drop instincts.

Between World War I (1914-18) and World War II (1939-45) the Cattle Dog breed was in disarray. Competing breed standards had replaced Kaleski's and show ring exhibitors found much else to complain about. Kaleski, himself, was critical of many of the exhibits at the Sydney Royal, particularly of the heavier, shorter-legged types he saw. He described them as "piggy" in his review of the Sydney Royal entry of 1933.[16] Breed standards weren't unified until the 1960s but the Cattle Dog breed, itself, grouped behind *Little Logic*, his son *Logic Return*, and the influential *Logic*-derived *Wooleston* Kennels of the 1950s. Most, if not all, Australian Cattle Dogs now living are descended from *Wooleston Blue Jack*. The influence of *Wooleston* Kennels (and later, *Tallawong* Kennels) changed the direction taken by the Australian Cattle Dog breed but not by the Australian Stumpy Tail Cattle Dog. As an indirect consequence of decisions taken by the Canine Control Council (Qld) the Australian Stumpy Tail Cattle Dog developed independently of *Wooleston* and *Tallawong* lineages. The "Stumpy", as he is fondly known, remained closer in type to the Cattle Dogs of Kaleski's youth (*Nipper* and *Danger* for example) than the heavier, shorter-legged type favoured by Australian Cattle Dog breeders after World War II such as *Bobby Blue* [1944]. (Year following a dog name is year of birth.)

Questioned as individuals, many Australian Cattle Dog and Australian Stumpy Tail Cattle Dog breeders and owners reject much of the misinformed "information", derived from Kaleski's later publications, that "explains" the history and development of their breeds. This has not translated upwards through breed clubs to the Australian National Kennel Council's state affiliates and to the ANKC itself. At the international level the Fédération Cynologique Internationale may accept only information supplied by the of the country of origin and, as a result, the ubiquitous Dalmatian infusion, for example, is entrenched in the FCI standard for the Australian Cattle Dog. The Australian Stumpy Tail Cattle Dog, similarly, suffers from the "official" conviction that the short-tailed breed couldn't possibly be related, historically or genetically, to its long-tailed look-alike. The problem would seem to be intractable given that some of those who reject the misinformation in conversation perpetuate it on their web sites.

1

THE AUSTRALIAN DINGO

We Australians are proud of our unique country, particularly of the native animals and their marked differences from so much of the greater world animal population. Even our first dog did things the Australian way, arriving unexpectedly and late to the party over 6,000 years ago, but still late in comparison with his counterparts on other continents. Humans were already on the Australian scene when the dingo arrived. They settled over 65,000 years ago.[1] The dingo also chose his job. He agreed to be tamed, and to live comfortably with humans if it suited him, but not to be a fully domesticated servant to man. He was, and is, an independent soul.

Canids – the dog family *Canidae* that includes dingoes, wolves and domestic dogs – have been associated with man on every inhabited continent for perhaps 30,000 years but Australia is the one exception. Archaeological evidence, including bones and rock paintings, suggests that Australia's first canid was the dingo. The earliest dingoes arrived between 6,000 and 8,000 years ago, probably by way of the land bridge that connected New Guinea and Australia, and spread over the north-western part of Australia. These earliest dingoes were closely related to the New Guinea Singing Dog.[2] Later immigrants, from a related but different lineage, colonised the south-western part of the continent. They came with visiting seafarers at least 4,000 years ago. Dingoes became an accepted part of the aboriginal communities already in occupation. Indian mariners may have brought the later dingoes to Australia or perhaps the seafaring Lapita people who spread eastward into the Pacific from East Asia. Traders from Timor and Taiwan, who sailed throughout Southeast Asia, may also have brought dingoes with them. Recent studies, however, combining genetic data and archaeological evidence favour the Toaleans, a group of maritime hunters and gatherers from the southern peninsulas of the Indonesian island of Sulawesi.[3, 4]

Canids that lived with agricultural peoples developed multiple copies of the starch-digestion gene, AMY2B, in response to the starch-rich diet that they shared with their humans. A few canids, including dingoes, that lacked starch in their early diet, also lack multiple copies of this gene. This genetic difference between dingoes and most other canids tends to rule out seafarers from India, Taiwan and Timor. This leaves the Lapita and Toalean people. The Lapita were known for their pottery and for travelling with pigs and chickens. No evidence of Lapita pottery has been found in Australia – much less of Lapita pigs and chickens. Pigs and poultry didn't arrive in Australia until 1788 with the first of the convict fleets. This excludes the Lapita and leaves, as the most logical, the hunter-gatherer Toalean people of Sulawesi who were also notable mariners.

These later dingo arrivals were tame and coexisted comfortably with humans although domestication of livestock wasn't on the Toalean agenda nor that of other hunter-gatherers. Whether the dingoes were reluctant to endure more sea travel, or whether a few litters had increased their numbers beyond canoe capacity, or whether the Toaleans no longer desired dingo company is a matter for conjecture, but the dingoes left behind by the Toaleans probably formed close relationships with indigenous Australians soon after arrival. They were used to living with humans and sought them out. In time the dingo population grew. Eventually there were both "wild" dingoes and tame "camp" dingoes, some of the tame dingoes having drifted off into the wild, probably to whelp. Some of the later camp dingoes were taken from the dens of wild dingoes and reared as pets with a variety of roles including provider of warmth on cold nights, camp scavenger, and hunting companion. Dingoes may have contributed to the extinction of the Thylacine ("Tasmanian Tiger") on mainland Australia although it survived into the 1930s in Tasmania.[5] Dingoes never colonised Tasmania. Bass Straight became impassable some 12,000 years ago, well before the arrival of the earliest dingoes.

William Dampier – buccaneer, maritime explorer and writer – was the first to focus British attention on the Pacific region. His accounts of his voyages to the South Seas, published in 1697 and 1699, established him as an authority on the southern Pacific Ocean. In 1699 Dampier made landfall on the west coast of New Holland (Australia). His description of the land animals he sighted on the Australian northwest coast, in August 1699, includes the first recorded observation made by a European of a dingo.

> There are but few land animals. I saw some lizards; and my men saw two or three beasts like hungry wolves, lean like so many skeletons, being nothing but skin and bones ...[6]

Twenty years later Captain James Cook explored the east coast of the continent. The exploration party included the wealthy and influential English naturalist, Sir Joseph Banks, and his protégé, the Swedish naturalist, Daniel Solander. Solander's was the second dingo report, following Dampier's. Cook's *Journal* for 1 May 1770 notes:

> In the woods between the Trees Dr. Solander had a bare sight of a Small Animal something like a Rabbit, and we found the Dung of an Animal which must feed upon Grass, and which, we judge, could not be less than a Deer; we also saw the Track of a Dog, or some such like Animal.[7]

Banks described the same shore excursion and the "dog or wolf" tracks. His greyhound was probably the first domesticated dog to visit Australia.

> The Captn, Dr Solander, myself and some of the people, making in all 10 musquets, resolvd to make an excursion into the countrey. We accordingly did so and walkd till we compleatly tird ourselves, which was in the evening, seeing by the way only one Indian who ran from us as soon as he saw us ... We saw many Indian houses and places where they had slept upon the grass without the least shelter; in these we left beads ribbands etc. We saw one quadruped about the size of a Rabbit. My Greyhound just got sight of him and instantly lamd himself against a stump

which lay conceald in the long grass; we saw also the dung of a large animal that had fed on grass which much resembled that of a Stag; also the footsteps of an animal clawd like a dog or wolf and as large as the latter; and of a small animal whose feet were like those of a polecat or weesel.[8]

The *Endeavour* continued northward but went aground on the Endeavour Reef, part of the Great Barrier Reef complex, on 10 June 1770. The next few weeks were spent on repairs but Banks and others not involved in repair work explored the area. On 29 June 1770 there was another possible dingo sighting.

One of our Midshipmen, an American, who was out a shooting today saw a Wolf, perfectly he sayd like those he had seen in America; he shot at it but did not kill it.[9]

The midshipman may have been thinking of a Carolina dog which is similar in colour and type to a dingo.[10] The following day the second lieutenant "saw 2 animals like dogs but smaller, they ran like hares and were of a straw colour."[11] After that there were no more animal sightings. The *Endeavour* continued her voyage northward and out of Australian waters leaving Australia undisturbed by Europeans until 1788. The Australian dingo was very much at home when the First, and later Fleets brought with them the dingo's distant relations: domestic dogs.

Australia began as a penal colony, the colony of New South Wales, with the arrival of the First Fleet in 1788 under the command of Captain Arthur Phillip, its first governor. Journals, kept by colonial administrators and military, continue the story of man and dingo in Australia; in this case, of European man and dingo. An early colonial sighting of a dingo, a puppy, was described by John White, Surgeon-General to the colony.

[21 July 1788] The natives had with them some middling-sized dogs, somewhat resembling the species called in England fox-dogs. A servant of Captain Shea being one day out shooting, he found a very young puppy, belonging to the natives, eating part of a dead Kangaroo. He brought it to the camp, and it thrives much. The dog, in shape, is rather short and well made, has very fine hair of the nature of fur, and a sagacious look. When found, though not more than a month old, he showed some symptoms of ferocity. It was a considerable time before he could be induced to eat any flesh that was boiled, but he would gorge it raw with great avidity.[12]

White realised that these tame dogs, dingoes, were accepted members of aboriginal groups. The puppy would not otherwise have been allowed to eat of their kill. Late nineteenth century writers describe aboriginals hunting with dingoes on mainland Australia. The dingo came into his own hunting smaller prey such as bandicoots, small macropods (kangaroos and wallabies) and goannas, often hunting in the company of women, but he also helped the men hunt larger game.[13, 14] John Hunter, captain of the H.M.S. *Sirius* (flag ship of the First Fleet convoy) and Phillip's successor as governor of the colony, met with no more success than White in his attempts to modify dingo behaviour.

> Of those dogs we have had many which were taken when young, but never could cure them of their natural ferocity; although well fed, they would at all times, but particularly in the dark, fly at young pigs, chickens, or any small animal which they might be able to conquer, and immediately kill, and generally eat them. I had one which was a little puppy when caught, but, notwithstanding I took much pains to correct and cure it of its savageness, I found it took every opportunity, which it met with, to snap off the head of a fowl, or worry a pig, and would do it in defiance of correction. They are a very good natured animal when domesticated, but I believe it to be impossible to cure that savageness, which all I have seen seem to possess.[15]

White and Hunter may, or may not, have brought their own dogs to the colony but they were compassionate towards their dingo pups. For the dingo, the arrival of the First Fleet was the end of his unique position as the only canid in the entire continent of Australia. His future as a predator facing extinction was not yet in view. The Cattle

Dog historian, Robert Kaleski, however, idolised the dingo and was convinced that the dingo was an ancestor of the Cattle Dogs that he sponsored into the show world in 1903. A number of later twentieth century breeders, mislead by Kaleski's version of breed origins, believed it essential to infuse dingo into the breed.

2

NEW SOUTH WALES COLONIAL DOGS

The first domestic dogs to arrive in New South Wales came with the First Fleet in 1788 and the colonial dog population grew rapidly. The immigrant dogs included the ancestors of the Tasmanian Smithfield and the Halls Heeler. The ancestors of the Tasmanian Smithfield may well have been the first dogs used for stock work in Australia, herding cattle at pasture and bringing them home to their yards at night. Dogs in personal ownership are rarely mentioned in early colonial diaries and official records, the Governor's greyhounds being one exception and the luckless dog on the *Coromandel* being another but dog ownership was taken for granted and too unremarkable for mention by most diarists. By 1807, however, not quite twenty years after the First Fleet's arrival, the dog population was out of control and the Governor ordered the destruction of stray and ownerless dogs.

> The increase of Dogs in these Settlements having long been a great Nuisance, being at all times injurious to Stock, extremely dangerous to Children, and no less to persons on horseback, the GOVERNOR finds it expedient to recommend in the most decisive manner, that all Curs and other useless Dogs of every description be destroyed.[1]

And again in 1812, earlier decrees having been ineffectual or insufficiently enforced. The annual races, of course, were not to be imperilled by stray dogs.

> THE Extraordinary Increase of Curs and Mongrel Dogs of a base and worthless Description (not withstanding the Public Notice given on that Subject on the 11th of August, 1810), rendering the Streets of Sydney dangerous to all Persons passing through them, whether on Foot, Horseback or in Carriages, it is necessary

to call the Attention of the Inhabitants at large to the Redress of this serious Evil. His Excellency the GOVERNOR is therefore pleased to express a Hope, that the Inhabitants of Sydney will take immediate Measures for the Destruction of those degenerate and useless Animals, or at least for the Confinement of them within the Limits of their own Premises so as to prevent their continuing a public Annoyance in the Streets, and thereby do away with the Necessity for resorting to other more compulsory Measures for the preserving the good Order and Safety of the Town.

As the Annual Races will commence with the ensuing Week, the Inhabitants are particularity called on to secure such of their dogs as they do not destroy, so that they shall not Wander to the Course, where they will not only interrupt the Sport, but may also be productive of fatal Accidents to the Riders. During the Race Week, the Constables and their Assistants are strictly enjoined to destroy all Dogs of whatever Description which they may find on the Course, or within the Limits of the Racing Ground.[2]

Free men and women contributed substantially to the colonial population even though New South Wales was established as a penal colony. The free population included civilian administrators and marines (and their families and personal servants) and the earliest voluntary free settlers. The First Fleet escort vessel, H.M.S. *Sirius*, for example, arrived in Sydney with some sixty-odd marines (and wives and children) on board, and each of the other convict transport ships carried thirty or more marines.[3] The *Lady Penrhyn* transported forty-one marines, as well as 101 convicts and three marine officers. The marines and their families expected to remain in New South Wales for a few years. Some remained in the colony as free settlers; others left when their regiments were sent to a new posting (usually India). Especially for the wives and children of marines, dogs would have met a deeply felt need as companions in an unknown country, distantly remote from the "civilisation" they had left behind them. The gentlemen of the colony – the marine and naval officers, and senior government administrators – preferred sporting dogs appropriate to their social status, such as greyhounds. For other ranks in the marines, and their women folk, any dog would have provided companionship and security of sorts. The first free settlers, five single men and two families, arrived in 1793 and their numbers steadily grew.[4] Some of them, too, may have brought dogs with them, particularly those who intended to take up land and farm.

One of the First Fleet arrivals, Watkin Tench, a marine officer on the transport ship *Charlotte*, enjoyed kangaroo hunting with greyhounds. It was both a sport and a welcome addition to food supplies.

> Our methods of killing them were but two; either we shot them, or hunted them with greyhounds. The greyhounds for a long time were incapable of taking them; but with a brace of dogs, if not near cover, a kanguroo almost always falls, since the greyhounds have acquired by practice the proper method of fastening upon them. Nevertheless the dogs are often miserably torn by them. The rough wiry greyhound suffers least in the conflict, and is most prized by the hunters.[5]

Canine immigrants ranged from ladies' lap dogs to mastiffs. Bull Dogs were popular as was the sport of bull baiting. Occasional misbehaviour on the part of the ladies' pets provided entertaining copy for the *Sydney Gazette*.

> A little useless member of the tribe too delicately reared to put up with an ordinary fare was a day or two ago arrainged [sic] upon the capital charge of devouring sixteen fine young goslings, on suspicion of which an innocent cat had been accused and executed. But the example of such made no impression upon the little barbarous epicure, who having killed 15 without detection, was surprised in the very act of tearing the last to pieces.[6]

The "Curs and other useless Dogs" that troubled the New South Wales colony, as well as the gentlemen's greyhounds and other sporting or hunting dogs, had their origins in Britain. The term "Cur" was used to refer to a nondescript working dog, rather than to a particular type of dog or as a term of disparagement.[7] They were too unimportant to attract the interest of writers and publishers until the late 1700s. Nineteenth century England was, however, remarkable for an increase as the century progressed, in the volume and diversity of books published. Histories and travel accounts were popular, and also natural history. Thomas Bewick was a leader in the field with his celebrated *A General History of the Quadrupeds* in 1790. Sydenham Edwards' *Cynographia Britannica* appeared in 1800 and (published anonymously by W. Taplin) *The Sportsman's Cabinet* appeared in 1804. *A General History of the Quadrupeds* includes twenty dog breeds, or breed types, that the dog world would distinguish (at least by name) in the late nineteenth century including Beagle, Bull Dog, Dalmatian, Fox Hound, Newfoundland, Pug and English Setter; mostly breeds that were preferred by the British upper classes, particularly by the sportsmen. *Cynographia Britannica* lists only twelve. *The Sportsman's Cabinet*, as its name suggests, is limited to dogs of interest to its author (mostly sporting dogs), but Taplin also included the drover's dog or cur. The illustrations (they were wood engravings, some hand coloured) in these early nineteenth century publications are a tribute to the engraver. The text was not necessarily first hand information and, in many cases was not. Edwards used Bewick's material, with generous elaboration, and Taplin re-worked Edwards. The output of the canine press was a new publishing genre, "books about dogs", and its authors had few pre-existing publications on which to draw, except on one another.

Early nineteenth century dogs were identified primarily by the purpose or function for which they were used. The early publications described types of dog but the various types didn't necessarily breed true. The few exceptions include the gentlemen's hunting and sporting dogs, some with origins in antiquity. The modern concept of "breed" didn't dominate the dog world until the second half of the nineteenth century – after the advent of dog shows in the 1850s. With the insight of an acute observer, Bewick emphasised the variation seen among dogs. Only their basic anatomy was constant:

> Of all animals, the Dog seems most susceptible of change, and most easily modified by difference of climate, food, and education; not only the figure of his body, but his faculties, habits and dispositions, vary in a surprising manner: nothing appears

> constant in them but their internal conformation, which is alike
> in all; in every other respect, they are very dissimilar: they vary
> in size, in figure, in the length of the nose and shape of the head,
> in the length and direction of the ears and the tail, in the colour,
> quality and quantity of the hair, etc.

> To enumerate the different kinds, or mark the discriminations
> by which each is distinguished would be a task as fruitless as
> it would be impossible ... To an attentive observer of the canine
> race, it is truly wonderful and curious to observe the rapid changes
> and singular combinations of forms, arising from promiscuous
> intercourse, which everywhere present themselves.[8]

He made it clear in his "Advertisement" (his preface) that the dogs
he described and illustrated were, in most cases, representatives
of groups of dogs that were defined by function or purpose rather
than by type. Bewick chose "the most remarkable (that is, the most
noteworthy) of the different kinds", not particular types that were
distinguishable as breeds, in the modern sense: types that bred true.

> We have selected the most remarkable of the different kinds, and
> given faithful portraits of them, drawn from the life; and there
> are still others, not unworthy of attention, which might have
> been added; but to have noticed all the variations and shades of
> difference observable in the canine race, would have swelled our
> account, already large, and have left us too little room for others
> of equal importance, in a comprehensive view of this part of the
> animal creation.[9]

Bewick described one particular terrier as being "remarkable" but by
the 1880s more than a dozen terrier varieties were recognised in the
show ring.

The daunting "variations and shades of difference" are nowhere
more apparent than among eighteenth century British working dogs,
the heterogeneous group that included the shepherds dog and the cur.
The earliest working dogs in the New South Wales colony would
have came from this group. Bewick emphasised the dogs' working

characteristics, and who worked them and how, but said nothing about their appearance.

> THE SHEPHERD'S DOG. This useful animal ... reigns at the head of the flock ...

> In those large tracts of land, which in many parts of our island, are solely appropriated to the feeding of Sheep and other cattle, this sagacious animal is of the utmost importance. Immense flocks may be seen continually ranging over these extensive wilds, as far as the eye can reach, seemingly without controul: their only guide is the shepherd, attended by his Dog, the constant companion of his toils: it receives his commands, and is always prompt to execute them; it is the watchful guardian of the flock, prevents them from straggling, keeps them together, and conducts them from one part of their pasture to another ... This breed of Dogs, at present, appears to be preserved, in the greatest purity, in the northern parts of Scotland.[10]

Bewick's engraving of a shepherds dog and his accompanying text distantly suggest the Border Collie but was intended as an example, only. His shepherds dog, as described, was an example from a general "kind" that worked sheep, a group that later included the Border Collie and the rough- and smooth-coated collies when these, much later, became defined as breeds and recognised in the show ring. He was unconvinced about the cur but emphasised its value to those who owned and worked them, regardless of their appearance.

> THE CUR DOG is a trusty and useful servant to the farmer and grazier; and although it is not taken notice of by naturalists as a distinct race, yet it is now so generally used, especially in the north of England, and such great attention is paid in breeding it, that we cannot help considering it as a permanent kind. In the north of England, this [the cur dog] and the foregoing [the shepherds dog] are called *Coally* [i.e. black] Dogs. They are chiefly employed in driving cattle; in which way they are extremely useful. They are larger, stronger and fiercer than the Shepherd's Dog and their hair is smoother and shorter. They are mostly of a black and white colour; their ears are half pricked and many of them are whelped with short tails, which seem as

> if they had been cut: these are called *Self-tailed Dogs*. They bite
> very keenly; and as they always make their attack at the heels, the
> cattle have no defence against them ...[11]

The cur and the shepherds dog were used for different kinds of work
– the cur was a droving dog (a heeler, who "[made] his attack at the
heels"), the shepherds dog, a herdsman – but both were black, or
black and white, and were collectively known as "coally" or black
dogs, "coally" being a reference to black colour not to a type of dog,
the later colley or collie.[12] Their use distinguished them, not their
appearance. Bob-tailed ("self-tailed") dogs were not uncommon in
seventeenth and eighteenth century England and were, in fact valued.
A tax on dogs was introduced in 1786 but working dogs, identified
by docked tails, were exempt from the tax.[13] Owners of naturally
bob-tailed working dogs were spared the need to dock their dogs'
tails in order to avoid being taxed and owners of naturally bob-tailed
non-working dogs likewise avoided the tax.

Bewick also described a dog that was used specifically for driving
cattle, a drover's dog, and in doing so left behind a succinct statement
about British dog breeding practices (emphasis added). Working dogs
were bred for their utility, their purpose, not for their appearance.

> Similar to the Cur, is that which is commonly used in driving
> cattle to the slaughter; and as these Dogs have frequently to go on
> long journeys, great strength, as well as swiftness, is required for
> that purpose. They are therefore generally of a mixed kind, and
> unite in them, the several qualities of the Shepherd's Dog, the
> Cur, the Mastiff, and the Greyhound. Thus, *by a judicious mixture
> of different kinds, the services of the dog are rendered still more
> various and extensive, and the great purposes of domestic utility
> more fully answered.*[14]

Edwards was reluctant to assign a country of origin to the shepherds
dog because it was "so universally disseminated". He did, however,
give a detailed description to accompany his illustration. His
description of the cur plagiarised Bewick and it is not impossible
that Edwards' illustrations were also adapted from Bewick.

The Shepherd's Dog seen so universally disseminated, that it would not be easy to name the country to which it belongs. The useful obtains a universality, denied to that which is sought only by the idle for amusement, or by the great for pomp and pleasure. To restrain the flock on the pathless plain, and recall the bold straggler, to obey the commands of an humble and unlettered master, were not likely to procure distinction and a name; yet his properties, peculiar to himself and essential to the wandering shepherd, must have early spread his breed wherever the pastoral life prevailed. The Shepherd's Dog is about fourteen inches high, nose sharp, ears half pricked, coat moderately long, somewhat waving; thick about the neck and haunches, tail bushy with an inclination upwards towards the point, seldom erected; colour all black, black with tanned muzzle and feet, or black with a white ring about the neck and white feet.

The Drover's Dog or Cur stands higher on his legs, is larger and fiercer than the Shepherd's Dog; colour black, brindled or grizzled, with generally a white neck, and some white on the face and legs; sharp nose, ears half pricked or pendulous; coat mostly long, rough and matted, particularly about the haunches, giving him a ragged appearance; many are self tailed [i.e. bob-tailed].

Edwards was contemptuous of the drover's dog and had no idea of how much was demanded of him. Droving was "of little importance" and didn't demand a dog "of superior mind". He was a botanical and animal draughtsman from an ecclesiastical family and obviously had no interest in droving nor understanding of the difficulties associated with "urg[ing] tame cattle along a beaten path". Droving was of no importance to the social class into which Edwards was born.

Inferior agents are never used, but when affairs of little importance are to be carried on; it would appear to be even a waste of animal intelligence to employ a Dog of superior mind simply to urge tame cattle forward in a beaten path, higher properties being unnecessary, chance has produced the Drover's Dog, from probably a comixture of Shepherd's Dog, Lurcher, Mastiff or Dane; his restless manner, shuffling gait, incessant barking, vagabond appearance, and perpetual return and reference to his master, bespeak him incapable of any great design, or regular chain of action, and mark him complete mongrel; being of little value, his place easily be supplied in other countries by other mongrels, and he appears peculiar to England, being rarely found in Scotland. He is useful to the farmer or grazier, for watching or driving their cattle, and to the drover or butcher for driving cattle and sheep to the slaughter ...[15]

Taplin was also contemptuous of the "Drover's Dog or Cur", and of the human company he kept. Even so, he reluctantly admired the cur's working ability. The work, itself, was beneath his notice, not the dog.

This dog, though with some points of similitude, is both larger and more ferocious than the shepherd's-dog, to whom, in appearance, he evidently seems a kin. In colour, the cur is of a black, brindled, or of a dingey-grizzled brown, having generally a white neck, and some white about the belly, face, and legs; sharp nose; ears half pricked, and the points pendulous; coat mostly long, rough, and matted, particularly about the haunches, giving him a ragged appearance, to which his posterior nakedness greatly contributes, the most of this breed being whelped with a stump-tail. The simplicity of his exterior seems admirably adapted to the easy insignificance of his destination, as it would be neither more or less than a prostitution of ability, to employ a dog of superior powers and penetration in the trifling office of urging tame cattle forward, in a beaten-path, where both speed and energetic action are so little required.

The social distinctions of the time were rigid and the upper classes usually found the activities of the lower orders beneath their notice. This attitude carried through to their perception of dogs. The dogs preferred by the gentlemen were obviously of superior intelligence to those used by the farmer or drover and this intelligence should not be "prostituted".

This dog ... is seldom seen but in the hands of drovers, carriers, and travelling adventurers; for his use being solely appropriate to a single purpose, the breed is cultivated merely by the farmer, or grazier, to whom alone he's useful in watching and driving their cattle; as well as to their delegate, the drover, in driving their cattle to market, or sheep to the slaughter ... In travelling with cattle, if a drove become huddled together, so as to retard their progress, he resentfully dashes amongst, and separates them 'till they form a line, and travel more commodiously to each other. If a sheep is wild, or refractory, he soon overtakes him, and seizing him by the ear, or fore-leg, speedily brings him to the ground. The bull, or ox, he forces to obedience by baying and baiting, most dexterously avoiding their heels and their horns. This dog, in uniformity with the subordinate rustic with whom he acts, ranks but low in the estimation of society.[16]

There was little published about British working dogs of the eighteenth and early nineteenth centuries that pointed to future working dogs, except for the shepherds dog of Bewick with its distant Border Collie similarity and the several descriptions of the cur. They ranked "but low in the estimation of society".

In 1897 Walter Beilby published *The Dog in Australasia*, the first book on dogs to be published in Australia. Intended as a general source of information, particularly for the guidance of newcomers to the dog fancy, Beilby included chapters on kennel management, breeding and veterinary treatment, as well as chapters on some seventy-odd dog breeds. He emphasised, not surprisingly, the importance of imported animals and included pedigrees and photographs in most breed chapters. He, himself, bred Fox Terriers from imported stock. The breeds that Beilby discussed in detail include the Collie, the Old English Sheepdog and the Kangaroo Dog, but the extent of his personal knowledge of some breeds was variable. In Beilby's opinion the Collie was of particular value to the Australian colonies. His identification of the Kelpie as a collie variant is, however, an unusual one.

No breed of dog is so extensively used in these colonies ... and none is more necessary. The collie was one of the first of the canine race to be introduced for work by the early settlers, where he was required for work by the early settlers, long before the goldfields were discovered ... I think it most probable that the first were imported into Tasmania. I know that good working strains were brought from Tasmania to Victoria by some of the earliest settlers ... A strain known as the Kelpie, that came from the island colony, are still plentiful in many parts of the Riverina [southwestern New South Wales] and Queensland.[17]

Beilby also praised the Old English Sheepdog, which he identified as a drover's dog.[18] Known as the "bob-tail", the Old English Sheepdog could not be bettered for work according to one of Beilby's informants. Beilby also mentioned the kangaroo dog. Commonly a "cross of deerhound and greyhound" the kangaroo dog was "any large mongrel which can catch or assist in running down kangaroos".[19]

Between the early British dog publications (Bewick 1790, Edwards 1800, and Taplin 1804) and Beilby (in 1897) there was nothing in print that could shed much light on the early New South Wales colonial dog population. Bewick, Edwards and Taplin wrote of the British dog population whence the early New South Wales population came. Beilby described the same population as it was more than a century later, and as the show-orientated dog fancy saw it. The Cattle Dog historian, Robert Kaleski, attempted to fill the hiatus by identifying possible Cattle Dog ancestors from published descriptions. Kaleski also focussed attention on the Australian dingo but not as an object of hatred and contempt as Beilby did. Kaleski admired the "noble" dingo and was convinced (incorrectly) that the nip-and-drop heeling instinct of his Cattle Dogs was inherited from the dingo. The dingo also found its way into *Cynographia Britannica* and *A General History of the Quadrupeds*.

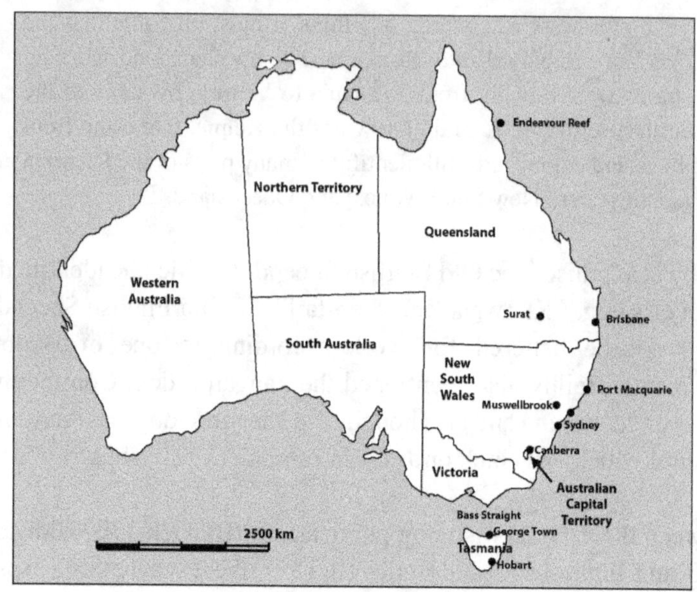

Reference map of Australia

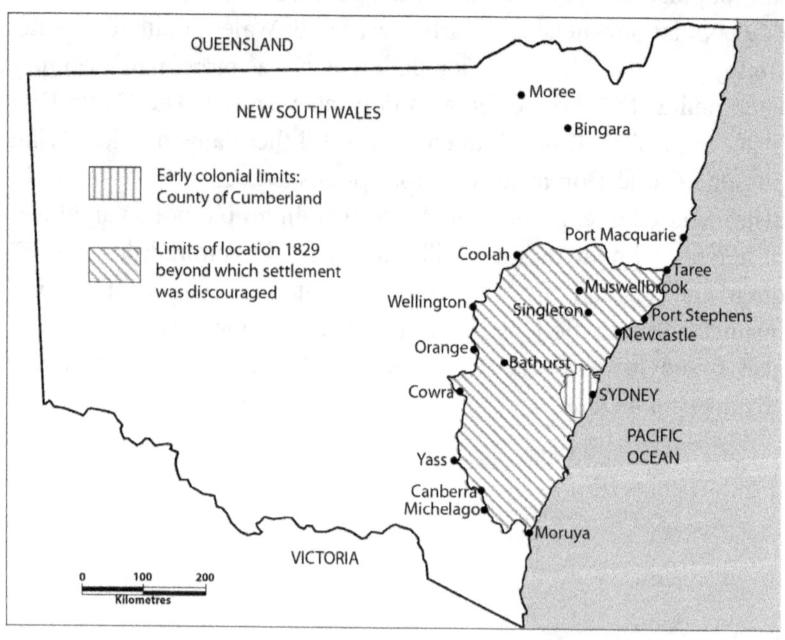

New South Wales showing the early colonial limits (County of Cumberland) and the limits of location, the "Nineteen Counties", established in 1829.

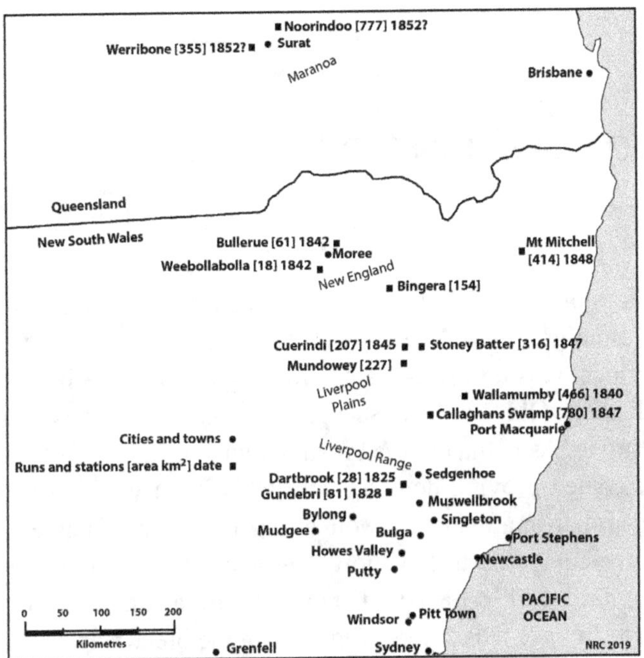

Locality map showing some of the properties held by the George Hall Estate in southeast Queensland and northeast New South Wales. Areas in km² and date of establishment if known.

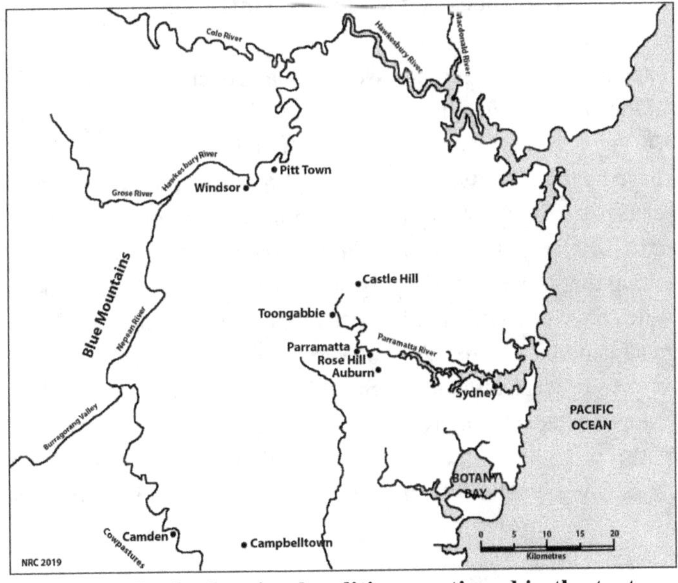

Sydney Basin showing localities mentioned in the text.

3

THE TASMANIAN SMITHFIELD

The ancestors of the Tasmanian Smithfield were among the first canine immigrants to New South Wales. The "Smithie", as he is known locally, is a coarse-coated working dog breed with probable (but distant) Old English Sheepdog ancestry. He has a strong following in Tasmania but the breed remains outside ANKC control. Coarse-coated droving dogs are still to be seen working cattle on the Australian mainland as well as in Tasmania. Their ancestors may have competed in the show ring against the Cattle Dogs that Kaleski described in his breed standard but, lacking the promotion that Kaleski gave "his" breed, faded from the breed ring.

In his *The Dog in Australasia* Beilby described the Smithfield cattle dog as a drover's dog of possible Old English Sheepdog derivation, offering a possible ancestry for the Tasmanian Smithfield.

> It seems strange that this, essentially a drover's dog, should so seldom be seen in our colonies, though occasionally animals bearing a resemblance to the dog named may be observed. There have certainly, not been any directly imported for many years past. I understand a few were introduced into Tasmania, and also Queensland, a long time ago, and it may be from this source that those occasionally seen in Victoria and New South Wales have descended ... In parts of Queensland, New Zealand, and Tasmania, I believe a few were bred several years ago, and for a time were known as "Smithfield cattle dogs" but of late years they have been bred out to such an extent as to show little of the original character, either in colour, shape, or coat. Of course the climatic influence upon the latter would soon assert itself.

> The "bob-tail" [that is, the Old English Sheepdog] is said to excel
> as a cattle dog, and for this reason he would be a great acquisition
> to certain parts of our continent, but, taken on the whole, I do
> not think he is a suitable animal for bush work, carrying as he
> does such an abundance of coat. He is far more suitable for cold
> climates, and would do much better in New Zealand and Tasmania
> than in Victoria, New South Wales, or Queensland. He generally
> gallops with his head down, having a peculiar springing style of
> movement, and his whole make and shape of body should strike
> one as being very much after the style of a bear ...[1]

It came as a surprise to Beilby that Old English Sheepdogs were not
in general use in the colony. He blamed climate for this omission.
"Animals bearing a resemblance" to Old English Sheepdogs could,
however, have been more numerous than Beilby realised and they
may have been descendants of early colonial immigrant dogs rather
than descendants of the later imports "a long time ago" to which
Beilby referred. That is, the [Australian] Smithfield, known to
Beilby, may have had ancestors among the early New South Wales
colonial dogs as well as, or instead of, early Old English Sheepdog
imports. Their earliest ancestors may have been found among any of
several, now-extinct, British working dogs including the Smithfield
Sheepdog (a shaggy-coated drover's dog).[2]

The Smithfield Sheepdog gave its name, and perhaps its ancestry,
to the [Australian] Smithfield. The [English] Smithfield was "like a
leggy Old English Sheepdog, usually sporting a full tail".[3] *Jack*, an
exhibit at Sydney's Agricultural Exhibition in 1898, was possibly of
this type. Betty Southall's *Geraldmine* Kennels would later become
well known in Queensland for working and exhibited Australian
Cattle Dogs but her childhood memories included a visit to her
grandfather's property in Ardlethan, southern N. S. W., when she
was "a little girl" (probably c.1920) and his Smithfield. She wrote:

> My grandfather, Mr William Elly, owned ... a Smithfield dog, the
> old black, rough coated, square bodied dog with a white collar
> and bob-tail.[4]

Southall's description of Elly's Smithfield recalls the photo used by Beilby to illustrate an Old English Sheepdog – as does Kaleski's description of the Black Bob-tail in his article in *The Bookfellow* (1907) and later reproduced in *Australian Barkers and Biters*.

> The Black Bob-tail was the first dog used for cattle in Australia; he was (and is) a big, rough-coated, square-bodied dog, with a head like a wedge, a white frill around the neck and saddle-flap ears. He got over the ground like a native-bear. Faithful enough, handy and sensible; but he couldn't stand the heat and long trips.[5]

Kaleski's reference to the Black Bob-tail's bear-like gait and heat intolerance also suggests familiarity with Beilby. His description of the Black Bob-tail may have been taken from Beilby's photo and not from personal observation although, like Southall, he may have seen Smithfields himself.

European settlement in Van Diemen's Land (Tasmania) dates from 1803. The Van Diemen's Land colonies, including Hobart (on the Derwent estuary) and George Town (on the Tamar River), were administratively part of New South Wales until 1825 when Van Diemen's Land became self-governing. The name change to Tasmania accompanied the colony's advancement to self-government. Until they became self-supporting the Van Diemen's Land settlements drew all their supplies from the mainland, including livestock – and dogs. Kangaroo dogs were particularly sought after. According to Beilby, a kangaroo dog was "any large mongrel which can catch or assist in running down kangaroos" but particularly a cross of deerhound and greyhound. Intending Van Diemen's Land buyers advertised in the *Sydney Gazette*.

> WANTED to PURCHASE for a Gentleman at a different Settlement, a good Kangaroo Dog, that must be warranted to kill and shew. A liberal price will be given.[6]

The forebears of the Tasmanian Smithfield also moved south from Sydney when there was need for them in the Van Diemen's Land settlements. Some families in Tasmania, including Graham Rigby's family, have been breeding and working Tasmanian Smithfields for several (human) generations. Rigby has compiled a Smithie breed standard, as a general (but not proscriptive) description of the breed.

THE TASMANIAN SMITHFIELD
Graham Rigby, Campbell Town, Tasmania.

The Tasmanian Smithfield is an all-purpose working dog found in all parts of Tasmania. The breed is not recognized by the ANKC. In the absence of an official breed standard, there is not complete agreement among Tasmanian Smithfield breeders as to what is "ideal" in the breed. There are also some strains that are less "pure" than others; relatively recent infusions of "non-Smithfield" are acknowledged by their breeders. If a breed standard were to be compiled for the Tasmanian Smithfield, however, there would probably be general agreement on the following.

General Appearance: Strong looking, long shaggy coat.

Characteristics: Should be alert, watchful, lively, friendly. Some can be late starters where working ability is concerned.

Temperament: Sociable, eager to please.

Head: Not overly broad, should be in proportion to the body.

Eyes: Brown.

Ears: Medium sized, usually hanging on side of the head, partly lifting when alert. Semi-erect ears preferred by some breeders, but never pricked.

Body: Should look in proportion, not overly long. Some taller, some a more solid build. Not leggy or short legged.

Height: Typically 50 cm at withers; body length approximately equal to height.

Tail: Some are naturally tailless; and incidence of taillessness seems to be increasing. Breeders are apparently selecting towards natural taillessness.

Coat: Good hair covering on the whole of body, legs, feet, head and tail. Length can sometimes vary but normally long and shaggy.

Colour: Because of the influence of other breeds, colour is variable. Colours most commonly seen include grey/blue, sandy/brown; some tri-colours and bi-colours. Breeders select for working ability and consider colour of little importance.

The Tasmanian Smithfield works most types of stock in varied working conditions – he is an all-round working dog. Smithies are equally at home working stock in bush country, paddocks, doing yard and shed work, also loading and un-loading Stock Trucks. They are not seen very often in Yard Trials these days due to their sometimes "more energetic" working style, which can run them foul of the rules that they are judged by. However, they get the job done just as efficiently as their more "robotic" workmates.

Of recent years, the Smithie has gained popularity as a family pet. His fun-loving, easy-going nature adapts well to the family home. This is a cause of concern as it may make the Smithie's future as a working breed precarious. Selection may become based on traits other than working ability.

A comparatively recent-comer to the breed, Matthew Larner, is one of the several Smithie breeders who are collecting pedigree records, supported by photographs. Larner also organises the annual Smithie Competition at the Campbell Town Show, an event with a large following of Smithie enthusiasts.

4

ROBERT LUCIAN STANISLAUS KALESKI
(1877-1961)

Robert Kaleski and Australian Cattle Dogs. The two are inseparable. Without Kaleski Australia's Cattle Dogs may have joined the Smithfield in obscurity. For more than a century Kaleski has been the unchallenged authority on the origin of the Australian Cattle Dog and other colonial working dogs. A dog enthusiast from childhood, Kaleski rose to prominence in the Sydney dog world when he published the first breed standard for Cattle Dogs in 1903. Later publications consolidated his position as an expert on dogs. Little else, however, is known about him. Kaleski's childhood was a fractured one. Much of his adult career was itinerant and in marked contrast to the professional and business interests of his siblings.

Robert Kaleski's father, John Stanislaus Kaleski, was an assayer[1] (Peter Kaleski,[2] pers. comm. 1995). At odds with local politics he left his native Poland and moved to Germany where he held academic appointments at the universities of Heidelberg and Bonn. With no hope of returning to Poland he emigrated to New South Wales. At the time of his death John Kaleski was an insurance agent.

A few of Robert Kaleski's childhood years were spent at Holsworthy (now a southwestern Sydney suburb but rural in Kaleski's day).[3] When he was 11½, so he tells us in his "Schoolday Reminiscences", he went to a school in Croydon (Sydney suburb, near Burwood). The school was "kept, run, or otherwise managed by the Rev. Joseph Newton".[4] School life was much to his liking until 1888 when the "Presbyterian Young Ladies' College" (now P. L C. Sydney) opened its doors opposite Newton's school. It seems that the young ladies had a demoralising effect on many of his school mates. Kaleski left

Newton's for the Sydney High School where he stayed until c.1893. The *Australian Dictionary of Biography* suggests that Kaleski began law studies but abandoned them in favour of "bush work". He did, however, attend Sydney Technical College and completed a course in agriculture in 1898.

Kaleski's inventive genius ranged from his settler's knife to a tip-wagon. The settler's knife (early 1900s) foreshadowed the Swiss Army Knife and Leatherman Tool, and his tip-wagon (1919) made an important contribution to bulk wheat handling. *The Sydney Stock and Station Journal* and *Country Life Stock and Station Journal* published his articles on agriculture regularly and he ran an information service from the offices of both journals, advertising that "All questions on agriculture ... will be answered in these columns."

Kaleski was passionate about native wildlife. Readers of *Smith's Weekly* and *The Sun* looked forward to sensitive and beautifully written stories such as "White Spot: the Tiger Cat", "Darkie: the Black Bream", and "Bronze-Wing: the Scrub Pigeon". His commitment to the environment was acknowledged when he was appointed Honorary Ranger under the Wild Flowers and Native Plants Protection Act. As a contributor to *The Bookfellow* and *The Bulletin* he enjoyed the friendship of prominent literary figures such as Dame Mary Gilmore, Henry Lawson and A. B. "Banjo" Paterson.

And then, of course, there were his many writings on dogs.

Kaleski's published work spans fifty-five years, from the Cattle Dog breed standard in 1903 to his article on Cattle Dogs in *The Australian Encyclopaedia* in 1958. The Royal Agricultural Society of New South Wales and the New South Wales Department of Agriculture accepted articles from him and he wrote prolifically for magazines and newspapers including *The Bookfellow*, the *Sydney Mail*, the *Sydney Morning Herald*, *The Bulletin*, *The Land* and *Walkabout Magazine*. *The Bookfellow*, a weekly, literary newspaper published in Sydney, launched Kaleski's career as a writer. The inaugural issue of *The Bookfellow* in January 1907 published Kaleski's 'The Australian Cattle

Dog: a champion breeder's account of him'. This, Kaleski's article of faith, was reprinted in various regional newspapers in New South Wales and finally in the new edition of *Australian Barkers and Biters* in 1933.

Australian Barkers and Biters – his bank manager suggested the title – is Kaleski's best known work. The first edition, 1914, was a small booklet with entertaining line drawings by Hugh Maclean. The 1914 text was substantially enlarged for the rare second edition, 1922, and sketches by D. H. Souter joined those of Maclean. This edition was not publically released but Kaleski revised the 1922 text for a new edition. This was published in 1933 with photographs replacing drawings. The new edition is the best known of Kaleski's publications. It was first reissued as a facsimile edition in 1987 by Margot Bakmain, Kaleski's literary executor.

Kaleski was highly regarded by the Cattle Dog breed fancy and his opinions sought and respected. In 1922 James Moore, president of the Sheep-dog and Cattle-dog Club of Australia, wrote:

> After I started the Sheepdog and Cattle-dog Club of Australia, one of the first things we did was to adopt [Kaleski's] standard as our guide. He then became a member to help us along and to give us the benefit of his experience, but holds no office of any sort. I might say that the Cattle and Sheep Dog Club of N.S.W. some years ago elected him as a life member in recognition of his services to those breeds.[5]

Kaleski's breed standard for Cattle Dogs (1903, reissued 1910) and *Australian Barkers and Biters* (new edition 1933) have earned him immortality but, at the same time, he is an object of ridicule. Although much younger than Kaleski, Tony Parsons (1931-   ), author and Kelpie breeder and historian, shared with Kaleski a common interest in working dogs. He described Kaleski as a "strange old fellow with some weird theories" whose thinking was rooted in the nineteenth century, not the twentieth, and who was preoccupied by similarities (Parsons, pers. comm. 2000). "He lived in a dream world", said Parsons. "He was not clear in his head and was losing touch with reality. He knew nothing about dog breeding." Parsons also wrote:

> For more than fifty years there was hardly a major publication that did not carry stories by Kaleski about the Kelpie and the Cattle Dog. He was an institution, and although scientists disagreed with many of his theories, he occupied an almost unchallenged position as an authority on Australia's working dogs. Much of what Kaleski wrote (and did) was of great value; the difficulty lies in deciding where he was right and were he was wrong ... I knew Robert Kaleski personally and I appreciated then, as I do now, how much he loved our working dogs; without him, the Kelpie and the Cattle Dog would have lacked an effective voice.[6]

Much of what Kaleski published in the first three chapters of *Australian Barkers and Biters* is demonstrably incorrect, but only in the light of research carried out since the book was published – almost a century ago. It is therefore inappropriate to criticise Kaleski's science from a twenty-first century perspective. As to his publications on Cattle Dogs Kaleski, admittedly, exaggerated the virtues of his Cattle Dogs and at the expense of other working dog varieties; but after all, the Cattle Dogs were very much his. Setting aside storytelling, however, a critical and chronological study of his publications (they span the years 1903 to 1958) reveals a discontinuity of thought and recollection: a date after which Kaleski's memory and grasp of subject became increasingly confused – very much as Parsons recalled. The discontinuity lies somewhere in the late 1920s, after he had finished the revisions for the new edition of *Australian Barkers and Biters* but before its publication.

Take Cattle Dog working ability, for example. Kaleski's descriptions in *Australian Barkers and Biters* and earlier publications (pre-discontinuity) tell of a dog that could work cattle almost without the drover's assistance. The dog needed the drover's help only with gates and slip-rails. After the late 1920s (post-discontinuity) a Kelpie infusion became essential because the Cattle Dog's working ability was deficient. Pre-discontinuity descriptions are generally consistent with one another. Post-discontinuity descriptions commonly contradict pre-discontinuity descriptions and often contradict one another as well. Kaleski's identification of Hall's supposed imported dog is another issue in which later versions conflict with earlier ones. Supposedly "new information" – "information" introduced later than *Australian Barkers and Biters* – also furnishes evidence for the discontinuity. The alleged Dalmatian infusion is the most pervasive piece of "new information". This infusion was attributed to the Bagusts who were closely associated with Kaleski from the 1890s or earlier. It was not, however, until 1935 that the Dalmatian infusion appeared in Kaleski's publications. It is reasonable to ask why Kaleski didn't remember the Dalmatian infusion until 1935, and why, in later publications (after 1933), the reasons for this unlikely infusion vary from publication to publication?

Recognition of this discontinuity – what it represents, and how it affects interpretation of Kaleski's publications on Cattle Dogs – resolves Parsons' "difficulty that lies in deciding where [Kaleski] was right and where he was wrong". Some medical or other trauma, the results of which first became evident in the late 1920s, seems to have compromised Kaleski's judgmental capabilities. Nothing relevant is known to the present Kaleski family to support this speculation except that, in his later years, Kaleski was described as "eccentric". Kaleski's memory and grasp of his subject material evidently deteriorated after the late 1920s as comparison between his pre-discontinuity and post-discontinuity publication show. Parsons (1931-) is not old enough to have known Kaleski until long after the publication of *Australian Barkers and Biters* in 1933. He never knew Robert Kaleski until long after Kaleski's mental processes became grossly impaired. Kaleski's publications on Cattle Dogs are critically reviewed, in chronological order, in Chapter 11 and reproduced in full in Appendix 1.

The text (but not the publication date) of *Australian Barkers and Biters* falls on the early side of the discontinuity, together with the Cattle Dog breed standard with its extended introduction (1903 and 1910), his article in *The Bookfellow* (1907) and his publication on Cattle Dogs in the Royal Agricultural Society's *Annual* for 1911. These writings are lucid – a declaration of Kaleski's admiration for his breed of choice and, indeed, his love of the breed that dominated his life and to which he gave so much.

5

KALESKI'S "BURROWING"

A century after Bewick published *A General History of the Quadrupeds* Robert Kaleski wondered where, in the British dog population, he might find the ancestors of his breed of choice: the Cattle Dog. He looked to the nineteenth century authors for guidance. Kaleski systematically "burrowed" (his word) in the late nineteenth century dog literature, looking for a British dog tht might have been ancestral to the Halls Heeler, the Cattle Dog's Australian ancestor.

The introduction and growing popularity of dogs shows – the first was held in England in 1859 in Newcastle-upon-Tyne – forced formal breed names, breed descriptions, and breed standards upon the dog fancy. Speculations on breed origins were also advanced and debated. Three major illustrated compilations, in particular, responded to what must have been an urgent need. John Henry Walsh, writing as "Stonehenge", published articles in the *Field* newspaper during the 1860s and these were reprinted several times after 1867 as *The Dogs of the British Islands*. Hugh Dalziel's *British Dogs* appeared in c.1879 and Vero Shaw's *Illustrated Book of the Dog* came out in 1881. New South Wales publishing caught up in 1897 with Walter Beilby's *The Dog in Australasia*.

During his search for the Halls Heeler's ancestors the Welsh collie attracted Kaleski's attention. He found useful references in Shaw and Dalziel and was even "acquainted" with the breed although his acquaintance may have been via Shaw and Dalziel, only, and not personal knowledge. Walsh included a chapter on "The Colley and other Sheepdogs" in *The Dogs of the British Islands* (1882). He made no mention of shepherds dogs but described the colley in detail with accompanying illustration. The shepherd's dog of Bewick had become the colley. Shaw particularly emphasised regional variation among the

dogs used by shepherds, variations that were driven by the need to suit dogs to intended purpose, and probably to terrain and climate, as well.

> In Scotland and the north of England, as well as in Wales, a great variety of breeds is used for tending sheep, depending greatly on the locality in which they are employed, and on the kind of sheep adopted in it. The Welsh sheep is so wild that he requires a faster dog than even the Highlander of Scotland, while in the lowlands of the latter country a heavier, tamer, and slower sheep is generally introduced. Hence it follows that a different dog is required to adapt itself to those varying circumstances, and it is no wonder that the strains are as numerous as they are. In Wales there is certainly, as far as I know, no special breed of sheepdog, and the same may be said of the north of England, where, however, the colley (often improperly called Scotch), more or less pure, is employed by nearly half the shepherds of that district, the remainder resembling the type known by that name in many respects, but not all. For instance, some show a total absence of "ruff" or "frill"; others have an open coat of a pied black and white colour, with a setter shaped body; while others, again, resemble the ordinary drover's dog in all respects. A mottled strain, one of which I have selected as the type of the smooth colley, is highly valued in the North of England and also in Wales.[1]

Dalziel, in *British Dogs*, also described a mottled, smooth-coated collie, the Welsh heeler.

> [The smooth coated colley is ...] in all points, except coat ... a facsimile of the more fashionable rough-coated ones, indeed, rough-coated and smooth-coated are often found in the same litter ... The mottled, marbled, mirled, or Harlequin variety are nearly always smooth-coated ... the Harlequin or mottled dog is often termed the 'Welch [sic] heeler'. The variety is, I believe, rather popular in Wales, but it is by no means confined to the Principality, but found scattered all over the United Kingdom.[2]

In his *Illustrated Book of the Dog*, Shaw admitted the Scotch collie, only, to the ranks of recognised working breeds, but drew particular attention to the mottled Welsh collie.

> There is one strain of smooth Collie which calls for particular attention, and that is the variety called sometimes the Welsh collie, and at other times the Highland 'heeler'. In colour this dog is a peculiar sort of greyish hue, to which the term 'harlequin', 'plum-pudding', tortoise shell', are all applied. He is usually found with one eye (sometimes both) 'wall-eyed' or 'China-eyed', which is a great additional attraction on the show bench ...[3]

Tenuous evidence but it appealed to Kaleski. His burrowing had been rewarded by descriptions of dogs with possible similarities to *Nipper* and other Cattle Dogs that he saw in the show rings of Sydney during the 1890s and early 1900s! The Welsh collie was a "mottled, marbled or mirled" dog, a "heeler" of a "peculiar sort of grayish hue". From these descriptions he inferred that the Welsh collie or heeler was known in the New South Wales colony and was the British import from which Thomas Hall developed the Halls Heeler. The "blue-gray Welsh merle" (with some variations on the name) became entrenched in Cattle Dog dogma, Kaleski Dogma, as the parent of the Halls Heeler and the Cattle Dogs' ancestor, with no more evidence than coincidental similarities turned up in Kaleski's burrowing. Kaleski also burrowed in Beilby's *The Dog in Australasia* (1897). He found support for his Welsh collie proposal in Beilby: "the collie was one of the first of the canine race to be introduced for work by the early settlers ..." but he ignored Beilby's contempt of the dingo and recommendation for its extermination. Kaleski admired the dingo and insisted that it contributed to Cattle Dog ancestry.

Kaleski's burrowing did not extend to the Hall family. He attributed development of the Halls Heeler to Thomas Hall of Dartbrook but never discovered more about the pioneering family whose enormous land holdings made them reliant on the dogs that came to bear their name.

1788   First domestic dogs arrive in New South Wales with the First Fleet.
George Hall applies for an assisted passage to New South Wales.

1790   Second Fleet arrives in New South Wales.
Bewick: *A General History of the Quadrupeds* published.

1791   Third Fleet arrives in New South Wales.

1793   First free settlers arrive in New South Wales.

1800   Edwards: *Cynographia Britannica* published.

1802   George Hall and the other *Coromandel* free settlers arrive in New South Wales.

1803   George Hall's first Hawkesbury Valley grant: 100 ac (40 ha).
First settlement in Van Dieman's Land.

1804   Taplin: *The Sportsman's Cabinet* published.

1807   New South Wales government proclamation, to destroy "curs and other useless dogs".

1809   1809-1828 all incoming mail to New South Wales posted in the *Sydney Gazette*. No mail for any member of the Hall family.

1819   John Howe's first expedition to the Hunter Valley.

1820   John Howe's second expedition to the Hunter Valley.

1821   George Hall's holdings now 1,500 ac (607 ha) in the Hawkesbury Valley.

1825   George Hall applies for 3,000 ac in the Hunter Valley.
Thomas Hall sets up Dartbrook.
AACo imports sheep, Shorthorn cattle, etc.

1826   George Hall now holds 4,040 ac (13 km^2) in the Hunter Valley.
Earliest date for Halls Heeler development.

1828   Thomas Hall: 1828 census: 4,700 ac (19 km^2), 700 cattle, 2 horses. 8 convicts.
Gundebri taken up.

TIME LINE 1830-1903

1830   George Hall's holdings now exceed 5,823 ac (24 km²).

1835   Dartbrook House completed.

1838   1838-1840 drought.

1840   George Hall (b. 1764) dies.
        Wallamumby run taken up.

1842   Bullerue run taken up.
        Weebollabolla run taken up.

1845   Cuerindi run taken up.

1847   Stoney Batter run taken up.
        Callaghan's Swamp run taken up.

1848   Mt Mitchell run taken up.
        Weribone run taken up.

1851   First gold discovery in New South Wales.

1852   Mundowey run taken up.

1859   First dog show: Newcastle-upon-Tyne.

1877   Robert Kaleski born (d. 1961)

1879   Dalziel: *British Dogs* published.

1881   Shaw: *The Illustrated Book of the Dog* published.

1882   Stonehenge: *The Dogs of the British Islands* published.

1897   Beilby:*The Dog in Australasia* published.

1898   *Jack* exhibited in Sydney as a cattle dog.

1899   *Nipper* whelped.

1901   *Floss* whelped.

1903   Cattle Dog breed standard published.

1903   *Danger* whelped.

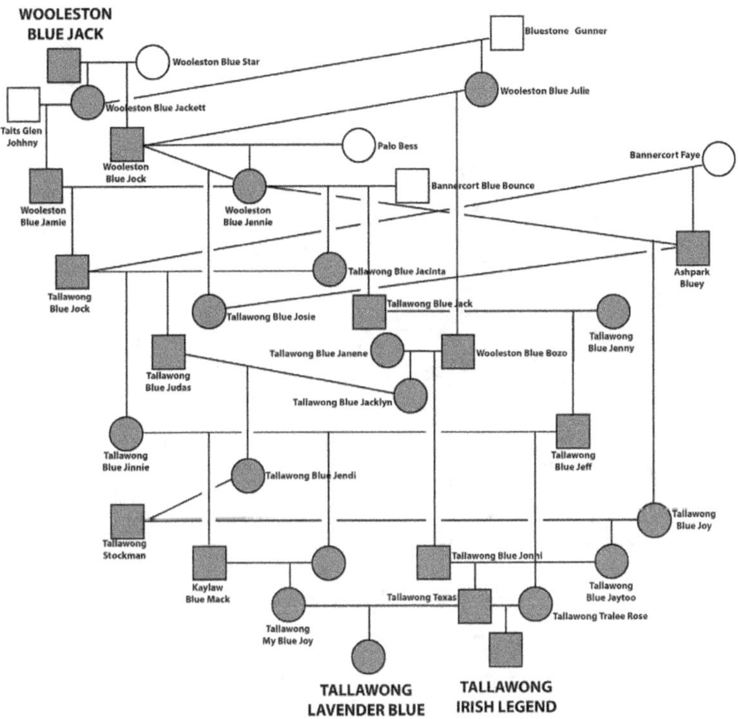

Family tree of *Wooleston Blue Jack* showing descent from *Little Logic*. Dogs shown as squares, bitches as circles. Shaded squares and circles show descendants of Little Logic.

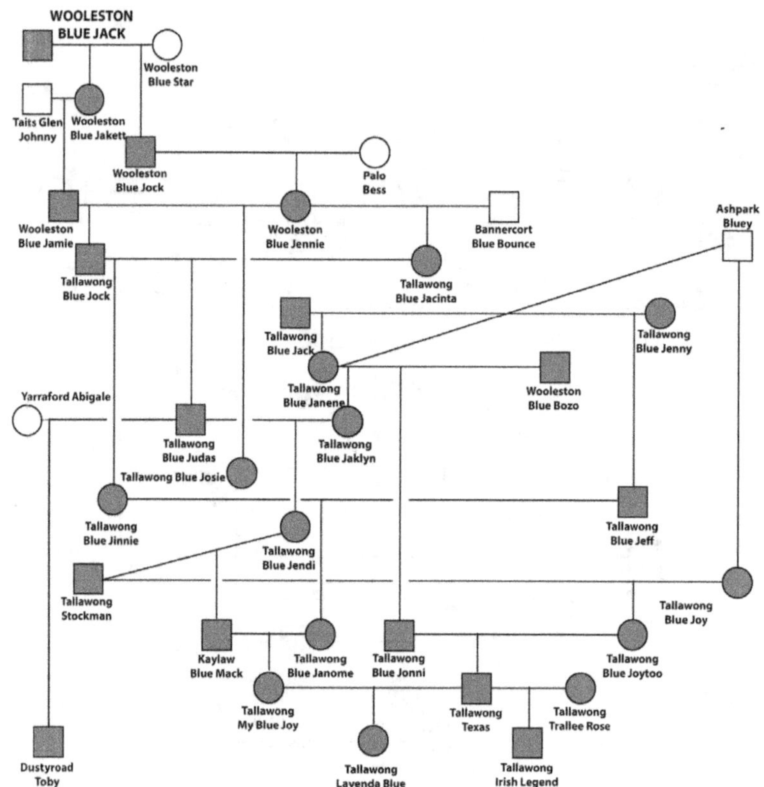

Family tree of *Tallawong Irish Legend, Tallawong Lavenda Blue* and *Dustyroad Toby* showing descent from *Wooleston Blue Jack*. Dogs shown as squares, bitches as circles. Shaded squares and circles show descendants of *Wooleston Blue Jack*.

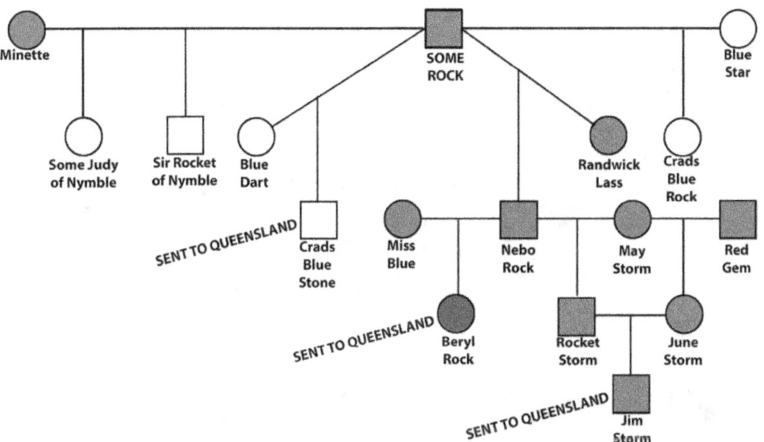

Part of the *Some Rock* lineage. Shaded circles (bitches) and squares (dogs) are animals born in New South Wales; open circles and squares are animals born in Victoria. *Some Rock* was one of the several New South Wales Cattle Dogs that made a substantial impact on the Cattle Dog populations of Queensland and Victoria.

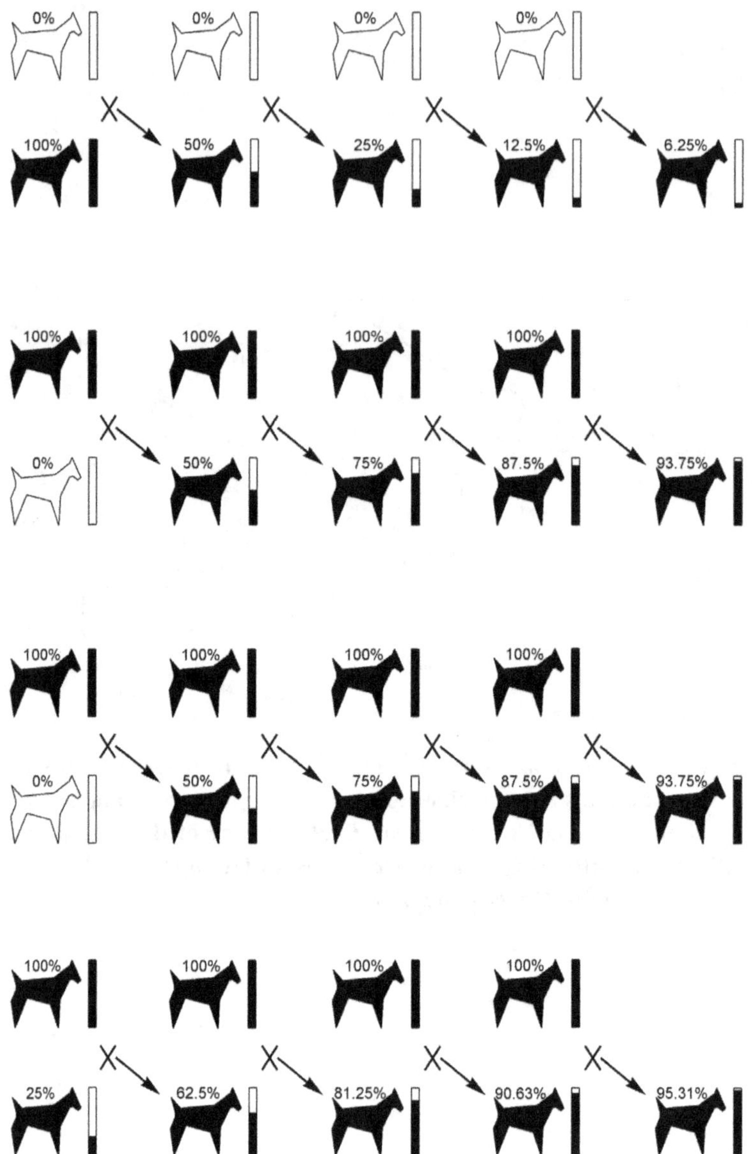

Repeat matings from dogs with different percentages of "blood" and the outcomes. Percentage "blood" was used as a measure of purity in the Stumpy Tail Cattle Dog upgrade program. (Helen Hewson-Fruend)

6

GEORGE HALL (1764-1840)

Kaleski identified Thomas Hall as the developer of the Halls Heeler but that honour may well belong to Thomas's father, George. It was immigrant George's ambition and thirst for land that founded the vast New South Wales and Queensland land holdings that were held in his name and inspired the development of the Halls Heeler for their management. The young George Hall left his native Northumberland in 1788, the same year that the First Fleet completed its epic voyage to New South Wales. With no thought of emigrating to a distant penal colony George set out for London carrying with him letters of introduction to Presbyterian congregations there and his trade qualifications as a carpenter and joiner.

The Scottish Presbyterian ministers, when George was a boy, came from Scottish kirks that had their own schoolhouses and schoolmasters and were noted for their own educational qualifications. Compulsory education for Presbyterian children after 1696 gave them a higher rate of literacy than was generally the case in England. Support networks between congregation and congregation developed to meet social change and particularly the effects of enclosure legislation and the Industrial Revolution. The young George Hall benefitted from the educational advantages available to him through his church and, in adulthood, from the Presbyterian support network in London. The effects of the Enclosure Acts and the Industrial Revolution shaped his life after he finished school.

It was usual for most boys in England, from George's social stratum, to leave school at the age of twelve. George's exceptional ability was, however, evident to his teacher and he was encouraged to attend night school for another two years. His school days were over when he was fourteen and he was apprenticed as a carpenter and joiner.

Later he completed another apprenticeship, in agricultural machinery, complementing his boyhood familiarity with agricultural practices. Despite his having grown up in a farming community there was little in the way of a farming future for George in Northumberland.

The London of the 1770s was growing westward from the City of London; a dynamic city, a city of architectural elegance and culture and of vigorous economic endeavour. George prospered. The housing shortage in London was to his advantage – his carpenter and joiner apprenticeship served him well – and he was able to build under lease agreements making him landlord as well as builder.[4] By 1791 his finances were sufficient to support a wife. He made a hurried trip home to marry Mary Smith, finalising a long understanding between them. Like George, Mary came from a farming background.

Meanwhile the New South Wales colony was in need of men with building trades and farming experience – skills that were missing in the convict population. A government offer of free land in New South Wales to qualified settlers was published in 1798. George was among those who responded to the offer in September 1801.

Intending settlers had to bring only themselves with their families and clothing and some of their personal possessions.[5] Identifying themselves with the transport vessel on which they eventually sailed, George and his associates became known as the *Coromandel* free settlers.[6]

George, Mary and their companions left England on 12 February 1802 and arrived in Sydney on 13 June. Their worst expectations could not have prepared the *Coromandel* settlers for the squalid little settlement that was Sydney Town. They were fortunate to be shipped to Parramatta (some 20 km up river) and thence to Toongabbie (another 10 km or so) soon after arrival, even if all that awaited them was the most basic of accommodation. George's diary records:

> Got all our luggage and families on board. Proceeded up the river
> and arrived at Parramatta in the dusk of evening. Had a large

> bread bag stole full of bread, meat and other things of value. Rum
> seized by the soldiers. Great trouble in getting our goods into the
> stores and saving them from being stole.[7]

The Sydney of 1802 was only a few hectares in area. It huddled around Sydney Cove and the Tank Stream, its water supply, and meandered westward along the Parramatta Road. Livestock wandered its streets and stray dogs were a public nuisance. Governor Phillip established the first government farm at Rose Hill, on the Parramatta River, in November 1788 and the township at Rose Hill became an administrative and market centre and the settlement expanded around it. In 1792 a new township was laid out further up Toongabbie Creek and Toongabbie became the colony's main food source. By the late 1790s, however, thoughtless cultivation had exhausted the Toongabbie farmlands and land clearance was under way at Castle Hill to replace them. Nevertheless, individual land grants at Toongabbie were made from 1794 and into the 1800s, and included those to the *Coromandel* immigrants.[8, 9] The *Coromandel* settlers were disappointed and dissatisfied with their Toongabbie grants and they were given farms in the Hawkesbury Valley on the north-west fringes of the settlement. George Hall's first Hawkesbury grant, in 1803, was 100 acres (40 ha) and two sheep. He took with him from Toongabbie his two convict servants. They had been involuntary passengers with him on the *Coromandel*.

George and his household were entitled to be "on stores" for three years, that is to receive government supplied basic victuals, but by 1805 his grant was self-supporting and his land holdings had increased. By c.1830 his self-declared assets included 1,050 acres (425 ha) by grant, 1,652 acres (668 ha) by purchase from other settlers, and 3,000 acres (1,214 ha) by purchase from the Crown (Dartbrook in the Hunter Valley). He was running 30 horses, 700 head of cattle and 150 sheep, and maintained a workforce of 10 free servants and 18 convicts. The earliest Halls Heelers probably worked George's stock.

The colony's population increased rapidly, both from convict arrivals and free settlers: 7,014 in 1802, the year George and Mary arrived in New South Wales; 10,682 ten years later; 19,595 twenty years later. (For comparison: some 15,000 spectators pack the stands around the Wimbledon Centre Court.) The colony's inhabited area increased, too, and roads followed in the wake of explorers. John Howe, one of the *Coromandel* settlers, was chief constable at Windsor from 1814 to 1821 and during his tenure discovered a route from the Hawkesbury to the Hunter Valley. By 1823 the route Pitt Town – Howes Valley – Bulga (originally known as Howes Track) was well-travelled. It was part (Putty Road) of the only land route from Sydney to Newcastle until 1930. The astute George would have been aware of Sydney's population growth and its implications for him as a primary producer. He intended to be a major contributor to Sydney's and other colonial dinner tables as the colony expanded. As soon as he was well established in the Hawkesbury Valley, he made plans for northward expansion, into the Hunter Valley and beyond.

George directed land acquisition and management from the Hawkesbury Valley until his death. When his sons reached adulthood they became his lieutenants, particularly William and Thomas. There is no evidence that George, himself, ever travelled north of the Hawkesbury Valley. He died on the night of 26 October 1840, his larger visions unrealised, on his way home from the Macquarie Arms, a public house run by his daughter Mary.

7

THE HALL EMPIRE c.1810-c.1840

The Halls, and other farmers who settled early in the Hawkesbury Valley, provided Sydney with almost half its food supply. Most of their produce was carried by boat down the Hawkesbury River and thence to Sydney. The Hawkesbury Valley settlers also depended on the river boats for supply of all goods that were not available locally. Tools, cooking utensils, medical supplies and milled flour; most came up the river from Sydney. Shipping movements were reported in the *Sydney Gazette* and watched with concern at both ends of the trade route. The condition of colonial roads did not encourage their use, particularly in the early 1800s, and the river trade continued until roads improved. A thriving ship building industry grew up on the Hawkesbury; sailing ships at first but, from the 1830s, steamers as well. George Hall was connected by marriage to one of the most successful ship builders, John Grono. George's oldest son, George Smith Hall, married Grono's daughter, Frances.

Lachlan Macquarie became the colony's governor in 1810. Inadequate roads and a shortage of cattle available on the open market were of particular concern to him. During his first tour of the colony Macquarie appraised the colony's wild cattle, the descendants of the 1788 escapees, and their potential value to the colony. Both of these issues had implications for George Hall's long-term planning and land acquisition. In 1810 there were roads, of sorts, connecting Windsor and Sydney but under Macquarie's direction they were upgraded to turnpike roads. The tolls may not have been welcome but the upgraded roads were passable to carriages (carriages could even pass one another) and to droves of stock. Improved roads were to George's benefit. His Auburn farms, bought in 1810 for their future value as holding and/or fattening paddocks close to Sydney's markets, were now connected by road (with military protection from convict escapees and aboriginal hunters) to his Hawkesbury Valley lands.

Macquarie estimated that 4,000 to 5,000 wild cattle roamed the Cowpastures area, south-west of Sydney. He recommended to London that no new intending free settlers be promised grants west of the Nepean River. Macquarie intended to preserve the wild cattle and facilitate their increase. A government edict, in 1812, made this clear.

> ...that no Persons whatever (excepting the Families of Messrs. McArthur and Davidson, and their Shepherds or Servants) shall pass over, or travel into the Country westward of the Nepean River, unless with a written Pass from HIS EXCELLENCY, or, in his Absecence [sic], from the LIEUTENANT GOVERNOR. The Public are further hereby informed, that the whole of the Wild Cattle grazing to the Westward of the River Nepean, being the Property of the Crown, are to be distinctly and clearly understood as such; and any Person or Persons who shall be detected in hunting, stealing, or killing of them will be prosecuted for Felony, and punished in the most exemplary Manner.[1]

The wild cattle were not of obvious benefit to the colony but Macquarie's reasons for preserving them later became apparent. A political agenda was at play: protection of John Macarthur's interests and the development of the merino wool industry. In 1805 Macarthur had been granted 5,000 acres (20 km^2) in the Cowpastures area, his future Camden estate. Later, in 1815, Macquarie began to build stockyards in the Cowpastures area to tame or slaughter wild cattle. Later still, between 1819 and 1820, almost 900 wild cattle were tamed and incorporated into the government herds and in 1824 the last of the wild cattle in the Cowpastures were removed so that Macarthur could take possession of 10,400 acres (42 km^2) of land at Cawdor (south of Camden) that he had acquired by grant and purchase.

A shortage of tame cattle for sale on the general market was also brought to Macquarie's attention. Government assistance was promised to those who felt disadvantaged by the high prices asked by established cattle growers and, in July 1811, Macquarie decided to sell off some of the tame government cattle to remedy the position. A public notice informed the fortunate.

> ... those settlers who have already obtained [the governor's] promise to grant them a proportion of horned cattle from the government herds shall attend at the Commissary's office on Monday, the 26th of August next, accompanied by their required securities, in order to perfect the prescribed bonds; on which occasion orders will be issued to the superintendent of Government herds to out them in the possession of the cattle so contracted for.[2]

Macquarie explained his decisions to the Foreign Secretary in London.

> The assignment of cattle which I have lately made from the Government herds to the old and newly established settlers have considerably reduced their numbers; but, notwithstanding this diminution, the horned cattle belonging to Government in the tame herds are not fewer than three thousand six hundred of all descriptions. The preserving of these tame herds I consider to be of the utmost importance, and, therefore, should, in my opinion, be persevered in for several years to come, as well for the benefit of the Crown as for the great assistance derived from them by the new settlers, who seldom possess the means of purchasing cattle from other individuals, who generally hold them, not only at high prices, but demand prompt payment; whilst, on the other hand, the settlers by purchasing from Government at a moderate price, and on a liberal credit, are enabled to acquire herds and wealth to themselves, and to pay Government at the end of eighteen months or two years, either in money or in kind, as may best suit their convenience.[3]

Another sell-off of government cattle went ahead in 1812.

> HIS EXCELLENCY the GOVERNOR having furnished the ACTING PRINCIPAL COMMISSARY with a List of those

> Persons to whom he has been pleased to extend the indulgence of drawing a certain Portion of Cattle from the Government Herds, on Credit, Notice is hereby given, that such of the following Persons as have executed the necessary Bonds are to attend on Mr. Jamieson, Superintendent of Government Stock, at the Stock Yard at Parramatta, on Thursday, the 1st of October next, to receive the said Cattle; viz. [28 names]. And such of the following Persons as have executed the necessary Bonds are to attend in like manner, at the Government Stockyard, at the Seven Hills, on Thursday, the 8th of October, to receive the Cattle signed to them; viz. [32 names incl. George M'Ginnis and Henry Fleming].[4]

George Hall didn't seek Macquarie's assistance but interests related to him did. Henry Fleming and George McInnis were both successful applicants. Henry Fleming married George's oldest child, Elizabeth, and the emancipated convict, George McInnis, would become George Hall's son-in-law twice over. McInnis was Thomas Hall's father-in-law, and also father-in-law of Thomas's youngest brother, Ebenezer. Macquarie again authorised sales of cattle from the government herds, in 1814 and 1816, but payment in kind ceased to be an option in 1816 because of unpaid debt. George Smith Hall and William Hall, George's oldest sons, were among those to benefit from the "reasonable terms" in 1816. Some two hundred settlers bought government cattle but a number of them defaulted on their repayments. Macquarie ended the scheme in1820.

During 1819 and 1820 John Howe, one of the *Coromandel* free settlers, led the expeditions that found a route from the Hawkesbury to the Hunter Valley: "Howes Track", the present Putty Road. Howe's journeys, they were no pleasure trips, foreshadowed droving difficulties between the Hawkesbury and Hunter Valleys should George Hall take up land in the Upper Hunter. The rich agricultural lands of the Upper Hunter Valley upstream from Singleton, and of the Liverpool Plains further north, weren't well known and fully appreciated until after "Howes' Track"[5] became a road. Singleton was established in 1820 but commercial transport to the area was mostly by water. The discovery of coal in Newcastle brought coastal shipping to the port on the "Coal River", as the Hunter was then known, and smaller vessels plied their trade upstream from Newcastle to the early Singleton settlement and surrounding grants. In 1824 surveyors followed the Hunter to its branches beyond Singleton, including Dart Brook, which they followed to its source. Their exploration took them as far as the Liverpool Plains. They reported enthusiastically on the agricultural potential of the Upper Hunter – Liverpool Plains region and realised that a continuation of the Putty Road would give good access to the region, right through to the Liverpool Plains.

> Two gentlemen who are attached to the Surveyor General's department, lately [1824] made an attempt, after they had completed the survey of some townships on the upper banks of Hunter's River, to trace that river to its source. They found that the river divided into several branches; and they succeeded in reaching the source of one branch, to which they gave the name of Dart Brook. The main branch of the river appeared to come from the Eastward. That which they traced came from the Northwest. The country which they passed over, particularly the flats on the banks of the river, are described as being remarkably rich and increasing in fertility, as they proceeded upwards.

> With the exception of the river flats, it is broken into a gentle undulation of hill and dale, moderately clothed with box and gum, but possessing, a rich covering of grass, so that besides being a fine sheep and cattle country, it is admirably adapted to cultivation. From Dart Brook they proceeded on to Liverpool Plains, across the dividing range which separates the waters of Hunter's River from the waters of the Western country ... They reached Dr. Bowman's farm, which is the highest on Hunter's River, on the third night from Liverpool Plain, having met with very little difficulty in crossing the dividing range, which is by no means rugged, and is for the most part covered with grass to the very summit. It is clear, therefore, that a road might be constructed from this part of the colony to Liverpool Plains ... without any difficulty and, in such manner, as to be but a continuation of the road from the Hawkesbury to Hunter's River ...[6]

George Hall would have read this report with considerable interest. His ambitions went far beyond mixed farms on a few thousand acres. Once comfortably settled in the Hawkesbury Valley he looked northwards, not only towards the Upper Hunter Valley but beyond the Hunter to the Liverpool Plains and the New England region. Most of the land in the Sydney Basin, the gently undulating region enclosed by the Blue Mountains to the west of Sydney and highlands to the north and south, was under either in private or government ownership or unsuited to agriculture by c.1810. There was no more room for George, except beyond the highlands immediately to the north of the Hawkesbury Valley.

Out of their long friendship, from the *Coromandel* voyage to their Hawkesbury Valley grants, John Howe may have encouraged George to apply early for grants in the Upper Hunter or, at least, to send his sons to make their own assessment of the region. Caution, however, prevailed. George waited until 1825 before applying for land in the Upper Hunter for himself and his sons even though the Putty Road opened to traffic in 1823. A shortage of tame cattle, with which to stock future Hunter properties, may have informed George's decision. All the cattle in the colony were in government or private ownership and most were of Cape or Indian descent. It would have been unwise for George to plan property expansion if he weren't sure that he could stock his new holdings. Roads, established transport routes, were essential to his plans, not only for stock movement but for more general transport: the stores and equipment needed for setting up new stations. The unknown element was whether there would be a market for the cattle grown on his future holdings. This was a risk that he was obviously prepared to take. The future held promise of an exported salt beef industry as well as domestic markets.

George made his first application to the Governor in April 1825.

> I humbly solicit your Excellency may be pleased to permit me
> to become the purchaser of 3,000 acres of land at Hunter River.[7]

Later in 1825 the government surveyor was ordered to survey 3,000 acres for George Hall in the Hunter Valley. The survey was completed in May 1826 and blocks were also surveyed for four of George's sons: William, John, Thomas and James. In addition George was given ownership of a disputed claim. The Halls ended up with 4,040 acres (16 km^2). Even though the surveys were in 1825-1826 and the deeds not issued until 1831 the Halls probably occupied Dartbrook before the survey was completed.[8] Other acquisitions followed. By the time George died, in 1840, the Halls held some 36,000 acres (146 km^2) in the Upper Hunter Valley as well as their Hawkesbury properties, plus some 600 acres in the present Dural area (~40 km north-west of Sydney) and their Auburn paddocks.

Thomas Hall may have settled at Dartbrook in 1825 or 1826; he was certainly there at the time of the 1828 Census. The Census return shows him to have been in charge of 4,700 acres, 700 cattle, 2 horses and 8 convict workers.[9] He made the 300 km journey from the Hawkesbury Valley to Dartbrook on foot, with a couple of horse-drawn carts to carry stores for the journey and tools for use in building, housing, stock yards and fencing. He would have taken his assigned convict workers with him and his brothers Matthew and Ebenezer who also had land grants in the Hunter Valley. Thomas undoubtedly took cattle, too, on his first journey to Dartbrook. He needed both killers and breeders. There were several men with him and that number could have driven a mob of forty or fifty head, or more. Coming from the restricted acreage available to them in the Hawkesbury Valley, George's cattle would have been used to handling. However, the trek through the highlands between the Hawkesbury and Hunter Valleys would have taught Thomas and his companions much about the realities of moving cattle through rough terrain, despite the advantages of a surveyed road and tame stock.

The Birth of the Halls Heeler

Dogs? Of course there were dogs on that trek to Dartbrook. Dogs were an integral part of nineteenth century life, particularly of rural life. Some of the "Curs and Mongrel Dogs" that infested Sydney inevitably followed settlers to the Hawkesbury Valley and on to the grants of George Hall and other farmers. Those for which George saw a use, stayed. Whether George Hall chose dogs, or whether dogs chose him, is immaterial. Dogs would have become a part of George's household as soon as he and his family were settled in the Hawkesbury Valley. Always practical, George would have preferred dogs that were useful to him: vermin hunters, guard/watch dogs, and dogs with aptitude for stock work of whatever kind. Some of the family's dogs, those showing potential for stock work, would certainly have accompanied Thomas to the Hunter. The dogs that proved their worth, working Thomas's cattle day after weary day along the Putty Road, would have more than justified their place in Thomas's household. These dogs were the "imported" Halls Heeler ancestors to which Kaleski referred. Some may have been dingo hybrids. Dingoes preyed on the colony and would not have overlooked a bitch in heat.

During his first year or so at Dartbrook Thomas's priorities were forest and scrub clearance and building basic farm infrastructure. He returned to Pitt Town occasionally for stores and equipment, and to discuss progress with his father and William and other brothers. Close cooperation and communication within the family was the foundation on which George's agribusiness was built. Discussion of droving difficulties through rough timbered country can hardly have been avoided during Thomas's Pitt Town visits. Future problems with infrequently handled stock were an expectation and one to be planned for. The wild cattle that had roamed the Cowpastures were a warning to them about how quickly tame cattle can become unruly and dangerous if free to range, unrestricted, over large areas. The management of semi-wild cattle on large unfenced areas (only Dartbrook and Gundebri at first) was a challenge ahead. Dogs would be essential. Breeding from the dogs that had proven themselves on the trek to Dartbrook would become one of Thomas's responsibilities. The earliest of the Halls' working dogs may have been whelped either at Dartbrook or in the Hawkesbury Valley but developed, as a more or less defined breed, at Dartbrook. This supposition sits comfortably within the larger context of the Halls Heeler story.

The development of the Halls Heeler is unlikely to have been systematically planned. Thomas Hall was not a dog breeder, in the sense we now understand dog breeding. The concept of breeding to a formal breed standard was half a century into the future. Thomas was concerned, solely, with producing a dog suited to a particular job: that of working cattle. Similarities of type and overall appearance emerged but coincidental to selecting for working ability. Thomas was skilled in the practicalities of animal husbandry and he brought these skills to developing the Halls Heeler. It is unlikely that the dingo contributed to the Halls Heeler other than coincidently. Kaleski, himself, drew attention to viciousness in some dingo crosses.[10] The heeling instincts that Kaleski so admired in his Cattle Dogs were those that were common in British drovers' dogs – indeed, essential to their survival – but those instincts were not in the dingo's make up. The dingo was never a drover's dog and was not a "biter", a nip-and-drop biter, like European drovers' dogs and Kaleski's Cattle Dogs.

> A good biter should always bite the hind foot which is resting on the ground supporting the weight of the animal's body, and should drop flat immediately after biting so that the hoof goes over him.[11, 12, 13]

The first Halls Heelers may well have been bred at Dartbrook under Thomas's direction but, as the Halls took up more lands in the Hunter Valley and further north, distance forced decentralised breeding. From necessity Halls Heelers were bred on properties that were remote from Dartbrook, to meet the needs of Hall stockmen in the New England region and further north.

The formation of agricultural companies in the 1820s offered settlers a new and publically available source of livestock. The proposed activities of the Australian Agricultural Company (AACo), announced in 1824, cannot have failed to influence George Hall's planning. The AACo was to be based in the Hunter region and held out promise as a source of British cattle with which George could stock his Hunter Valley properties. During his early years in the Hawkesbury Valley George Hall favoured Teeswater sheep, a breed familiar to him from the north of England.[14] His preference for British livestock almost certainly included cattle breeds, particularly Shorthorns, that would have been familiar to him from his youth in Northumberland. His dreams may have been of mobs of Shorthorns, rather than Cape and Indian cattle, grazing his future Hunter lands and waited until these became more readily available to him. George's second son, William, recognised the particular suitability of Shorthorns to open range cattle raising because of their docile temperament. His judgement influenced the Halls' early preference for Shorthorn cattle.[15]

Britain was greedy for wool and also hopeful that the colony would eventually import its woollen textiles. The AACo was formed to support the growth of the colony's fine wool industry but the company's stated aims were broader.

> 1st. From the growth and export of fine wool from Merino sheep of the most approved breed.
>
> 2ndly. From the breeding of cattle and other livestock, and the raising of corn, tobacco, etc., for the supply of persons resident in the colony.
>
> 3rdly. For the production at a more distant time of wine, olive oil, hemp, flax, silk, opium, as articles of export to Great Britain.
>
> 4thly. From a progressive advance in the value of the land as it becomes by cultivation, and by an increased population.[16]

One million acres (4,047 km^2) were surveyed for the AACo at Port Stephens and, at the end of 1825, two ships brought in sheep, Shorthorn cattle, horses and other stock.[17] Earlier in 1825 Thomas Potter McQueen of Segenhoe, only a few kilometres northwest of Dartbrook, had imported a stud bull to enhance his Shorthorn herd.[18]

George Hall's plans had fallen neatly into place. He had title to land in the Hunter Valley. Thomas and two of his brothers were settled at Dartbrook. He had access to Shorthorn cattle from the AACo and also from private breeders such as John Lee of Bylong, from whom he bought stock in the late 1830s.[19] It was left to Thomas to provide working dogs, and in sufficient numbers. The need for effective working dogs assumed new urgency in the 1830s. In 1833 convicts made up forty percent of the New South Wales population but criticism of the convict transportation system was becoming louder and convicts didn't necessarily bring with them skills (particularly rural and trade skills) that were needed in the colony. The Molesworth report to the British Government in 1837 recommended abolition, describing transportation as "not just exile but slavery as well". For pastoralists like the Halls this foreshadowed labour shortage. Their convict workforce, when its members had served out their sentences, would become free men and there would be no convict replacements. Some former convicts were available for hire and may have remained with the Halls but others may have been given grants of land or followed other business interests.

Capital inflow from Britain during the 1830s fuelled rapid growth in the New South Wales colony. Both the pastoral and whaling industries expanded. Downturn began in 1840 with the 1838-1840 drought.[20] A wave of bank failures in the early 1840s appears not to have affected the Halls – they were financially secure – but the economic conditions and the drought itself checked George's plans for northward expansion. George's death in 1840 might have halted those plans permanently had not his family decided to carry on as George would have wished and when conditions favoured them, in the name of the George Hall Estate: business as usual under the management of William and Thomas Hall. For the Halls the late 1830s and early 1840s was a period of consolidation. The George Hall Estate would take up more property in the Hunter Valley, and further north, when the time was right.

The Order-in-Council ending transportation to New South Wales was signed in 1837 and the last convict ship to Sydney arrived late in 1840. Powerful land owners, such as W. C. Wentworth, agitated for reintroduction of transportation. They feared that the flow of free immigrants, attracted to the colony by the prospect of land grants and assigned convict labour, would dwindle. Closer to home, they were reluctant to lose convicts as a labour supply for a growing wool industry. (Wentworth needn't have been concerned about immigration. Gold attracted 370,000 immigrants in 1852 alone.[21]) Wentworth's lobby had considerable clout and a small number of transportees were sent to New South Wales during the later 1840s but the last convicts arrived in New South Wales in 1850.

The impact of loss of convict labour was exacerbated by the labour shortages following the gold rushes. For the Halls, this meant fewer men available to operate increasingly large land holdings. The time of the Halls Heeler had come.

8

THE HALLS AND THE HALLS HEELER AFTER 1840

In 1836 George Hall, then aged seventy-two, made a new Will. His wife, Mary, had died in 1827 but eight of their children were still alive. (Elizabeth, their oldest, died in 1834.) According to the practice of the times the Will was just. George divided his estate among his seven sons; his remaining daughter had a husband to support her. Two of the sons, George Smith and James, lived in the Hawkesbury Valley and were rewarded by way of individual bequests. For his other five sons, William, John, Thomas, Matthew and Ebenezer (those most active in the management of his properties) George created a Trust to exist for ten years after his death. William and John, both of whom lived locally, and the Rev. John McGarvie (first minister at the Ebenezer Presbyterian church) were to be George's executors.

George died in 1840, his vision of vast land holdings stocked with Shorthorn cattle unrealised, but his death made little difference to the Hall family's activities. The same sort of cooperation, that had existed between family members during George's lifetime, continued. William and Thomas managed the enterprise and, in the name of the George Hall Estate, extended its holdings as George would have wished. They added to Gundebri and Dartbrook and purchased other properties in the Hunter including St Heliers of 14,635 acres (5,932 ha). By 1848 George Hall Estate lands extended into the New England region of New South Wales – Bingera, Stoney Batter, Mundowey and Cuerindi with an area of over 820 miles^2 (2,124 km^2) – and into Queensland, including two runs[1] on the Balonne River: Noorindoo Station of 300 miles^2 (777 km^2) and Werribone Station of 137 miles^2 (355 km^2). George's sons, except for William and John in the Hawkesbury Valley, and Thomas permanently resident at Dartbrook, were overseers on various stations and some of the younger generation, George's grandsons, worked for their fathers and uncles. These younger men became increasingly important to the operations of the George Hall Estate in terms of labour but, with future labour shortages looming, the time of the Halls Heeler had indeed come. William Hall's protégé, James Butler, recalled that the Halls would never have been able to take up so many stations, nor cope with the amount of stock work involved, without their dogs.[2]

James Butler (c.1841-1917) was as a son to the childless William Hall. In 1847 William had learned of the death of Sylvester Butler, a farmer in the Macdonald Valley where he, too, had land. Butler's widow was struggling to raise a large family and William made it his business to call on Mrs Butler. Perhaps he could offer assistance? James, her six-year-old son, so impressed William that he suggested that the boy return to Percy Place with him. James could make himself useful feeding fowls and dogs, collecting eggs, and other odd jobs around the farm. The mother agreed. James lived at Percy Place until William's death and cared for him during his semi-invalid later years. William was the only father James remembered. He was devoted to William and to Hall interests and, in adulthood, became known as "Hall's General". In his own later years James was given to reminiscing and found a keenly interested listener in his son who, in turn, passed James's stories on to his own son, Neville. Neville not only enjoyed listening to his father's re-telling of James's recollections but wrote them down. Neville later inherited Myall Station from his father. Part of the former Hall property, Bingera, Myall Station was a selection[3] that James had taken up after the Hall properties dispersed in the 1870s. Neville inherited dogs with the property and believed them to have been of Halls Heeler descent.

The Halls' stations, according to James Butler, were not contiguous but were close enough for stock to be moved easily from station to station and for stockmen to travel between station and station when cattle work (mustering, branding) needed extra hands. The Halls boasted that they could travel from their Queensland runs to the Hawkesbury Valley and camp on their own lands every night. The properties were selected for management efficiency and with an eye to access to the main markets of the 1860s: Sydney, Brisbane, Newcastle, and Port Macquarie.

A hut and stockyards were built on each station, on level ground near permanent water. Hut and yards were both enclosed within a fenced (dog-leg[4] or two-rail) horse paddock of some thirty or forty acres. This paddock was cleared of all cover to give a clear view of the approaches to the hut. Aboriginals and escapee convicts were an omnipresent threat. The rest of the station remained unfenced. Topography (watersheds, rivers) and distance from water kept stock from straying. A station did not need many men to run it: an overseer, a hut keeper, and three or four stockmen. The overseer, one of the Hall family or a particularly trusted stockman, managed the station and kept in touch with other stations. He passed messages, usually by letter, back to Dartbrook in the Hunter Valley or to Percy Place in the Hawkesbury Valley. The hut keeper looked after the sleeping hut, doled out rations, cooked and looked after the spare horses. Three or four stockmen completed the permanent work force. James Butler's recollections tell much about the Halls' planning and cattle- and man-management but nothing of dog-management. It is, however, obvious that the hut keeper's duties would have included feeding the dogs, caring for any that were injured (but expected to recover), looking after bitches in whelp, and minding pups that were too young to be introduced to cattle.

After 1840 the Hall stations fanned outward from Dartbrook. This forced decentralised, but cooperative, dog breeding. Practices still known in western New South Wales were probably those of the Halls' and their stockmen. Each of the various stations kept dogs of one sex, only. This avoided fights and the obvious distraction offered by a bitch in heat. When a mating was intended the necessary arrangements were made and pups later supplied where needed. Over-supply of pups was unlikely. Injuries inflicted by cattle would have accounted for many deaths; so would parasite infestations and the inevitable snakes. Dogs who were unsatisfactory as workers did not long survive. The dogs' outward appearance (phenotype, in genetic terms) was immaterial; the offspring of particularly prized workers would have been sought after, regardless of their appearance. The Halls Heeler travelled. From his nominal origin at Dartbrook he spread through the Hunter Valley, south into the Hawkesbury Valley, north into New England, still further north into the Maranoa region of Queensland, and beyond. He travelled wherever the Halls and their stockmen needed him. Eventually there ceased to be any reliance on Dartbrook for replacement Halls Heelers.

George Hall intended the Trust set up under his Will to end ten years after his death (that is, in 1850) but the five brothers allowed it to continue; a grave error of judgement as it turned out. After Thomas's death in 1870 and William's in 1871 only two of the original five brothers named in the Trust were alive but George's great-grandchildren were many. The resulting litigation was complex and protracted. At least one family member was left impoverished and Anne, Thomas Hall's widow, paid rent for her continuing occupation of Dartbrook until she was able to purchase the property at auction. Court proceeding dragged on for twelve years at the end of which all former Hall properties were in non-Hall ownership except for Dartbrook (Anne Hall) and Gundebri (Matthew Hall). Most of the New South Wales stations were auctioned in 1873. *The Sydney Morning Herald* for 29 March 1873 reported:

> The sale of the Messrs. Hall's stations, at the Exchange, on the 26th instant, attracted a very large number of buyers, nearly 200 being present, before the commencement of the sale, all the different lots offered met with keen competition, and the prices realised were very satisfactory. The stations sold as follows.—Lot 1. Weebolabola and Bullerrue, in the Gwydir district, together with about 3600 cattle (1000 of which are to be paid for at £3 15s a head), at £6 1s 6d — Messrs. A. and W. Munro, purchasers. Lot 2. Bingera, in the Gwydir district, together with about 2,500 head of cattle, at £3 7s 6d — Mr. G. McDonell purchaser. Lot

3. Cuerindi and Mundowey, in the district of Liverpool Plains, together with about 2,000 head of cattle, (and about 5,000 sheep to be taken at 8s 6d per head) at £4 12s 6d, Mr. J. Scroggie, purchaser; Lot 4 : Stoney Batters in the New England district, together with about 8,000 head of cattle, at £5 3s, Messrs. J. and T. Cooper purchasers; Lot 5: Wallamumbi Station in the New England district, together with about 4,000 head of cattle, (and about 5,000 sheep to be taken at valuation) at £3 10s 6d, Mr. J. Fletcher purchaser; Lot 6: Mount Mitchell in the New England district, together with about 2,500 head of cattle, at £3 9s 6d, Messrs A. and R. Amoss purchasers ...[5]

Judith Wright, the poet, grew up on Wallamumbi, the station having been bought by her grandmother, Charlotte Wright. In "South of My Days" Judith Wright wrote of drought, droving and death; scenes that would have been all too familiar to the Halls.

> Droving that year, Charleville to the Hunter,
> nineteen-one it was, and the drought beginning;
> sixty head left at the McIntyre, the mud round them
> hardened like iron; and the yellow boy died
> in the sulky ahead with the gear, but the horse went on,
> stopped at Sandy Camp and waited in the evening.
> It was the flies we seen first, swarming like bees.
> Came to the Hunter, three hundred head of a thousand -
> cruel to keep them alive - and the river was dust.

The Hall family faded from the rural scene and so did the Halls Heeler, but in name and ownership only. Stock and land were sold together. Some of the station hands and stockmen stayed on the stations under their new ownership and with them, their dogs. Some, like James Butler, selected property on former Hall stations. Others moved on taking their dogs with them. The dogs became freely available and some became associated, in name, with particular stockmen such as John Timmins and his "Timmins Biters".[6]

But who was he, the Halls Heeler?

The Kaleski Dogma

The Kaleski Dogma was laid down in 1903 in Kaleski's introduction to his breed standard and elaborated on in his *Bookfellow* article of 1907. "Mr Hall or Wall of Muswellbrook" imported a "blue-gray Welsh merle for working cattle".[7, 8, 9] The Kaleski Dogma has remained almost unchallenged since publication but it rests on incorrect assumptions. Kaleski assumed that the Halls had maintained contact with family and friends in England. (They didn't.) Kaleski also assumed that mail delivery times between Australia and England were much the same as in his own time. (They weren't; in Kaleski's day, about six weeks; in the Halls' day, more than four months.) Obviously the Halls Heeler's ancestors were "imported". All the colonial dogs were "imported" but Kaleski Dogma states, specifically, that Thomas Hall imported dogs (presumably from Britain). The probability of Hall's having done this is vanishingly small; no known contacts in England and two-way correspondence times of around eight months. In any case, the concept of a breeding program (and of importing dogs to support it) would have been foreign to Thomas Hall.

Postal records show that the Halls' contact with England ended when they sailed on the *Coromandel*. All incoming mail to the colony was advertised, as awaiting collection, in the *Sydney Gazette*. The duties of the colony's first Postmaster, appointed in 1809, included taking charge of mail arriving by ship and authorising the *Sydney Gazette* advertisement. This arrangement continued until 1828 when mail deliveries were introduced.[10] George Hall was not among the few whose names were advertised as mail recipients during the years up to 1828 nor did any other members of the Hall family receive mail. George was unlikely to have enjoyed the friendship of some colonial official returning to England, who might have acted as his intermediary. The class distinctions of the time were rigid; George was an immigrant tradesman, not one of the colony's "gentlemen". Shipping records for 1820-1840 do not include any record of dogs being imported.[11]

Kaleski's attempts to discover the Halls Heeler's British ancestor in late nineteenth century publications were misguided. A century separated the Cattle Dogs, for which he wrote the breed standard, from the "Curs and other useless dogs" that arrived with the convict fleets and other ships that docked in Sydney during the early colonial years. During that century the British dog population changed dramatically in response to the pressures of a growing dog-show-orientated dog fancy; a change from dog breeding focussed essentially on purpose (vermin control, hunting, droving) to focus on type as prescribed in a breed standard.[12] Increasing mechanisation as the nineteenth century progressed also changed the dog population. Many distinct working dog types, known in the early nineteenth century and earlier, vanished when they were no longer needed. Kaleski did little more than emphasise the obvious: the British ancestors of the Halls Heeler existed in the British dog population. Working sheepdogs, similar in type and colour to Australian Cattle Dogs, are still to be found in the British dog population.[13]

Kaleski's identification of the "blue-gray Welsh merle" as the ancestor of the Halls Heeler was not only misguided but also introduced a long-standing confusion between the ticked/speckled/ mottled colouration, seen in both Cattle Dog breeds, and the colour pattern associated with the merle mutation, seen in breeds such as the Australian Shepherd Dog: irregular dark blotches against a lighter background of similar pigmentation.[14] The merle mutation does not occur in the Australian Cattle Dog or in the Australian Stumpy Tail Cattle Dog.

Kaleski remained convinced that the Halls Heelers (and therefore Cattle Dogs) inherited their heeling instincts from the dingo. In curious but explicit contradiction, he condemned dingo crosses unless the cross were selective, to "good working stock"! Almost an admission, on his part, that dingoes were intractable and didn't nip-and-drop as a heeler should. "A good working strain" was essential in a dingo cross, if a controllable nip-and-drop biter was wanted in the offspring.

> Anything of the dingo cross is very hard, but, unless crossed
> to a good working strain, they are very hard biters, and
> uncontrollable.[15, 16]

Despite the contradiction Kaleski said he introduced (or reintroduced) dingo into his Cattle Dog breeding and many others have followed Kaleski's questionable example since. Roy Barratt (see below) was probably not the first and certainly was not the last, but at no time during the past 6,000 years (an estimated date of its arrival in Australia) has the dingo been a droving dog. Camp follower and hunting companion too, but never a drover's dog. A dingo infusion could not, and cannot, introduce heeling instincts into the resulting offspring.

Kaleski credited the butcher, Fred Davis (father of his dog-breeding partner, Alex) with having brought Halls Heelers to Sydney, c.1875, from the Hunter Valley, to work in his cattle yards and move cattle from sale yards to abattoir.[17, 18] Very unlikely, but Davis may have done so. Halls Heelers must have been in Sydney long before 1875, working stock on the Halls' Auburn farms and driving stock from the Hawkesbury Valley to Sydney. The ancestors of the Halls Heeler remain obscure except that they arrived in New South Wales with the early convict transport convoys and other shipping of the time.

Kaleski's version of the Cattle Dog's origin, as published with his breed standard, was not uncontested. The pseudonymous "Sir Bedivere" penned a fortnightly column, 'The Kennel', in *The Town and Country Journal* (a Sydney newspaper). In 1903, and probably predating[19] the first publication of Kaleski's Breed Standard, he showed his considerable familiarity with the nineteenth century classical writers on British dogs. He knew that the description, "drover's dog", described the dog's function, not a type of dog, and noted that variations in type were often regional.

> Dogs used for droving purposes were, when all the stock were
> shifted by road, common to all parts of Great Britain, though
> most plentiful, perhaps, in the more important stock-rearing

districts. That these were used for cattle as well as sheep is indicated by the word 'heeler'. No doubt to a great extent a common build prevailed, but some favoured one kind of coat, and some another, and similarly with ears and colour, different preferences prevailing in different districts.[20]

Quoting from Dalziel (from an edition later than the one cited in Chapter 5) Sir Bedivere also drew attention to working dogs in the English population with similarities to Cattle Dogs although his speculations on Cattle Dog ancestry were, as he admitted, "hazarded".

In his later edition, [Dalziel] refers to the 'Sportsman's Cabinet', by the celebrated artist Reinagle, there described as a Highland Sheep-dog, but which Dalziel, who had an intimate knowledge of Highland dogs, believes to have been really of southern origin.[21] Its description tallies to a very great extent with that of the earlier Australian Cattle-dog. It was grey and white in colour, in height and length nearly equal, not so deep in chest as the Collie, rounder in skull, the muzzle shorter and broader, coat rough and harsh, and free from curl, long all over the body and on the back of legs (here there is some divergence), shorter from the neck downwards, and shorter, but still rough on the face. When, therefore, it is hazarded that the Australian Cattle-dog is a cross between the Coolie, Coally, Smithfield, Yorkshire Collie, or the like, it probably means that certain separate strains of the same breed have been reunited, and the cleaner legged dogs and later the short haired ones, selected to suite the climate and country.

Sir Bedivere mentioned Harry Bagust and praised his breeding activities, but was unconvinced about the dingo.

Mr. H. Bagust, of Canterbury, believes Dingo blood to have been resorted to because of their prick ears. As, however, these so frequently recur in many domestic breeds, they cannot of themselves be accepted as evidence of such a cross. Mr. Bagust's own efforts have been committed to building up a well-defined strain by careful selection of stock from among recognised Cattle-dogs, and so well has he succeeded that there is in his strain comparatively little variation in type or colour.[22]

G. W. Bagust's *Nipper* and J. G. Bagust's *Floss* illustrate Sir Bedivere's article. Kaleski was yet to become well known. Sir Bedivere's may be the first published use of the breed name, "Australian Cattle Dog".

A wildly divergent view of Cattle Dog antecedents came from Joseph Rose. Rose judged Cattle Dogs at the Sydney Royal for a few years and published a breed history in 1908. It is a convincing breed story – from which Hall and dingoes are completely excluded. It is probably fictitious, written for his own self-aggrandisement and to discredit Kaleski. That there was animosity between Rose and Kaleski is obvious from correspondence in the *Sydney Mail* during 1922 (see Chapter 13).

> Many years ago, in and around the County of Cumberland, cattle were worked by black-and-tan collies, short-coated, pricked-ear dogs. Several of the stock owners wanted something a trifle harder and a cross of the above was tried by the late Judge Cheek [sic] and my respected father, which brought about the pricked-ear dog. The cross was a blue Smithfield cattle dog (imp.) on a black-and-tan bitch, the progeny of which came to fill the bill of an ideal cattle dog. They were bred at Campbelltown (N.S.W.) and in time drifted all over New South Wales and Queensland. This dog has been neglected for years, but a few of the old hands, viz., Messrs Kaleski, Bagaust [sic], Pettitt [sic] and the writer, have kept the breed pure, and have formed a club to register all sires, so as to keep them pure. Several breeders have tried the cross with the dingo dog. They were biters, very severe biters, but always whip-shy. A friend of mine near Muswellbrook bred a litter of this kind. During his first trip to town with cattle, the dogs accompanied him. As soon as the exhaust of a railway engine was heard – well!! he hasn't seen them since. This example does not speak well for the dingo cross.[23]

Despite Joseph Rose's determined effort to compete with Kaleski, Kaleski's version of cattle dog breed origin (slightly modified) remained the most convincing: that the Halls Heeler was developed by Thomas Hall from unidentified colonial dogs, obviously "imported", with possible coincidental dingo infusion. This, essentially, was the view of Atoa (probably pseudonym of Captain G. E. Simcocks, prominent in the Brisbane dog world of the 1920s and 1930s).

> It is suggested by some writers that a cross with the dingo was sought purposely, but this I cannot accept. The dingo was always the stockman's enemy, to be killed on sight, owing to the devastation wrought amongst sheep and calves and it is hard to believe that they would take the risk of bringing the enemy within the gates. The infusion of dingo blood, and there cannot be any doubt that this took place, could come about naturally and unsought.[24]

Even as late as 1941, however, Hall's role was still in dispute despite Kaleski's publications, but the dingo was allowed to maintain its position as parent to the Halls Heeler. The Sydney breeder and exhibitor, Roy Barratt (sometime owner of *Nebo Rock*), wrote:

> It is still a matter of conjecture as to how the Australian cattle dog was produced but it is beyond doubt that one of the contributing parties was the native dog called the dingo.[25]

Barratt was strongly in favour of re-infusing dingo into the cattle dog breed. The belief, that dingo blood should be re-infused, was (and continued to be) widely held although few breeders have been as open about their activities as Barratt.

> In order to maintain rigidly the correct type I recently obtained a particularly fine specimen of dingo which was mated to a short, well-set, close-coupled cattle dog bitch – winner of the 'open' class at the Royal Agricultural Show, Sydney, in kind the world's greatest exhibition. The progeny are progressing wonderfully well; and by careful line breeding, success in maintaining the standard is assured.[26]

Barratt, in 1941 (above) echoed Kaleski, 1903 and 1910 (below) in emphasising the need to cross dingo to good working cattle dogs. Barratt, like Kaleski, was aware that dingo crosses were often vicious and uncontrollable:

> Anything of the dingo cross is very hard, but, unless crossed to a good working strain, they are very hard biters, and uncontrollable. Finding the strain is beginning to run out a little in shape and head, we are now crossing with a pet dingo of mine to get these points back again, and though we will get a little too much red in at first, I think the increased vigour and shape will more than repay us.[27, 28]

That is, the dingo infusion was basically unsatisfactory – dingo hybrids were uncontrollable, vicious biters – but need for dingo infusion (or re-infusion) was written into Kaleski Dogma and taken on board by Barratt and others without question. A New South Wales veterinarian, Allan McNiven, was another who accepted Kaleski Dogma as holy writ and embarked, during the 1940s, on a breeding program that was aimed at introducing dingo into an Australian Cattle Dog lineage. The experiment, which persisted into the 1960s, failed to gain traction in Australia but attracted some American interest.[29] Later in the 1960s Joe Tait (*Taits Glen* Kennels) introduced dingo into his breeding, as photos of *Taits Glen Bonita* and *Taits Glen Susy* attest. Several other much later dingo infusions are alleged and anecdotal evidence abounds.

The Halls Heeler is inferred to have been a speckled or mottled animal, either blue or red, with tail length varying from tailless to normal length. Those unidentified colonial ancestors, that contributed to the Halls Heeler, must obviously have been of a type that is consistent with *Nipper* and *Floss* and later dogs such as *Gibson Lady Blue* and Neville Butler's dogs.

The esteemed British writer on dogs, David Hancock, proffers an opinion on the Australian Cattle Dog's ancestors and some of the entrenched beliefs held about the breeds origins.

> The Australian Cattle Dog is often stated to have come from a mixture of smooth merle collies, dingo, Dalmatian, and black and tan Kelpie. The dingo blood is stated, in one Australian publication, to have introduced silent working, the red coat colour and the herding instinct. The last point is explained in these words:

'A dingo trait is to silently creep up behind an animal and bite, and these cross pups followed this style of heeling.' A reasonable response to this, to me, incredible statement, would be: British working sheepdogs work silently; red merle is in the collie gene pool – it doesn't need an infusion of dingo blood; and the heeling instinct was present in British herding dogs before any Europeans reached Australia, ask any Welsh Corgi or Lancashire Heeler breed historian. As for the infusion of Dalmatian blood, can you truly imagine any hard-bitten, weather-beaten cattle farmer introducing the blood of a spotted coach dog to, as the Australian publication puts it, 'give the progeny a love of horses and a sense of responsibility for guarding his master's possessions'?[30]

Calthorpe (formerly Dartbrook) House c. 1890. Family group includes Thomas Hall's widow, Anne.

Robert Kaleski (1877-1961).

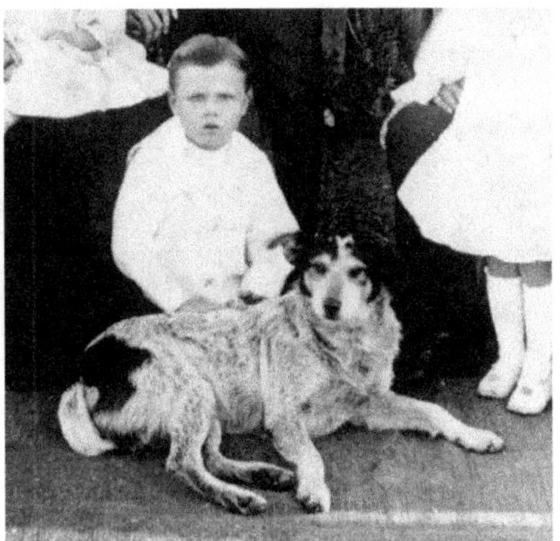

Jack, exhibited as a cattle dog at Sydney's Agricultural Exhibition in 1898.

Halls Heeler, born c.1890, from an Allen family photograph. The Allen family lived on Blairmore, a former Hall property near Aberdeen, N.S.W.

Rowdy [1899] (dog at rear assumed) and *Blue Fly*.

Nipper [1899]

Floss [1901]

Ch *Danger* [1903] owned and bred by Joseph Rose. Kaleski praised the dog as being of good type.

Ch *Nugget* [1908] owned and bred by Robert Kaleski.

Silent Jack [1919] on the job: a nip-and-drop biter.

Working cattle dog with possible Smithfield ancestry, Garangula Station, Harden N.S.W.

Robert Kaleski's *Thornhill Tiger* [192-]

Gd Ch *Some Rock* [1927].

Interstate Gd Ch *Nebo Rock* [1929].

Interstate Gd Ch *Nebo Rock* [1929].

Gibson Lady Blue [1929]. Bred by John Friend, Gibson Island, Brisbane.

From left: Gd Ch *Tisiphone* [1929]. Gd Ch *Eurydice* [1933], Gd Ch *Minos* [1929]; bred and exhibited by C. B. George.

Mrs W. W. Campbell was one of the few woman judges of Cattle Dogs in New South Wales during the 1920s and 1930s. The dog was probably Gd Ch *Miss Valentine* [1925].

Stumpy Tail Cattle Dog, illustration by Ian McBain in the *Courier Mail* Dog Book.

Gd Ch *Little Gem* [1926] grandsire of *Little Logic*.

Judge/breeder, Arch Bevis, with Ch *Bonnie Blue* [1942], left, and Ch *Kenwyn Tiger* [1942]; granddaughter and son, respectively, of *Little Logic*.

Ch *Little Logic* [1939].

Ch *Oatley Peter* [1942].

KC & KCC Ch *Young Autocrat* [1942].

Qld Gd Ch *Bobby Blue* [1944]. Example of the heavier-bodied type preferred after World War II.

RAS & CCC Ch *Logic Return* [1949].

Ch Kalamundi *Rex Regis* [1949].

KCC Ch *Neangah Royal Mitzi* [1949].

KC & KCC Ch *Trueblue Patches* [1951].

Ch *Hillview Brighton Boy* [1953].

Broombees Bobby [1953], a descendant of the stumpy-tailed Gd Ch *Blue Bess* [1923].

RAS Ch *Wooleston Blue Jack* [1954].

Berrilyn Nettle [1955] with foster kids.

Berrilyn Happy [1959].

Ch *Wooleston Blue Jock* [1965].

Ch *Wooleston Blue Jenny* [1967].

Berrilyn Breton [1970].

Ch *Tallawong Blue Jenny* [1973].

Ch *Dustyroad Toby* [1979].

Taits Glen Susy [1965] was registered as *Taits Glen Johnny* x *Taits Glen Bonita* but allegedly had a dingo sire.

Taits Glen Bonita [1962] is understood to have had two dingo grandparents.

Working cattle dog of probable Halls Heeler descent, c. 1940, owned by Neville Butler, Myall Station, Bingara N.S.W.

Working cattle dog of probable Halls Heeler descent, c. 1940, owned by Neville Butler, Myall Station, Bingara N.S.W.

Sunny Boy [1944] ancestor of *Glen Iris Red Ember* and *Glen Iris Stumpy*.

Glen Iris Red Ember [1973].

The Cur dog, from Bewick 1807.

The Shepherd's dog, from Bewick 1807.

A Scotch Bob-tailed Sheep Dog, from Shaw 1881.

Old English Sheep Dog, from Beilby, 1897.

Early engraving of the dingo. "The New South Wales wolf has been called a dog; but its wild and savage nature seems strongly to point out its affinity to the Wolf." From Bewick 1807.

Halls Heeler born c.1890 on Blairmore, a former Hall property.

9

KALESKI: THE STORYTELLER

To the dog world Kaleski was the authority on Cattle Dogs – except to those who disagreed with him. To farmers, he was a source of information on agricultural issues by way of his association with *The Sydney Stock and Station Journal*, the *Country Life Stock and Station Journal* and other publications. Readers of Sydney's literary publications, however, looked forward to his short stories and shared with him his love of native animals and their very different world. "Bronze-wing the Scrub Pigeon" is one of the several stories that Kaleski published during the 1920s and 1930s.

BRONZE-WING, THE SCRUB PIGEON
By Robert Kaleski
The Sunday Sun and Guardian, Sunday 25 November 1934, p. 21.

It is mid-afternoon in mid-autumn on the Green Hills. The day is clear, the sky cloudless; no hint of the approaching winter thrills the air. The sun shines hotly on the far end of the Hills, where the wattles grow thickest and tallest, each striving to outgrow its neighbor. Their long, feathery, green branches droop down wards, weighted by the heavy brown pods now open and empty, the black hard seed which they enclosed lying thick on the ground under the trees.

At the bottoms of the stouter trees, in against the trunk, lies what seems to be a thick, gossamer veil, covering a mass of little brown round seeds. It is the nest of one of the Destroyers, made between dark and dawn by the big grey goat-moth. Beneath that veil, and in the rough crevices of the bark, she laid her eggs; and soon, secure from one of the Destroyers, Red-Ant the Hunter, the little grubs hatch out from the brown seed-like eggs and begin to eat their way into the trunk and destroy it. Each nest means scores of young destroyers if allowed to hatch out, so that they would soon overrun the wattles and destroy them utterly; thereby throwing the ground open to the sun again, and spoil the making of the forest-floor, but for preyers set over them to keep the balance even.

From afar in the scrub and timber comes a long, low call, audible miles away. "Tah-moor," "tah-moor," "tah-moor." It is answered by one closer to the edge of the clearing. A whir-r-r of wings from the edge of the timber bordering on the open space of the hills, and out from it fly two birds, the sun flashing on the burning copper of their wings as they fly. They alight under the nearest wattle, and stand for a moment, listening and looking for danger, as all wild things must do, ere they begin feeding, if they wish to survive. By their cameo-like brown heads, white beneath the eyes; bodies the size and shape of a large tame pigeon; and their bronze-barred wings, you may know them for Bronze-wing the Scrub-Pigeon and his mate — destroyers of wattle-grubs, eaters of wattle-seeds, and one of the keepers of the balance of life even. Sure that no danger threatens, they begin to pick up the little black seed lying so thickly on the grass. Soon they leave them, and go to the butts of the trees, where they find the young grubs sheltering behind the webs, safe from Red-Ant and his kin, who cannot penetrate the web. These they speedily devour, regardless of the sticky web, so that soon nothing is left of the grubs but a few fragments on the grass, which will speedily be found and devoured by Red-Ant and his kin. At dawn they begin their feeding afresh, stopping every now and then, with brown beaks thrown forward to listen for danger. A stick cracks sharply a few yards away. They look up, ready for instant flight, and then resume feeding. It is only a settler's horse, picking at the grass amongst the wattles, and they have learnt that these four-footed things are harmless to them and their kin.

When the sun begins to show the hour of noon they leave the wattles and fly along the forest edge, keeping close to the timber for fear of hawks, till they come to the big rocky water-hole where the sand stone formation ends and the shale country of the Green Hills begins. A huge grey gum grows beside the water-hole; into its broad, spreading top they fly, and squat on one of the smaller branches, unseeable to the keenest vision. Sharply they look round for sign of danger; then, seeing none, fly down to the water, and drink their fill. Rising again, they fly back into the forest, and perch on the lofty branch of a red gum till late after noon, when it is time to begin feeding again.

They are in the haunts of Warrigal the Red Dog and his mates, and Spotty the Tiger-Cat; while Brownie the Range-hawk flies over here now and then, and likes their white flesh as much as the others. So they feed and watch, listening for crack of stick or rustle of leaf betokening an enemy; and feeding against the little wind that plays through the forest, to keep their lovely feathers unruffled, and gain sign of enemy. Presently Bronze-wing, listening keenly, hears a faint rustle, as of a bough being pressed back. With a low, quick call he warns his mate, and the pair watch keenly for a few seconds, till they catch a glimpse of black and white fur lying flattened against a log, just out of springing distance. Instantly they run a few yards at right angles to where they stood, and launch themselves into the air with a loud beating of wings as the foiled tiger-cat lands just where they stood. They fly swiftly in a semi-circle through the forest for a half-mile space, in case the tiger-cat should follow, and then begin their feeding afresh. The country is more open here, and they feed together, against the wind as before, till the laugh of Kookaburra the Snake-killer and his mates tells of sunset, and they make their perch for the night.

Day follows day, and week follows week. The cold, windy days and still, dark nights of winter pass into the fresh, clear days and balmy nights of spring, and still Bronze-wing and his mate, unhurt by hawk or tiger-cat, feed and play amongst the scrub and wattles. As the days grow warmer, heating their blood, and the richer food gives them more strength than they need, they prepare to follow the Law, and bequeath it to future generations.

So Bronze-wing and his mate make a rough nest of crossed sticks, loosely but skilfully thrown together, in the fork of a tall grey-gum, in the densest part of the forest. In the nest she lays two small, white eggs on which she sits patiently, sometimes relieved by her mate, till in due time the little creatures inside have strength to break the thin shells enclosing them and peer out into the world. Now begins an anxious time for their parents. The tender, toothsome little things are the most sought-of out of all young fledglings by the preyers, and were it not that the nest is so cunningly placed, and the sticks harmonise so well with the bough's coloring that it is almost invisible, their shrift would be a short one.

The baby bronze-wings thrive and grow, till they are large enough to leave the nest, and be carried by the parents to the shelter of a small tree growing close by, where they perch, still guarded and fed by their parents, till they are old enough to fly with them through the forest and out amongst the wattles in the Green Hills, to gather the black seed there, and help to control the wattle's growth. They are part of the Law, and are themselves governed by the Law that some day will strike them as it strikes all— great or small.

10

SHOW TIME

The Cattle Dog contributed a chapter to the 1914 edition of Kaleski's *Australian Barkers and Biters*. Who better to describe the dog shows of the 1910s and the antics of those associated with them, than the Cattle Dog, himself?

The "Enfield mob" probably included C. S. Petit, a prominent Cattle Dog breeder of the 1910s who used the prefix *Brooklyn*. "Timmins" can't be identified, beyond his association with Kaleski's "Club" but "Old Peak" may be the Peake that, according to Kaleski, introduced Bull Terrier into his Cattle Dog breeding (see Appendix 1: The Working Dogs of Australia). Kaleski knew that the famed Timmins Biters were bred from Halls Heelers stock by the drover, Timmins. It is possible that Kaleski learned about "Mr Hall of Muswellbrook" from one of the Timmins family.

SHOW TIME
By the Cattle Dog
Australian Barkers and Biters. N.S.W. Bookstall Co.,
Sydney, 1914, pp. 115-124

The man I stop with (he calls himself my owner) has a number of mates with whom other cattle and sheep dogs live. The whole lot meet every evening under a lamp-post at the corner in summer-time, and the nearest pub, in winter, and talk about us. The other people in Balmain who do not care about dogs, call them the Kennel Club. The great fault I have with them is that they are too opinionated. Each of them insists that he has the best dog in Australia; whereas it is well known that I am that myself. He takes the stand that he is not arguing with the others, but telling them; so mostly the meetings are dissolved by the police. One man particularly annoys me. He has a

wild eye, a rush of language to the mouth, and a voice like the Day of Judgement. A Deaf man can tell when he has finished by the way the gas flickers. At first he tried to catch me by the neck to show the Club that my nose was short by two inches; but he lost two fingers over it, so hasn't tried it since. I hate being pawed about like a girl. He comes from the back country, and is never tired of insisting that the drop-eared dogs are the best (mine are pricked); and that we Sydneyites are "slorter-yard dorgs." He was imported into the Club as a set off to old Peak, who is always trying to back his bitch against anything in the world for a fiver, and annoys the Club by constantly producing the money.

This is our usual way of living; then, one night, I hear my host asked casually if he is going to show me. He says not, explaining that there is nothing in it, and that he is tired of the trouble of getting me up. The rest of the Club agree cordially; they think it very sensible. Visiting their yards through the week I find all their best dogs tied up at home; the kennels nicely cleaned and strawed, and a full saucepan of meat beside them. Some of them have been recently bathed; Peak's bitch in hot blue water and suds, so she tells me. At the next meeting I notice Timmins (who has the next best dog) furtively feeling my coat to see if I have been washed. The others carefully avoid all mention of their dogs, and wonder whether any of our cousins from the bush will be in. The Enfield crowd and others are denounced as bad sportsmen; they won't show because they don't get first every year, and denounce the Club as a "click". "Let the best dog win," my host says, looking at me; this sentiment is warmly applauded by all.

The next week I am chained up to a well-strawed kennel, and liberally fed on boiled meat, carefully and constantly washed in blue water, and led out in the afternoons for exercise by a corpulent little boy, son to my host. I had great fun with him at first, towing him up to other dogs for a friendly fight and roll in the road; but now he always has two mates with him, and I find the three too heavy. After a few weeks of this I am rugged when taken out, so as to make my coat lie well. The infant population of Balmain follows me, fighting with each other for the honour of holding my chain. The corpulent little boy and his two mates get so many ginger-beer and fruit bribes that they nearly burst; no doubt in after years they will think of me as the best friend they ever had.

I never see the Club at this time; but nearly every day one or the other of them peers through the fence at me, Timmins being the most regular visitor. On Sunday mornings, some of them come round and chat at the gate.

"Nipper's inside, tied up; sick," my host explains evasively. "I might take it into my head to show him; but I don't know. There's nothing in it these times."

The morning of the show we start early; the little boy with my number ticket in his pocket, and he and his two mates on my chain. I could have great sport on the road tripping up elderly people and biting them, but the little cowards warn them off me. Just the same at the gate; every time I edge near the attendant for a good nip, they caution him, and he sidles off.

When I get to our bench, I find the whole of my mates there; all fat and shiny, with new collars and chains on. After climbing up to my place, and making my bed comfortable (these attendants seem to have absolutely no idea of spreading straw), I settle down for a look around. The main thing noticeable is our Club. They saunter up and down in front, each eyeing the dog likely to beat his own. Each affects surprise at seeing the other's dogs, and explains that he only brought his dog in just to give the show an entry. Then they all bunch up at one end of the bench and talk about cows. The few women exhibitors are different. They keep stroking and brushing their dogs all the time, with one eye watching for the judge. After an hour or two the steward comes round; then we follow the Club out to the ring side. Each exhibitor leads his dog by its new chain and numbered collar; the steward calls out the class he wants, and we trot into the ring. Each owner walks round the judge, parading his dog, shaking its chain, and clicking at it to make it look fierce. After a lot of this, the judge looks us all over, examines our mouths, and then puts the blue ribbon on me, and the red and yellow on others. Then we are led back to our bench, and the next batch comes on.

After they are all back, the Club surges round our stand like waves of the sea, shouting and arguing till the stewards put them outside for a couple of hours to cool. After that, the attendants come round and tack up our prize cards, and we have to put up with the incessant yelping of the public and other dogs for some days. Then, the last thing on Saturday night, we are let out to freedom – till the next show comes round.

The first things you notice at the show are the other dogs. They are all sorts, sizes, and colours, black, brown, and brindle, with yellow and white thrown in for luck. The fox-terriers and collies are the noisiest, yapping incessantly; the bull-dogs the most restless. Somehow we are always benched back to back with these brutes. As soon as they get there, they begin to work themselves into a ridiculous passion over nothing, till they are all foam and lather. Then they either die in a fit, or some one throws water over them and they recover. When I was younger I used to argue with them about it; show them how useless it is trying to bite till there is something to bite at; but they could never see it. The bull-terriers are much more sensible. (I believe they are distant connections of mine). They just wait quietly, with eager, red-rimmed eyes; then, when a hand comes along, they grab it.

The big dogs, like St. Bernards, are slow and sleepy, like big bullocks. Pugs and terriers I have no time for; especially the Scotch and Welsh terriers. The first of these, if you happen to be tied up next to him, always tried to get half your straw as well as his own, by a quiet, one-sided exchange of bones, whilst the Welsh terrier, if you don't watch him, will steal everything within reach. The little creatures called silky terriers make me sick. They live on velvet cushions, never do an hour's work, and have maids and silver-backed hair-brushes. All the women crowd round them and kiss them. If I could only get a chance to settle one! Some shows actually have cats in them, with prizes for the heaviest tom, the finest tabby, the liveliest tortoiseshell, and so on. Such nonsense. At one show I let most of the dogs loose the first night, and we pulled their cages to pieces and killed them all; so they only have them there the last day now.

After the dogs come the public, of course. It is extraordinary what variety there is in the crowds. Men, women, children, journalists, and lovers; no two are alike either in dress or character. Some only gape at you and pass on; others try to be familiar, and pull you about; some even try to guess your value. The only sensible ones are the farmers and drovers. They come in and look at us all day; brown bearded men mostly, bringing back memories of red soil plains, dry water-holes, and the cattle feeding off the camps in the cool of the morning.
The journalists I treat with contempt. They come round, notebook in hand, murmur to themselves "Cattle and sheep-dogs were well represented," and go off to spend half an hour amongst the useless collies.

Lovers are the most irritating. They make silly little remarks to you, and laugh and giggle to each other. I have only had one chance at them so far; the girl pushed her lover against my bench in fun, making the partition rattle; so of course I bit him on the shoulder. Next instant she brought her umbrella down on my head. I pulled it from her and tore it up as a warning against temper. I don't suppose the man would profit by it, though.

Towards evening, the people thin out, and the little dogs get tired, so that one gets time to yarn with his mates and find out how they got on. When night is falling, and the public has gone home the place gets quiet. Instead of the yapping of man and beast, all you hear are mates yarning to each other across the benches, and an odd mastiff or bully growling himself to sleep. Sometimes a rat or mouse slips out of a hole in the floor and creeps about looking for scraps or dog-biscuit. Then all is quiet again; nothing breaks the silence till morning but the rattle of a dreaming dog's chain as he curls about in his straw, or the whimper of hounds hunting in their sleep. The faint grey light of dawn creeps in; stock begin to trample in their stalls, and the show wakes to life again.

I have been in a great many shows. To see one is to see the lot; the only difference is the size of it. In a little show only a big local man can win; in a larger one any local man; and in the Sydney or big country shows anyone with the best animal. Heavens, how I have been cheated by some of these country places. Once I was given second to a dog which died of distemper an hour after it left the ring; another time to a dog which never turned up to be judged at all (it belonged to the Mayor). Several times I have had to rescue my owner from enraged local exhibitors. They always wait till the outsider goes to take his animal away; then three of four club together, and knock him down and jump on him. Being patriots in a sort of a way, they can't stand seeing the prize go out of the district. Once, and only once, I was unfairly beaten, and glad of it. This is how it happened.

I was at Bathurst show one year. I was sent up by myself, and got there the evening before judging day; had a look round as usual, to see what was against me. It was a poor lot; only one dog there with any show points at all. He happened to be benched next to me, so I started a yarn with him. Like most country dogs, he was very shy at first; then after a while we got very friendly. He was in sore trouble, he told me. "It's this way," he explained mournfully, "I want to win badly. The squatter I live with has a very pretty daughter. She's as good as she's pretty, and her lover's the same. He's got to judge us to-morrow, and ask the old boy for her to-morrow night. The old chap's set his heart on getting first with me; if he only gets second, he'll most likely part them for good. You know what these pig-headed old idiots are. Of course we know the standard up here; as soon as I saw you I knew I had no chance. She's been very good to me, and —" his head sank sadly between his paws.

I made up my mind to help him if possible, and had a long yarn with him. Told him all the show tricks, then got him to hold my collar so that I could slip out of it (it's an easy trick when you know it). Once loose, I slipped over to the water-trough, wet myself well, and rolled in a heap of sawdust I saw in the corner; then went back to my bench, slipped my collar on again, and fell asleep.

As soon as the show opened, a fine pair of lovers came in to see us. The girl was as pretty as a picture, with grey eyes and brown hair. Her cheeks were like ripe peaches when the sun shines on them. (I never eat these myself; they disagree with all our family.) After she had a look at me I saw tears start in her eyes, and her mouth quivered. "I'm afraid poor Bonny has no chance with the Sydney dog," she said sorrowfully to her companion. He turned away without speaking. I smiled up at her and wagged my tail. After seeing her I was determined to get second. So when they came to lead us out, I behaved disgracefully. First of all I lay down and rolled on the floor; then I had to be dragged into the ring, with my ears flat and tail between my legs. My coat was on end, and full of dirt and sawdust. I absolutely refused to parade the ring, snapped savagely at the judge every time he came near me; and finally broke from the boy holding me, and bolted from the ring altogether, and kept away till I saw the girl's dog come out with the blue ribbon; then I slipped away, cleaned myself thoroughly, and went back to my bench. The girl's dog had just began to smother me with gratitude, when she and her lover came up to us. I smiled up at her again, and wagged my tail. I am sure she knew, because she stooped down and kissed me twice, right on my broad flat forehead. Then they went away somewhere, hand in hand. My owner has never been able to make out, to this day, how I came to get second.

Now that I am retiring as champion, I don't mind telling you the tricks of the trade. The first thing, of course, is to have all the show points; the next is to show the judge that you have them. That is all there is in it. The first comes by nature, of course; the second by experience and brains. So that in the ring, the main thing is to carry yourself and chain well. Head up, ears up, tail up, and a walk in the ring as if you owned the earth. Possession is nine points of the law; self-possession is the tenth. It is all the better if you make an occasional leap at the next dog, with your mouth open; this shows the judge you have plenty of spirit. Always keep yourself before the judge's eye; don't let another dog get in between. When the judge calls you, chum up to him; if he throws anything up for you to snap at, snap quick but don't bite. (I lost a first once through biting a pet pipe in halves, and the taste stopped in my mouth for weeks.) When he opens your mouth, hold it so that he can admire your tusks; when he lets go, wag your tail afterwards. When leaving the ring with the ribbon, put on an extra burst of side. This impresses the people around, and pleases the judge. Always make any arrangements with the other dogs about places or prizes before going into the ring; you may get a fussy judge or steward, which gives you no time.

Of all the shows I have ever seen, nothing pleases me so well as the show of beef in front of a butcher's shop.

11

KALESKI ON CATTLE DOGS

Robert Kaleski's publications on Cattle Dogs are
collected in Appendix 1.

Apart from *Australian Barkers and Biters* (1933) Kaleski's
publications are not readily accessible. Many of his publications
are to be found only in the collections of major Australian libraries.
An exception is his article in the *American Kennel Gazette* which is
limited to American sources. As a result most attempts at compiling
breed histories of long-tailed Cattle Dogs have relied heavily on
Australian Barkers and Biters and *The Australian Encyclopaedia*
(1958). An otherwise unknown article by Kaleski, said to have
been published in 1935, *The Australian Cattle Dog: his share in the
pioneering of Australia and his origin*, became well known, at least
in Sydney, after Cheryl Edwards reproduced it in her book *Australian
Cattle Dogs: old timers* in 1995. (Kaleski never recognised the short-
tailed variety). Kaleski's fifty-five year long published output on
dogs, and particularly Cattle Dogs, was formidable and includes:

Introduction to the Cattle Dog breed standard 1903 and 1911.

The Australian Cattle Dog (*The Bookfellow* 1907).

The Working Dogs of Australia (*RAS Annual* 1911).

Australian Barkers and Biters 1914.

Australian Barkers and Biters 2nd ed. 1926: printed but never
publically released.

Whence came Australian Dogs? *American Kennel Gazette* 1930.

Australian Barkers and Biters new ed. 1933.

The Australian Cattle Dog (1935? provenance unknown, reprinted
by Cheryl Edwards).

> Foundation dogs of Australia (*Sydney Mail* 1938).
>
> The Cattle Dog *(Dogs of the World* 1947).
>
> The Cattle Dog (*Walkabout Magazine* 1949).
>
> Our prosperity rests on dogs (*The Sunday Herald* 1950).
>
> *The Australian Encyclopaedia* 1958.

A long article introduced Kaleski's Cattle Dog breed standard in 1903,[1] a slightly edited version of which reappeared in 1910 when the standard was reissued.[2] Essentially, the article was breed promotion – promotion of a new breed with a supporting breed standard that was making its show ring debut. Kaleski went to enormous lengths to emphasise the need for effective cattle dogs in almost any cattle working situation and to show that "his" Cattle Dogs met all the requirements: steady, game, faithful, enduring, and intelligent. Kaleski placed such enormous emphasis on correct biting, nip-and-drop biting, that one wonders whether this instinct was missing in other dogs that he saw working cattle. Not one to shrink from offering advice Kaleski was generous with his. Breaking-in a pup with a steady old dog is still relevant and if Kaleski's training methods appear unduly harsh, twenty-first century Australian Cattle Dog owners should remember that their Cattle Dogs have a much softer temperament than the Cattle Dogs of 1903.

Kaleski was unsuccessful in his attempt to give Cattle Dogs a distinctive name, "merlin", although his alternative, "blue heeler", has persisted in informal use. He also wished to distance "his" Cattle Dogs from the Smithfields mentioned by Beilby.[3] Smithfields were probably common in the show rings of the time and *Jack*, exhibited as a cattle dog at Sydney's Agricultural Exhibition in 1898, may have been one of them. Kaleski probably saw this dog in the show ring competing against "his" Cattle Dogs. Kaleski's acquaintance with the "Welsh heeler or merle" was probably from the late nineteenth century dog literature.

Kaleski's article in *The Bookfellow* introduced the Kaleski Dogma to a larger audience, to the literary world as well as to the dog fancy. It was reprinted in other newspapers and was parent to the Cattle Dog chapters in the later editions of *Australian Barkers and Biters*. In

The Working Dogs of Australia Kaleski emphasised colour as well as working traits – a response to the Cattle Dog's new status as a benched breed. Type, including coat colour, was to be as described in the breed standard. This 1911 article has particular historical significance. Here Kaleski, himself, associated Halls Heelers with the Timmins family. The famed Timmins Biters were Halls Heelers descendants.

> They [Halls Heelers] soon got scattered about the Hunter and New England. The well-known droving family of Timmins got some of them and produced some wonderful workers.[4]

By the late 1920s the basic Kaleski Dogma was in place, the text of the 1933 edition of *Australian Barkers and Biters* being little changed from the 1926 version.

The Kaleski Dogma insisted that:

- The black bob-tail was the among the working dogs first used in Australia. Various attempts to develop a working dog suited to Australian conditions were attempted but abandoned. Dingo crosses, in particular, were vicious and unreliable.
- Hall, of Muswellbrook, imported merle working dogs: Welsh merles in 1903, smooth Highland collies in 1907 and 1911, "called by ignorant people 'Welsh heelers'".
- The imported dogs were noisy and headstrong, and were crossed with dingo. This cross, Kaleski was convinced, introduced nip-and-drop heeling traits. He, himself, called Hall's dogs "Halls Heelers" and recognised them as the ancestors of the Cattle Dogs for which he compiled the first breed standard. Unlike other dingo hybrids, the Halls Heeler was an unqualified success as a working dog; neither vicious nor unreliable.
- Halls Heelers were breeding true by the 1840s.
- Besides being excellent workers of cattle, Kaleski's Cattle Dogs were vigilant guardians and protectors of their owners' property.

Kaleski's Dogma, except for Hall of Muswellbrook, was largely his own creation: a plausible story devised to give his Cattle Dogs the dignity of a history.

- No dog can be identified as the first working dog in Australia. Kaleski's guess is as good as any. The early colonial herdsmen would have been grateful for any dog that proved useful to them. We know little of the British working dog population of the late eighteenth century that supplied the immigrants – other than what Bewick, Edwards and Taplin wrote about them (see Chapter 1). We can infer only that among the immigrant dogs there were some that were ancestral to the Smithfields, (known to Betty Southall and probably to Kaleski), to the Tasmanian Smithfield, and to the Halls Heeler.

- Kaleski was convinced that Cattle Dogs' characteristic nip-and-drop heeling trait was a dingo inheritance. It wasn't. The dingo was, and is, a predator, not a droving dog. Having attributed nip-and-drop to the dingo Kaleski then had to insist that Thomas Hall's dingo hybrids were excellent working dogs but other dingo crosses were vicious and intractable.

- A dingo contribution to the Halls Heeler, if any, is most likely to have been accidental not intentional. The dingo had little to offer as a working dog, except being acclimatised to New South Wales conditions, but Kaleski admired the dingo and gave it qualities that it didn't possess – least of all, that of a heeler.

- Some of the "several attempts to make pure breeds of cattle-dogs" are so outrageous as not to be taken seriously. The Russian poodle[5], for example, was probably a standard poodle, a soft-mouthed retriever; a most unlikely candidate for a stock dog. Dogs described as Russian poodles were exhibited in Victoria in the 1860s.

The Kaleski Dogma remained much the same from its earliest statement in 1903 until the end of the 1920s. (The relevant text in *Australian Barkers and Biters* was written in 1907 for *The Bookfellow*.)

[1903, 1910] This breed was first made, as far as I can ascertain, by a Mr Hall or Wall of Muswellbrook, about forty years ago [that is c.1860]. He imported the blue-gray Welsh merle for working cattle, but finding they were unsuitable on account of barking too much, crossed them with the dingo and founded the present variety, which, by selection and careful breeding, became a distinct breed and throws true to type.

[1907] So Mr. Hall, of Muswellbrook, imported some blue smooth Highland collies or merles; called by ignorant people Welsh heelers. These were a lot better than the common collie; but still had some of the barking at-the-head business in them. So they were crossed on the dingo.

[1911] About fifty years ago, a Mr. Hall of Muswellbrook imported some smooth Highland collies (merles) for working cattle. These proved too noisy and headstrong and were crossed by him with the dingo to get the latter's idea of creeping up silently behind and biting. The cross proved a great success as workers and came blue or red speckled as the dingo or the collie predominated in them.

Then the Dogma changed. A post-1930 Kaleski Dogma emerged which contradicted the original Dogma and which was confused and internally inconsistent as well. It left one wondering, as Tony Parsons did, whether Kaleski knew anything at all about dogs and dog breeding. In 1930 Kaleski published in the *American Kennel Gazette*. In this article he introduced the assertions that have most earned him contempt: the needless Dalmatian and kelpie infusions, his "utility points" and the assertion that the Halls Heeler was a "direct cross" lacking distinctive, fixed type. In the post-1930 Dogma Kaleski insisted on red speckled legs, so as not to show dust, and brought to us the legendary (and imaginary) Tom Bentley's dog. The revelations that began in 1930 were eventually knitted together, to emerge in his disastrous article in *The Australian Encyclopaedia* in 1958.

[1930] About 20 years after Hall's importation some of these dogs were brought to Sydney by Alexander Davis, and they attracted much attention at Homebush sale-yards, where they were taken up by various drovers and butchers. As they were the result of a direct cross, a distinctive type was not fixed.

- Not a distinctive type, after twenty years of development? Little wonder that Parsons (pers. comm. 2000) said that Kaleski knew nothing about dog breeding. Kaleski's American readers would have been astounded by this revelation, if not frankly disbelieving.

[1930] The next move was, therefore, to infuse the blood of the Dalmatian, or spotted carriage-dog, and subsequently that of the kelpie. The result, in the hands of skillful breeders, was a compact, active dog identical with the pure dingo in type and build but with peculiar markings found in no other dog in the world.

- Even more unbelievable: the assertion that infusing Dalmatian and kelpie into a cross-bred dog lineage could produce the Cattle Dog for which Kaleski wrote his standard.

[1930] The face and ears are black or red, with a tan spot over each brown eye and a white stripe down the middle of the forehead; the body is a dark blue, evenly speckled with a lighter blue – whence the name "blue-speckle" – there may be a black saddle or spot on the tail-butt, no more black being allowed, the tail and under part of the body are a lighter blue, the legs, from feet to elbow, and hock, red-speckled. Blue-black or from light to white colors are barred; also "wall" or white eyes.

- By the time he wrote this, in the late 1920s, Kaleski was obsessed with colour. These colours and markings were of enormous importance (to Kaleski). They were his "utility points", invested with incredible significance as predictors of working ability, stamina, keen eye sight and, above all, descent from the mythical Tom Bentley's dog.

[1930] Rigid adherence to these markings is necessary, since they are "utility" points. The black head shows kelpie strain, and hence keen working qualities; the red head, dingo strain, and hence great hardiness; the brown eyes show keen sight; the white stripe down the forehead and the black spot on the tail-butt show descent from "Tom Bentley's dog" – one of the most perfect workers ever known.

- Parsons recalled that Kaleksi was obsessed by similarities. His obsession included assigning some particular (and imaginary) significance to colour and markings – none more nonsensical than "brown eyes show keen sight" or irrelevant than "red-speckled legs do not show the red dust".

  [1930] The dark-blue color is indispensable to a dog doing so much biting – and therefore liable to get kicked – since dark blue is invisible, especially at night. Black, on the other hand, is very conspicuous in daylight, and white is so by either day or night. The red-speckled legs do not show the red dust in which the dog is so often working. The dingo type is insisted upon because it denotes the strength and speed which are the results of natural selection during untold years under Australian conditions.

- The Kaleski who described these "utility points" was a man struggling painfully and unsuccessfully to capture fugitive recollection but succeeding only in writing disconnected rubbish.

In 1995 Cheryl Edwards reprinted an article by Kaleski, said to date from 1935: *The Australian Cattle Dog: his share in the pioneering of Australia and his origin* (1935).[6] Its stirring tribute to colonial pioneers is more evocative of the opening up of the American West (as portrayed in the myths of film and fiction) than it is of Australian colonial exploration. The reality was less glamourous. The wool grower did, indeed, make Australia's fortune but the country was opened up to him by the early explorers – many of whom lost their lives in the attempt. Despite the best efforts of several early exploration parties the New South Wales colony was confined to the coastal area around Sydney for twenty-five years. Several attempts to cross the highlands to the north, west and south of the colony met with defeat. Even after the Blue Mountains were crossed in

1813 there was no great rush westwards. Government, in fact, tried to prevent it. "Gentlemen, or other respectable free persons" could visit the area provided they were given the governor's permission. A military guard was posted on the road west, probably at the present Victoria Pass, to ensure that no unauthorised person could visit, or worse, "squat" (establish himself without government approval) in the unauthorised area.[7]

A series of droughts and caterpillar plagues during the late 1810s and early 1820s forced the issue. Expansion was essential and inevitable but, even so, government policy confined the colony to the "limits of location", the "Nineteen Counties": an area within about 200 km of Sydney. Settlers were allowed to take up land only within this area but, from the outset, there was always some unauthorised occupation (squatting) on Crown Lands both within and outside the Nineteen Counties.

As well as romanticising colonial history the 1935 article developed the post-1930 Kaleski Dogma.

> [1935] Then in 1840 a squatter named Thomas Hall who owned the "Dartbrook" property at Muswellbrook, Hunter Valley, N. S.W., imported a pair of blue Smooth Haired Collies from Scotland. They were called "Merles" (or mottles) because of the dark and light blue being mixed in patches on them. (These dogs were originally a cross of the Rough Haired Scotch Collie and the Blue Italian Greyhound; this is where the blue colour came from) ... The Greyhound in them kept them nearly silent ... The Dingo instinct gave them the idea of creeping up silently behind a horse or bullock and biting the foot on which the weight was resting at the moment, so that they could not be kicked. They came red mottle, blue mottle or plain red as the Dingo or merle predominated in them ... Hall continued his experimental matings until his death on the 28th May 1870.

- The blue Italian greyhound became part of the Dogma in this 1935 article. Kaleski apparently confused the slate blue of the Italian greyhound (diluted black) with the "blue" seen in Cattle

Dogs which is an expression of the Ticking gene. How the Italian greyhound cross was to produce a silent dog was not explained and, unless the Italian greyhound of Kaleski's day was a larger and much more robust animal than those of the present day, the Italian greyhound was a most unsuitable infusion to a breeding program if a working dog were to result.

The *Sydney Mail* published "Foundation Dogs of Australia" in 1938. This added little to the emerging post-1930 Dogma but is notable for its mention of the colony's earliest dogs.

[1938] In the first few years of settlement many English dogs, sporting and working, were brought out, mostly by officers and immigrants, either as pets or because they might be useful in the new land. The officers appear to have favoured coursing dogs (greyhounds) for the native game, and bull terriers for fighting purposes.

Although this is obviously what occurred, Kaleski remained convinced that Hall imported the Halls Heeler's ancestors.

Kaleski published nothing on Cattle Dogs during the twenty years between 1938 and 1958 except for a chapter in *Dogs of the World* in 1947, an article in *Walkabout Magazine* in 1949, and a short note in *The Sydney Morning Herald* in 1950. During the late 1950s, however, he was invited to contribute to *The Australian Encyclopaedia*. First published in 1958 *The Australian Encyclopaedia* was reprinted in 1963 and 1965. It was an important event in Australian publishing and enshrined and gave misplaced authority to the post-1930 Kaleski Dogma. Although his contribution was titled "Cattle Dogs" Kaleski wrote:

[1958] The Australian blue-speckle cattle-dog was established as a pure breed in 1890, after a long period of experiment by cattle-owners and dog-breeders to produce a dog suitable to Australian conditions.

- The breed name "Australian blue-speckle cattle-dog" was a Kaleski invention. The breed was known as "Cattle Dog" until the ANKC breed standard of 1963 gave formal recognition to "Australian Cattle Dog". Kaleski didn't recognise the stumpy tail variety.
- There were no experiments "to produce a dog suitable to Australian conditions". The unlikely, but abandoned, cross-breeding attempts, that Kaleski suggested, were probably accidental not intentional – if indeed they occurred.

The editors of *The Australian Encyclopaedia* knew only of Kaleski's past prestige and early publishing record when they sought him as a contributor.

If pre-1930 publications are studied together <u>as a group</u> and compared with later publications, also studied together <u>as a group</u>, it becomes evident that the two groups are inconsistent with one another and that the publications comprising the later group are inconsistent, one with another as well. That is, there is a discontinuity in Kaleski's grasp of his subject matter: apparent loss of memory, confusion, contradictions. A possible health concern, causing a decline in mental capacity, is a persuasive explanation although no such illness is known to the present Kaleski family.

Kaleski's later publications, excluding *Australian Barkers and Biters* (1933) should be rejected as misleading and valueless: the writings of a failing mind. Kaleski still wrote with the confidence of an established authority after the late 1920s but his grasp of subject became increasingly, and obviously, unreliable and fanciful.

Posterity has taken Kaleski completely literally. His knowledge of the nineteenth century publications on dogs was profound but, in his enthusiasm to develop an ancestry for the Halls Heeler, he used his knowledge uncritically. According to Kaleski's publications prior to 1930, Hall imported merle collies and crossed them with the dingo. There is some variation – "blue-gray Welsh merle", "smooth Highland collies (merles)" – but the basic theme remains.

Hall imported merle dogs and crossed them with the dingo. Kaleski's identification of the "imported" ancestor was apparently taken from nineteenth century publications and he attributed to Thomas Hall the breeding practices and concept of breed that were accepted in his own time, but not in Hall's.

After the late 1920s the story changed. Kaleski's thinking became confused. Welsh merles and Welsh Heelers were heard of no more. Hall imported "blue Smooth Haired Collies" with origins in the English mastiff or, alternatively, with a cross between the "Rough Haired Scotch Collie and the Blue Italian Greyhound". At first, the dogs were called "merles" because of their mottled colour, "dark and light blue being mixed in patches". Then they were described as blue, their colour being inherited from the Italian Greyhound. Next, they were "either all red like the dingo, or covered with rusty grey blotches, shot with black". Finally, they were blue mottled merles. The following extracts from Kaleski's later writings supposedly describe the same event but demonstrate his muddled thinking. They are inconsistent with one another and with pre-1930 articles.

> [1930] In 1840, a squatter named Hall of Muswellbrook, New South Wales, did a good deed for Australia when he imported a pair of blue-gray "merles" – marbled or mottle smooth-haired Scotch dogs – which were said to be good at working cattle. This breed had its origin in a blend of the old English mastiff – which protected the herds from wolves – the greyhound, and the Scotch collie.

> [1935] Then in 1840 a squatter named Thomas Hall who owned the 'Dartbrook' property at Muswellbrook, Hunter Valley, N. S.W., imported a pair of blue Smooth Haired Collies from Scotland. They were called 'Merles' (or mottles) because of the dark and light blue being mixed in patches on them. (These dogs were originally a cross of the Rough Haired Scotch Collie and the Blue Italian Greyhound ...

> [1938] At last, in 1840, a squatter named Hall, at Muswellbrook, in the Hunter Valley, imported a pair of blue, smooth- haired

collies from Scotland 'Merles', a new breed, then becoming fashionable. These dogs were originally a cross of the true (rough) Scottish collie and the blue Italian greyhound, from which they derived their blue colour.

[1947] Then, on a lucky day for Australia, a squatter named Hall, breeding cattle at Muswellbrook, on the Hunter-River, N.S.W., imported a pair of blue, smooth-haired collies ("Merles" or "Mottles") from Scotland in 1840. These dogs were originally a cross of the rough Scotch collie and the blue Italian greyhound; were blue mottled with black ...

[1949] Then in a fortunate year for Australia (1840) a squatter named Hall, of Muswellbrook on the Hunter River N.S.W. ... imported a pair of blue "merle" (smooth-haired mottled) Scotch collies. These dogs were poor biters, but light-coated and active in all weathers ...

[1950] ... a pair of the breed made by Hall, a squatter at Muswellbrook, from a cross of the Dingo and smooth blue Scottish Collie in 1840. They were known as "Hall's Heelers". These dogs were tireless workers and heelers, but poor colours: being either all red like the Dingo, or covered with rusty grey blotches, shot with black.

[1958] A better dog was produced in 1840. A squatter named Hall, who had a cattle station at Muswellbrook, N.S.W., heard of a good strain of working "merles", blue-mottled, smooth Scotch collies with "wall" (white) eyes, and he imported a pair from Scotland. These were an improvement on the ordinary collie, although their barking and "heading" style of working were not altogether suitable for cattle. To eliminate these defects, Hall crossed the breed with the dingo ...

Not only did the Halls Heeler ancestry change but their working ability as well, particularly between 1949 and 1958. The "poor biters" of 1949 became "tireless workers and heelers" in 1950 – only to degenerate in 1958, condemned for their "heading style of working".

The infamous Dalmatian infusion is a particularly notable example of the progressive decay in Kaleski's thinking. There is no mention of a deliberate Dalmatian infusion in Kaleski's earliest publications and only a disparaging remark in *Australian Barkers and Biters* but the Dalmatian infusion would later become essential to "improving" the Cattle Dog breed. The particular Dalmatian was even identified, by owner and address. For reasons unexplained, it was essential that the Cattle Dog should "love" horses. A love of horses, it seems, was a prerequisite to the dog's guarding horses and saddlery from theft. Forgotten were Kaleski's 1903 "requirements of a good [cattle] dog". After the 1920s Kaleski was increasingly preoccupied by coat colour and apparently unable to distinguish Dalmatian spots from Cattle Dog speckle or mottle. The colour description of 1930 and Kaleski's insistence on markings being "utility points" reappeared in *The Australian Encyclopaedia* in 1958, including the "Tom Bentley's dog" tale: a tall story of the tallest.

It is difficult to explain the contradictions between Kaleski's early and the later publications, and the inconsistencies within the latter except by appeal to some medical or other trauma that progressively affected his judgemental capabilities from the late 1920s.

Berenice Walters, of *Wooleston* Kennels, was only too aware of the misinformation in circulation during the 1970s and that much of it originated with Kaleski. Nevertheless, she recognised a debt to Kaleski. Her opinions of fifty years ago have a modern ring.

> Unfounded garbage about the breed as has been written about the breed, and is still being written, has done untold damage to the breed and caused those who write such stories and Australian dog breeders generally to be treated with ridicule. As early as the 1920s articles were appearing in overseas papers on Australian Cattle Dogs, laughing that this breed claimed to be the greatest cattle dog ever that had to have Dalmatian infused to give it a love of following horses (this in a breed that had been claimed by stockmen as the ideal drovers dog); another reason given was that as the Dingo-Collie cross did not breed true to type (after forty-odd years of working and breeding) a rank outside breed was brought in "to fix the breed".[8]

Walters took exception to Sydney bench breeders "claim[ing] for themselves the glory of the Halls Heelers (or Blue Heelers or Queensland Heelers)", adding "No wonder Queensland breeders claimed their strain of the original Hall cross as superior."

Walters recalled that Alan Forbes,[9] was of the opinion that, "although there is some disagreement as to the breeds used it is generally thought that the cattle dog developed chiefly from cross-breeding between a Dingo and a Blue Merle Collie, with a later injection of Bull Terrier blood". The Dalmatian and the Kelpie stories can be dismissed. Kelpie infusions, accidental or intentional, have occurred from time to time but probably not as attributed to the Bagusts by Kaleski and by way of Maiden's Kelpie. Coat colour genetics, in particular, disposes of the Dalmatian.[10]

In early studies of canine coat colour the Dalmatian type of solid spotted pattern was attributed to an independent gene but Little showed it to be a modification of ordinary flecking.[11] The basic Dalmatian genotype is therefore $s^w s^w$ TT. That is, the coat is mostly or completely white due to the s^w gene and liberally covered in coloured spots due to T. The spots are solid in the Dalmatian pattern, whereas they are interspersed with white hairs in Cattle Dogs. A gene is present in the Dalmatian that prevents the occurrence of white hairs in the spots.[12, 13] This gene is inherited as a recessive to flecking. Denoting the gene for interspersion of white hairs (flecking) by F, the gene for solid spots will be f. The genotype for Dalmatian type spotting at this locus is ff whereas in Cattle Dogs it is FF.

And Kaleski? Regardless of the misinformation and dated information for which he was responsible, Kaleski campaigned tirelessly for recognition of Australia's working dogs and kept them before the public eye. Whatever it was, the misfortune that overtook him and compromised his mental capabilities, we should accord him our greatest respect for the support he gave to the Cattle Dog breed. And no one else identified "Mr Hall of Muswellbrook".

Thomas Simpson Hall (1808-1870). Portrait owned by Mrs Enid Ross.

Ch *Glen Iris Stumpy* [1990] a descendant of *Sunny Boy*.

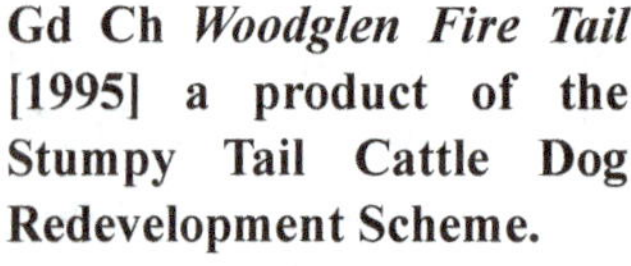

Gd Ch *Woodglen Fire Tail* [1995] a product of the Stumpy Tail Cattle Dog Redevelopment Scheme.

Gd Ch *Ambajaye High Tail It* [1999] a product of the Stumpy Tail Cattle Dog Redevelopment Scheme.

Blue working dog of a type found in Britain c.1990.

Working cattle dog with possible Smithfield ancestry Cunnamulla, Qld. 2015.

Ch *Geraldmine Ugy Bear* [1994].

Tasmanian Smithfields with about four months coat growth.

Tasmanian Smithfields Smithies are usually clipped in warm weather.

T Ch & O Ch *Tirlta Peace of Mind* UDX [2002-2016], left, and Ch & O Ch *Tirlta Dartbrook* UDX [2009]. Bred by the author, exhibited, trained and handled by Sue Dickerson.

Tirlta Wasting Light [2011] aged seven months. Bred by the author, owned and exhibited by Kath Williamson.

Tirlta Gem of the South [2009-2021]

Rock painting of a dingo and ancestral figure, Laura region, Queensland.

The Shepherds Dog and the Cur, from Edwards 1800.

The dingo, or the Dog of New South Wales, and the Pomeranian Dog, from Edwards 1800.

Cover of *Australian Barkers and Biters* 1914.

12

BREED STANDARDS

Breed standards for both Cattle Dog breeds
are collected in Appendix 2.

Kaleski's breed standard for Cattle Dogs was first published in the *Agricultural Gazette of N.S.W.* for August 1903. It was reissued in 1910 in the Department of Agriculture's *Farmers' Bulletin* 38. Following the practice of some early British breed standards Kaleski included points for each characteristic described. A description of "feet" was missing from the first version but added in the reissue. The general article on the Cattle Dog that preceded the standard in the 1903 version reappeared in the 1910 version with the text unchanged except for the omission of the last few paragraphs. The omitted paragraphs advanced Kaleski's proposal for tattoo identification – useful but never followed up – and included some extravagant claims about the Cattle Dog's show ring success. That is, "his" Cattle Dogs were competing successfully in the show ring, against "cattle dogs" – any dog that worked cattle. There were no working dogs particularly identified as defined as Cattle Dogs until Kaleski produced a standard. After 1903, Cattle Dog classes, at least in Sydney, were judged as per standard. A definitive point in the breed's history and development and one that stands to Kaleski's lasting credit.

The standard was not a unilateral statement of Kaleski's personal opinions although his opinions carried considerable weight. The provenance of the standard, however, emerged in a larger debate in the *Sydney Mail* during 1922 that ranged from quality of cattle dog exhibits to dog poisoning. Kaleski wrote:

A standard was drawn up by me in 1897 because, like many others, I had been severely victimized when showing almost perfect dogs by judges giving the prize to crossbreds and mongrels at his own sweet will. Like Mark Twain's Riley, I got full of this, and drew up what I considered to be the perfect standard for working sheep and cattle dogs, got it endorsed by the leading breeders and the original Kennel Club of N.S.W., and published it, with a description of the breeds, in the N.S.W. 'Agricultural Gazette'. It was generally in use up to about 1912; by then some of the breeders had developed into dealers (this was the downfall of the old Kennel Club, of which I was a councillor for some years), and the standard did not suit their book; so they managed to get it more or less ignored at the shows. This has been going on up to the present time: hence the low ebb in type and quantity. Also, a lot of breeders rear the dogs in their back yards, and never attempt to work them, with the usual result — disease and loss of working qualities. A number of old and new fanciers have revived our original club (the Cattle and Sheep Dog Club of Australia) with a view to bringing the dogs up again. The first thing it did, after forming, was to adopt my old standard, and set out that the dogs must be judged by it. By this means, it is believed, the club is assured of success.[1]

Kaleski's article drew irritated response from Joseph Rose.

As a reader of the "Mail" for many years I must take exception to some of the statements made by Mr Kaleski re the cattle-dog. He says he formed the judging standard; whereas he was only one of those present when the standard was formed by Messrs Bagast [sic] J Burns, J J Yabsley, C Pettit [sic], and myself, also Mr E J Gibb of Mortlake, I like to give credit where it is due but this is over the odds. ... My dog was the standard of the club, and the only dog to win the Cattle-dog Cup.[2]

The Cattle Dog breeder and judge, Joseph Yabsley, argued with Rose.

I was one of the original members of the Club when we passed Mr Kaleski's standard. We discussed it point by point, and passed it as being as nearly perfect as possible. By the way, Mr Rose has not got the names right in his letter. Mr Gibb was never a member of the club, and those present were Messrs. P. Barrett, H. Baggars [sic], J. Baggars [sic], W. King, W. Crane, and R. Kaleski.[3]

Kaleski eventually replied to Rose, himself, having been "too busy" to do so earlier.

> What he means by 'forming' the standard is best known to himself. I drew up the standard without any assistance from any person whatsoever in 1897 – several years before the first meeting of the Cattle and Sheep Dog Club of Australia – and showed it first to my breeding partner, Alec Davis, now a well-known carcase butcher at Enfield, to see if he could suggest any improvement in it. His opinion was that it could not be bettered, so I circulated it amongst the breeders, and in 1903, published it in the Agricultural Gazette of N.S.W. It was endorsed by the Cattle and Sheep dog Club of Australia, of which I was hon. Secretary, and later by the old Kennel Club of N.S.W. This was the first endorsement, without the scale of points. The second endorsement of the standard, taking in my scale of points and adding a new one (feet), completing the standard as it is to-day, took place in 1910, and was published in a special pamphlet on cattle-dogs and sheep-dogs by the N.S.W. Department of Agriculture.

> About Mr Rose's dog being the standard of the club. No dog was ever a standard of the club while I was hon. Secretary, which was from its inception till 1912, when a majority of the members changed its name to that of the Sheep and Cattle Dog Club of N.S.W. What Mr Rose apparently refers to was my putting his old dog *Danger* on the club envelopes as 'correct type', which he was; but which kept me in hot water with most of the other members for a long time afterwards.[4]

Kaleski and Rose may have been at daggers drawn but that didn't stop Kaleski from very publically admiring Rose's dog Ch *Danger* [1903], a dog of particularly modern appearance. Even so, Rose wrote again to the *Sydney Mail* on 1 November 1922.

> I crave space to reply to Mr Kaleski's remarks regarding the
> Cattle Dog Club. Re the standard, he says that no mention was
> made of feet. I drew attention to this. He wanted to give 20 points
> for ears. I had it reduced to 10. Mr Yabsley bears me out on this.
> If Mr Kaleski had said the club framed the standard the statement
> would have been correct.[5]

James Moore, president of the Sheep-dog and Cattle-dog Club of
Australia, closed correspondence on the standard with a tribute to
Kaleski. Clearly, in 1922, Kaleski was highly regarded in the Cattle
Dog breed fancy (except by Joseph Rose) and his opinions sought
and respected.

> ... the Sheepdog and Cattle-dog Club of Australia, I formed
> myself. [Kaleski] had nothing to do with it. After I started it, one
> of the first things we did was to adopt his standard as our guide.
> He then became a member to help us along and to give us the
> benefit of his experience, but holds no office of any sort. I might
> say that the Cattle and Sheep Dog Club of N.S.W. some years
> ago elected him as a life member in recognition of his services
> to those breeds. I would like Mr Rose to tell us what he has ever
> done for the benefit of our dogs ...[6]

Rose never replied.

Dalziel's *British Dogs* (1879?) was subtitled "their varieties, history,
characteristics, breeding, management and exhibition". Kaleski
intended no less for his Cattle Dogs when he published the standard.
A long article introduced the standard and another was published in
The Bookfellow (both in Appendix 1). Kaleski eulogised the Cattle
Dog's working ability, described the breed's general characteristics,
advised on training and diet. He provided them with a history
(Mr Hall's imported dog crossed with dingo) and added useful
information for breeders: "The pups are *white* when first born, but
turn blue after a few weeks, and are surprisingly uniform in colour
and markings. Their ears do not prick till they are a few months old."
The Cattle Dog was a nip-and-drop biter, Kaleski explained. One
wonders whether the nip-and-drop trait was unique to Cattle Dogs

in nineteenth century New South Wales and distinguished them from other dogs used for cattle work. The standard reappeared in 1933 in *Australian Barkers and Biters*, unchanged, except for the point score for height that was missed in the earlier versions. This later version included explanations for each of the standard points.

The Australian agricultural shows of the early twentieth century were parochial in outlook and state orientated. Standard after standard followed Kaleski's and it was not until the formation of the Australian National Kennel Council that competing interests were finally resolved. The agenda of the first official meeting of the ANKC, in 1949, was a long one. Items for discussion included the unification of breed standards but this was not achieved until the 1960s.

The present Australian Cattle Dog standard, dated 14 December 2009, differs little from the 1963 standard except in occasional choice of words and stifle description. Concern about stifle angulation (too many straight stifles were seen in the show ring) prompted the change, in 1981, to stifles well turned. Stifle angulation was certainly a major concern in the 1970s as the judge, Alf Seymour, pointed out in 1978.

> Probably the most evident fault in the body area would be insufficient turn of stifle. It must be realised that the Standard calls for moderate turn of stifle, but surely this does not excuse the many straight stifles evident today. Often accompanying straight stifles we see high tail sets and lack of slope over the rump. This causes lack of drive in movement and stilty rear ends.[7]

In 1986, after the amendment to well-turned stifle, Bill Crowley (judge and sometime member of the ANKC) commented:

> A few short years ago member bodies of the Australian National Kennel Council were so concerned about straight stifles that they amended the Standard from 'a moderate turn of stifle' to the present 'stifles well turned'. The major reason for this was that owners of otherwise good dogs used the term 'moderate' to excuse straight stifles. There is no real evidence yet that this has

brought about any substantial change but eventually it should. The one thing that even the most casual judge can detect is a straight stifle. If he doesn't see it at once, he will quickly identify it by the short, choppy or stilted movement as the dog goes around the ring, taking twice as many steps to cover the same ground as the well angulated competitor. This poor movement is accentuated when the dog moves into specials against other free moving dogs.[8]

Well intentioned amendments of this kind, however, are not the purpose of a standard as Hewson-Fruend pointed out, and this one was unnecessary. Under "Movement" the 1963 standard stated that "straight stifles [and] bow hocks must be regarded as serious faults".[9] Unfortunately, FCI-Standard No. 287 for the Australian Cattle Dog still (2021) asks for a well-turned stifle, as does the American Kennel Club and The Kennel Club, UK. The ANKC has yet to seek update of the overseas standards in line with country of origin.

The coat colour of red Australian Cattle Dogs remains a matter for continuing debate. Early discrimination against red animals may be historical: Kaleski excluded them from his standard even though he was aware of them (at least by 1910). More recently the ANKC standards have described red Cattle Dogs as "red speckled", implying that red Cattle Dogs must be speckled but blue Cattle Dogs may be of more even colour (evenly ticked). There is no reason why red animals must be speckled although frail excuses have been advanced. (Dingo shooters need the speckle to distinguish red Cattle Dogs from dingoes? Tell that to a dingo shooter!) The ambiguous "not white or cream" is an inheritance from the NSW Stock Club Standard, 1928.

> The colour should be of good even red speckle all over, including the undercoat (not white or cream) with or without darker red markings on the head.

Between the first publication of Kaleski's standard in 1903 and the ANKC standard of 1963, competing standards proliferated. Most were variations on Kaleski and did not recognise a stumpy-tailed variety. The standard published by the Cattle Dog and Kelpie Club of Queensland in 1923 was a rare exception. This standard described the long-tailed variety first and dealt with the short-tailed Cattle Dog by additions.

> The description for the long tail variety applies, except as to tail, and with the following additions. Tail must be naturally stumpy.
>
> Disqualifications: under or overshot mouth, docked tails.
>
> Objections: tail exceeding four inches in length; dew claws on hind legs.

During the 1920s the Cattle Dog and Kelpie Club of Queensland obviously considered long-tailed and short-tailed Cattle Dogs to be two varieties within a single breed. This view was apparently endorsed by the ANKC when it issued a standard for the Stumpy Tail Cattle Dog. Although it recognised long-tailed and short-tailed Cattle Dogs as two separate breeds the differences between the two standards of 1963 are small except for tail descriptions. The colour specifications for both breeds are similar, including tan markings.

Blue Australian Cattle Dog 1963: The colour should be blue or blue-mottled with or without other markings. The permissible markings are black, blue or tan markings on the head, evenly distributed for preference. The forelegs tan midway up the legs and extending up the front to breast and throat, with tan on jaws; the hindquarters tan on inside of hind legs, and inside of thighs, showing down the front of the stifles and broadening out to the outside of the hind legs from hock to toes. Tan undercoat is permissible on the body providing it does not show through the blue outer coat. Black markings on the body are not desirable.

Blue Stumpy-tail Cattle Dog 1963: The dog should be blue or blue mottled, whole coloured. The head may have black markings with or without tan. Black markings on the body are permissible. *The forelegs may have tan midway up the legs and running up the front of the throat. The hindquarters, tan on the inside of the hind legs and inside the thighs, showing down the front of the stifles and* *broadening out to the outside of the hind legs from hock to toe. Tan, the richer the better.*

Red Speckle Australian Cattle Dog 1963: The colour should be of a good even red speckle all over, including the undercoat (not white or cream) with or without darker red markings on the head. Even head markings are desirable. Red markings on the body are permissible but not desirable.

Red speckled Stumpy-tail Cattle Dog 1963: The colour should be of a good even red speckle all over, including the undercoat (not white or cream) with or without darker red markings on the head. Even head markings are desirable. Red markings on the body are permissible.

Blue Stumpy-tail Cattle Dog updated 2009: The colour should be a good even blue mottle or blue speckle, with or without black marking on the head and body. *Blues should not have a red undercoat or any appearance of red throughout the coat or head.*

Red Speckle Stumpy-tail Cattle Dog updated 2009: The colour should be a good even red mottle or red speckle, with or without red markings on head and body. Reds should not have a blue undercoat or any appearance of blue throughout the coat or head. *Irrespective of the colour of the dog, tan markings are not permissible in either the blue or red dogs, under any circumstances.*

Tan in Stumpy Tail coats became a fault only after the implementation of the 2009 standard; that is, after the Stumpy Tail Cattle Dog Redevelopment Scheme was inaugurated. According to Margaret Davis (pers. comm. 2021) judges, such as herself, who took part in Redevelopment Scheme grading days made their assessments according to the 2009 standard. Although tan in blue Stumpies seems to have become uncommon by the 1980s – only three registered: *Glen Iris Bush Idol* [1981], Ch *Glen Iris Bush Mate* [1981] and *Glen Iris Small Talk* [1987] – one wonders whether the Collis standard influenced condemnation of tan.

In her self-published book, *Australia's First Working Dog* (1999), Laurel Atwell (writing under the pseudonym, Joyce Herald Collis) produced a breed standard for the Stumpy Tail Cattle Dog, allegedly dated 1934, for which she cited neither provenance nor any evidence that any breed club or show organiser adopted the standard. In the absence of provenance it is plausible to wonder whether the standard was a fraudulent attempt by Atwell to advance her own opinions, the Atwell Dogma. There was no historical reason to depart from the Cattle and Dog Club of Queensland standard of 1923 but Atwell was obviously intent on promoting the Stumpy Tail Cattle Dog as a separate breed, completely unrelated to the Long Tail Cattle Dog. This is evident from her book. Who compiled this standard? Evidently it had little or no authority when it was issued, or its colour preference would not have been so flagrantly disregarded.

13

DOGS, SHOWS AND BREEDERS TO 1950

Within twenty years of the first dog shows in England, Australia had taken up the sport. For Cattle Dogs, with no pedigreed, imported ancestors and no formal early ownership records, their documented history starts with show catalogues. The first large agricultural shows in Australia were held in the capital cities of the various colonial states.

The Agricultural Society of New South Wales (later the Royal Agricultural Society of New South Wales) held annual Metropolitan Intercolonial Exhibitions in Sydney and the National Agricultural and Industrial Association (later the Royal National Agricultural and Industrial Association) held annual National Exhibitions (later, Royal National Exhibitions) in Brisbane. These shows became known as the Sydney and Brisbane "Royals" and are referred to as such in this text, regardless of date, except in the case of specific shows. (The Brisbane Royal is also known locally as the "Ekka"; i.e. Exhibition.)

Few show catalogues survive other than those of the Royal Shows. The most informative for Cattle Dogs are those from Sydney and Brisbane. From c.1900 the Royal catalogues gave name of exhibit as well as name of exhibitor. Name of breeder, parentage of exhibit, date of birth and colour were sometimes included. Results from lesser shows were occasionally published in the daily newspapers and in the dog world press that emerged during the 1920s, but these commonly list the exhibitor, and sometimes name of exhibit, only. The photographic record is poor except for Cattle Dogs exhibited at the Sydney Royal. The *Brisbane Courier* and the *Sydney Morning Herald* (both daily newspapers) covered the Royal shows in their respective cities and listed the results of dog judging but photos of dogs are few. New South Wales working dogs fared better. Articles by Kaleski and other writers, often with photographs, were regular features in the *Sydney Mail*.

Queensland pedigree records are the most complete of any state. Stud Books were issued from 1922 by the Kennel Association of Queensland. Most Stud Book entries include three-generation pedigrees and among the Stud Book entries are many dogs that were never exhibited at a Royal Show. For the period to 1939 some 1,160 Cattle Dogs are recorded to Queensland owners including thirty-five dogs bred in New South Wales. With three exceptions, the New South Wales dogs were whelped in 1929 or later. The New South Wales pedigree record for the corresponding period is largely dependent on the catalogues for the Sydney Royal.

Many early shows were arenas both for display and sale of stock. Cattle dogs were no exception. Classes for exhibition and sale of cattle dogs were scheduled from the 1870s. The Brisbane Royal catalogue for 1891, for example, advised exhibitors:

> Public sales of such exhibits as owners may desire to dispose of shall be held at the exhibition on such days and in such order as shall be duely [sic] notified.

The asking prices were high, in the monetary value of the day, and reflected the value placed on the dogs exhibited. These were usually around £5-0-0 but exceptional exhibits were priced higher. The highest price placed on any Cattle Dog exhibit during this period was £100-0-0 for Byrne's *Ringer*, at the 1913 Brisbane Royal. Byrne's *Lassie* (one of four, with the same name, that he exhibited) was offered for £50-0-0 at the same show and, in 1917, George Griffith asked £40-0-0 for his stumpy-tailed bitch, *Blue Bell*.

New South Wales

Classes for cattle dogs were scheduled from the 1870s but few exhibits are recognisable as Halls Heeler descendants; some are definitely not. Three of the six cattle dog exhibits entered at the 1870 Metropolitan Intercolonial Exhibition in Sydney were described as "imported" or "from imported stock".[1] Their exhibitor, E. W. Rouse of Rouse Hill, also entered a sheepdog "imported from Scotland". Cattle dog entrants to a later Metropolitan Intercolonial Exhibition, 1875, included *Coolie*, a Scotch collie and a *Roolo*, German "collie", but also *Wonga*. The 2½ year-old *Wonga* was described as 1ft 10 ins (55 cm) in height and weighing 38 lbs (17 kg). His breeding was "by *Driver* from *Judy* by Mr Timmins *Bluey*". *Wonga* may have the distinction of being the first Cattle Dog of Halls Heeler ancestry exhibited at a Sydney Royal.

Nipper [1890] was exhibited by G. W. Bagust at the Metropolitan Intercolonial Exhibition in 1890, along with *Flora*, exhibited by J. Bagust, *Spot* [1899] exhibited by A. W. Davis, *Bluey* (J. R. Bowditch), *Phill* (P. Anderson) and Robert Kaleski's *Tiger*. There were three entries, only, in 1901 – *Floss*, *Nipper* and *Tiger* – but, encouraged by Kaleski's breed standard, numbers grew rapidly. Between 1900 and 1909 seventy-nine Cattle Dogs were exhibited and, during the next decade, 370 Cattle Dogs were displayed to the Sydney public including Joseph Rose's *Danger*. Most of the exhibited dogs were described as blue although there were a few red speckled Cattle Dogs among them. Thirty-eight of the exhibits were black-and-tan. The tan may have been derived from Kelpie or from a Halls Heeler ancestor. Most New South Wales owners and breeders came from localities that are now inner suburbs of Sydney but a few were from more distant addresses in the Camden and Wollongong areas. One Sydney exhibitor obtained his dog from Longreach in Queensland.

Among the Cattle Dogs entered in the Sydney Royal between 1900 and 1919 eighteen have present day descendants. None of these were owned by the Bagusts, Kaleski, Davis or Yabsley but four of them were from the kennels of Charles S. Pettit. Pettit began showing Cattle Dogs in 1907, usually under the informal *Brooklyn* prefix, and became increasingly prominent in the bench Cattle Dog world during the years that followed.

Queensland

Sixty-two Cattle Dogs were shown at Brisbane Royals during the pre-1900 period, nearly all of them by exhibitors with addresses in and around Brisbane. Most of the exhibits were blue; some were described as "yellow". Long-tailed and stumpy-tailed types were not distinguished in the catalogues. None of the pre-1900 exhibits made documented contribution to the Australian Cattle Dog of the present day.

Although the Brisbane Royal included classes for cattle dogs from 1890 this was not common at smaller shows. The Queensland Kennel Club, for example, did not schedule a class for Cattle Dogs at its 1910 show although provision was made for an "any other varieties" class. Cattle Dog classes were scheduled at the Brisbane Royal in 1901 but there were no entries. From 1902, however, entry numbers grew and between 1902 and 1909 fifty-six cattle dogs were shown, most of them described as blue. A few Queensland breeders began a long association with Cattle Dog breeding and exhibiting at this time, among them William Byrne, one of the several Cattle Dog breeders in the Ipswich area. Byrne was among the first Queensland breeders to import from New South Wales. Bred by the Bagusts, *Rowdy* [1899] was sent to Byrne by Joseph Rose in the early 1900s.

Between 1910 and 1919, 128 Cattle Dogs were exhibited at Brisbane Royals. Colour was recorded for very few of them but there were many "blue" names. At least nineteen and probably more were stumpy-tailed; there were separate classes for Stumpy Tail Cattle Dogs from 1917. The exhibits included Byrne's Gd Ch *Blue Bess* [1923] who has descendants in the present day Australian Cattle Dog population via *Broombees Bobby* [1953]. The 1917 Cattle Dog entry was unusually large and in March 1918 the *Brisbane Courier* commented:

> The cattle-dog is evidently regaining the popularity this
> Australian production enjoyed a decade ago, and enquiries for
> such dogs are becoming numerous. This may be accounted for by
> the great commercial value this breed of dog possesses.

The columnist added:

> There are two very valuable breeds (both Australian natives),
> the cattle dog and the Kelpie. The dogs are absolutely necessary
> commodities to the handlers of cattle and sheep and their worth
> on the large and small stock stations in Australia cannot be
> overestimated.[2]

The Brisbane Royal of 1917 attracted thirty-one Cattle Dog entries,
eleven (35%) of which were short-tailed. During the 1920s, however,
many Cattle Dog breeders in Queensland followed the trend set
earlier by William Byrne with his purchase of the New South Wales
dog, *Rowdy*. Byrne, and other breeders with show ring ambitions,
evidently saw success in terms of dogs bred in New South Wales and
progressively replaced their Queensland foundation stock with dogs
from New South Wales. New South Wales judges, such as Charles
Court-Rice, were invited to judge Brisbane shows and promoted
the New South Wales (Kaleski) standard or later New South Wales
standards based on Kaleski's. (Court-Rice, himself, produced a
standard based on Kaleski's.) During the 1930s the number of
Brisbane breeders preferring dogs from Sydney kennels increased.
In 1950, "Cattle Dogs (short-tail)" contributed only four (12%) of
the Brisbane Royal entry of thirty-five. The contribution of early
Queensland Cattle Dogs to the benched Cattle Dog population in
Queensland became increasingly attenuated.

Victoria

Victoria's first dog show, the Victorian Dog Show, was held in
1864 under the auspices of the Acclimatisation Society of Victoria.
The entry was dominated by poodles, including a Russian Poodle
– one of the more unlikely Cattle Dog ancestors that appeared
in Kaleski's later (and unreliable) writings. Sheepdogs were

exhibited in 1864 but it was not until 1865 that cattle dogs were shown and these were described as Smithfields. Seven dogs were exhibited as Cattle Dogs at the Annual Exhibition of the Royal Agricultural Society of Victoria (the Melbourne Royal) in 1913. The colour descriptions of four of them suggest that they belonged in the Cattle Dog class but three of them were of foreign coat colour: black and tan; yellow; black and white. The following year, 1914, the Royal attracted only two entrants but both were blue. There were no entries in 1915. From 1916 to 1933 entry numbers varied (from three to ten) and, until 1927, included some that were neither blue nor red.

Other than the catalogues of the Melbourne Royals only one show catalogue survives from the 1920s, a September 1927 show organised by the Victorian Poultry and Kennel Club and combined clubs affiliated with the Victorian Kennel Association. E.V. Craddock of Ballarat exhibited *Blue Chap* [1926] and *Blue Chum* [1926?]. From these modest beginnings, Craddock became one of the most influential early Cattle Dog breeders in Victoria, particularly after he acquired the New South Wales dog, Gd Ch *Some Rock*, and stood him at stud.

The 1932 Lord Mayor's Charity Dog Parade Cattle Dog entry was dominated by Mrs E. V. Willis (West Brunswick): Ch *Sir Rocket of Nymble* [1931], Ch *Some Judy of Nymble* [1931], Ch *Trixie of Nymble* [1929] and Ch *Lady Minette of Nymble* [1931]. These were all, variously, offspring of Ch *Some Rock* and/or Ch *Minette* [1925], a New South Wales bitch that Willis purchased. She bred and exhibited Cattle Dogs throughout the 1930s. In 1934 the Royal Agricultural Society of Victoria celebrated its centenary. The Centenary Exhibition attracted fifteen Cattle Dog entries and included three dogs from New South Wales, among them Gd Ch *Nebo Rock*. Willis owned and or bred nine of the exhibits and Craddock, two.

Melbourne Royal entries continued to increase (forty-eight in 1950) and interstate exhibitor interest was maintained. KC & KCC Ch *Young Autocrat* was shown in Melbourne in 1946. KC Ch *Oatley*

Peter was shown in 1946 and 1947. The Centenary Exhibition also introduced a new breed name, Australian Heeler. The classes in the centenary catalogue were headed: "Australian Heelers (Late Cattledogs and Queensland Heelers)". They remained " Australian Heelers" until 1956.

Dog registrations were not a requirement in Victoria until the formation of the Kennel Control Council in 1930. The Kennel Control Council sought parentage on early registration applications but, evidently, was not greatly perturbed when these details were not supplied. *Sir Peter*, registered in 1934 with parentage unknown, was described as bred by S. Hodge, a "travelling showman".

The *Sun Dog Book,* published in Victoria (its co-author described as a "noted Interstate Judge of Dogs") included a poorly informed section on Cattle Dogs.

> Many people are under the impression that the title cattle dog includes all dogs that will work cattle, and numbers of those seen at the shows, particularly in Victoria, are of a rough, almost Sheepdog type. In Queensland, where the breed has been developed and a more uniform type bred for, owners have a more definite idea of what is needed. In both Queensland and New South Wales large classes are seen at the various shows, and the type is more definite and even than that seen elsewhere. These dogs are strongly built, wonderful workers, and are being bred mostly blue merle in colour, which would suggest that at some time there was a cross of the blue merle Collie. A Kelpie-Collie cross is also suggested. In Victoria a few breeders exhibit the Queensland type of dog and these are generally accepted as the true Cattledog.[3]

In fact Victoria looked towards New South Wales for breeding stock. *Some Rock* [1927], *Young Autocrat* [1942] and *Oatley Peter* [1942] were among the New South Wales Cattle Dogs that contributed substantially to Cattle Dogs in Victoria.

The Power of the Press

Regular columns, such as "The Kennel" in the *Brisbane Courier*, reported on the affairs of the Queensland dog world from the 1890s. These columns advertised forthcoming shows, some show results and other general news but the amount of detail varied and probably reflected the amount of interest taken in the column by the readership and the journalist of the time. During the 1920s, however, a number of periodicals, devoted partly or entirely to the dog world, appeared. A review of what is preserved, both in the general and the dog press, gives some insight into the tensions and concerns of the Cattle Dog world between the two World Wars. The major kennel clubs in New South Wales were endeavouring (with signal lack of success) to form a single controlling organisation for canine affairs and Queensland was having similar problems with competing major clubs.

The weekly *Sydney Mail* showed particular interest in Australian working dog breeds and gave Kaleski and other correspondents a voice. Kaleski campaigned tirelessly for public recognition and appreciation of the importance of Australian working dogs to the rural industry. His Sydney Royal critiques, with accompanying photographs, were an annual *Sydney Mail* feature during the 1920s and 1930s. His appeals for increased prize money should be read in their economic context. Australia was moving towards economic depression and some of the country areas were hit harder, and earlier, than the cities. Transport and other costs made exhibiting at the Sydney Royal beyond the financial means of some country Cattle Dog breeders. Unemployment levels were high. For many men, enlistment for World War II service in 1939 was the first fully employed work that they had known for many years.

The quality of judging and inattention to breed standards came under scrutiny by Kaleski and others. In general, Kaleski was not favourably impressed by the dogs he saw exhibited. He was also critical of the Royal Agricultural Society of New South Wales under more than one heading. He aired some of these issues after the 1921 Sydney Sheep Show. As an exhibitor to the show, himself, he refrained from commenting on the exhibits or judging beyond saying that the entry was small and that fine animals were few. This he attributed to insufficient prize money, to the judge's name being withheld until just before judging, and to uncertainty as to the standard to be adopted. Kaleski was also adamant that the best Cattle Dogs were working Cattle Dogs, not pet animals.

> Breeders of sheep and cattle dogs, to be successful, must of necessity be workers of them as well, or be in a position to pay to have them worked, so as to ensure that shape, stamina and intelligence are retained in them. If kept in back yards or as pets for a few generations these dogs lose these qualities and become as useless for work as a show collie. This being so, the best breeders are usually drovers or stock-dealers of small means, to whom pulling a dog out of its work, fattening it, and getting it up means a serious loss, for a good dog saves a man's wages in handling stock, and it is not easy to get a substitute.[4]

Kaleski's *Sydney Mail* article in July 1922 restated many of his objections in more forceful and detailed terms. The letters in reply are revealing of Kaleski's prestige among (some, at least of) the members of the Sydney Cattle Dog fancy. On the other hand, Joseph Rose's standing appears to have been somewhat doubtful. Evidently, there was no love lost between Kaleski and Rose (see also Chapter 8). Kaleski wrote:

> Up to about 1912 good working sheep and cattle dogs of pure strains were available in large numbers at very reasonable prices. Since then they have shown a steady decline in numbers, in purity, and in quality, til now it is very difficult and costly to get a dog true to type and a good worker. The reasons for this state of affairs are fourfold: (1) Lack of interest by the general public; (2) baits [malicious poisoning]; (3) not judging to standard; (4) carelessness of breeders. This is mainly the result of the first three.

> The first reason is a very serious one. The main offenders in this are the newspapers and the agricultural and dog societies. The newspapers are to blame in that they give little publicity to the

doings of these dogs, and the general public show no interest in them. If the press featured all working dog classes at the shows and encouraged articles on the dogs' work and general utility on the road, farm and station (where it is safe to say, each dog saves a man's wages) it would not take the public long to see that here was a field of interest far beyond the imported picture show. Once the press woke up, agricultural societies would cater specially for these dogs, and give prize-money and classes worthy of them. Then breeders would have some incentive to spend their money and time breeding dogs true to type and standard, and letting the public know that they had them. After a few years the cattle and sheep dogs would become one of the main features of every agricultural show in the Commonwealth, and deservedly so.[5]

The *Sydney Mail* took up the cause as far as printed promotion was concerned although the daily newspapers remained uninterested. The agricultural societies saw no value in promoting Australian working dogs and special prizes remained few.

The dog world press was less inhibited than the general press. Complaints of one sort or another, criticism of judging and even allegations relating to misappropriation of funds and trophies were reported. Defamation and libel would appear not to have been sensitive issues in the 1920s and 1930s and character assassinations were fairly routine. Descents to the level of E. E. Dodd's open letter to C. B. George in 1934 were, however, infrequent. (Dodd bred and exhibited *Nebo Rock* but later sold the dog to Roy Barratt.)

You officiated as a 'judge' of Cattle and Kelpie Dogs at the General Dog Fanciers' Club's show on August 25 [1934], and in the Open Cattle Dog class you placed the super dog, Interstate Grand Champion Nebo Rock, third in a class of three, notwithstanding this dog is a challenge winner on 58 occasions, including the Royal Agricultural Society, Sydney, twice, and the Royal National Exhibition, Brisbane twice, or four Royals in a row, under exactly fifty different judges. Your decision was so utterly absurd that you were held up to ridicule and became the laughing stock of the ring-siders competent to criticise your lamentable attempt at judging. There are quite a lot of questions which you might be good enough to answer for public information. Have you ever perused the standard laid down for this breed of dog? If so where did you obtain it and did you ask any competent judge to explain to you what was actually meant when the different points of the dog were referred to in such standard? What are your qualifications to judge? How often have you judged a 2-Point Championship show and where? Were you influenced in your absurd awards by the following facts: -

(a) Will you deny that this super dog Nebo Rock, which I had the pleasure of breeding, has been placed over your own dog on no less than twenty occasions under seventeen separate judges and that the only occasion your dog was placed over Nebo Rock was when the latter was covered in bare patches, the after effects of ringworm, and that the judge who officiated then told you on a subsequent meeting why he reversed his decision, and that your dog was not the equal of Nebo Rock?

(b) Will you also deny that you publically questioned me when officiating as judge at the Hyde and District Canine Fanciers show on the 18th August, to point out to you where Nebo Rock 'was a superior dog to your own'?

(c) Did I not go over the dogs from muzzle to flag, and do this to your satisfaction and which coincided with so many other competent judges?

(d) Were you grieved at my remarks?

(e) Do you regard yourself as an expert in these breeds and are you egotistical enough to really think the fifty gentlemen referred to, including the leading local, Queensland and Victorian judges are incompetent and that you yourself are the past master in this regard? Perhaps you will leave the public to answer this question for you, as surely you cannot even attempt to do it yourself?

As you have had the temerity to accept an invitation to perform a duty you have shown so flagrantly your incompetency to fulfil, I hereby challenge you to publicly debate the merits of Nebo Rock with your own or any other dog showing for a side wager of £20 (twenty pounds), the Kennel Association of New South Wales to be asked to kindly nominate six of its recognized and competent judges to officiate as referees, and the winner to donate the winnings to the public hospitals. To correct our standard we want your knowledge badly. Come along, Mr. George, you have already had one 'think', and will be due for another after you have accepted this challenge and deposited your £20 with the secretary of the Kennel Association of N.S.W., 10 Bligh St., Sydney. It is always better to stand down than attempt a job you cannot satisfactorily perform, instead of injuring yourself and the club for which you officiate.[6]

George's reply was courteous, concise and to the point.

The reason the dog was placed third is that there were two better dogs in the open class. That is not the only occasion when the dog was beaten under competent cattle dog judges. In answer to his numerous questions, I beg to inform Mr. Dodd that the standard followed by me is the one recognised by the Standard Stock Club of N.S.W. I don't think it should interest him where I obtained a copy of the standard. I can inform Mr. Dodd that I am qualified to read and understand plain English and the points of a dog from muzzle to tail. My other qualifications are these: I have bred and worked cattle and sheep dogs for fourteen years and handled them from my youth. The next part of the letter is a tirade about my dogs. Mr. Dodd is not correct in saying that my dogs have beaten the dog in question on one occasion only. One occasion was at the R.A.S. Show, 1933, when one of my dogs won from puppy to open class and champion and best cattle dog or kelpie at the show. This breaks the four Royal wins in succession which he claims. For the other occasions I advise him to apply to the K.A. in case I make inaccurate statements as he does. Surely he does not mean that the dog he refers to was passed by a vet. surgeon and exhibited when suffering from the after effects of a disease and covered with bare patches. I don't know of any judge who would handle a dog in such a condition. At Ryde I was not satisfied with Mr. Dodd's comments on my dog. He did not examine the dog from muzzle to tail. I consider myself an expert in these breeds after twenty year's experience in Queensland and N.S.W.

Let me inform Mr. Dodd that I do not criticize other judges through any paper.

As to his challenge of £20, what authority has he to issue a challenge for me to publicly debate the merits of another man's dog? I am ready to show under any cattle dog judges appointed by the K.A. whom the Standard Stock Dog Club recognizes as competent.[7]

Judging of Cattle Dogs and Kelpies at the Sydney Royal of 1936 was the subject of an equally angry but better substantiated attack. David Moore, a judge himself as well as editor of *Dog World of Australasia*, commented:

We are afraid that the judge did not cover himself with glory in the judging of this breed [Cattle dogs]. In his remarks to the Press he stated that it should always be remembered that this dog is essentially a working dog and should only be judged from that standard. We heartily agree with that in theory and practice. He should certainly, as a biter of heels of cattle, have a full complement of teeth. That suggests that the judge should examine the mouths of the dog brought before him. This phase was sadly neglected. In fact, dogs were awarded premier honours which were, and are, practically toothless. Very many dogs were put down and unsound dogs put up. Perhaps the judge can explain a remark he made to the effect that it is a pity that we cannot fit a dog with false teeth like humans, which went to indicate that he knew that certain dogs appearing before him were unsound in this vital respect, and then dispense the highest award to such a dog. [Nebo Rock] is almost seven years old, being whelped on June 14, 1929. He has large bulging eyes, in addition to a bad mouth. His ring temperament is unsound, spending the major portion of the time in the ring spread-eagled, challenging to a fight. In our opinion there were many more dogs more closely conformed to the standard.[8]

Moore was similarly unimpressed by the Kelpie Challenge bitch. He provided a photo to make his point and suggested that the judge favoured the owner.[9]

T. A. Stibbard, president of the Standard Stock Dog Association of N. S. W., voiced his club's displeasure by way of an open letter to the judge of Cattle Dogs and Kelpies at the Sydney Royal of 1936, C. D. Lawrence.

The 'Sydney Morning Herald' reports you as having said that the Open Dog, Cattle Dog class, 'was a revelation to you of all-round quality and that the Challenge-winning dog possessed excellent type and, though ageing, won with ease.' You are also reported as saying that 'the Cattle Dog is essentially a working dog, and should be in suitable condition.' 'A short, thick-set body and speckled coat are important features of the breed.' For the information of breeders and exhibitors of Cattle Dogs we would be pleased if you would define type, as your awards were a contradiction of your Press comment, inasmuch as you awarded first, second, and third in many classes to dogs each of which showed a different type, and dogs which conformed more to the standard type were not placed in your awards. The standard drawn up and adopted by this club in 1931 and also adopted by similar clubs in Victoria and Queensland and recognized by all leading breeders and exhibitors, says nothing whatever, that the dog must be short, thick-set. In actual fact, the relative measurements should be in length 10 as is to 9 in height. In other words: if a dog is 18 inches high, he should be 20 inches long. The standard also says that 'the teeth should be sound and strong.'

We take it that you will agree that this is as it should be if the Cattle Dog is to fulfil the object of his existence (i.e., a biter). Will you now inform us how a dog with both upper and lower incisors worn away (only stumps level with the gums remaining) can be a biter? Further, is not a dog in such condition an imperfect dog? And is it not against all canons of judging to award an imperfect dog a prize? The standard says, regarding the eyes: 'They must be neither prominent nor sunken.' We take it that you will not deny that the Challenge-winning dog has prominent eyes, similar to a Pug or a Peke. That being so, it is now up to you to explain how 'he won with ease.' You are also reported as saying that 'no more than one point separated first and second prize-winning dogs in other classes.' Being that you have demonstrated by your awards and remarks that you are unacquainted with the standard as adopted by the clubs catering for the breeds, will you please explain how you assess points? Further, it might interest you to know that point judging implies judging by compartments. Judging by compartments infers that the compartments are greater than the whole which is neither logic nor good sense.

> Your remark that 'the Cattle Dog is a working animal and should
> be shown in suitable conditions', we think you will agree, applies
> equally to the Kelpie. That being so, how do you justify your
> award to the Challenge-winning Kelpie bitch, which would have
> done justice to herself in the pig section. Taking into account
> your awards and remarks on the judging, we are of the opinion
> that the standard you are acquainted with is the 'one-man
> standard' issued about 1904, and consequently 38 years behind
> the times, and would advise you to procure the latest up-to-date
> and comprehensive standard adopted by this club.[10]

Public confrontations such as these undoubtedly assisted sales of the
periodicals concerned but they also point to considerable vigour and
freedom of expression in the dog world of the 1920s and 1930s, as
well as to the internal friction that engendered it and, despite the
abuse hurled at *Nebo Rock*, the *Some Rock* (sire of *Nebo Rock*)
lineage made an important contribution to the Cattle Dog breed,
particularly in New South Wales and Victoria.

Competing breed standards were a continuing source of
dissatisfaction. In his open letter, above, Stibbard specifically referred
to Kaleski's standard as being out-of-date. There were similar
complaints about variant standards in other dog world publications
during the 1930s. Unification of breed standards was not achieved
until the ANKC standards of the 1960s were issued. The earliest
variants on Kaleski's standard included the Queensland Kennel Club
standard of 1906, Court-Rice's version, 1911, and the Cattle Dog and
Kelpie Club of Queensland with its stumpy-tail standard, 1923 (see
Chapter 14). Later standards include the Cattle and Sheep Dog Club
standard, 1925, the NSW Stock Dog Club standard, 1928, and the
Kennel Control Council, Vic., 1936 and 1950.[11, 12, 13, 14, 15, 16, 17, 18] One
early, and strongly-worded complaint, and one that was not limited
to competing standards but included references to incompetent and
improper breeding practices as well, was published in *Our Dogs and
Feathers* in 1925.

> Kelpies and Cattle Dogs have opposition clubs and, apparently,
> judges and standards. These local breeds could make NSW

famous, but they are jealous to nonsense, and will not agree on types, and it is folly to put up breeders or workers as judges who never studied anatomy or perfection of symmetry. Outsiders used to finding the make and shape of breeds would judge more uniformly. And it is high time they bred by pedigree. Our stud book is a curiosity, like a Witch's Cauldron for unknown things, yet they claim to compete with pure breeds for specials, not themselves settled into a breed and not acknowledged by any authorities. Like breeds like very truly but they need clean breeding and Dingo will no longer work sheep or breed Kelpie. The kelpie man asked for a note that a Kelpie Bitch was working well at a trial. I said, 'Yes, wrong colour, how's she bred?' He gave it away simply. 'By a Border Collie.' Kelpies seldom win now, they are too keen. Then cattle dogs should have title. There are lots of cattle dog breeds besides these. They also are mostly mysteriously bred but follow type well – Dingo type. We like them much but owners are indifferent and won't put them straight. Classes are big and good at the 'Royal' but the best are seldom in show form. How can they – workers![19]

Interstate preferences

The Halls' runs in the New England region of New South Wales, and in the Maranoa region and elsewhere in Queensland, were the closest source of Halls Heelers for breeders intending to exhibit in Brisbane and surrounding areas. Photos of *Gibson Lady Blue* [1929], and other Cattle Dogs bred by John Friend (Gibson Island, Brisbane) offer the only clue as to their breed type but suggest similarity to earlier Sydney dogs such as *Nipper* [1899]. The most significant and lasting difference between the early Queensland and New South Wales Cattle Dogs was that Queensland accepted short-tailed Cattle Dogs and litters that included both long-tailed and short-tailed pups. Queensland breeders took the presence or absence of tail for granted. Short-tailed cattle dogs were also known in northern New South Wales but in Sydney, under the influence of Kaleski's breed standard, short-tailed pups may have been culled as defective. Kaleski, himself, may have objected to (or been unaware of) short-tailed cattle dogs – and he compiled the first breed standard.

Roy Barratt's promotion of *Nebo Rock* during the 1930s focussed interstate attention on New South Wales Cattle Dogs. Barratt entered *Nebo Rock* (a *Some Rock* son) and *Beryl Rock* (a *Nebo Rock* daughter) in the Brisbane Royal of 1933 taking the Challenge for that year with *Nebo Rock*. *Beryl Rock* (later KAQ Gd Ch), remained in Queensland. By that time *Some Rock* had moved south to the Ballarat (Vic.) kennels of E. Craddock. Following Barratt's successes in Brisbane, Craddock sent *Crads Blue Stone*, another *Some Rock* son, to Queensland. The lineage was obviously well thought of in Queensland. Belle Young (*Harlaxton* kennels) later bought *Jim Storm*, a New South Wales bred *Nebo Rock* grandson.

The *Some Rock* lineage was one of several Sydney lineages that made substantial contributions, both to the Queensland and Victoria Cattle Dog population between the two World Wars. The *Maroubra Lad* [1930] lineage was particularly strong in Queensland and made an important contribution to Belle Young's *Harlaxton* breeding. Queensland admiration of New South Wales Cattle Dogs was explicitly stated in the *Queensland Kennel Club Yearbook*, 1946.

> In the southern States the breeders have retained the true type of this breed, but in Queensland, probably due to the introduction of kelpie blood, the breed has deteriorated and has lost a lot of its type and stamina, being too light in head, foreface and lower jaw, also too coarse in ears and too light in bone. There are, however, at least two good types of the breed in Brisbane at present, and we hope their progeny will improve the breed in future.[20]

This blatant kennel promotion points to *Hillview* Kennels (Arch Bevis, and owner of *Little Logic* and *Logic Return*), and to one or other of *Harlaxton* (Belle Young), *Standard* (William Byrne) and *Logic* (Thomas Maher). All were prominent in the Cattle Dog world of Queensland. The association between Bevis, Byrne and Maher seems to have been particularly close.

There was no corresponding movement of Queensland- or Victoria-bred dogs to New South Wales until after World War II. In the post-war period most of the dogs transferred from Queensland to New

South Wales were descendants of New South Wales dogs sent earlier to Queensland. Queensland's explicit early preference for blue Cattle Dogs underwent change in the 1950s when Sydney bred red Cattle Dogs became sought-after by some Queensland breeders. The earliest known transfer is *Artmar Miss Camcyn*. Others, such as *Hillsdale Red Flame*, followed. Belle Young (*Harlaxton* Kennels), Queensland owner of *Hillsdale Red Flame*, had sufficient prominence in the show ring to lead a trend in favour of red Cattle Dogs if leadership were necessary.

Working Cattle Dogs were probably known in other Australian states in country areas. Benched Cattle Dogs in states other than New South Wales, Queensland and Victoria, were, as far as is known, derived from the three eastern states. Stumpy Tail Cattle Dogs are said to have been exhibited in Tasmania as "Smithfields", in the late 1940s or early 1950s, by Mr and Mrs E. S. Byard of Mole Creek, Tasmania, but they may have been Tasmanian Smithfields. The numbers of Cattle Dogs exhibited, both at the Sydney and Brisbane Royals, continued to increase during the period between the World Wars. Similar shows were held in other state capital cities but Cattle Dog exhibition in other states lagged behind Sydney and Brisbane.

First export?

In 1930 *Leilavale Silent Chief* ended a distinguished show career by becoming the first recorded Cattle Dog intended for export. The national monthly, *Our Dogs of Australia*, reported on the Queensland Kennel Association's show under the heading "Silent Chief for England ".

> Cattle Dogs. Ryan's *Gr Ch Leilavale Silent Chief*, 1st and challenge. Good muzzle, front legs … He is going home to England where a club is to be started to foster the breed.[21]

There is no record of his having arrived in England and the club never eventuated. If he did in fact, reach England, the Kennel Club may have suffered culture shock and rejected him as a "pure breed".

Described as "blue and tan", *Leilavale Silent Chief* was exhibited at Brisbane Royal shows from 1924 to 1930, gaining his Grand Champion title in 1926.

Women in the Cattle Dog world

Dog shows were, until the 1900s, strictly male preserves. The first assault was won by the ladies when they were allowed to exhibit toy breeds. This small victory encouraged general rebellion and Ladies Kennel Clubs in various Australian States were inaugurated. To the considerable embarrassment of the gentlemen the shows organised by the ladies were a great success. One of the later clubs, the Ladies' Canine Society of NSW, emphasised the position by allowing gentlemen to join as "associate members" with all membership privileges except management involvement.[22]

The names of Cattle Dog owner/breeders in New South Wales during the 1920s and 1930s include that of Mrs W. W. Campbell of Croydon, Sydney, who was one of the first women to judge Cattle Dogs in New South Wales. Campbell judged the inaugural show of the Standard Stock Dog Association (aka Standard Stock Dog Club) in April 1931, awarding Challenge Dog to *Little Gem* and the Bitch Challenge to *Lady Mascot*.[23] One earlier woman Cattle Dog judge is known in New South Wales; Miss Agnes Mackay judged the Sydney Royals of 1918 and 1919. Mackay also exhibited a Cattle Dog at the Ladies' Kennel Club of New South Wales show in 1911 at which Kaleski judged. Whether she handled the dog in the ring is not known but in her "Notes on Australian Stock Dogs" she wrote about Cattle Dogs and Kelpies with an enthusiasm that almost exceeded Kaleski's.[24]

Dog names

Most early dog names were fairly commonplace but some are memorable, even if they did show a complete disregard for pedigree. Among the memorable are *Cobber* by *Thistle* out of *Nettle*; *Larrikan* by *Napper* out of *Tandy*;[25] and the cheerfully blasphemous *Sign of the Cross* by *Peter* out of *Beware*. Some tributes were made to the stage, too. The Australian musical comedy and light opera singer, Gladys Moncrieff, "Our Glad" (1892-1976), is remembered in *Moncrieffe Blue* and *Rio Rita*, the latter a role played by Moncrieff. *Ada Reeve* and her pup, *Goodie*, were both exhibited at Sydney Royals. Ada Reeve walked the stage as well as the Sydney show ring. Ada Reeve (1876-1964) was acclaimed in London's East End theatres and also made four Australian tours between 1897 and 1922. Like her Cattle Dog namesake, Ada Reeve had a daughter, Goodie. Goodie Reeve was, from the late 1930s to early 1950s, well known in Sydney for her programs on Radio Station 2GB, such as the one for blind ex-servicemen returned from World War II, and a children's session, "Chickabiddies". She also wrote the first musical commercials ever put to air in Sydney (Goodie Dawson, aka Goodie Reeve, pers. comm. 1952). In Victoria the Australian actress and singer Nellie Stewart (1858-1931) had admirers in the dog world. *Nellie Stewart* was an entrant in the Melbourne Royal of 1918. "Our Nell" began her long and distinguished career at the ripe age of five. She toured internationally, playing in roles from pantomime to grand opera. Her most memorable role was as Nell Gwynne in the play "Sweet Nell of Old Drury".

14

THE AUSTRALIAN CATTLE DOG
SINCE WORLD WAR II

Between World War I (1914-18) and World War II (1939-45) the Australian dog world was in disarray. Competing dog clubs vied for supremacy and the Cattle Dog fancy, itself, was in no better position. The absence of an agreed upon and generally implemented breed standard and uncontrolled judging had their effect on the Cattle Dog breed from the 1920s onward as Kaleski reported in many articles. It is evident from the pages of the *Sydney Mail* that, although Kaleski's was the loudest voice of protest, others shared his concerns. Kaleski's perseverance may not have been rewarded in the ways he wished but he left behind him an invaluable historical record – including his comments (mostly uncomplimentary) on Sydney Royal exhibits.

The photographic coverage of Cattle Dogs, particularly between wars in the *Sydney Mail*, documents changes in type. Two forms were developing. The first, a lean, leggy dog, and a second, a heavier-bodied, shorter-legged animal with intermediate forms in between. Among early Cattle Dogs, *Nipper* [1899] was typical of the lean, leggy type. Later examples include *Gibson Lady Blue* [1929] and Ch *Kalamundi Rex Regis* [1949]. *Bobby Blue* [1944] was typical of the heavier-bodied, shorter-legged type.

It took a dog, not a judge or breeder, to unify the Cattle Dog breed.

Hailed as the "Father of the Breed" *Little Logic* was bred in Sydney in 1939 but sold, as a pup, to the Queensland kennels of Arch Bevis. Bevis promoted *Little Logic* during the World War II years, gaining for the dog his Grand Champion title in 1947.[1] *Little Logic* had a strong genetic influence on the Australian Cattle Dog population, particularly in Queensland, where many of his offspring survived World War II. Only one photograph of the dog remains but it shows him to favour the lean, leggy type. Post-war, however, the Cattle Dog fancy seems to have preferred the heavier-bodied type, such as *Bobby Blue* [1944]. *Bobby Blue*, owned and exhibited by W. Hough (Qld) was awarded Best of Breed at three successive Sydney Royals and two Brisbane Royals. The judge at the 1949 Sydney Royal, A. Fisher, wrote:

> Mr. W. Hough's *Bobby Blue* is one of the finest specimens of the breed it has been the writer's pleasure to handle. He has the soundest possible legs and feet, and, to quote our old friend, Robert Kaleski, "has a bite like bad whisky", extremely powerful jaws, big, strong teeth, with typical Cattle Dog expression. His head is a model, and few would find fault with his make and shape.[2]

By the end of the 1950s, *Little Logic* was in the pedigrees of most registered Australian Cattle Dogs but usually by way of his son, *Logic Return* [1949] – also a typical exemplar of the heavier-bodied shorter-legged type. Both dogs were promoted by Arch Bevis (*Hillview* Kennels, Brisbane). Bevis started breeding Cattle Dogs in the early 1930s. He registered both long-tailed and short-tailed Cattle Dogs but changed his breeding preference in favour of Cattle Dogs with New South Wales ancestry during the late 1930s. (The *Hillview* prefix was registered in 1938, in the name of Bevis's wife, Ada.) Bevis obtained *Little Logic* (born in 1939) from J. Schofield of Rockdale (Sydney suburb). He chose well. The dog's pedigree is only partly known but his ancestry includes dogs whose titles indicate that they were greatly esteemed by the judges of the time. Bevis was aggressive in his promotion of both *Little Logic* and *Logic Return*, and the *Logic Return* son, *Hillview Brighton Boy*, but "the real champion" as he said, himself, was *Little Logic*.[3] The Cattle Dog fancy, however, favoured the heavier-bodied, shorter-legged type of *Logic Return*.

Logic Return was born in 1949 from one of the last litters registered to *Little Logic*. His breeder, Thomas A. Maher (Kingaroy, Qld.) sold the dog to Bevis who exhibited him until the mid-1950s. The dog was later owned, and stood at stud, by Ray Moss (*Mossdale* Kennels, Sydney) and, finally, by S. Robinson (*Gwenray* Kennels, Sydney). Two of *Logic Return's* offspring, *Trueblue Patches* and *Harlaxton Gem*, were exhibited at the Sydney Royal of 1953. A favourably impressed Tom McGorien (author and judge) wrote:

> The noted Queensland dog, *Logic's Return*, scored a real triumph when his two sons, champion *Trueblue Patches* and *Harlaxton Gem*, won the champion and reserve award, defeating their sire. *Patches* later won the award for best of breed. He is owned by Mr A. Ouley, of Arncliffe [*Turrella* Kennels], and is a great dog. He has typical cattle dog conformation, big ribbed and sturdy throughout, yet with plenty of elegance and is favoured with the head we like, broad skull, clean strong jaw, with well-placed eyes and ears.[4]

McGorien obviously preferred the heavier-bodied shorter-legged type.

The influential *Wooleston* Kennels emerged during the 1950s. Bernie and Berenice Walters chose *Broombees Bobby* (a direct *Little Logic* descendant) and *Turrella Lass* (a *Logic Return* descendant) as the foundation of their breeding program. This combination produced *Wooleston Blue Jack* [1954]. Nearly all *Wooleston* dogs and most, if not all, Australian Cattle Dogs whelped since 1990 are descended from *Wooleston Blue Jack*. According to Berenice Walters (pers. comm. 1997) she and Bernie wished to breed Australian Cattle Dogs that were successful, both in the breed ring and as workers. *Turrella* Kennels (Sydney) was a bench kennel but W. Roth (*Broombees* Kennels, Mudgee, N. S. W.) is said to have been a drover. In breeding from *Broombees Bobby* and *Turrella Lass*, both *Wooleston* goals were realised. For some twenty years *Wooleston* Kennels supplied breeding stock to kennels in Australia and overseas. More than thirty-five championship titles are credited to *Wooleston* and there was a ready market among local stockmen for dogs that were not of show quality (Berenice Walters pers. comm. 1997).

Breeders of the 1950s seemed to want either *Logic Return* offspring or a pup from *Wooleston* Kennels. This preference changed the direction taken by the breed. The heavier-bodied shorter-legged form prevailed and was further consolidated, from the 1970s, by *Tallawong* Kennels in Victoria.

From their start in the late 1960s with *Wooleston Blue Jenny* [1967] as foundation bitch, Ken and Helen Dickson bred into *Wooleston* by purchase of other bitches and stud use. By the end of the 1970s *Tallawong* was, effectively, a closed but extended kennel – almost a closed breeding colony built on *Tallawong*. Non-*Tallawong* names appearing in later *Tallawong* pedigrees are those of dogs with strong (or exclusive) *Tallawong* ancestry. No other Australian Cattle Dog kennel in Australia has achieved an extended kennel of such extent and operated with so tightly planned a breeding program. Between 1990 and 2000, over 90% of all "successful" Australian Cattle Dogs (that is, dogs that were used for breeding) were descendants of *Wooleston Blue Jenny*.

Although some exhibiting breeders advertise prominently and campaign vigorously in the show ring, no individual dog or bitch of the early 1990s, or since, can be identified as having made particular impact on the Australian breed population. Most exhibiting Australian Cattle Dog breeders in Australia seem reluctant to promote prefixes other than their own and show-prominence does not necessarily reflect breed-prominence.

After World War II, consensus on Breed Standards began to emerge. Re-drafted breed standards assisted the transition to the heavier-bodied shorter-legged type.

- From 1903 to 1935, the Australian Cattle Dog's general appearance was described as: "that of a small thick-set dingo."
- Between 1936 and 1962, general appearance read: "a well-proportioned dog showing great suppleness of limb, neither massive nor heavy, but showing great substance in small compass and at the same time free from any suggestion of weediness. It must not approach the greyhound type."

- From 1963 to present: "a sturdy, compact, symmetrically built working dog. With the ability and willingness to carry out any task however arduous, its combination of substance, power, balance and hard muscular condition to be such that it must convey the impression of great agility, strength and endurance. Any tendency to grossness or weediness is a serious fault."

Following the publication of the 1963 Standard judges accepted a dog of greater substance than formerly was the case. Warnings were, however, voiced, that the working capacity of the Cattle Dog should not be compromised.[5] In a lecture to intending judges, c. 1966, Alan Forbes (*Pacific* Kennels) commented:

Today, with motorised transport of live-stock, internal slaughtering centres, etc., our dependence on the Cattle Dog has eased considerably. This has influenced the gradual trend towards a heavier, more attractive dog, slightly shorter on the leg than his working counterpart of years ago.[6]

In 1992, Betty Southall (*Geraldmine* Kennels) wrote sadly:

When the Cattle Dog was first developed, cattle were mainly quiet and the holdings small. Cattle were moved about: by horse and dog. Gradually the cattle industry expanded and so did the size of the holdings or stations. Most of these were hundreds of square miles ... Initially, these were stocked with British breed cattle which were quiet when released, but, it being impractical to muster more than once a year, it didn't take long for them to become wild and the progeny very wild. It took top stockmen, top horses and especially top dogs to flush these beasts out of scrub and forest and drove them to branding yards and railheads in harsh country and over great distances. The feats of these people, horses and dogs are legend.

The next development was the introduction of the Brahman and related breeds of cattle. These were introduced for their greater stamina, their ability to travel large distances between water and feed with less stress and their greater tendency to tick resistance.

But along with these attributes came lithe, long legged athletes who could, and nearly always did, travel like the wind in any direction but that required, combined with a cunning alternative – to head for the nearest patch of impenetrable scrub and lie doggo. Faster, wilder cattle required faster horses and horses with better staying power. So thoroughbred horses were put over station horses to solve this problem. The Cattle Dog also had to be able to travel fast and have great endurance to deal with this development and, consequently, they were selectively bred to achieve the leg length and angulation necessary if they were to be of any use at the task for which they were bred. Heavy, short legged, "square" show dogs that are exhausted in the shade waiting to enter the show ring cannot fulfil the purpose for which they are supposedly bred. It doesn't matter whether the task is mustering, droving or yarding up, the Cattle Dog travels many more miles than the person on the horse and it takes a damned fine dog to be able to out-travel a specially bred stock horse.

The Cattle Dog was, once, such an animal ... I think we need to get back to the real Cattle Dog in our breeding, the dog capable of performing the function for which it was bred. I think we should be selecting for a little more leg, less bulk and not bull heads. How does the [General Appearance statement of the Standard] fit in with those huge hulks we all see being lifted into car or trailer after a show? Where in the standard does it say a cattle dog should be woolly? ... [Moreover] a thick shouldered, head heavy, short legged, straight-stifled apology for a Cattle Dog couldn't do [the work for which it is intended].[7]

Helen Hewson-Fruend was critical of judges and breeders alike.

The impact of *Little Logic* and *Logic Return*, together with breeder- and judge-acceptance of the heavier-bodied shorter-legged dogs, has been far reaching and enduring, in spite of well intentioned warnings and pleas.[8]

15

BETTY SOUTHALL (1914-2008)

Bessie Southall (better known as Betty) grew up on Derby Station, near Goondiwindi, Qld. After a shooting accident and the extended hospitalisation that followed, Betty's father was forced to sell Derby.

Betty married Gerald Southall in 1934. Her mother arranged the marriage – not an uncommon practice in those days – "but I came to love him", said Betty, and she remembered him when she registered her breeder's prefix, *Geraldmine*, in 1970. Betty returned to Derby with Gerry after they married and they managed the station until World War II when Gerry enlisted. After the war Gerry was given a soldier settlement farm in the Atherton Tablelands. Nominally intended for dairying and mixed farming, it would have suited mountain goats admirably. Gerry and Betty struggled on together until Gerry's death in 1961.

Betty's last years were in Tolga, Qld, also in the Atherton area, but her heart and memories remained in Goondiwindi.

MUSTERING IN WESTERN QUEENSLAND
Betty Southall

Up early morning – stir the campfire – put the billy on to boil. Someone went to bring the horses in, then a quick breakfast: damper and salt beef, and a pot of black tea. Horses saddled, away by sun-up, and a hard day's riding. We would see a mob of cattle in the distance and would then split up. Some of us would go to the left and others to the right so as to get around them before they saw us. They were wild. They would take off, running, as soon as they saw us so we had to be on good, fast horses, with our Cattle Dogs close by.

When we finally got around the mob the cattle would ring around and around, then a wild bull would break out and try to make it to the scrub. This is where the dogs came into their own. They would heel the bull but wait until he bellowed. Then one of the dogs would race around to get on the bull's nose and try to hold the beast. Two men would be close by. One of them would get hold of the bull's tail, to swing him off his feet and throw him to the ground. The other would get his head and hold him down. The "tail man" would put the bull strap on the bull's legs, so that he couldn't get up, then castrate him. Most of the cattle had long horns, so the horns were sawn off at the same time.

The dogs and horses had a spell while all this was going on, but, Oh Boy! Watch out when the bull was free again! One man would take the bull strap off his legs while the other was holding the head. Then the men would run for their lives. The bull would charge anything in his way, as soon as he was free. This is where the dogs took over, until the bull was back with the mob again – and given half a chance, he would break out again. Sometimes there were more young bulls than cows in the mob and a few more would have to be thrown before the whole mob was herded into the yard, a small wire-fenced paddock.

If you were lucky, you would have time for a damper and corned beef sandwich for lunch. Most times, you ate while riding.

Once the mob was yarded, one man would ride around them and the others could let their horses go and get the night horses saddled and ready for the night watch. Someone would keep riding around the cattle all night. If there were enough of us, each man would do a two-hour shift. There was dinner to be cooked, too, and damper for the next day. That was my job. The meal generally consisted of corned beef, potatoes (in their jackets) and sometimes stew, made from corned beef, onions and dried vegetables. Dumpling in syrup was a treat. Sometimes the dogs would get a rabbit or two and we would share with them. We roasted rabbit in the camp oven and sometimes roo. Then roll out the swags and try to get some sleep before the cattle decided to rush.[1]

Most nights were good but sometimes there would be a rush. The cattle would hear something and take off at full gallop – sometimes through the camp. If there was a rush, everyone got his night horse and took off after the galloping mob, to try to get around them, calm them down, and bring them back to the yards.

Next morning the horse-tailer would have the horses mustered, just on daylight, and re-shod if necessary. Because the country was stony, and rough on horses' hooves, all our horses were shod. After breakfast, most of us would ride around the cattle while one or two men, on good camp draft horses, would cut out each beast into its allotted mob – sale cattle in one corner, branders in another and bush, in a third – while other riders kept them in place. Then there would be branding. It was called "Bronko branding". The branding iron was heated in a fire and a rope tied around the horns of the beast to be branded. The Bronko horse would pull the beast up to a post or tree, near the fire and irons, the beast would be thrown to the ground and branded, castrated and earmarked, and then sent back to his herd.

The sale cattle were handed over to a drover, with his own team of men, horses (including packhorses) and dogs.

16

THE AUSTRALIAN STUMPY TAIL CATTLE DOG

The Australian Stumpy Tail Cattle Dog, the Stumpy as he is affectionately known, is closely related to the Australian Cattle Dog. Both share a common origin in the Halls Heeler and both share their early history with the immigrant, George Hall and his family and particularly with Thomas Simpson Hall of Dartbrook in the Hunter Valley.

The long-tailed Cattle Dog and the short-tailed Cattle Dog started on their separate ways after 1903 and the publication of Kaleski's breed standard for Cattle Dogs. The separation of long-tailed and short-tailed Cattle Dogs as distinct varieties came of their emergence as show exhibits. Kaleski was either unaware of the two types or deliberately excluded short-tailed types from his standard. He may have (correctly) viewed the short- or bob-tail as a defect although he would not have recognised it as being heritable. Outside the immediate influence of Kaleski's standard Queensland breeders took the presence or absence of tail for granted. Both short-tailed and long-tailed Cattle Dogs were exhibited in Queensland from the 1890s. The earliest benched Cattle Dogs in New South Wales were owned and/or bred in Sydney but some of the earliest benched Cattle Dogs in Queensland probably came from the Halls' runs in north-west New South Wales and south-west Queensland. These runs were the closest to breeders intending to exhibit in Brisbane and surrounding areas. *Gibson Lady Blue* [1929], and other Cattle Dogs bred by John Friend (Gibson Island, Brisbane) offer the only clue as to their breed type. Although they were bred much later there is a similarity in type to early Sydney dogs such as *Nipper*. No photos of early short-tailed exhibited Cattle Dogs are known.

Until the 1910s short-tailed Cattle Dogs were numerically strong enough to justify classes for them at Brisbane Royals (see Chapter 13). From the 1920s, however, the growing Queensland popularity for New South Wales dogs had its effect on the short-tailed type. Their exhibited numbers at Brisbane Royals decreased although classes were still scheduled for Stumpies at some local agricultural shows and kennel clubs. At some of these smaller shows long-tailed and short-tailed were exhibited in the same classes. After kennel controls were established, however, the Stumpy Tail Cattle Dog became a recognised breed in its own right and Cattle Dog classes, if scheduled, distinguished between the two types.

The Stumpy's survival as a benched breed came under different threat during the 1950s. Following his first judging appointment in Queensland, a New South Wales judge revealed his ignorance of the Stumpy's history as an established breed. In a published critique he described Stumpies as: "an abomination that needed to be eliminated from the face of the earth" (Davis, pers. comm. 2021.)[1]

Shortly after this critique was published the Canine Control Council (Qld) posted a notice that "on the advice of some judges" it was de-registering all Stumpy Tail Cattle Dogs. Naturally, Iris Heale (*Glen Iris*) and other Stumpy breeders objected to this but Heale alone had the determination and financial resources to take the CCCQ to court. Subsequently the CCCQ's ill-considered decision was overturned. Heale announced her success in a letter to the editor of one of the Brisbane newspapers but also complained that other Stumpy breeders had not helped her with the court case. In reply to Heale's letter, one of the other Stumpy breeders objected to her complaint stating that, although he and others were supportive of Heale, they simply did not have the money to spend on legal fees. These breeders had apparently been mislead and given the impression that each of them, individually, would have had to take the CCCQ to court if they wanted to have their dogs registrations reinstated. This was incorrect. After the breed had been reinstated all Stumpies would have been reinstated automatically. The source of this misinformation is unknown but may have been encouraged from within the CCCQ itself. (Some within the CCCQ may have hoped that the Stumpy breed would die out and remove the embarrassment that Heale represented.) The end result was that dedicated breeders and the bloodlines they represented were permanently lost.

Heale, herself, attributed the CCCQ's attempt to deregister Stumpies, at least in part, to another administrative decision (Heale, pers. comm. c.1997). This decision related to bringing Queensland litter registration practices into line with other states.

By the 1940s kennel controls were established in Victoria, New South Wales and Queensland and dog registrations became a requirement. In Victoria and New South Wales, the breeder registered some, or all pups, in each litter. Buyers of pups could re-register the pups in their own names if they so desired. Queensland opted for a different system. The breeder registered a <u>litter</u> but the buyers registered pups in their own names if they wished to do so. A litter bred to two short-tailed parents would be registered, by the breeder, as Cattle Dog (short-tail) but any long-tailed pups in that litter could be registered (incorrectly) by their new owners, as Cattle Dog (long-tail). Whether this occurred in practice is far from certain but, prior to the 1940s, it would have been common to mate long-tails to short-tails: they were the same breed! They were differentiated only in the show ring Eventually the CCCQ decided to abandon its "old system" of litter registration in favour of a "new system", so as to conform with Victoria and New South Wales. When the "new system" was implemented in October 1958, the presence of registered Cattle Dogs (long-tail) with parents registered as Cattle Dogs (short-tail) was allegedly detected.

The attempted Stumpy deregistration action of the CCCQ and the subsequent reinstatement of *Glen Iris* kennels left *Glen Iris* in a unique position: the one and only registered Stumpy Tail Cattle Dog kennels in existence. From then on Heale refused to sell registered bitches. Whether this was her revenge on the, by this time, deregistered Stumpy breeders who hadn't supported her legal action or whether it was her reaction against perceived victimisation by the CCCQ is far from clear. She knew that the Stumpies, as a benched breed, would die with her and it probably saddened her. Heale was, however, very aware of the dangers of extreme inbreeding and later mated long-tailed dogs to her short-tailed bitches. Her own kennel facilities were very limited and she was not in the position to develop a breeding colony. (Later she actively supported the Stumpy Tail Cattle Dog Redevelopment Scheme, see below.) The last known 1950s Stumpy litter registered to a prefix, other than to *Glen Iris*, was whelped on 27 March 1955. This suggests a 1956 date for the Stumpy re-registration drama. The CCCQ implemented its "new system" of litter registrations, in line with other states, in October 1958. This undoubtedly affected *Glen Iris* Stumpy registrations after the court action. Heale may have been asked to "prove" pure Stumpy ancestry for a *Glen Iris* litter, born on 31 December 1957.

During the 1980s some members of the Australian working dog fancy realised that Heale, born 1919, was not getting any younger. Representations to the ANKC resulted in the implementation of the Stumpy Tail Cattle Dog Redevelopment Scheme. At its Darwin conference in October 1988 the ANKC decided to introduce an ongoing program to ensure the preservation of the Stumpy Tail Cattle Dog. A press release in the *KCC Kennel Gazette* announced its terms of reference.

> Many people claim that apart from its value as an all-rounder, the Stumpy-Tail is one of the best working cattle dogs ever produced. Wide publicity and enquiries throughout Australia indicate that at this point of time there is only one single registered breeder, located in Queensland. In the past ten years only 50 Stumpy-Tail puppies (23 dogs and 27 bitches) have been registered with the eight Canine Controls. At a rate of five puppies per year, it is obvious that unless positive action is taken, this attractive breed could disappear. However there does appear to be a substantial number of pure-bred Stumpy-Tails which, for a variety of reasons, are not entered in the ANKC Register. There are also indications that a substantial market could be developed if registered, pure bred dogs become available. With the support of the eight Controlling Bodies, the Australian National Kennel Council has decided that:

1. It will set up a "Development Breeding Programme" using specially selected stock.
2. That when the progeny of these selected dogs reach a satisfactory standard they will be entered in the pure bred Register.
3. That in each State and Territory there be set up a "Breed Selection Committee" including at least one person with wide experience in the cattle dog field.
4. This Committee will examine and photograph Stumpy-Tail dogs and bitches for use in the breeding scheme. It will also research and record any relevant breeding details already available.
5. In addition, the ANKC has appointed a Supervisory Committee (comprising Mr R. Kennedy of the ACT and Lt Col. R. Underwood of Queensland), to oversight and coordinate the operation.
6. All Stumpy-Tails entered into the programme shall be tattooed in the ear or the flank for positive identification.
7. Inspection of potential breeding stock shall take place at selected centres and, if possible, at arranged "Field Days".
8. No dogs other than Stumpy-Tail Cattle Dogs shall be used in the programme.[2]

Selection of possible candidates for the program was by inspection, by a panel of three Working Dog Group judges. Grading days were organised at various centres across Australia. For a few years, until poor health overcame her, Iris Heale replaced one of the judges comprising inspection panels in Brisbane.

In the Upgrade Program that was subsequently developed, percentage "blood" was used as a measure of purity. Four different categories were recognised with regard to percentage "blood" and various Grades were assigned on this basis. The theory underlying this categorisation relies on the fact that each animal gives 50% of its genetic information (here called "blood") to its progeny.[3]

A pure bred dog is 100% "blood" for its breed.
Pups from a cross breeding will be only 50% "blood" for that breed.
A cross bred dog that is 50% "blood" will, when mated to a pure bred animal (100% "blood") give rise to up-graded pups; that is, 25% plus 50% = 75%.

Grade 1. Registered pure bred animals = 100% pure "blood".
Grade 2. Unregistered pure bred animals = 100% pure "blood".
Grade 3. Apparently pure bred animals (typey) with at least three grandparents known to be pure = 75%.
Grade 4. Apparently untypey animals with at least 1 grandparent known to be pure bred (may carry tan markings) = 25%.

The Upgrade Program recognised three groups. In general use, if not officially, alphabetical designations replaced the numerical ones.

Summary of Grades 1988

Grade	Description
A former Grade 2	Unregistered males and females, known to be pure bred from background information. Unregistered males of exceptionally good quality.
B former Grade 3	Of sufficiently good quality to make an immediate contribution to the Upgrade Program.
C former Grade 4	Requiring upgrade through two generations.

In any mating using graded animals, offspring could only be graded one grade higher than the lower graded parent.

Mating outcomes

Mating	Outcome
Registered x A	Eligible for pure bred registration, subject to inspection.
A x A	Eligible for pure bred registration, subject to inspection.
A x B	Nominally Grade A, subject to inspection.
A x C	Nominally Grade B, subject to inspection.
B x C	Nominally Grade B, subject to inspection.

Inspection procedures for pups were formalised. The first inspection was to be made within fourteen days of whelping by a veterinarian or Breed Warden to certify that tails were not docked. The second inspection, by a Breed Warden, was to be made at not less than three months of age. A stringent view was to be taken of type, and particularly of tail-length. Lack of pedigree data was not to influence classification. The ANKC was criticised for ending the scheme prematurely and breeders were criticised for making insufficient use of B and C Grade animals. The scheme did, however, succeed in its aim of preserving the Stumpy Tail Cattle Dog as a registered breed.

As an accident of its history, Iris Heale's thirty-year monopoly of the breed, the Australian Stumpy Tail Cattle Dog developed independently of the *Wooleston* and *Tallawong* influences of the 1950s and 1960s that reshaped the Australian Cattle Dog. The Stumpy has remained more faithful to the lean, leggy dog of Kaleski's days than has the Australian Cattle Dog. In type, the Stumpy more closely resembles the pre-*Wooleston/Tallawong* type, such as *Kalamunda Rex Regis* [1949], than post-*Wooleston/Tallawong* cattle dogs such as *Dustyroad Toby* [1979].

The name change to Australian Stumpy Tail Cattle Dog became effective on 1 January 2002 and the following year the breed was accepted by the Fédération Cynologique Internationale. Regrettably, the breed history supplied to the FCI followed the prevailing "generally agreed" received wisdom promulgated by Laurel Atwell writing as Joyce Herald Collis.[4] No thought was given to whether the individual breed types expressed by the supposed ancestors of the Stumpy, proposed by Collis – dingo, red bob-tails and German Coolie – were consistent with the breed type seen in the Australian Stumpy Tail Cattle Dog; Gd Ch *Ambajaye High Tail It*, for example. The improbable breed history supplied to the FCI reads:

> It is generally agreed that the Stumpy Tail Cattle Dog descended from the original cross of a Smithfield with an Australian Dingo. Credit for this cross goes to a man by the name of Timmins of Bathurst, NSW. This occurred about 1831 and the progeny, red bobtail dogs were known as "Timmins Biters.[5]

Close, but not far from what Atwell/Collis wrote:

> It is generally agreed that the Stumpy Tail Cattle Dog descended from the original cross of a Smithfield with an Australian Dingo

and a British Smithfield (Timmins Biters). These red bobtail progeny were then crossed with a smooth coated, blue merle Collie, resulting in the dog we know today as the Stumpy Tail Cattle Dog (Hall's Heelers). [6]

According to Beilby the Smithfield probably had Old English Sheepdog ancestors. According to Kaleski the Timmins Biters were Halls Heelers. (Appendix 3 provides excerpts from Atwell/Collis. Much of her writing is plagerised from Kaleski's publications.)

The Stumpy Tail Cattle Dog fancy seems to have believed every word of the Atwell Dogma and assisted her in her excommunication of the Stumpy from his long-tailed cousins. Atwell's breed history ignores the pedigree data included in the Brisbane Royal catalogues of the 1910s. These data show very clearly that Cattle Dogs were considered to be a single breed with two varieties, long-tail and short-tail, not two separate breeds.[7] This is far from the "two breeds with different origins" notion proposed in the Atwell Dogma.

In her chapter on tail-length inheritance in *A Dog Called Blue* Helen Hewson-Fruend reviewed the inheritance of taillessness, with particular reference to the Australian Stumpy Tail Cattle Dog. She wrote:

> The Australian Stumpy Tail Cattle Dog has the genetic makeup to produce a natural tail, 10 cm or less in length [as required by the breed standard]. Nevertheless, breeders of the Australian Stumpy Tail Cattle Dog will experience the frustration of producing some longer tailed or apparently normal, long-tailed dogs. This is due to the nature of expression of the allele of the gene involved in causing the loss of some of the coccygeal vertebrae. Robinson[8] and Willis[9] both report on the mode of inheritance of taillessness and/or stumpy-tail (stub tail) – sometimes referred to as bob-tail in early cattle dog literature.[10]

She attributed the variable tail length to the variable expression (incomplete penetrance) of the dominant allele, T^1. Studies at the molecular level, however, have since demonstrated that taillessness in the Australian Stumpy Tail Cattle Dog is dominant in its inheritance, with complete penetrance.

Taillessness in the Pembroke Corgi has since been shown to be dominantly inherited with complete penetrance, due to a dominant mutation (C189G) of the T-box transcription factor T gene.[11,12] This mutation has been found in seventeen other stock dog and hunting breeds including the Australian Stumpy Tail Cattle Dog. The homozygous double-dominant, T^1T^1, (G/G) is apparently lethal, causing embryonic death or early post-partum death as a result of developmental deformities.[13] The heterozygous carrier, T^1t^1, (C/G) produces a varying degree of shortened tail length and was found in all tested short-tailed Australian Stumpy Tail Cattle Dogs. The homozygous double-recessive, t^1t^1 (C/C) – mutation absent – occurs in long-tailed individuals of the breeds tested.[14]

The eighteen breeds in which this mutation (C/G) occurs, and their wide geographical distribution, suggest an ancient ancestral origin for the mutation and its dispersal during various phases of Eurasian migration. Most of the breeds are stock dogs or hunting breeds and include:

Austrian Pinscher	Jack Russell Terrier
Australian Shepherd	Karelian Bear Dog
Australian Stumpy Tail Cattle Dog	Pembroke Welsh Corgi
Bourbonnais Pointer	Polish Lowland Sheepdog
Brazilian Terrier	Pyrenean Shepherd
Brittany Spaniel	Savoy Sheepdog
Croatian Sheepdog	Schipperke
Danish/Swedish Farmdog	Spanish Waterdog
Hungarian Mudi	Swedish Vallhund

Six other breeds, in which short tailed phenotypes occur, have been tested but in these breeds the C189G mutation is not present.

Boston Terrier,	Miniature Schnauzer
English Bulldog	Parson Russell Terrier
King Charles Spaniel	Rottweiler

Hancock has pointed out that migrant peoples were more commonly accompanied by pastoral breeds and hounds than by other types of dog.[15] There is speculation, for example, that Welsh Corgis were taken to Wales by Viking invaders via the Swedish Vallhund.[16] There is, however, little doubt that the European ancestors of the Halls Heeler contributed taillessness to the Australian Stumpy Tail Cattle Dog.

In Sydney, and anywhere else in the early 1900s where Kaleski's standard had influence, selection against taillessness (the dominant allele, T^1) would have resulted in that allele vanishing from the local Cattle Dog population. Apparently, this is exactly what happened. From a breeder's point of view, extinguishing a dominant trait is relatively easy. Kaleski, and those breeders influenced by him, had only to exclude from breeding (and showing) short-tailed Cattle Dogs. Problem solved. In Queensland, where discrimination against taillessness was not an issue, the dominant allele, T^1, persisted in the early Cattle Dog population.

17

GATHERING THE THREADS

Robert Kaleski gave Australia's Cattle Dogs their future. Without Kaleski's continuing support Cattle Dogs may not have survived as an identifiable breed.

Dogs, described as cattle dogs, were exhibited in the Australian colonies soon after enthusiasm for dog shows spread from England but, until Kaleski's standard was adopted by judges, any dog that worked cattle was a cattle dog. Most defied association with any particular lineage. Dogs of Halls Heeler descent were, however, Kaleski's breed of choice – the breed that he ushered into the show ring by way of his breed standard and to which he gave his lifetime support. Among the ignored working cattle dogs were dogs with possible Old English Sheepdog ancestry, including the Smithfield, but no one was interested in promoting the Smithfield or any other working cattle dog type as a benched breed. Kaleski's Cattle Dogs captured the breed name for themselves. If they complied with Kaleski's standard they were Cattle Dogs.

Kaleski's Cattle Dogs lacked the dignity of a history. Some of the older British breeds were mentioned by the scholar, Dr John Caius (1510-1573) physician to Queen Elizabeth I, and in earlier manuscripts as well, but Kaleski couldn't find early cattle dogs in the eighteenth and nineteenth century books that he consulted. Curs and heelers were there, and various sheep dogs but no cattle dogs, so Kaleski provided his Cattle Dogs with a history of his own making. It was a history with little foundation in fact, the Kaleski Dogma, that remained unchallenged from its first publication in 1903. In its original form the Kaleski Dogma proposed that Thomas Hall, of Dartbrook, imported working dogs. At first Kaleski described the imported dog as a "blue-gray Welsh merle" but later preferred to identify Hall's supposed imports as "smooth Highland collies". According to Kaleski, Hall crossed his imported dogs with dingo and from this cross developed the working cattle dogs that Kaleski, himself, called "Halls Heelers".

Except for their association with Thomas Hall, Kaleski seems to have been poorly informed about the Halls Heelers. He never realised that Hall stations and runs extended from Sydney in New South Wales to Surat in Queensland in a discontinuous chain hundreds of kilometres long and that Halls Heelers were worked on all of them. From the 1870s, and probably earlier, other stockmen were breeding and working Halls Heelers – among them the drover, one John Timmins. The Halls Heelers, worked and bred by Timmins, become known as "Timmins Biters" and were greatly admired by stockmen. Kaleski may have learned of Thomas Hall and the working dogs associated with him from one of the Timmins family – perhaps the Timmins who was a member of the early Cattle Dog fancy in Sydney – but appeal to what is (or is not) possible shows Hall's alleged import of collies, or of any other working dog, to be an impossibility. The Hall family lost all contact with England after sailing on the *Coromandel* in 1802 and import arrangements, made by mail, would have taken years to finalise. Letters between New South Wales and Britain were months on the way. The ancestors of the Halls Heelers came to New South Wales with the convict transports and other early shipping. Kaleski realised that the early colonists brought dogs with them but didn't appreciate how quickly the colonial dog population grew or grasp that it must have included the Halls Heeler's ancestors.

Kaleski's insistence, that dingo contributed to the Halls Heeler's ancestry, was misguided. Although he admired the dingo he condemned dingo hybrids as vicious and intractable, with the single exception of the Halls Heeler. He insisted that the dingo cross was successful only if to "a good working dog strain"; a somewhat circular argument. According to Kaleski, the dingo contributed the nip-and-drop biting trait but other working characteristics were dependent on a dog of "a good working dog strain". The Cattle

Dog's characteristic nip-and-drop heeling instinct, that Kaleski so admired, is an inheritance from its European ancestors. The dingo is, and was, a predator and never a stock dog. It may be that Kaleski knew of instinctive nip-and-drop heelers only among Cattle Dogs and proposed an improbable ancestral origin for the trait. He certainly admired the dingo, even to the extent of giving it virtues it didn't possess and of using it in his own breeding.

Kaleski was sure that Halls Heelers were brought to Sydney from the Upper Hunter by the butcher, Davis, but Sydney butchers such as Davis would have looked closer to home than the Hunter for beef and mutton purchases on the hoof. Halls Heelers were probably first seen in Sydney, working stock in the Halls' Auburn paddocks, or droving between the Hawkesbury Valley and Sydney. Unknown to Kaleski, Halls Heelers spread through Queensland from the Halls' most northern properties, as well as through the Hunter and New England regions from Dartbrook.

Kaleski published voluminously until about 1930 but then his writing output almost ceased. His few later publications were probably invited and include his contribution to *The Australian Encyclopaedia* (1958). His versions of the history and development of the Cattle Dog in these later publications are confused and contradictory, and inconsistent with one another and with his earlier versions. This persuades the conclusion that some medical or other trauma affected his memory and mental acuity. He was described as "eccentric" in his later years. Kaleski's later publications, and particularly their emphasis on a Dalmatian infusion, should be disregarded. In his breed standard, Kaleski scorned Dalmatian as "objectionable".

Although Kaleski credited Thomas Hall with the development of the Halls Heeler that honour belongs to George Hall, Thomas's father, as much as it does to Thomas. It was George, not Thomas, who inspired and drove the land acquisitions that eventually comprised George Hall Estate cattle empire. George and Mary Hall and their four children arrived in New South Wales as free settlers in 1802. By 1805 George's 100 acre (40 ha) Hawkesbury Valley grant was self-supporting and by 1821 he owned over 1,500 acres (600 ha). During the next ten years he added land in the Upper Hunter Valley, including Dartbrook, the station that would become Thomas's future home. The Halls also acquired dogs including the ancestors of the Halls Heeler – probably self-invited stray dogs from the miscellaneous domestic dog population that infested the early colony. George Hall gave his son, Thomas, the task of setting up Dartbrook station and may also have charged him with the task of developing the Halls Heeler.

Thomas Hall set out on the 300 km journey from the Hawkesbury Valley to Dartbrook on foot, in 1825 or 1826, following the, then, recently completed Putty Road. He took his convict workers with him and his brothers, Matthew and Ebenezer, who also had grants in the Upper Hunter. Their two horse-drawn carts were laden with necessities (whatever was needed to establish settlement on Dartbrook) and cattle as both killers and breeders. And dogs, chosen for their droving aptitude. By 1828 Thomas had charge of 4,700 acres (1,900 ha.), 700 cattle, 2 horses and 8 convict workers. Dartbrook House was probably completed by 1835 to receive Thomas's wife, Ann McGinnis.

Development of the Halls Heeler was part of the over all development of Dartbrook and was selective. The best workers were kept and nurtured. The failures weren't. Inevitably a more or less distinctive type emerged. After the late 1840s most of the George Hall Estate properties were too far from Dartbrook for the Halls' stockmen to be able to rely on Dartbrook for dogs when replacements were needed. Halls Heeler breeding became decentralised and, with the passage of time, Halls Heelers bred in northern New South Wales and Queensland may have differed slightly in type from those bred at Dartbrook and further south.

The show ring eventually distinguished two regionally separate types. The most obvious difference between the "Queensland" and "New South Wales" types was tail length. Both short-tailed and long-tailed Cattle Dogs were accepted and exhibited in Queensland but not in New South Wales. Kaleski's standard made no provision for short-tailed types but the Cattle Dog and Kelpie Club of Queensland, for example, recognised two Cattle Dog varieties, short- and long-tailed. Early in the 1900s, however, the Queensland breeder, William Byrne, bought *Rowdy* [1899] from the Sydney breeder, Joseph Rose. From then on, the increasing popularity of New South Wales Cattle Dog lineages in Queensland was a major contributor to the decline of the short-tailed Cattle Dog.

Lesser shows continued to be well patronised during World War II even though the Royal shows were suspended. Older breeders, too old or unfit to enlist or in protected industries, carried on regardless. The Brisbane breeder, Arch Bevis, added the Sydney-bred pup, *Little Logic*, to his kennels in 1939 and exhibited the dog during the war years 1939-1945. *Little Logic* was a Grand Champion by 1947 and his impact on the long-tailed Cattle Dog population in Queensland was far reaching. During his phenomenal stud career, from 1941 to 1949, *Little Logic* sired more than 130 registered pups from forty-odd litters including Ch *Kenwyn Tiger* and his most influential son, *Logic Return*. Hilton Sinclair, *Berrilyn* Kennels, was one of the Sydney breeders whose first exposure to *Little Logic* was at the 1948 Sydney Royal. Exhibits included Ch *Kenwyn Tiger* [1942]. Sinclair (pers. comm. 1999) recalled his excitement when he first saw *Little Logic* offspring at the Sydney Royal in 1948. He immediately set out to introduce *Little Logic* into his *Berrilyn* breeding lines and was outstandingly successful in doing so. The *Berrilyn* lineage continued from the 1940s into the 1990s, the longest lived and one of the most productive of the post-war kennels. Les Dowsett (*Oatley* kennels) was also an important contributor to the breed during the 1940s and he, too, included *Little Logic* in his later breeding. In Queensland, Belle Young followed the beat of the *Little Logic* drum as did William Byrne. Young's *Harlaxton* prefix was active from the late 1940s until the mid-1970s; Byrne's *Standard* prefix from the early 1940s to the late 1950s. *Little Logic* and other dogs from the *Standard* Kennels also contributed to post-war prefixes in Victoria including *Kalamunda*, *Neangah* and *Tallangatta*: all active from the late 1940s to the late 1950s.

The ground was prepared for the emergence of *Wooleston* Kennels in the 1950s with the Walters' choice of *Little Logic* descendants, *Broombees Bobby* and *Turrella Lass*, as their foundation stock. The first *Broombees Bobby* x *Turrella Lass* litter was whelped in 1954. This litter included *Wooleston Blue Jack*. Nearly all *Wooleston* dogs and most if not all Australian Cattle Dogs whelped since 1990 are descended from this dog. During the next thirty years, the Walters registered some two hundred pups from more than eighty litters. Helen and Ken Dickson became the Walters' most influential clients. The *Tallawong* lineage was built on the Dicksons' *Wooleston* acquisitions, *Wooleston Blue Jenny* [1967] and *Wooleston Blue Jemina* [1970]. The Dicksons registered their first *Tallawong* litter in 1969: *Wooleston Blue Jamie* x *Wooleston Blue Jenny*. Most later *Tallawong* litters were from *Wooleston* or *Tallawong* parents, or from other-prefix dogs with *Tallawong* parents such as *Kaylaw*, *Merrigal* and *Carundon*. In practice, *Tallawong* became an extended closed kennel with a breeding output that exceeded *Wooleston*. During the thirty years, 1969-1999, the Dicksons registered around two hundred pups from over one hundred litters, mostly during the 1980s. Both *Wooleston* and *Tallawong* Kennels were successful in the show ring and both kennels exported, particularly to the U.S.A. Although strongest in Victoria, *Tallawong* influence spread north and west to other states.

The short-tailed Cattle Dog, as a benched breed, came under threat of extinction during the 1950s when the CCCQ deregistered all short-tailed Cattle Dog breeders. Iris Heale (*Glen Iris* Kennels) succeeded in overturning the CCCQ decision and became unique as the only remaining breeder of registered short-tailed Cattle Dogs. Heale maintained this position until 1988 when the Stumpy Tail Cattle Dog Redevelopment Scheme was implemented. Heale's thirty-year monopoly of the breed, however, insulated the short-tailed Cattle Dog from the major, and enduring, changes to type that overtook the post-war long-tailed Cattle Dog – initially by way of *Little Logic* and *Logic Return*, and later by way of the breeding activities of *Wooleston* and *Tallawong* Kennels.

Little attention was given to breed histories until the 1970s. George Holloway[1] lectured to the Australian Cattle Dog Society of NSW Breed Seminar on breed history in 1978, mostly basing his discussion on *Australian Barkers and Biters* and Kaleski's contribution to *The Australian Encyclopaedia*, and Angela Sanderson published *The Complete Book of Australian Dogs* in 1981.[2] Sanderson also drew on the more readily available Kaleski publications. Although she noted that the Australian Cattle Dog and the Stumpy Tail Cattle Dog "are too alike for there not to be similarities in their breeding" Sanderson otherwise perpetuated the Kaleski Dogma with some variations of her own. Bert Howard proposed the entirely imaginary Northumberland Blue Merle Drovers Dog in 1990 and a Kaleski-based ANKC breed history for the Australian Cattle Dog accompanied the Breed Standard Extension 1998 (reaffirmed 2009.)[3] The ANKC breed standard for the Australian Stumpy Tail Cattle Dog was not supported by a breed extension but Dogs NSW, an ANKC affiliate, added an historical note, of sorts, to the Stumpy Tail page on its web site. None of these latter day histories have had any particular impact on either Australian Cattle Dog breed beyond attracting disbelief, contempt or resignation, according to the views of their readers.

Changing breed standards have, however, mirrored the change in breeder perception of desired type in the Australian Cattle Dog, a change largely driven by the impact of the *Wooleston/Tallawong* influence since the 1960s. As early as 1966, Alan Forbes drew attention to "the gradual trend towards a heavier, more attractive dog, slightly shorter on the leg than his working counterpart of years ago".[4] Comparison between dogs of the 1940s and 1950s (*Kalamundi Rex Regis, Trueblue Patches, Broombees Bobby*) and dogs of the 1960s and 1970s (*Wooleston Blue Jenny, Tallawong Blue Jenny, Dustyroad Toby*) illustrate the trend since World War II.

The Stumpy Tail Cattle Dog Redevelopment Scheme (1988) inaugurated lasting change of type. The ANKC 1963 standard permitted tan on blue animals, "the richer the better", and as late as 1981 Iris Heale registered "blue, black and tan" Stumpies including Ch *Glen Iris Bush Mate* [1981]. By 1994 tan was no longer acceptable to the ANKC and the 1994 standard seems to have been the version in place during the implementation of the Stumpy Tail Cattle Dog Redevelopment Scheme. Recent ANKC standards condemn tan as a "serious fault". Historically, there is no reason why tan should have been excluded.

The larger story of Australia's working dogs is poorly known and piecing it together relies mostly on identifying and dismissing impossibilities. The story begins with their arrival in Australia; there were no domestic dogs in Australia until 1788. The New South Wales colonial dogs arrived with the convict fleets. About half the earliest settlers were free settlers not convicts: the wives and children of the military and administrators, and some voluntary free settlers. Some brought dogs with them. Dog ownership was so taken for granted that colonial journals rarely mention dogs but dogs did come with the early settlers and found New South Wales to their liking. Within twenty years the stray dog population had reached nuisance level and the Governor urged colonists to confine their own dogs; strays were to be destroyed by government order. The dog population obviously included the ancestors of the Tasmanian Smithfield and Halls Heeler.

The history, such as it is known or inferred, of today's Tasmanian Smithfield and the two Australian Cattle Dog breeds, differ in one important respect. The Smithfields known to Beilby were apparently used for cattle work in most of eastern Australia, from southern Queensland to Tasmania. They were bred locally, and at need, with few constraints on their colour or general type. Although their descendants still work stock in mainland Australia they gained informal (non-ANKC) breed identity only in Tasmania. In contrast, the Australian Cattle Dog breeds developed from the Halls Heeler. The Halls Heeler seems to have emerged later than the Smithfield and remained largely under the control of a single family, the family of George Hall and his sons, for half a century before appearing in the show world with its emphasis on type as prescribed in a breed standard. Even less is known of the Halls Heeler's ancestors than of the Tasmanian Smithfield's except that its type must have been consistent with that of its descendants, such as *Nipper* and *Floss*, the Allen family's dog, Rose's *Danger*, Kaleski's *Nugget*, and Neville Butler's dogs. They were genetically tailless although some individuals had normal tails. Like the ancestors of the Tasmanian Smithfield, the ancestors of the Halls Heeler were among the ownerless stray dogs that followed the early settlers wherever they went and took up residence wherever they could. Some evidently made George Hall's grant in the Hawkesbury Valley their home. Vermin hunters, watchdogs and stock workers would have been made welcome by the Halls and other Hawkesbury Valley settlers.

By the 1810s most of the region bounded by the Blue Mountains to the west, and the highlands to the north and south of Sydney, was in government or private ownership or unsuited to agriculture. The colony needed to expand. John Howe (like George Hall, one of the *Coromandel* free settlers) led one of the several exploration parties that pushed the known limits of the colony outwards. Howe found a route from the Hawkesbury Valley to the Hunter Valley in 1819. The road (Howes Track, later, the Putty Road) was opened to traffic in 1823 and, in 1825, George Hall purchased land in the Upper Hunter Valley. Thomas, one of George Hall's most able sons, settled at Dartbrook, one of George's first Hunter Valley stations, probably in 1825. Thomas, his younger brothers Matthew and Ebenezer, who also made their homes on Dartbrook, and Thomas's eight assigned convict workers, walked the first cattle to Dartbrook; forty or fifty head, possibly more.

Thomas would have taken dogs that showed aptitude for stock work with him to Dartbrook. He needed them. He is understood to have been a notable stock breeder, particularly of Shorthorn cattle. He was equally successful in breeding the working dog that, long after his death, became known as the Halls Heeler, and that gave essential support to the Halls' stockmen and drovers for over thirty years. After the George Hall Estate properties went to auction in the 1870s Halls Heelers became freely available and were sought after by stockmen and drovers including members of the Timmins family.[5]

The Timmins Biters (Halls Heeler descendants) were particularly admired. After the 1890s the Halls Heeler story becomes the Cattle Dog story, better documented and with photographic support.

The defining event in this story was the acceptance of Kaleski's breed standard in 1903. It established Cattle Dogs as a benched breed but it had a darker side: its exclusion of short-tailed cattle dogs. This split the breed. Queensland and New South Wales Cattle Dogs became separate entities. Queensland breeders took the presence or absence of tail for granted – as the Halls must have done – but in New South Wales, where Kaleski's breed standard first prevailed, short-tailed pups were apparently excluded from exhibition.

In New South Wales the Cattle Dog breed developed according to Kaleski's standard although variant standards later superseded it. In Queensland, particularly during the 1920s, many Cattle Dog breeders in Queensland followed a trend set by William Byrne, an influential Brisbane breeder and judge. Byrne and other breeders with show ring ambitions saw success in terms of dogs bred in New South Wales, long-tailed Cattle Dogs, and replaced their Queensland foundation stock with dogs from New South Wales at the expense of the short-tailed lineage. Victoria also looked towards New South Wales for purchases. Offspring from highly regarded Cattle Dogs, such as *Some Rock* [1927], were soon to be seen in Queensland and Victoria as well as in their native New South Wales. There was no corresponding movement of Queensland- or Victoria-bred dogs to New South Wales until after World War II. In the post-war period most of the Cattle Dog movement from Queensland to New South Wales and Victoria was of descendants of New South Wales dogs sent in earlier years to Queensland.

Competing breed standards, both in New South Wales and in Queensland, had their effect on the long-tailed Cattle Dog breed. Photos of Sydney Royal exhibits from the 1920s and 1930s and Kaleski's critiques of them suggest that there was lack of consensus as to type.[6] In 1935 an anonymous country judge commented:

> Loss of type is an ever-present danger, and the breeding out of the working instincts of many breeds is a real tragedy ... The ignorance regarding type at many country shows is appalling. On several occasions I have judged cattle dogs where not one in the section was worthy of a prize.[7]

Lean, leggy types, reminiscent of *Nipper*, were still being exhibited during the 1920s and 1930s but also heavier-bodied, shorter-legged dogs. After World War II (1939-45) breeder preference favoured the heavier-bodied, shorter-legged type. *Little Logic* was hailed as the father of the Cattle Dog breed but the dog's impact was substantially via his son, *Logic Return*: a typical exemplar of the heavier-bodied, shorter-legged type.

The influence of *Wooleston* and later *Tallawong* Kennels also supported the trend towards the heavier-bodied, shorter-legged type. Breeders of long-tailed Cattle Dogs in the 1950s seemed to want either *Logic Return* offspring or a pup from *Wooleston* Kennels. This changed the direction taken by the breed. The heavier-bodied shorter-legged form prevailed and was further consolidated, from the 1970s, by *Tallawong* Kennels in Victoria.

In Queensland, the short-tailed cattle dog had been progressively declining as a benched breed since the 1920s but during the 1950s it faced extinction. This was not the result of breeder preference, however, but of official edict. The short-tailed type was isolated, for thirty years, from the long-tailed type by decisions taken by the CCCQ in the late 1950s and the monopoly that Iris Heale subsequently imposed on the Stumpy Tail Cattle Dog. The Stumpy was rescued from extinction as a benched breed when the Stumpy Tail Cattle Dog Redevelopment Scheme was proposed in 1988. As a result of Heale's thirty-year Stumpy Tail Cattle Dog monopoly the Stumpy Tail Cattle Dog was scarcely influenced (if at all) by the breeder enthusiasm for the *Wooleston* and *Tallawong* lineages after the 1950s and 1960s. This is evident in the type dissimilarities that distinguish the redeveloped Australian Stumpy Tail Cattle Dog from the present day Australian Cattle Dog.

The *Little Logic - Logic Return* lineage hardly touched the Australian Stumpy Tail Cattle Dog.

Robert Kaleski remains a towering figure in the history of Australia's Cattle Dogs even though he spurned the Smithfield and invented a history for "his" Cattle Dogs. Without him the Halls Heelers may have vanished from the rural scene and never have achieved identity as the Cattle Dogs that played an essential role in stock management during the late nineteenth and the early twentieth centuries. Kaleski's support for Australia's working dogs was a lifetime commitment and nothing can or should detract from admiration for his commitment. *The World's News*, a Sydney newspaper, included biographical notes with a review of *Australian Barkers and Biters*.

> Bob was born in Burwood, and started breeding prize setters when he was six; has bred and worked dogs ever since. An old [Sydney] High boy, he went into the country when the banks crashed [1890s] and later started a big poultry run near Guildford, now a suburb of Sydney [but] then in the bush. Kaleski then went in for scientific agriculture, began research work along that line at Granville Technical School, and has carried on agricultural investigation ever since. He has written standard books on settlement, nature study, dogs and forestry, and is supposed to know more about land and dogs than any one else in Australia.[8]

This may have been Kaleski on Kaleski but the view was generally endorsed. *Australian Barkers and Biters* (the 1933 edition) was enthusiastically received and widely praised. The revised text of *Australian Barkers and Biters* and most of Kaleski's other publications, however, were written before the 1930s. That is, the prolific author of earlier years almost stopped writing after the 1920s. Kaleski's 1958 article in *The Australian Encyclopaedia* was invited and it is probable that all his publications, from 1930 on, were also requested by their various publishers. Comparison between Kaleski's early and later publications persuade the conclusion that some medical or other trauma affected his mental processes. Kaleski's obvious declining interest in writing for publication after the 1920s supports this view.

Regardless of how questionable and out-of-date some of his opinions were, Robert Kaleski identified Thomas Hall as the early developer of the Halls Heeler and produced the first breed standard for the Cattle Dog. Both were monumental achievements in the history of the Australian Cattle Dog breeds. Without Kaleski neither Cattle Dog breed would have survived to the present day.

APPENDIX 1

Kaleski's publications on dogs 1902-1958

CATTLE DOGS

Introduction to the Cattle Dog breed standard 1903 and 1910

In travelling about this country handling stock no observant person can fail to be struck, on both practical and humanitarian grounds, with the amount of suffering entailed on our dumb animals by the use of bad dogs, either cattle or sheep. Confining myself, in this article, to remarks on the former, how often it will be noticed of anyone handling cattle, especially in the old settled districts, that instead of one well-bred good-working dog handling them without noise or trouble, the drover will have about half-a-dozen mongrels which worry and harass the unfortunate creatures almost to madness, and necessitate a constant flow of blasphemy and whip-work from the frenzied drover to get the mob to its destination. Residents on the travelling routes between Flemington and Glebe Island, or Flemington and Canterbury, can feelingly endorse my remarks on this point, especially if, as sometimes happens, they have been unable to get out of their front gate for a few hours owing to an overdriven beast, with its three or four canine attendants, having temporarily taken charge of the street and turned it into a little Armageddon of its own. On how many dairy farms in this State may be seen at milking-time two or three lop-eared mongrels hanging round the bails biting milkers, springers, and poddies with strict impartiality, and working on and off at their own sweet will. As we have not yet reached the Golden Age when we can dispense with dogs in handling cattle, the next best thing is to use dogs that will work them with the least trouble and suffering.

It is with that object in view that I am writing this article. As I have been breeding and working cattle-dogs since I was 9 years of age, in different parts of the State, and have had some pretty tough times handling different classes of cattle in rough places – Burragorang Valley, for example – I can speak with some little experience on the subject. Whilst to my mind there is nothing so objectionable as the sight of cattle being knocked about by bad dogs, so there is nothing prettier than to see a couple of good ones steering, with almost superhuman sagacity, a big mob through wild, difficult country.

Requirements of a good dog

The main requirements of any dogs for working cattle are that they should be steady, game, faithful, enduring, and intelligent. *Steady,* because the best worker in the world is useless, and very often dangerous, if headstrong and unwilling to obey orders, especially when working cattle through broken country. *Game,* because a cow-hearted dog, on being kicked or severely handled, will slink off into the scrub and leave his owner to work the cattle by himself. *Faithful,* because if not, you will find he has cleared out with some stranger that has taken his fancy just when you wanted him particularly; and if you have left him to watch your saddle or gear in your absence that will have gone too. *Enduring,* because a dog that knocks up easily is only a nuisance, and you are better without him. *Intelligent,* because a dog has to learn a lot to be a good worker, and it is a heart-breaking task teaching a stupid pup.

It must never be forgotten that, as with sheep-dogs, you have to suit your dogs to the class of cattle you usually handle, and breed with that object. I have seen pounds knocked off the value of dairy cattle, especially in the Camden district, by the using of savage cattle-dogs accustomed to working wild station cattle, and which had made the dairy cattle confirmed kickers and afraid of a dog. For wild cattle you require a silent biter, very hardy and severe. These dogs should not be worked on horses, if possible, as they make confirmed kickers of them. They are all the better for being a bit on the big side, as they have often to stand a terrible lot of knocking about, especially when droving bulls or stags, which would spoil the best dog God ever put breath into. For handling horses, working bullocks, dairy cows, and quiet cattle of any sort, a medium-sized dog, with just a little voice, and who rather nips than chops, is the best, though cunning old dairy cows will make the sweetest-tempered dog chop them, as they are so beastly cunning at edging out of the mob, round the head of a dead tree or through the broken panels in a fence. For springers, heifers and calves, a very steady easy dog is required, which will only nip under great provocation, and which will come off instantly when whistled or called, as nothing makes young stock knock up easier when tired than a dog that is perpetually following them up and heeling them; and carrying knocked-up calves across the saddle and minding the tail of a mob at the same time is inclined to make one think sarcastically of the poet's assertion that " The drover's life has pleasures that the townsfolk never know."[9] For trucking and yard work, a dog with plenty of voice is essential; for scrubby country it is also better if your dogs are broken to bark a little when working out of your sight, as should a beast elect to stand and keep charging them on breaking out of the mob any distance, you know where he is. To be a first-class worker, a cattle-dog should be able to work either side and the tail of a mob, or both sides if the drover minds the tail; should be able, if the drover has to go ahead to open gates, &c., to bring the mob along after him; to gallop to the head of a mob and swing it by the leaders back on itself when there is danger of boxing with another lot, or to swing it in any direction necessary; to draft with its owner at gates or slip-rails; to bail up a horse that refuses to be caught, and make him stand; to make any horse or beast lead, and to guard any article which may be left with him for that purpose, from a team to a tub of feed.

In the matter of breaking-in a pup, every man has his own ideas on the subject. Personally, I prefer to break a pup in with a steady old dog, which cannot be spoilt, on a quiet lot of cattle. The pup will imitate the old dog, except that he will try to do about six times more work than there is any need for. After a few trips he will discover that there is nothing in overdoing things, and the old one can be called behind and the young dog allowed to do all the work. When the pup can work a mob by himself, leave the old dog at home, and take care to keep the pup constantly at work for twelve months or so, if possible, so that he will not forget his work. Break in with a big mob if possible, and have quiet cattle, as old bulls or stags will kill or maim a careless pup. Do not break him in on horses on any account, as they will nearly always kick out a pup's tusk teeth, which renders him useless for biting; and never allow anyone to feed or handle him but yourself. Never beat a pup severely, no matter what the provocation, as it will cow and spoil him nine times out of ten; and never, under any circumstances, correct him with the whip, or you will make him whip-shy, and ruin him for working with a whip. I have broken many old ones of this habit, but it takes a terrible lot of time and patience. To correct a pup, keep a short piece of green bough, and after cutting him with it a few times make friends with him again before letting him go; it cows a pup to be sulky with him. Do not put a heavy collar or piece of chain round his neck to steady him if he is too eager, as it only hampers him in working, does no good, and makes it easier to steal him. Train him to avoid strangers by blunting a big needle, and when he runs up to be stroked advance your hand (with the needle in it) and gently prod him on the nose with it. After a few trials he will soon learn to distrust any person's hand approaching him. If he does not take to watching anything he is told naturally, then make his bed alongside a tub or box of feed and chain him short up to it when stock are knocking about, so that if he lets any animal approach he stands in danger of being trodden on. He then realises that as he cannot get out of the way he must keep any intruder away in self-defence, and soon acquires the habit of biting anything which comes to interfere with him when on guard.

A good biter should always bite the hind foot which is resting on the ground supporting the weight of the animal's body, and should drop flat immediately after biting so that the hoof goes over him. A little experience will soon teach him to bite each foot alternately if necessary, even when the beast is going at full speed. Some dogs bite from the side instead of the back, but as a rule they die early. If wanted, a good dog should bite either foreleg or hind; if sent to turn a single beast, and unable to swing him by the heels, he should turn him by running up on the opposite side, and jumping and snapping at his neck, well behind the horns.

Varieties

The varieties of cattle-dogs I am acquainted with in New South Wales are as under, placed in order of merit, as I have found them to work:

The merlin or blue heeler, erroneously known as the Smithfield.

The Welsh heeler or merle, erroneously known as the German collie.

The red bob-tail, often called by drovers Timmins' breed.

The black bob-tail, apparently the old English cur-dog.

Mongrels and crosses, generally the bull, fox-terrier, or dingo, crossed with the collie.

The black sheep-dog, called the barb, I have also seen used, but they can only work cattle as they would sheep, and I would not be bothered with them myself, as cattle or horses require to be worked with a dog that can bite.

The Merlin or Blue Heeler

This breed was first made, as far as I can ascertain, by a Mr. Hall or Wall, of Muswellbrook, about forty years ago. He imported the blue-gray Welsh merle for working cattle, but, finding they were unsuitable on account of barking too much, crossed them with the dingo, and founded the present variety, which, by selection and careful breeding, became a distinct breed and throws true to type. After having tried all varieties, about ten years ago I took up this breed as the best of the lot, and in company with a few more enthusiasts have been breeding them ever since. The standard we breed to (approved of by the Kennel Club of New South Wales) is as follows ... [in Appendix 2].

THE AUSTRALIAN CATTLE-DOG
A champion breeder's account of him
The Bookfellow vol. 1 no. 1 January 3 1907 pp. 10-11.

Reprinted in *The Maitland Daily Mercury* 14 January 1907 p. 2 and in *The Northern Miner* 31 August 1910 p. 7; part of the article was also reproduced in *Australian Barkers and Biters* 1933 pp. 77-81.

Very few people in this country, outside butchers and drovers, know what a cattle dog is; but they would have to pay nearly as much again for their meat if there were none. Handling cattle without them would be costly indeed. Usually, one cattle dog is as good as two men: in rough or bad places he is better than a dozen. He can go easily where a horseman cannot; quick as lightning, too.

The best time to see his value is when the cattle try to get away from the drover – whether at an awkward corner in broken country or through scrub or crowded streets. Then, as the leaders swing away, with the mob to follow if they are successful, the drover whistles; like an arrow his dog shoots up to those leaders. Snap ! snap ! at the throat of the one he wants to turn, and it swings from him as on a pivot, jamming the other leader over as well. Nip ! nip ! at their heels; and they dart along the right track, followed by those behind, whilst the dog stands watching at the weak point, till all are past. No human being could work like that; the cattle would be tearing down the wrong track, unheadable, before he would be half-way to them.

Or again; a dark, drizzling night, with the drover pushing on to reach a favourite camp, or to deliver the cattle. He rides ahead of the mob, trusting to instinct; the night is black as the Pit. Behind him follow the cattle; unwilling, but forced along by the determined watcher behind. As the "rogues" fall back, in hopes of standing till the mob has passed, they get a series of heel-nips which make them bellow again, and dart in to the mob for shelter. There may be a thousand head behind the drover; but never a one will be missing at the slip-rails, thanks to the cattle dog.

How the breed arose

Nothing in the bush makes so good a mate as the cattle dog. Besides working cattle and horses, he is a great fighter, a good game dog, a retriever, and the finest watch dog possible. There are many dogs called cattle-dogs; but, only four sorts are genuine – the others are mere amateurs. First of the four come the blue-speckled heelers: then their cousins, the red speckles; then the red bob-tail; and, lastly, the black bob-tail. The black bob-tail was the first dog used for cattle in Australia; he was (and is) a big rough-coated, square-bodied dog, with a head like a wedge, a white frill round the neck, and saddle-flap ears; he got over the ground like a native bear. Faithful enough, handy, and sensible; but he couldn't stand the heat and long trips. Besides, he bit like an alligator, and barked like a consumptive. The other faults were bad but the last was a finisher. How could a man borrow any of his neighbours' cattle with an advertisement like that behind them? So one Timmins (who was in the trade) got the idea of crossing him with the dingo, so as to shut his mouth, and let a man ride about in peace. The result was the red bob-tail; it was nice and quiet, but a horribly severe dog. If it could get out of the drover's sight with a calf, over a hill or in scrub, it would have it half eaten by the time he got to it. The cross was too violent. The pure collie was tried next, but cattle were out of his line. Being always used to turn sheep by barking at their heads, he couldn't understand why cattle wouldn't work in the same way. Those who survived the horns were put back on sheep, as their barking made the cattle break and rush like the dickens, fats doing this would run three or four pounds of tallow off themselves before they got cool again.

So Mr. Hall, of Muswellbrook, imported some blue smooth Highland collies or merles; called by ignorant people Welsh heelers. These were a lot better than the common collie; but still had some of the barking at-the-head business in them. So they were crossed on the dingo. (The early settlers had a great respect for that animal.) This turned out all right; the pups came blue-speckled or red-speckled as the merle or dingo was stronger in them. Instead of yapping like the collie, they had the old dingo style of creeping silently up behind and biting. It is this dingo idea, which makes the blue and red speckles the best cattle dogs in Australia to-day. These speckled heelers are like a small thick-set dingo to look at, barring the colour; if you met one in the bush you would shoot it for its scalp. And yet they don't want to go hunting at all; working cattle or horses is all they care about. Give them plenty of that, about half enough feed for an ordinary dog, and a bag on the lee side of the stable to sleep on, and they're in paradise. Just the opposite to the collie, which will hunt like a beagle if he gets the chance.

There have been several attempts to make pure breeds of cattle-dogs; but the only survivors are the blue and red speckles. The others soon died out. About the first was a cross of the Russian poodle and collie – a middle-sized blue, brown, or black dog, smothered in hair like an otter hound. It bit like bad whisky and had no sense; that and its coat have sent it to limbo. The next was the bull-terrier and collie cross. This was a lumpy white or light brown dog; faithful and sensible, but too slow, severe, and heavy. So it had to go. Then some one tried crossing the kangaroo-dog and bull; when these weren't eating sheep they were killing calves; so they died out. The last experiment has been to try the black sheep-dog called the barb. This joker shoos frightened cattle along nicely, but is helpless, if they turn to him; for he is no biter and can't stand being kicked.

Rearing and training

All cattle-pups are picked and reared in the same way, whatever their breed or colour. The great thing is to get a thick-set hardy prick-eared dog, with a wide flat skull (for sense), and a sharp nose (for clean biting). Look for these points in the pups; to get the colour, turn them on their backs, and look at their foot-soles. These show what the dog's colour will be. If pink he will run from light to white; if reddish or brown, he will be that colour; light blue, dark blue; black, the same. I don't know why it should be so, but it is. We breeders of the speckles pick all our pups in that way, as our pups are all born white and don't get their true colour till a few months old. So if we hadn't that guide to go by, we would have to keep the whole litter till they turned, to get the colour we wanted; for litters always run mixed from light to very dark.

In rearing, as soon as weaned, the pups want a cooked meat diet to make them fierce and hardy. Feed them on milk and such slops, and you get a lanky, loose-jointed dog, with about as much life in him as an india-rubber doll. Some breeders never seem to learn that a dog's natural food is meat. If fed on raw meat, though, they got distemper which is fatal; because even if you do bring them round with Turkey rhubarb or other stuff, they are always shaky and unreliable. Half each of pollard and bran, mixed in with the meat, keeps them in great order. They must have plenty of big bones to gnaw as well, so as to strengthen the jaws; small bones often lodge in the throat, or spoil them. It is best to rear pups in a big yard or paddock free from stock; otherwise the little things will try instinctively to heel the stock, and perhaps get their baby brains kicked out. Also, rear two or more together, so as to let them practice heeling on each other, thereby becoming quick as lightning with their teeth.

When about six months old, a pup is fit to break in. There is some art in this, but still, breaking in a pup, is like breaking in a child. If he's got it in him, he'll pretty well train himself; if he hasn't he will take up all your time and patience, and then never make a dog. The only thing is to give him a fair chance to prove himself. To do this, have a good old dog, and a big quiet mob of cattle. Without both, you can't break in a young pup to work. With no old dog to tell him it takes him about six months to learn your orders; with a wild lot of stock, he will most likely get killed or maimed through ignorance before he learns the tricks of the trade. If you can't get dog and mob your self, find out someone who has them, and borrow their job for pup's benefit. If you send him away with drovers, you will never see him again. If you break him in to a couple of head of stock, they get cunning to him, and he learns to bark at their heads to move them, which is a vile habit. Don't beat him too hard, or you will break his heart past mending, just like a bullock's; though the more he gets knocked about by stock, the more, eager he gets to bite. Never touch him with the whip on any account, or he won't work with it.

The Virtuous Dog

When a pup has got a fair idea of work (putting stragglers back into the mob, bringing the mob along behind the drover through gates and slip-rails; turning the mob from wrong lanes and corners, you want to leave the old dog at home, and work the pup by himself; it gives him confidence. Keep him at this for six months at least; then he won't forget his work. Pups are just as flighty as children. In between whiles, when he has become a reasonable biter, take him out with horses. Let him get used to making a horse lead, or watching it for you when tied up. Teach him to watch your horse's feed for you (some publicans are terrors to take the feed away if you are inside), also to jump into the saddle and ride lying across it, if he cripples his feet in any way. The only trouble about this last idea is that, if a pup is naturally lazy, the trick becomes chronic.

Besides being a good worker, a cattle dog must be faithful, sensible, hardy, and obedient. Faithful, or he will desert you in time of need; sensible, or he is too much trouble to break in; hardy, or he can't do the work; obedient, or he may disobey orders, and kill the drover and cattle both. When you are getting a cattle pup, you have to suit his build and disposition to the class of cattle you generally work. A decent, gentlemanly dog, used to persuading quiet dairy cattle along with easy, infrequent nips, is no use at all for wild scrubbers, stags, or bulls. These are all full of low, pot-house tricks, that no respectable beast could be guilty of; such as backing stealthily into a corner, and trying to hook the dog with a dirty horn; lodging him up against a stump, so as to kick his brain out; pretending to feed, and then suddenly running forward to stamp on him.

Kindness is wasted on these brutes; the dog to deal successfully with such offal is a heavy, quick one, with a snap like an alligator's; one that brings blood at every bite. Yet such a one used on quiet, dairy cattle, would drive them mad in half an hour, and their owners when they saw then. For calves you hardly want a dog at all; they knock up so quickly when bitten, and then have to be carried across the saddle, making dismal travelling. The only cattle dogs which can be worked on all these sorts of cattle any time are the blue speckles, and then only when well seasoned.

Cattle dogs vary in disposition somewhat like human beings. Most are honest and faithful, a few pointy and treacherous. It is very rarely that any of them are lazy. Some are born clever, others only learn sense by experience. All the females rather like being beaten by their owners than otherwise. I have one now, the best biter in Australia; if she gets a fortnight's spell, she does every thing wrong out of cussedness, just like a girl. Then I catch her and give her a good belting. This makes her as happy as Larry, and she works A1 till she gets another spell. To bachelors thinking of matrimony, a course of breaking in cattle pups should be invaluable.

When and how to bite

The way a true cattle dog bites is to dart up behind the animal and nip it on the heel of the foot which is then carrying the weight; the second after the bite he drops flat, and the hoof whistles harmlessly over him. Next second he is out of danger. If he bit at the lifting foot, he must rise instead of dropping and would meet the hoof half-way. An amateur jumps for the tail, or bites sideways, or the wrong foot; he always dies very early. In working, it is wonderful how little they mind being kicked. Sometimes an extra cunning old horse will catch one full on the skull, knocking him yards back. He just gives a howl, shakes himself a few times, and at it again. Heaven help the animal that kicked him then! It gets enough attention from that dog's teeth, in unguarded moments (It can't be always on the watch); to last a life-time. Sometimes one gets the blow on his jaw, breaking it, or knocking out the tusk-tooth. This makes him of very little use afterwards as a cattle dog's teeth are his living. It is wonderful what kicks they will re-cover from, though, I had a little lady once that got her skull split clean across, with the brains showing; kicked in the dark by a strange horse. Everyone assured me she would die; yet she was heeling calves in a fortnight.

Cattle dogs get kicked by rogue horses; these kick straight down into the ground (and on to the dog's head) instead of kicking back, and consequently overhead. When a good biter sees animals trying this he dashes in and chews their front legs; then out again before they can cow-kick. In every district there is such a rogue; generally an old team-horse, used to being harried by strange dogs. These will puzzle the best biter for a while, till he finds out the particular style of kicking, and suits himself to it. A good biter always feints a couple of times at a strange horse before coming in to bite. Then he sees what to expect. To see a good biter at a rogue, is better than watching a heavy-weight prize-fight. Each tries all the tricks he knows; but a good biter can always get the horse, if he has to feint and duck for half an hour to do it. To get it moving he circles round and round it, biting its nose till it gets giddy in twisting about to avoid him; then he can bite all he likes. Once he gets it moving he's right; he bites each weighted foot alternately, every few yards, so that the horse runs to the wagon or yard for shelter.

With a bullock team, the dog should know each bullock's place in it, and should fetch them up and put them in their places whilst the teamster has his breakfast. The bullocks soon get used to the dog and will walk into place naturally saving a lot of bother. A good dog never bites them in the yoke, as it makes kickers of them. The same with a horse team.

I have had some very intelligent cattle dogs. Drovers get into the habit of boasting about their dogs I know; still, mine are so good that I can't exaggerate about them. I had a little speckle dog once ... ["Lead us not into temptation", the editor of *The Bookfellow* cautioned!]

THE WORKING DOGS OF AUSTRALIA
RAS Annual 1911 pp. 201-209

Now, for the cattle-dogs. As I said before, these are of two colors, blue and red speckle. The markings of both are curious, and found in no other dog in the world. The blue speckles have the head black or red, usually with a white stripe down the middle of forehead; body dark-blue speckled on back, sometimes with black saddle, or black spot on tail-butt; lighter blue, sometimes mottled with white hairs on under part of body; legs blueish, with or without red spots mottled over them. A tan spot over each eye (which is *brown)* and tail lighter blue, sometimes with white tip. This is the general run of blue speckles.

There are, however, three strains (Messrs. Harry Bagust, Yabsley's, and mine) which have more fancy markings. We breed for *black* head only, black spot on tail-butt, or black saddle (all other black barred), legs to be all red speckles (only) to forearm and hock. This adds much to the appearance of the dogs, and as we only breed from the best workers, does not affect the working qualities. The colours are now so fixed that we practically never breed them out of markings.

The *red* speckle has red ears, sometimes a red saddle, and the rest of the body red speckles on a lighter ground. They are therefore much easier to breed to color than the blues. In some strains of blues, a red pup will be found in every litter; in the reds a blue; but usually they throw their own colors. For example, in my twenty odd years of breeding blues, I never bred a red speckle yet, and my experience is that of most breeders.

The speckle breed arose this way. About fifty years ago, a Mr. Hall of Muswellbrook imported some smooth Highland collies *(merles)* for working cattle. These proved too noisy and headstrong and were crossed by him with the dingo to get the latter's idea of creeping up silently behind and biting. The cross proved a great success as workers and came blue or red speckled as the dingo or the collie predominated in them. They soon got scattered about the Hunter and

New England. The well-known droving family of Timmins got some of them and produced some wonderful workers. As far as I can find out, they were first brought to Sydney by Mr. Fred Davis, of the well-known butchering family, about '75. After him came the Lees, the Peakes, and the Jubbs (the first-named are suspected of putting a cross of white bull-terrier through them.) Then a blue dog came on the field, called Bentley's dog who was crossed through these dogs and from whom all the latter-day blue dogs of any note claim their descent. He was owned by a butcher working on Glebe Island, called Tom Bentley, and was a marvel for work and appearance. Although his pedigree was never set out, we know beyond doubt that he was one of the pure Hall strain. From him on selected bitches, Messrs. Jack and Harry Bagust, C. Pettit, J. Brennan, A. Davis (Fred Davis's son, who was my partner in the blue dogs for years), many other breeders and myself, made a start breeding the blue dogs. About fifteen years ago we had them practically perfect. The third blood (bull-terrier) filtered through had set the breed thoroughly; though in some cases at the expense of shape and activity. Where more than a very slight infusion of bull was used, it was noticeable (and is to this day) in the rabbit ear, heavy jaw, and long low body lacking activity; also lack of sense and control, and snapping instead of sharp, clean biting. However, these were few and far between. The majority were beautifully marked blue or red speckled dogs, exactly like a small thick-set dingo, boiling over with work and as sensible as Christians.

Unfortunately, prices were so low (5/- was a big price to get for a pup) that many of the old breeders became disgusted and went out of the business altogether. I remember buying old Spot (our first champion at the R.A.S.) from behind a greengrocer's cart in Summer Hill, for half a crown. He was then only twelve months old. We found out his pedigree (he was a pure Bagust) and got many a fine pup from him. If he were alive today he would easily bring £30. He was, without exception, the best blue dog I ever saw, and his work was as good as his looks. Many a time when a sulky bullock broke from the mob and took to the water, I have seen him swim after it, and swim with it, chewing its tail till it took to dry land and the mob again. In his day he had no equal at cross roads or broken fences. He was the father of my blue dog Tiger (also champion at the R.A.S.) and great-great-grandfather of my present champion dog Nugget.

The blue and red speckles are equally good as workers, and both bite the same way; that is, they dart straight in behind the animal and bite the heel the weight is on, dropping flat the moment after to avoid a kick. A few crouch first and bite upwards; we call these tusk biters. They cannot bite at full speed, like the true heelers. If the dog bit the foot taking no weight, he would meet the lifting foot, and get laid out for a certainty.

Besides biting stragglers, the cattle-dog will bring the mob through gates when the drover is in front; work on either side required, where there are broken fences and cross-roads; gallop to the head of the mob and hold it when there is danger of any sort in front; make any horse or beast lead, and watch his owner's property when the latter is away from it.

A curious thing about all blue pups is that they are born *white,* and don't turn their proper color till a few months old. As blue is not *a fixed* color in breeding, the pups in a litter vary from light to dark blue. (With careless breeders they run from black to white.) The way we pick them for color at a couple of weeks old, is very simple, though scientifically it is still a puzzle to me. We turn each pup on its back on the grass, and look at its foot soles. If the foot soles are all dark blue, it will be a dark blue. If some *are pink,* the lighter the color. If all soles are pink, the pups will turn out *white,* and should be destroyed at once. White is the cattle-dog breeder's abomination; the dogs being soft, and so conspicuous as to be readily kicked or horned on the darkest night.

It is rather difficult now to get good pure blue or red speckles; owing to drovers crossing them on the barb, as the cross works cattle like sheep, and saves the drover a lot of riding. These cross-breds, however, won't stand being kicked and most of the second generation won't bite at all. There are lots of these (throw-backs) being sold as pure blues, from 10/- a head upwards. It is safe to say that the public will get just what they pay for, as a pure blue or red speckled dog ready to work can't be sold under a fiver, to pay the breeder.

WHENCE CAME AUSTRALIAN DOGS?

Necessity Was Responsible for the Evolution of Both Sheep
and Cattle Dogs
American Kennel Gazette 1 September 1930 pp. 26-28; 102-103
(Cattle dogs pp. 27-28; 102-103)

As the Australian sheep-breeder had to evolve a special breed of
sheep-dog by crossings, so did the cattle-raiser find it necessary to
evolve a new cattle-dog by a blending of the native red dog – the
dingo – and the smooth-haired Scotch sheep-dog.

Although of three different colors – blue-speckle, red-speckle and
plain red – this animal is essentially the same – a thick-set, prick-eared
dog; in shape, coat and size a replica of the dingo. His method of
working is also the same, no matter what his color may be; namely,
to follow horses or cattle and bite the hind heel, on which the weight
is resting, of any straggler, dropping flat immediately afterwards, so
that the consequent kick whistles harmlessly over him; to gallop to
the head of the mob and swing it in any desired direction by snapping
at the leaders' necks; to make any bullock stand to be yoked; to watch
his owner's property anywhere and at any time; and to be mate,
game-catcher, retriever, guard and companion to his master. Such is
the Australian cattle-dog, and it is interesting to follow the record of
his evolution.

The first colonists brought with them a dog known as the black
bob-tail; a few of his descendants are still to be found on farms
in the older-settled districts. This was the old English cur-dog, a
big, rough-coated – not grizzled – square-bodied animal, with a
wedge-shaped flat head and drop ears. Most of them had a white ring
round the neck, some had white feet. These dogs were faithful and
sensible, and in the early days, when the farms were small and the
cattle quiet, they served their turn. But when the country was opened
up and the stock had to travel long distances, they proved unsuitable,
their heavy frames and long coats being against them, particularly
in hot weather, as was also the barking to which they were addicted
and which made the cattle wild and difficult to handle. To overcome

these defects, a drover named Timmins conceived the notion of crossing this black bob-tail with the dingo, and thus originated the red bob-tail. But though this dog was a silent and hardy worker, he was a very severe biter and apt to kill calves when working out of the drover's sight. The next breed to be tried was a cross of the rough-haired collie and the dingo, but this type had the bad habit of running to the head and barking instead of working from the back and sides. A number of other crosses were tried, such as between the bullterrier and the rough-haired collie, between the kangaroo-dog and the bulldog, and between the rough-haired collie and various breeds of rough-haired terriers; but these were all very severe biters and proved uncontrollable.

On the big cattle-runs, which were coming into existence, a silent, tractable, clean-biting dog was indispensable. Consequently, in 1840, a squatter named Hall of Muswellbrook, New South Wales, did a good deed for Australia when he imported a pair of blue-gray "merles" – marbled or mottle smooth-haired Scotch dogs – which were said to be good at working cattle. This breed had its origin in a blend of the old English mastiff – which protected the herds from wolves – the greyhound, and the Scotch collie.

But though merles were a great improvement on the previous breeds, they still had the old collie habit of barking and running to the head. Hall, therefore, crossed them with the dingo. The result proved a great success. The progeny had the dingo habit of creeping up behind and biting. They were at first known as "Hall's heelers," then as "blue heelers"; and the puppies came red-mottled or blue-mottled according to the strain – dingo or merle – which predominated. Most of them were prick-eared and of the dingo type, and had the dingo brown eye, though, occasionally, there cropped up the "china" or white eye so prevalent in the merle.

About 20 years after Hall's importation some of these dogs were brought to Sydney by Alexander Davis, and they attracted much attention at Homebush sale-yards, where they were taken up by various drovers and butchers. As they were the result of a direct cross, a distinctive type was not fixed. The next move was, therefore, to infuse the blood of the Dalmation, or spotted carriage-dog, and subsequently that of the kelpie. The result, in the hands of skillful breeders, was a compact, active dog identical with the pure dingo in type and build but with peculiar markings found in no other dog in the world. The face and ears are black or red, with a tan spot over each brown eye and a white stripe down the middle of the forehead; the body is a dark blue, evenly speckled with a lighter blue – whence the name "blue-speckle" – there may be a black saddle or spot on the tail-butt, no more black being allowed, the tail and under part of the body are a lighter blue, the legs, from feet to elbow, and hock, red-speckled. Blue-black or from light to white colors are barred; also "wall" or white eyes.

Rigid adherence to these markings is necessary, since they are "utility" points. The black head shows kelpie strain, and hence keen working qualities; the red head, dingo strain, and hence great hardiness; the brown eyes show keen sight; the white stripe down the forehead and the black spot on the tail-butt show descent from "Tom Bentley's dog" – one of the most perfect workers ever known. The dark-blue color is indispensable to a dog doing so much biting – and therefore liable to get kicked – since dark blue is invisible, especially at night. Black, on the other hand, is very conspicuous in daylight, and white is so by either day or night. The red-speckled legs do not show the red dust in which the dog is so often working. The dingo type is insisted upon because it denotes the strength and speed which are the results of natural selection during untold years under Australian conditions.

THE AUSTRALIAN CATTLE DOG

His share in the pioneering of Australia and his origin 1935
Reprinted by Cheryl Edwards in *Australian Cattle Dogs:
Old Timers* 1997
Original provenance unknown and publication date unconfirmed.

If we Australians ever wake up out of our present mechanized sleep, and recover sufficient gratitude to do honour to the men (and their instruments) who settled this vast continent and made life possible here for us today, we will erect in a prominent place, two vast statues in everlasting bronze. The second statue will be that of an early wool-grower with a merino ram beside him and his faithful sheep dog at his feet. But the first one will be that of the pioneer, eight foot green-hide whip on shoulder, with his team of eight bullocks, his rough built old bullock dray and his fierce looking Cattle Dog beside him. The wool grower and his merino sheep made Australia's fortune; but the pioneer, with his bullock team and Cattle Dog had to go before him to break the way. Without him and his straining team to cut and tear the way through the pathless wilderness, there could have been no settlement; and without the wise, faithful Cattle Dog to watch his dray and bullocks and to shepherd the team to feed close to the safety of the camp, and gather them for the yoking in that fenceless, trackless wilderness of long ago, there could have been no settlement. Hostile blacks and fierce native dogs would soon have ended his team, his life, and his journey.

As soon as the pioneer settled on his land after his weary travel, his Cattle Dog became more indispensable than ever. He was needed at every moment to watch at night while the stock rested after their day's feeding; to warn his master of prowling blacks or bushrangers, or thieving tiger cats or possums. At dim dawn he had to muster the working bullocks for ploughing, or for carting posts and rails for the stockyards and later, the bark and slabs for his house. The small herd of cattle that supplied the beef, milk and steers for working bullocks had to be constantly mustered or they wandered and went wild; and it was the Cattle Dog's job to muster them. If the settler were a coastal man and therefore dealing solely with cattle, his dog had all the mustering and driving jobs to do as well; and working in the dense coastal scrubs, which were full of ticks, had to become immune to them or die in fever. When the settler made his annual trip with the bullock team to Sydney or his port town (perhaps five hundred miles away, with wool down and stores back) on his Cattle Dog fell the onerous work of minding it on the track; "heeling" the off-side bullocks when the dray or wagon, as often happened, bogged to the axle; watching them on the camps, and the dray as well, mustering them in the dawn for the yoking, and landing them safely back on the station without the loss of a single beast.

The first Cattle Dogs used in Australia were the old "Smithfields" or drovers dogs. They were big rough coated, square bodied dogs, with flat, wedge shaped heads, saddle flap ears and bob tails; and they generally had a white "collar" or frill round their necks – a mark of their collie breeding on one side. They were called "Smithfields" or more generally "Black Bob-Tails" and must not be confused with the Old English Sheepdog, though they probably had a strain of it in them. They were faithful, hardy, and sensible; but like all bob-tailed dogs, were heavy and slow on their feet and were great barkers and severe biters.

As the colony opened up and the herds increased, the need of a more active dog with less voice, became pressing. In about 1830 a Hawkesbury River drover named Timmins who used to bring cattle down from Bathurst over the Blue Mountains to the Homebush Saleyards in Sydney, conceived the idea of crossing his dogs with the red native dog or Dingo, to get the animal required, and thus originated the red bob tail, "Timmins Heelers", or "Timmins Red Bob-Tails" as they were sometimes called. Dogs of this cross were a great improvement on the Smithfield; they were very active and were good severe biters, and almost silent. But they had one bad fault – if they got out of the drover's sight they would chew a calf or beast nearly to pieces; the Dingo instinct coming uppermost when out of control. After a time, most of them died out and the rough haired Scotch Collie was tried next. They, except in rare cases, were a failure, as they tried to work the cattle as if they were sheep, rushing to the head and barking. This action made the cattle wild, and was particularly bad for fat cattle as they would "break" and rush in all directions with such a dog and so lose their condition. A cross of Rough Collie and Russian Poodle was tried next. A few of the survivors may still be seen today in the old country towns: a blue, rusty, brown or black dog with a coat like that of an Otterhound. It was a very severe dog, biting anywhere from head to tail, and its long coat spoilt it for our summers. It soon died out. Crosses of the Bull Terrier and Collie were tried but they proved too slow, severe and heavy. (None of the terrier cross are any good for Cattle Dogs, because they are "chewing" biters and cripple every beast they touch, unlike the true Cattle Dog which drives his teeth cleanly in and out again and never cripples). In places where the cattle were very fierce and wild, crosses of Bull Dog and Kangaroo Dog were tried; but they were only good for catching and throwing outlaws, and were quite useless for quiet cattle, so they died out too. A good job!

Then in 1840 a squatter named Thomas Hall who owned the "Dartbrook" property at Muswellbrook, Hunter Valley, N.S.W., imported a pair of blue Smooth Haired Collies from Scotland. They were called "Merles" (or mottles) because of the dark and light blue being mixed in patches on them. (These dogs were originally a cross of the Rough Haired Scotch Collie and the Blue Italian Greyhound; this is where the blue colour came from). Most of them had "wall" or "china" (white) eyes, and were known in the early days as German Coolies. They were a great improvement on the Cattle Dogs tried so far, being very active, passable biters, and not nearly so noisy as the Rough Collie. The Greyhound in them kept them nearly silent, but they still barked and "headed" when excited. It is not definitely known whether Hall himself first crossed them with the Dingo, but he got the credit for it, and the dogs became known as "Hall's Heelers". They were fine dogs, very brainy, hardy, tireless and active. The Dingo instinct gave them the idea of creeping up silently behind a horse or bullock and biting the foot on which the weight was resting at the moment, so that they could not be kicked. They came red mottle, blue mottle or plain red as the Dingo or merle predominated in them, and they became well known about the Hunter Valley. (Hall continued his experimental matings until his death on the 28th May 1870).

Then on a fortunate day for the breed, Alec Davis, one of the well known carcass butchering family, brought a pair of these dogs to Sydney. They attracted much admiration at the time (between 1870 and 1880), and several local men got pups for breeding purposes. Amongst these buyers were two men. Jack and Harry Bagust, who were really the founders of the present day, improved Australian blue speckled Cattle Dog, the only true breed of Cattle Dog in the world. Many other breeders claimed the honour, and no doubt many of them, such as the Lees, the Peaks and the Judds, did much, by careful mating and selection, to help the breed along, but the Bagust brothers did put the two other breeds through them – the Dalmatian and the Kelpie – which gave them the two qualities required and made them into a distinct breed, (they were, of course, only a cross before).

The two qualities they lacked were, first, they were not fond of horses (as might be expected from their origin) and therefore could not be depended on to watch the drover's horse when left saddled anywhere, and secondly, they had, through long use, become accustomed to working only the"tail" of a mob (in broken country it was the drover's custom to ride ahead of the mob, and let the dog bring it along behind him).

Now the Dalmatian, being essentially a horse dog, and bred for the purpose of minding the valuable carriage horses in their stable night or day, and not, as so many think now, merely as an ornamental appendage to trot behind the carriage, was the only dog suitable for crossing with "Hall's Heelers", for this purpose. Also his blue spots would blend with the blue mottle of the merle. So the Bagusts looked round for a Dalmatian, then a good deal in use in Sydney in those days of carriages and pairs. They found him, so I understood from them, in the stables of one of the Stephens, a very old Sydney legal family, who lived near Canterbury in one of those spacious old homes at the south end of Ashfield. Speaking from memory, he was an imported dog. His drop ears and whip tail were of course, disadvantages which occasionally bob up in a badly bred strain, but he gave to the breed the love of horses which it still has today.

Now, while this cross gave the love of horses, so essential to a drover's dog, and the attractive speckle colour, and also caused the disappearance of the annoying "wall" or "china" (white) eyes so prevalent in the merle, it had its disadvantages. The dogs, after constant selection of the best (the Bagust's motto being "we breed a lot and we drown a lot") still lacked the idea of working the sides and head, so the Bagust's put a Kelpie cross through them from some of the numerous fine black and tan Kelpies then working about Homebush Yards (this would be about 1890). They did not use the blue Kelpie for fear of breeding the speckles out.

This Kelpie cross had one disadvantage. It changed the colour of the head from Dingo red to black, made them a little fine in the muzzle, and made the body colour too dark. The dogs mostly came either all black, or blue with black patches all over them, which spoilt their appearance. Some had a tendency to have tan legs, instead of the red speckle lower legs which the Bagust's wanted so as not to show dust like the blue legs and feet did. Finally they got the perfect coloured and shaped blue Australian Cattle Dog as it is today – black or red ears and sides of face, the rest of the head blue, and a tan spot over each eye, dark blue (the invisible colour by night or day, so that they run little risk of being horned or kicked), body with black saddle, or spot at tail butt, lighter blue speckle under body and tail, red speckled feet and lower legs.

In a few years (about 1897) the imported breed had become very popular, and spread all over the Commonwealth and to New Zealand. Jack and Harry Bagust enjoyed the pleasure of breeding many prize winners and champion workers, that is, after I had successfully established the standard for them.

It was 1893 when I got rid of my cross bred Cattle Dogs and took up breeding the blues. I started showing in 1897, and it was then that I realized that there was no standard to bind the judges, so I drew up what I considered the perfect standard for Cattle Dogs, Kelpies and Barbs in 1897, had it endorsed by all the leading breeders and published in the Agricultural Gazette for N.S.W. in 1903. I then had the standards adopted by the original Kennel Club of N.S.W. and later by The Agricultural Society of N.S.W. The Agricultural Department of N.S.W. assisted by printing and distributing the standard in pamphlet form so that breeders and buyers everywhere came to know exactly what type to look for. Many attempts have been made to improve on these standards, but so far without success. The reason for this is that the shape and the coat of the dogs are taken from that of the wild dog of Australia, which, through evolution, is perfectly developed to suit our climate and conditions, and the colours and markings are a guarantee of purity.

FOUNDATION DOGS OF AUSTRALIA
Sydney Mail Wednesday 13 April 1938 p. 26 and 30
Illustration: Gd Ch *Some Rock*

It is fitting in these days when we are celebrating the laying of the corner stones on which Australia's fortunes have been built that we should turn a thought toward the four-footed friends whose part in the establishment of our great pastoral industry has been far more remarkable than most people realise. Among the world's great breeds of dogs, Australia possesses four that are now almost as distinctively our own as are our kangaroos and koalas. First there is the dingo, whose ancestry goes back some millions of years; then comes the kangaroo dog, evolved here in the earliest days of settlement when hunting for food was often imperative; the cattle-dogs, and the sheep-dogs, whose evolution was essential to the carrying on of the pastoral industry under the peculiar conditions obtaining in the vast hinterlands "beyond the Blue Mountains." Only one of these dominant breeds is native to the country, but the others, built on various lines of imported blood, are acknowledged the world over to-day as purely Australian.

In this article I do not propose to deal, except incidentally, with the dingo, but rather with those that have been moulded within the country since the coming of Phillip. Without our kangaroo-dogs, which kept the hungry settler in wild meat when beef and mutton were unobtainable; the cattle-dogs, without whose help in guarding his master's dray and stores from thieves, and mustering and helping to drive the working bullocks and grazing cattle, the teamster and grazier would have lost very often not only their stock, but their lives; and the most important of all, the sheep-dog, without whose constant care and shepherding Australia would have had no mutton sheep then, and probably no merino sheep to-day; without these dogs we should have been a hundred years behind. Let us, then, in bare justice to our four-footed friends, pause a moment to do them the honour they richly deserve, and trace up, like our merino sheep, their evolution from what they were in our first years to what they are to-day.

The First Dogs

In the first few years of settlement many English dogs, sporting and working, were brought out, mostly by officers and immigrants, either as pets or because they might be useful in the new land. The officers appear to have favoured coursing dogs (greyhounds) for the native game, and bull terriers for fighting purposes. At times a pair of hounds arrived; on a few occasions, bloodhounds for scent hunting. The immigrants, on the other hand, went in for utility dogs for working sheep and cattle – the old English sheep-dog (really a Russian collie), the black bob-tail (a cross with it and the smooth haired drover's dog), usually known as the Smithfield; and the long-haired Scottish collie. Sydney swarmed with ticks at that time, so many of the dogs must have perished before they got a chance to show what they could do; yet many survived and got out into the country. After a time one breed emerged from the ruck and laid the foundation of other breeds – the kangaroo-dog (the foundation of our present breed of sheep-dogs).

The kelpie and barb were evolved much later in our story, as also was the blue cattle-dog. The kangaroo-dog, especially before the

Blue Mountain barrier was conquered and the wide plains allowed unrestricted breeding, was perhaps the most important dog to the early settler, because butcher's meat, powder, shot, and guns were very dear, flour, fruit, and vegetables often very scarce; and the mainstay of the early settlers was billy tea and kangaroo meat. At first the kangaroo-dog was only a large, fierce greyhound, but the settlers soon found that he was no match for the "old man" kangaroo or his cousin the dingo, so a few Scottish deerhounds were imported to give him more weight and power, and occasionally a cross of collie was introduced to improve the scent. The resultant dog was a big, wire-haired, powerful animal, fit to tackle anything in the bush. In the course of time our hot climate made him smooth-haired, the splendid animal as we know him to-day.

The Cattle- and Sheep-Dogs

The cattle-dog in those early days of small farms and quiet stock, before the stampede through the road over the Blue Mountains, was the old Smithfield. Faithful, slow, and sensible, and able at a pinch to work quiet cattle, sheep, or horses, he filled his niche in his time, and is still doing it on a few farms in the older settled districts. With his long legs, short back and tail, flat wedge-shaped head and drop ears, he looked like a bit of Old England transplanted into a new country. The first step in improving the cattle-dog was taken by a drover called Timmins, who used to bring fat cattle from Bathurst to Homebush over the Mountains by Bell's Line. This would probably be about 1830. He crossed the Smithfield with the local native dog and got a red bob-tail, a much faster and more active dog than the Smithfield, and one that worked almost silently, a most important feature when handling fat cattle. The only fault of these dogs was that, out of the drover's sight over a hill or in scrub, they were terribly severe biters and would almost eat a calf or yearling. To get over this, Timmins crossed them with the Scottish collie. Some of these, in Timmins' hands, were wonderful workers: old hands talk about them to this day; but they would not "breed on" (transmit their good qualities to their progeny), and so the breed died out, though even to-day a "throw-back" may be seen. After Timmins' day, the rough-haired collie was tried, but was not a success; too much barking at the head and frightening the cattle. Then the Russian sheep-dog (the 'Owtchar' [sic]– generally misnamed the Russian poodle in the old days here) was crossed with the rough collie. It also was a failure from much the same cause, besides being too heavy-coated and very severe. Then crosses of the bull-terrier and rough collie were tried, but they were too slow, severe, and heavy. In places where the cattle were fierce and wild, a cross of bulldog and kangaroo-dog with collie was tried, but these also were a failure, fit only for catching and throwing wild cattle, and soon died out.

The Merles

At last, in 1840, a squatter named Hall, at Muswellbrook, in the Hunter Valley, imported a pair of blue, smooth- haired collies from Scotland 'Merles', a new breed, then becoming fashionable. These dogs were originally a cross of the true (rough) Scottish collie and the blue Italian greyhound, from which they derived their blue colour. Many of them had white eyes, and were often miscalled 'German collies'. They were a great improvement on the dogs tried so far for cattle, being very active, passable biters, and not as noisy as the rough collie; but they still barked and 'headed' a lot when excited. Hall, to eliminate this trait, crossed them with the dingo (the old hands always called them 'native dogs'), and these dogs became famous as 'Hall's Heelers'. They were very hardy, tireless, sensible, and controllable. The dingo cross made them almost silent workers and the collie instinct kept them under control. They were red mottled, blue mottled, or plain red, as the 'Merle' (Scots for mottled) or dingo predominated in them, and became well known all through the Hunter Valley. About 1875 (he could never fix the exact date) 'Pialla' Davis, one of a well-known butchering family in Sydney, brought a pair down to the family slaughter-yard at Canterbury. They were much admired for their work and looks. Several local men got pups to breed with. Amongst these men were Jack and Harry Bagust, who, by their skilful crossing and the blending of these pups with other selected breeds, were really responsible for the present-day blue or red speckled cattle-dogs.

To impart a love of horses and the well-defined speckles into the breed they used a selected Dalmatian; to get the clever head, and side working they used the black and tan kelpie, and, in their own words, 'bred a lot and drowned a lot' till they got the present type definitely set to breed true. By 1897 the breed had become very popular all over Australia, and after I had drawn up the standard for them in that year (and the kelpie and barb also), the cattle-dogs became one of the greatest attractions of the R.A.S. and kindred shows, and have completely ousted all other breeds and crosses of cattle-dogs from public favour.

CATTLE DOG
Dogs of the World 1947 pp. 11-15

The cattle dog was, and is, one of the greatest aids to pioneering in Australia. Without him the lot of the early settler would have been hard indeed on a country as vast, and so unfenced; to attempt to handle his cattle, horses and working bullocks without a reliable dog would have been only a waste of time. And as well as helping him with his stock, the cattle dog was guard, mate, vermin-killer, game retriever, an all-round dog. Many a settler's life in the early days of Australia was saved from blacks, snakes, bushrangers, floods and fires, by the watchfulness of his faithful cattle dog. Australia owes this dog, and his cousin, the Kelpie, a debt of gratitude it can never repay, although one town in N.S.W. (Gundagai) has done its share towards it by putting up a statue to him.

The first real cattle dog used in Australia was the old Smithfield — a black bob-tailed dog with a white ring round his neck, and sometimes with white on chest. (This dog, essentially an all-round English drover's dog, must not be confused with the old English bob-tailed sheep dog, which carries a coat of dense grizzled hair and is colored usually blue, blue-grey, or sandy.) The Smithfield was rough-coated, with long straight hair, and a big square body, long legs, a flat wedge-shaped head, honest brown eyes, and saddle-flap ears. From his build he was not suited to fast work, though very handy on short trips, or working on farms. He was very faithful and sensible and may be seen on odd farms in the old settled districts to this day. His faults were that he was rather a severe biter and barked a lot. To get over the barking a well-known drover called Timmins crossed him with the dingo and produced the Red Bobtail, generally known as "Timmins' biters". These dogs were silent biters, but very severe, though some of Timmins' dogs were wonderful workers; and did not come into general use. The rough-haired Scotch collie was tried next, but he proved a failure. He wanted to run cattle as he did sheep — by barking at them and running at their heads. This, of course, made quiet cattle wild, and wild cattle dangerous; making them rush and run all their condition off; so he had to be put back to sheep again. Various other crosses were tried, the bull-terrier and collie, for example, but none of then proved of any value.

Then, on a lucky day for Australia, a squatter named Hall, breeding cattle at Muswellbrook, on the Hunter-River, N.S.W., imported a pair of blue, smooth-haired collies ("Merles" or "Mottles") from Scotland in 1840. These dogs were originally a cross of the rough Scotch collie and the blue Italian greyhound; were blue mottled with black, and most had "china" or "wall" (white) eyes. They were, and sometimes still are, erroneously called "German coolies". Goodness only know why, the only German dog of their color is the Great Dane. They were a great improvement on any dogs previously used, but still barked and headed a bit. To get over this they were crossed with our dingo and the cross proved a great success. They were locally known as "Hall's heelers". Some came all red, like the dingo, others blue mottled, others, again, red mottled. A pair of blue mottles were brought to Sydney by Alec ("Pialla") Davis, of the well-known butchering family at Newtown, between 1870 and 1880 (old Alec could never remember the exact date for me) and sent to their slaughter yard at Canterbury. They were soon taken up by local breeders and drovers and two breeders in particular, Jack and Harry Bagust, of Canterbury; by putting the Dalmatians into them to get the love of horses so necessary for a drovers's dog (and incidently the spots changed their mottles to speckles) and also crossing the best of these with the black and tan Kelpie for head-work, may be said to have really founded the present breed of Australian blue speckled cattle dog — the best and only pure breed in the world to-day.

I got rid of my cross-bred cattle dogs in '93, and took up the blues, drew up the standard for them, and Kelpies also, in '97; had both endorsed by all breeders, and in 1903 had it published in the Agricultural Gazette of N.S.W. (Agricultural Department) and adopted by the original Kennel Club of N.S.W. (of which I was hon. sec.) and our R.A.S. Since then the breed has gone all over Australia, to New Zealand, South Africa, and (lately) to the United States; articles of mine on them have been published recently in the American Kennel Gazette – the leading dog magazine of the world. The editor, Mr Casanova, wrote me lately that a pair of them have been benched recently on the Pacific Coast, at a big show, for the first time in American dog history.

THE CATTLE DOG
Walkabout Magazine December 1949

Now that the history of the Australian Blue-Speckle Cattle-Dog (to give the breed its proper title) is fading into the dim past, it seems timely that the facts regarding it should be set down for the benefit of present and future Australians: particularly as one Australian State (Queensland) is beginning to claim the breed as its own, under the name of "Queensland Blues." Of the original founders and helpers of the breed (the only pure breed of cattle-dogs in the world) there are only three of us left: Alec. Davis, of Homebush, N.S.W., retired carcase butcher and my old partner in the blue dogs; Owen Nolan, retired property-owner of Clovelly, Sydney; and myself. Alec, has gone out of dogs altogether now; only Nolan and I are still breeding from the original stock and keeping the good old strain up.

Australia is mostly so fenced in and civilized now that it is difficult to make the present generation understand the true value of a good cattle-dog, but in the pioneering days it was truthfully said that "a good cattle-dog is a man's living." Our country then being mostly a wilderness, the settler had to depend on his dog to look after his fat stock, his milkers, his horses, his pigs and – most important of all – his team of working bullocks, on which he depended, when chained to his dray or wagon, to take his cedar or other timber to the mill or waterway, and his wool and produce to the nearest port, and to bring back his tea, sugar, flour and other necessities to keep him going till he was ready for another trip. To look after his stock in the wild bush of that time would have taken a small army of men, but with a good cattle-dog it was an easy job because, while the stock were not afraid of men, they feared the cattle-dog, with his speed and ready teeth, and so were easily kept under control.

The first cattle-dog used in Australia was the old black bob-tailed Smithfield butcher's dog; then came its cross with our dingo, the red bob-tail, generally known as Timmin's Bob-tails; then the rough-coated Scotch Collie, and then the crosses of the greyhound, bull-terrier, and so on, all of which had such serious faults that they were given up in despair as doing more harm than good and the settlers looked around in desperation for a breed of dogs that would really do the work under the altering conditions. The old black bob-tail was fairly useful at first, but as the country opened up from the original strip of coastline around Sydney, he could not stand the travelling; then followed the cross with our dingo to make the red bob-tail. He could travel all right, but was too noisy and severe a biter.

Then in a fortunate year for Australia (1840) a squatter named Hall, of Muswellbrook on the Hunter River N.S.W. (the family is still there), imported a pair of blue "merle" (smooth-haired mottled) Scotch collies. These dogs were poor biters, but light-coated and active in all weathers, and well under control. They were also too much inclined to go to the heads of the cattle and try to work them like sheep. This had a tendency to make the cattle wild and run the fat off themselves, so Hall crossed them with the dingo, and as the progeny grew up they proved a great success, having the old dingo instinct of creeping silently behind the cattle and biting their heels without getting kicked.

They were very brainy, hardy and tireless in all weathers. In colour they came red-mottled or blue mottled, according as the dingo or blue merle predominated in them. Most of them had black streaks or dots through them. A few came all red, just like the pure dingo, but, whatever their colour, they were all first-class workers, and became known all over the Hunter Valley as Hall's Heelers. Alec. Davis's father (known all over the Hunter and New England as "Pialla" Davis) was the northern fat-stock buyer for the family (the Davises were an old-established Sydney carcase and retail butchering company in those days with paddocks and a big slaughter yard at Canterbury). He saw these dogs of Hall's everywhere and brought a pair to Sydney for the firm's use, mainly to bring cattle over from the Homebush saleyards to the slaughter-house. This happened in the seventies (old Alec, could never remember the exact date for me). In common with most of the people of that time, young Alec, and I were inveterate dog-fanciers, and as we grew up, in common with most of the dog-breeders around there, greatly admired these dogs. They were, however, lacking in two essential qualities of the perfect cattle dog. The first fault was that, owing to their origin – dingo and collie – they had no love for horses or watching their owner's property, and hence could not be trusted to watch their master's saddle horse and gear if he left it (stealing horses, saddles and bridles was a very lucrative profession in those days). Secondly, they had from long use become accustomed to working the "tail" and "wings" of a mob, and could not be sent ahead to block or wheel it when wanted. Two notable cattle-dog fanciers that we knew well – Jack and Harry Bagust – lived close to the slaughter-yard. Neither of them worked cattle (Jack being a stonemason and his brother in the building line), but they loved good workers and determined to make a perfect and pure breed out of the foundation stock, which, of course, were only a first cross. To this end, with the help of us other fanciers, they got two breeds to use, which would, they believed, correct the faults. The first breed was of course the Dalmatian, to give them the love of horses and guard sense bred in them for centuries. The second breed was our Australian black-and-tan kelpie (Maiden's dogs, if I remember aright) to give them the headwork.

Using these two breeds brought in the necessary blood (third) to make a permanent breed out of what were crossbreeds more or less fixed by selection, but like most new bloods it had other advantages and disadvantages. The Dalmatian blood changed the dull-mottles to the present attractive blue speckles, and did away with the "wall" (white) eyes which now and then cropped up in the breed. It smoothed the coat, but had a tendency, in some strains, to bring out the drop ears of the Dalmatian and the "whip" (thin) pointed tail. The kelpie cross, while giving them the needed head-work, also gave some of them all-black coats instead of speckles and a tendency to light paws and forefaces ("snipy heads") instead of the strong dingo biting jaws. These defects were gradually corrected, the Bagusts doing most of the work, though all over Sydney area other fanciers were working in with them, till at last the perfect dog as we have it to-day was evolved. It took some years of breeding selection to do it, and the saying then was, "We breed a lot and we drown a lot." In a few years' time the improved and "set" breed had become very popular and pups were sent to buyers all over the Commonwealth and New Zealand.

In 1897 I drew up what I considered the perfect standard for cattle-dogs, at the request of the other breeders (incidentally, the standards for kelpies and barbs as well), had it endorsed by all the leading breeders and published in the Agricultural Gazette (Agricultural Department of N.S.W.) and in pamphlet form in 1903. I then got the three standards adopted by the original Kennel Club of N.S.W. (then a very powerful body of amateurs and affiliated with the Kennel Club of England) of which I was at that time honorary secretary, and later by the Royal Agricultural Society of N.S.W. Since then the breed has never looked back, and at the R.A.S. of N.S.W. annual show, one of the largest in the world, cattle-dogs and kelpies generally head the classes in numbers of exhibits.

OUR PROSPERITY RESTS ON DOGS
The Blue Speckle Cattle Dog
The Sunday Herald p. 9, 2 April 1950

I can speak with full authority on this breed, being one of the original founders of it, in 1880-1890. There are only two of us left now, my old partner Alec Davis, retired carcase butcher, and myself. Alec's father, "Pialla" Davis, fat stock buyer for the family, brought to the family's slaughter yard at Canterbury a pair of the breed made by Hall, a squatter at Muswellbrook, from a cross of the Dingo and smooth blue Scottish Collie in 1840. They were known as "Hall's Heelers". These dogs were tireless workers and heelers, but poor colours: being either all red like the Dingo, or covered with rusty grey blotches, shot with black.

We local fanciers, particularly Jack and Harry Bagust, also of Canterbury, determined to make them a pure, attractive breed; and to that end used the Dalmatian to get the speckles, and the black and tan Kelpie to get the working brains and tractability, till we got the breed as it is to-day.

CATTLE DOGS
The Australian Encyclopaedia 1958, 1963 and 1965

The Australian blue-speckle cattle-dog was established as a pure breed in 1890, after a long period of experiment by cattle-owners and dog-breeders to produce a dog suitable to Australian conditions. In the early days of settlement, once pastoralists began to move out from the poor land near Sydney to more fertile areas, there was an increase in cattle-raising. Beyond the small patches of cultivated land around settlers' homesteads the country was an unfenced wilderness, and it was into such areas that cattle strayed as soon as the edible grasses and shrubs near the homesteads had been eaten. To bring them home through the bush, dogs were necessary, and the settlers therefore began a search for a type suitable for the work.

The dogs first tried were brought from England, and were of the old Smithfield breed; to settlers they were known as the black bob-tail. The bob-tail was a square-built, long-legged, black dog, sometimes with white on the chest; it was wide between the ears, and had a sharp nose, drop ears, and a bob-tail. For slow work on a farm, with quiet stock, it was satisfactory, and it was faithful, hardy, and sensible. But its long legs and short body made it unable to run any distance, and its thick coat was not suited to hot summer conditions. As more land was settled, the need was increasingly felt for a more active type of dog, especially since cattle-raising began to be carried on more extensively. With the opening up of the grazing areas west of the Blue Mountains, the need for a lightly-built, thin-coated dog became acute.

"Timmins's heelers", or, as they were sometimes called, "Timmins's red bob-tails", were the result of an attempt by a Hawkesbury River drover to produce the type of dog required. Timmins crossed the Smithfield with the "native dog", as the dingo was called. The dogs from the cross were an improvement on the black bob-tail, but although they were very active and could withstand the hot weather they were severe biters and were hard to control. Timmins's own dogs had a reputation for handiness and brains, but other cattle-men were less successful in handling theirs. The dingo is by nature independent, and resents control. The Scotch collie was tried after the red bob-tail had been discarded, but proved useless. Its way of working sheep by running round them and barking was of no use with cattle, which became wild and difficult to handle, and soon lost condition. The graziers then tried a cross of the Russian sheep-dog (the owtcharka), known locally as the Russian poodle, and the collie. The progeny were wire-haired ("grizzle-coated"), somewhat resembling the otterhound; some were long-tailed, some bob-tailed. These dogs, however, were brainless and bit severely, and so they soon died out as a cross. Nevertheless, some of their descendants may still be seen on farms in old settled districts. The cross next tried was between the bull-terrier and the collie, the breeders hoping to get silence and biting-power from the first, and working qualities from the second. But this cross, like those preceding it, was unsuccessful;

the dogs were faithful and sensible, but too slow and heavy. Also, they proved to be "chewing" biters; that is, instead of biting cleanly and letting go at once, they would hang on to the bullock's or horse's heel and chew it, laming the animal. Sometimes they bit the flesh out. This cross, too, was discarded.

A better dog was produced in 1840. A squatter named Hall, who had a cattle station at Muswellbrook, N.S.W., heard of a good strain of working "merles", blue-mottled, smooth Scotch collies with "wall" (white) eyes, and he imported a pair from Scotland. These were an improvement on the ordinary collie, although their barking and their "heading" style of working were not altogether suitable for cattle. To eliminate these defects, Hall crossed the breed with the dingo, and the dogs resulting were very successful. They were blue-mottled or all red according as the merle or the dingo predominated; but both types were silent, tireless workers, with the instinct to creep up silently behind and bite low. They were known locally as "Hall's heelers", and became very popular all over the Hunter Valley.

In the 1870s Alexander ("Sandy") Davis, a well-known carcass-butcher, took a pair of the dogs to Sydney, where they were much admired by dog-fanciers. However, they had two faults: being a cross of the dingo and the collie they had no love of horses, or for protecting their master's gear; and their custom of working only the back and sides of a mob meant that they would not go forward to block or wheel it when required. Two notable dog-fanciers of Sydney, Jack and Harry Bagust, decided, therefore, to make a pure breed of the dogs (until then only an inbred cross) and to correct their defects. Aided by other fanciers, of whom Robert Kaleski was one, they put a Dalmatian cross through them to give them the love of guarding horses and gear, and to produce blue speckles instead of mottles; and then put a cross of black-and-tan kelpie into them to give them intelligence and the instinct for heading-in.

Inevitably, these crosses had their disadvantages. The Dalmatian strain introduced drop ears and the thin "whip" tail, and the kelpie introduced too much black in the colour and inclined some of the dogs to be afraid of being kicked. But by 1890, careful breeding having eliminated dogs not possessing all the required qualities, the breed as it is today was set. In 1897 Kaleski, at the breeders' request, drew up the standard for the "blues", and had it adopted by the original Kennel Club of New South Wales and the New South Wales Agricultural Department. With a few slight variations, this standard still obtains.

The Australian blue-speckle cattle-dog, besides being the only pure breed of cattle-dog in the world, is marked and coloured like no other. The face and ears are black or red, with a tan spot over each brown eye and a white stripe down the middle of the forehead. The body is a dark blue, evenly speckled with a lighter blue, and with perhaps a black saddle or spot on the tail-butt (no more black being allowed). The tail and under part of the body are a lighter blue, the legs from feet to elbow and hock red-speckled. Blue-black or light colours are barred; also "wall" eyes. Rigid adherence to these markings is necessary, since they are all utility points. The black head shows the kelpie strain, and hence keen working qualities. The red head reveals the dingo strain, and hence it has great hardiness. The white stripe down the forehead and the black spot on the tailbutt show descent from "Tom Bentley's dog" – one of the most perfect workers ever known. Dogs are about 20 inches high at the shoulder; bitches about 18 inches. The dingo type is insisted upon because it denotes the strength and speed that are the results of natural selection during untold years under Australian conditions.

[The Cattle Dog entry in the most recent edition of *The Australian Encyclopaedia*, 6th ed 1996, is an unsigned abridgment of Kaleski's original article.]

APPENDIX 2

Breed Standards

CATTLE DOGS
Robert Kaleski

The standard we breed to (approved of by the Kennel Club of New South Wales) is as follows:

	Maximum Points
Head: Broad between the ears, tapering to point at muzzle, full under eye, strong and muscular in the jaws.	15
Ears: Short and pricked, running to a point at tip, thick and set wide apart on the skull, with plenty of muscle at the butts. Should be as decidedly pricked as a cat's.	10
Eyes: Brown, quick, and sly-looking.	7
Shoulder: Strong, with good slope for free action.	7
Chest: Deep, but not out of proportion to body.	7
Legs: Clean, and fair amount of bone; great muscular development.	7
Feet: Small and cat-shaped.	7
Back: Straight, with ribs well sprung, ribbed up, and good loins; should arch slightly at loins.	7
Hindquarters: Strong and muscular, with back thighs well let down for speed; *no dew daws on feet*; tail fair length, dingo or "bottle" shaped.	12
Height: Dogs, about 20 inches; bitches, a little smaller.	7
Coat: Short, smooth, and very dense.	7

Colour: Head, black or red; body, dark blue on back,   7
sometimes with black saddle, and black spot on tail butt,
lighter blue, sometimes mottled with white hairs on under part
of body; legs bluish, with red spots mottled over them. Tail,
light blue, sometimes with light tip.

General appearance: That of a small thick-set dingo.

Faults: Over or under size, legginess, half prick or lopping
ears, overshot or under-shot jaws; anything likely to diminish
speed and endurance.

100

The pups are *white* when first born, but turn blue after a few weeks,
and are surprisingly uniform in colour and markings. Their ears do
not prick till they are a few months old. To get the best results, they
should be reared as much as possible on cooked meat – bullock's
heart for choice; and kept away from poultry, of which they are
ardent collectors. They usually require little or no training, the work
seeming to be instinctive with them.

The Welsh Merle or Heeler Is a blue-gray dog about the size and build
of a smooth-haired collie, generally with wall eyes. They make fair
workers sometimes, but are usually fearfully noisy and headstrong,
and have nothing like the endurance of the merlin.

The Red Bob-tail Is a square-bodied, long-legged dog, with a wedge-
shaped head, and saddle flap ears (sometimes pricked), and a bob-
tail. They are faithful and good yard dogs, and all right for short trips,
but will not stand much travelling, and are generally noisy.

The Black Bob-tail Is a big square-bodied thick-set dog, very like the
old Yorkshire sheep dog in general appearance, but smooth-haired,
with a similar head to the red bob-tail. Black in colour, with a large
white ring round the neck. Are rather scarce now. Very fair for short
trips and yards, but their weight kills them for road work.

Mongrels and Crosses I have seen a few good of these, and the
majority are useless. Their only idea, as a rule, is to run to a horse's or

beast's head and bark and snap at his nose till he either kills them or clears out to pastures new. The best cure for this is a .44 Winchester bullet put in behind the foreleg. Their best work is generally seen on a good meaty bone or a dead sheep. Anything of the dingo cross is very hardy, but, unless crossed on to a good working strain, they are very hard biters, and uncontrollable.

Advantages of the Merlins or Blue Heelers

Are very hardy, faithful, and good workers, no trouble to break, and always eager for work in any weather or any distance. I have never been able to knock one up. Very clean, quick biters, nearly silent, and can readily be changed from one class of cattle to another. Will stand more punishment than any dog I know, and do not hunt like the collie cross; splendid yard dogs and companions, great fighters, and very intelligent and biddable. I may here state to save inquiries, that I do not sell pups, preferring to save the cream of each litter only, rear them myself, and give them to reliable drovers, with the provision that I am to have their services at the stud any time I want it. By this means I am enabled to breed from none but the best workers. My fellow-breeders and myself never part with a bitch pup under any circumstances whatever, only occasionally exchanging one amongst ourselves.

Finding the strain is beginning to run out a little in shape and head, we are now crossing with a pet dingo of mine to get these points back again, and though we will get a little too much red in at first, I think the increased vigour and shape will more than repay us. I have had a good deal of experience with the dingo cross, and find it is all right if sufficient care be exercised in the selection.

[Omitted from the 1910 reissue of the standard:]

Wherever we have shown these dogs we have won against all classes, but prefer to keep them off the show bench. At the Royal Agricultural Show here for the last six years our blue dogs have won so consistently that they now have no competitors.

Having often had valuable pups stolen, I have been trying for years to find a way of marking them. [Kaleski proposed tattooing]. If successful, this will block dog-stealing; and if made compulsory in country districts, with a registered system of marks, will solve the burning question of identifying sheep-killing dogs.

In conclusion, I would like it clearly understood that because I have emphasised the fact that a cattle dog should be a quiet, clean biter, I do not mean he should rip a beast from hock to heel, or any such barbarity, nor that he should bite at anytime without occasion. At the same time, as every cattleman knows, a bite on the foot (at the right time) is worth a hundred lost beasts in the bush.

We will now take the standard point by point and explain it so that the judge and buyers can see the reason for each one.

Broad between ears: This ensures that the Dog has a large brain-box, hence has plenty of intelligence. If narrow there, the brain must be small and the intelligence feeble; hence a poor worker.

Tapering to a point at muzzle: This means that the least weight is at the business end, ensuring that the Dog can get his bite in quickly and drop out of danger, on the same principle as the boxer using light gloves instead of heavy ones – his hitting is much quicker.

Full under the eye: This ensures that the muscles which move the lower jaw are very strong, which is very necessary, as they correspond to the biceps of a boxer and give the dog power to do his work. A dog deficient there cannot continue biting long: his jaw-muscles become tired.

Strong and muscular in the jaws: If deficient there, when a dog is kicked by a shod horse he has his jaw broken because there is no cushion of muscle to protect the bone; hence, thus injured, he is useless.

Ears short and pricked: Short, so that they can be readily laid flat when biting or fighting; hence less likely to be damaged. Pricked, so as to catch sounds, such as whistles or words of command, best, especially from a distance. Running to a tip, V-or diamond-shaped, for two reasons: (1) the progeny are more likely to be prick-eared, the ear-muscles rising much higher in a diamond-ear than a "tulip" or spoon-shaped ear; (2) the spoon-ear is a sure indication of the Bull-terrier cross; set wide apart on the skull, so that the ear inclines outwards rather than forwards, for in the latter case they do not hear so well; hence cannot answer to the whistle or word of command as efficiently from a distance. They should be as pricked as a cat's for that reason.

Eyes: brown, because that is the Dingo colour, therefore the best. If blue or white, the animal is extremely likely to go blind or deaf, or both; in either case it will be useless for anything. Quick, because a dog has to judge his distance every time when coming in to bite, and the eye must be quick to do it. Sly-looking, because a hot-headed, rushing dog is useless as a worker, and the eye is the index to his character.

Shoulders: strong and well-sloped, so that the dog gallops easily and drops with ease when biting.

Chest, deep, but not out of proportion to body: Deep, because a shallow-chested dog has no heart-room and is easily thrown off his balance. If too deep, or "Bulldoggy" as we call it, he cannot travel at any speed.

Legs: Clean, because a hairy-legged dog becomes weighted with mud on soft roads and soon tires. Fair amount of bone to carry a fairly heavy body. If too light in bone he is top-heavy. Great muscular development, because without it he lacks the driving power to do the work; hence he is useless.

Feet: Small and shaped like those of a cat, because offering the smallest bearing surface for heat-blisters on hot roads, or thorns ("bindyi"); also when the foot is small the power is more concentrated, giving better results. The shape of the foot was a disputed point for some years, some breeders arguing that the dog with the splay or "hare" foot sank less in soft ground, having a greater bearing surface. However, experience has proved that the cat foot is the best all round.

Back: Straight, because a hollow-backed dog is always weak in the loins, and hence cannot drop or come back quickly enough when biting.

Ribs: Well-sprung or "casky" denote a strong, hardy constitution; "well-ribbed up" means that the last rib is close to the hip, thus enabling the dog to turn and twist his body easily.

Good loins, for the reason that they are the hinge of the body, and if weak the body is useless. Should arch slightly at loins, for the reason that the dog's hindquarters are then of the Greyhound shape, giving him more speed and activity than a straight-backed dog. If the reader looks at the prize-winners shown he will notice the slight arch in all of them. In my champion dog "*Nugget*" (as illustrated) the arch is more pronounced: he was nearly as fast as a Greyhound, though very powerfully built.

Hindquarters: Strong and muscular, because they are the "engine" or propelling power of the dog. Some dogs are perfect in front, but fail lamentably here; such dogs tire very quickly, and do not earn their salt for a drover. Back thighs well let down for speed, because the lower the hock-joint the longer the stride; hence more speed. No dew-claws on feet, because they catch in long grass or mud and tear the sinew, crippling the dog.

Tail: Fair length, for the reason that it regulates the dog's movements, being merely a continuation of the backbone covered with hair, and it serves to balance the dog in his gallop. If too short or too long, his speed and action suffer accordingly, just as with Greyhounds. Dingo, or bottle-shape, for two reasons: (1) this shape of tail indicates Dingo strain, as against a long, thin tail denoting Bull-terrier, or short tail the old Bob-tail; (2) a dog with a brush tail rests better than any other, as in a wild state the dog sleeps coiled in a circle, with the nose buried in the fur of the brush. I don't know why exactly, but believe that there is a physiological reason for it. Probably, by lessening the respiration in this way, the dog conserves energy on the same idea as hibernation – otherwise suspended animation.

Coat: Must be short, smooth and very dense, as the Cattle-dog has to work in all climates and all weathers. Like the Dingo, the coat consists of two – a loose outer one to turn the sun's rays, and a short inner one, close and fine as a seal's fur, to keep out cold and wet.

Height: About twenty inches has been found by experience to be the best height for working purposes. They work well in all heights, but do not stand the constant work like the dog of twenty inches; just as the medium-sized man is always the best for constant work, as against a big or little one. Bitches, of course, should always be a little finer and smaller than the dog.

Color: for two reasons: (1) That true blue color (neither light nor dark) is the most invisible color possible, particularly at night; hence a dog of this color is not easily seen by cattle or horses, and thus has the least chance of being kicked (2) The markings and colors as indicated stand for purity of breeding. In every strain of Blue Cattle-dog there is some peculiarity, and it shows in the color as well as in the shape, so that an expert can tell by looking at any Blue Dog how he has been bred. Some breeds have objectionable traits in their strains (Bull-terrier cross, etc.), and the color helps as a guide to pedigree. If the dog shows more black than specified he is probably a Barb cross and hence timid and unreliable. If he is a whitey-blue he shows Dalmatian cross, and is very likely to be kicked or gored, especially at night, as stock can watch him much better; also he is more liable to go blind and deaf.

General appearance: That of a small, thick-set Dingo, for reasons given before.

Faults are specified so that the standard shall be rigidly adhered to and faults as described not allowed to creep in.

AUSTRALIAN CATTLE DOG
Australian National Kennel Council, 1 January 1963

General Appearance: The general appearance is that of a sturdy, compact, symmetrically built working dog. With the ability and willingness to carry out any task however arduous, its combination of substance, power, balance and hard muscular condition to be such that must convey the impression of great agility, strength and endurance. Any tendency to grossness or weediness is a serious fault.

Characteristics: The utility purpose is assistance in the control of cattle, in both wide open and confined areas. Ever alert, extremely intelligent, watchful, courageous and trustworthy, with an implicit devotion to duty, making it an ideal dog. Its loyalty and protective instincts make a self-appointed guardian to the Stockman, his herd, his property. Whilst suspicious of strangers, must be amenable to handling in the Show ring.

Head: The head, in balance with other proportions of the dog, and in keeping with its general conformation, is broad of skull, and only slightly curved between the ears, flattening to a slight but definite stop. The cheeks are muscular, but not coarse nor prominent, the under jaw is strong, deep and well developed. The foreface is broad and well filled in under the eye, tapering gradually to a medium length, deep and powerful muzzle. The lips are tight and clean. The nose is black, irrespective of the colour of the dog.

Teeth: The teeth should be sound, strong and regularly spaced, gripping with a scissor-like action, the lower incisors close behind and just touching the upper. Not to be undershot nor overshot.

Eyes: The eyes should be oval shaped and of medium size, neither prominent nor sunken, and must express alertness and intelligence. A warning or suspicious glint is characteristic. Eye colour is dark brown.

Ears: The ears should be of moderate size, preferably small, than large, broad at the base, muscular, pricked and moderately pointed (not spoon nor bat eared). Set wide apart on the skull, inclined outwards, sensitive in their use, and firmly erect when alert. The inside of the ear should be fairly well furnished with hair.

Neck: The neck is of exceptional strength, muscular, and of medium length broadening to blend into the body and free from throatiness.

Forequarters: The shoulders are broad of blade, sloping, muscular and well angulated to the upper arm, and at the point of the withers should not be too closely set. The forelegs have strong round bone, extending to the feet without weakness of the pasterns. The forelegs should be perfectly straight viewed from the front, but the pasterns should show a slight angle with the forearm when regarded from the side.

Hindquarters: The hindquarters are broad, strong and muscular. The rump is rather long and sloping, thighs long, broad and well developed, with moderate turn of stifle. The hocks are strong, and well let down. When viewed from behind, the hind legs, from the hocks to the feet, are straight and placed neither close nor too wide apart.

Feet: The feet should be round and the toes short, strong, well arched and held close together. The pads hard and deep, and the nails must be short and strong.

Body: The length of the body from the point of the breast bone, in a straight line to the buttocks, is greater than the height at the withers, as 10 is to 9. The topline is level, back strong, with ribs well sprung and ribbed back. (Not barrelled ribbed.) The chest is deep and muscular, and moderately broad, loins are broad, deep and muscular, with deep flanks, strongly coupled between the fore and hindquarters.

Tail: The set on of tail is low, following the contours of the sloping rump, and at rest should hang in a slight curve of a length to reach approximately to the hock. During movement and/or excitement it may be raised, but under no circumstances should any part of the tail be carried past a vertical line drawn through the root.

Coat: The weather resisting outer coat is moderately short, straight and of medium texture, with short dense undercoat. Behind the quarters the coat is longer, forming a mild breeching. The tail is furnished sufficiently to form a good brush. The head, forelegs, hind legs from hock to ground, are coated with short hair.

Colour (Blue): The colour should be blue or blue-mottled with or without other markings. The permissible markings are black, blue or tan markings on the head, evenly distributed for preference. The forelegs tan midway up the legs and extending up the front to breast and throat, with tan on jaws; the hindquarters tan on inside of hind legs, and inside of thighs, showing down the front of the stifles and broadening out to the outside of the hind legs from hock to toes. Tan undercoat is permissible on the body providing it does not show through the blue outer coat. Black markings on the body are not desirable.

Red Speckle: The colour should be of a good even red speckle all over, including the undercoat (not white or cream) with or without darker red markings on the head. Even head markings are desirable. Red markings on the body are permissible but not desirable.

Size: The desirable height at the withers to be within the following dimensions:–

Dogs 45.7–50.8 cm (18-20 inches). Bitches 43.1–48.2 cm (17-19 inches). Dogs or bitches over or under these specified sizes are undesirable.

Movement: Soundness is of paramount importance. The action is true, free, supple and tireless, the movement of the shoulders and forelegs with the powerful thrust of the hindquarters in unison. Capability of quick and sudden movement is essential. Stiltiness, loaded or slack shoulders, straight shoulder placement, weakness at elbows, pasterns or feet, straight stifles, cow or bow hocks, must be regarded as serious faults.

CATTLE DOG

Cattle Dog and Kelpie Club of Queensland, current in 1923
The Kennel *Brisbane Courier* 1/12/1923 p. 12

LONG TAIL VARIETY

General Appearance: that of a small thick set dingo, but with better expression, head broad between the ears, slightly narrowing to the eyes.

Foreface: moderately long, with great jaw power, slight stop and well filled in under the eyes.

Teeth: level, sound, and powerful.

Ears: pricked, small, pointed at the tips, fairly thick in leather, placed wide apart at the outer corners of the skull.

Eyes: brown in colour, quick, and somewhat sly looking.

Shoulders: clean, muscular and sloping, elbows placed parallel with the body.

Chest: not too broad, but deep, with well-sprung ribs.

Forelegs: perfectly straight, well boned and muscular.

Forefeet: round, strong, deep in pads, with close knit, well arched toes and strong nails.

Back and loins: short, level, and strong.

Hindquarters and hind legs: powerful and muscular, with hocks fairly well let down, and placed parallel with the body.

Hind feet: close-knit and strong.

Tail: fair length, well clothed with strong hair, and carried gaily, but not curled.

Coat: fairly short, quite smooth and flat, with a hard outer coat, and immensely dense under jacket.

Colour: blue and black, blue, black and tan, blue-roan, or red-roan.

Height: Dogs, about 20 inches: bitches, slightly less.

Disqualifications: under or over shot mouth.

Objections: Dew claws on hind legs.

STUMPY TAIL VARIETY

The description for the long tail variety applies, except as to tail, and with the following additions.

Tail: must be naturally stumpy.

Disqualifications: under or overshot mouth, docked tails.

Objections: tail exceeding four inches in length; dew claws on hind legs.

CATTLE DOG (Stumpy Tail)
Breed Standard said to date from 1934
Collis, J. (1999). Australia's first working dog.

General Appearance: shall be that of a well proportioned dog of square appearance with sly expression.

Head: flat skull broad between the ears slightly narrowing to the eyes.

Foreface: of moderate length with strong jaws. Slight stop, well filled under the eyes.

Teeth: scissor bite, sound powerful, under or over shot a serious fault.

Ears: set high on skull, pricked, moderately small, pointed at tips. Fairly thick in leather.

Eyes: should be oval in shape of medium size, neither prominent or sunken they should show sly expression and be of dark brown colour.

Shoulders: clean, muscular, sloping with elbows parallel with the body.

Chest: not too broad but deep with well sprung ribs, barrel shaped ribs a serious fault.

Forelegs: straight, strong boned and muscular.

Back and loins: strong level, strong loins.

Hindquarters: powerful and muscular giving the dog somewhat square appearance.

Hocks: fairly well let down, and placed parallel to the body.

Stifles: well turned.

Tail: not to exceed 4 inches in length. Set on high.

Coat: medium length. Dense, harsh, with dense undercoat. Under no circumstances should the undercoat protrude through outer coat.

Colour: all blue on head or heavily marked with black. No tan at all.

Body: blue or blue with black markings.

Red speckled: head heavily marked with red.

Body: red speckled, medium size red spots on body not an objection.

Feet: round strong deep in pads with close knit well arched toes, strong toe nails.

Toe nails: white a serious fault.

Dew claws: on hind legs penalised.

Height: dogs 18-20 inches, bitches 17-19 inches.

Make sure reds have dark pigmentation, dark nose, lips, or otherwise if pink will have a soft mouth. Must be black on roof.

[Note added by Collis.] The 1934 standard states a definite colour for the Stumpy Tail Cattle Dog. This colour preference was disregarded and Blue/Black & Tans were exhibited, registered and bred from.

STUMPY-TAIL CATTLE DOG
Australian National Kennel Council, 1 January, 1963

General Appearance: Shall be that of a well proportioned working dog, rather square in profile with a hard-bitten, rugged appearance, and sufficient substance to convey the impression of the ability to endure long periods of arduous work under whatsoever conditions may prevail.

Characteristics: The Stumpy possesses a natural aptitude in the working and control of cattle, and a loyal, courageous and devoted disposition. It is ever alert, watchful and obedient, though suspicious of strangers. At all times it must be amenable to handling in the Show ring.

Head: The skull is broad between the ears and flat, narrowing slightly to the eyes with a slight but definite stop. Cheeks are muscular without coarseness. The foreface is of moderate length, well filled up under the eye, the deep powerful jaws tapering to a blunt strong muzzle. Nose black, irrespective of the colour of the dog.

Teeth: The teeth are strong, sound and regularly spaced. The lower incisors close behind and just touching the upper. Not to be undershot or overshot.

Eyes: The eyes should be oval in shape, of moderate size, neither full nor prominent, with alert and intelligent yet suspicious expression, and of dark brown colour.

Ears: The ears are moderately small, pricked and almost pointed. Set on high yet well apart. Leather moderately thick. Inside the ear should be well furnished with hair.

Neck: The neck is of exceptional strength, sinewous, muscular and of medium length, broadening to blend into the body, free from throatiness.

Forequarters: The shoulders are clean, muscular and sloping with elbows parallel to the body. The forelegs are well boned and muscular. Viewed from any angle they are perfectly straight.

Hindquarters: The hindquarters are broad, powerful and muscular, with well developed thighs, stifles moderately turned. Hocks are strong, moderately let down with sufficient bend. When viewed from behind the hind legs from hock to feet are straight, and placed neither close nor too wide apart.

Feet: The feet should be round, strong, deep in pads with well arched toes, closely knit. Nails strong, short and of dark colour.

Body: The length of the body from the point of the breast-bone to the buttocks should be equal to the height of the withers. The back is level, broad and strong with deep and muscular loins, the well sprung ribs tapering, to a deep moderately broad chest.

Tail: The tail is undocked, of a natural length not exceeding four inches, set on high but not carried much above the level of the back.

Coat: The outer coat is moderately short, straight, dense and of medium harsh texture. The undercoat is short, dense, and soft. The coat around the neck is longer, forming a mild ruff. The hair on the head, legs and feet, is short.

Colour (Blue): The dog should be blue or blue mottled, whole coloured. The head may have black markings with or without tan. Black markings on the body are permissible. The forelegs may have tan midway up the legs and running up the front of the throat. The hindquarters, tan on the inside of the hind legs and inside the thighs, showing down the front of the stifles and broadening out to the outside of the hind legs from hock to toe. Tan, the richer the better.

Colour (Red Speckle): The colour should be a good even red speckle all over, including the undercoat (not white or cream), with or without darker red markings on the head. Red patches on the body are permissible.

Size: The height at the withers should be within the following measurements: Dogs 45.7-50.8 cm (18-20 inches). Bitches 43.1-48.2 cm (17-19 inches). Dogs or bitches over or under these specified sizes are undesirable.

Movement: Soundness is of paramount importance. The action is true, free, supple and tireless, the movement of the shoulders and forelegs in unison with the powerful thrust of the hindquarters. Capability of quick and sudden movement is essential. Stiltiness, cow or bow hocks, loaded or slack shoulders or straight shoulder placement, weakness at elbows, pasterns or feet, must be regarded as serious faults.

[The present standard, 2009, explicitly condemns tan.]

Colour: Blue: The colour should be a good even Blue Mottle or Blue Speckle, with or without black marking on the head and body. Blues should not have a red undercoat or any appearance of red throughout the coat or head. Red: The colour should be a good even Red Mottle or Red Speckle, with or without red markings on head and body. Reds should not have a blue undercoat or any appearance of blue throughout the coat or head.

Tan: Irrespective of the colour of the dog, tan markings are not permissible in either the Blue or Red dogs, under any circumstances.

Faults: Cream or white undercoat. Any colour other than black on nose or toenails.

Serious Faults: Tan markings. Tan/red overlay on head and/or body in blue dogs. Blue muzzle and/or blue overlay on head and/or body in red dogs.

APPENDIX 3

Excerpts from Collis (1999)

Collis, J. H. (pseud. of Laurel Atwell) 1999.
Australia's First Working Dog. Yepoon. FASB Trading.

It is generally agreed that The Stumpy Tail Cattle Dog descended from an original cross of an Australian Dingo and a British Smithfield (Timmins Biters). These red bobtail progeny were then crossed with a smooth coated, blue merle Collie, resulting in the dog we know today as the Stumpy Tail Cattle Dog (Hall's Heelers). The Australian Dingo is Australia's first dog breed. His genes and working ability have been borrowed to develop The Stumpy Tail Cattle Dog.

The most popular working dog used by drovers and cattle owners of early Australia was the Smithfield or 'Drovers dog'. It was a big, rough coated, square-bodied dog, with a flat, wedge shaped head, saddle flap ears and a natural bobtail. It had a white "collar" or frill around the neck. It was called a "Black Bob-tail" and was similar in appearance to an Old English Sheepdog. It was faithful, hardy, and sensible, but like all bob-tailed dogs, was heavy, slow on its feet, a great barker and a severe biter. Bobtail is the key word when it comes to Smithfield and the Stumpy Tail Cattle dog. Both are born without a tail or just a gesture of one. The genetic inheritance of the bobtail allows us to trace the history of this breed through the centuries. Around the 10th Century, the English Crown levied a tax on dogs. The Crown realized that the herdsman and shepherds could not pay this tax, nor could they live without the help of a dog for certain tasks. An exemption from this tax was provided if the tail was a natural bob or docked. The term Cur was used for this natural or docked bobtail working dog. (Curtailing)

The History of the Smithfield in Australia began with the importation from England of animals to form the government herd in New South

Wales. By 1803, the government cattle herd numbered 1,530. In 1804 a consignment of 200 arrived in Hobart and early in 1805, 600 cows were sent to Port Dalrymple in Tasmania. The most popular working dog for these herds in Coastal New South Wales and Tasmania was the Smithfield. As the colony opened up, following the crossing of the Blue Mountains and the development of new grazing lands, the herds increased. In 1820 the cattle numbers had increased to 54,103. The need for a more active dog with less voice became pressing. In about 1830 a Hawkesbury River drover named Timmins conceived the idea of crossing his Smithfield working dogs with the Dingo. From this originated the red bobtail known as "Timmins Biters/Heelers", or "Timmins Red Bob-tails". Dogs of this cross were a great improvement on the Smithfield. They were very active, silent and good severe biters. They had one bad fault - if they got out of the drover's sight they would chew a calf or beast nearly to pieces. The Dingo instinct coming uppermost when out of control.

The next step in the development of the Stumpy Tail Cattle Dog was an effort to breed out the vicious bite of the red bobtail (Timmins Biters/Heelers). This was achieved by mating the red bobtail with a smooth haired, blue merle Collie. In 1840 a squatter named Thomas Hall imported a pair of blue, smooth haired Collies from Scotland. These were called "Merles" because of the dark and light blue being mixed in patches on them. This union of the red bobtail (Timmins Biters/Heelers) and the smooth haired, blue merle Collie produced the "Hall's Heeler". These two main instigators of this breed, John Timmins and Thomas Hall, saw no need to infuse any other breed into the Hall's Heeler. John Timmins continued his working life as a contract drover regularly driving herds from the Hunter Valley to the markets in Sydney using a string of excellent Hall's Heelers. Photos from the Allen Family, who lived and worked at Blairemore, a Hall property near Aberdeen, New South Wales, include shots of a Hall's Heeler. These photos show clearly the dog to be "bobtailed". This is clear indication that the Hall's Heeler is the Stumpy Tail Cattle Dog we know today.

Robert Kaleski, judge, and exhibitor of dogs and a renowned breeder of long tail Australian Cattle Dogs, started his breed development from the pure Hall line of dog. Kaleski makes clear indication of this in his writings. His breed development is the only known recorded breed development of the long tail Australian Cattle Dog. Photos in his book, Australian Barkers & Biters, show *Thornhill Tiger*, one of his own breed line, to be stumpy tailed.

[Far from being tailless *Thornhill Tiger* appears to have had his tail amputated by scissors when his image was cut out from its original photographic background.]

ABBREVIATIONS

AACo:	Australian Agricultural Company
ADB:	Australian Dictionary of Biography
ACDS of NSW:	Australian Cattle Dog Society of NSW
ANKC:	Australian National Kennel Council
CCCQ:	Canine Control Council, Qld
CSIRO:	Commonwealth Scientific and Industrial Research Organisation
FCI:	Fédération Cynologique Internationale
HRA:	Historical Records of Australia
HRN:	Historical Records of New South Wales
n.d.:	no date
NLA:	National Library of Australia
NSW:	New South Wales
NY:	New York
pseud.:	pseudonym
Qld:	Queensland
RAS:	Royal Agricultural Society of NSW
Sydney Gazette:	*The Sydney Gazette and New South Wales Advertiser*
VDL:	Van Diemen's Land (Tasmania)

REFERENCES

Arndell, R. M. 1984. *Pioneers of Portland Head: builders of Ebenezer Church and School, early settlers of the Hawkesbury and Hunter rivers and squatters of the north-west New South Wales and southern Queensland, including family genealogies.* 2nd ed. Epping, N.S.W., R. S. Arndell.

Banks, Sir Joseph. [n.d.]. *The Endeavour Journal of Sir Joseph Banks.* [Journal from 25 August 1768-12 July 1771]. Project Gutenberg Australia 0501141h.html. Downloaded 24/07/2019.

Barrat, C. and Latchford, L. A. c.1934. *The Sun Dog Book. The Sun,* Melbourne.

Baxter, C. J. 1989. Musters of New South Wales and Norfolk Island 1805-1806. ABGR, Sydney.

Sir Bedivere. 1903. The Australian Cattle Dog. *The Town and Country Journal* 9 September 1903.

Bewick, T. 1790. *A General History of the Quadrupeds.* (First edition 1790). Windward Reprint, 1980.

Beilby, W. 1897. *The Dog in Australasia.* George Robertson, Melbourne.

Clark, N. R. 2003. *A Dog Called Blue: the Australian Cattle Dog and the Australian Stumpy Tail Cattle Dog 1840-2000.* WriteLight, Blackheath, N. S. W.

Collins, D. 1798. *An Account of the English Colony of New South Wales,* v.1. London: Printed for T. Cadell Jun. and W. Davies, in the Strand. Project Gutenberg Australia. gutenberg. net.au/ebooks/e00010.html.

Cook, J. 1893. *Captain Cook's Journal During His First Voyage Round the World Made in H.M. Bark "Endeavour" 1768-71.* Elliot Stock, 62 Paternoster Row. Project Gutenberg Australia. gutenberg.net.au/ebooks/e00043.html#ch8. Downloaded 22/07/2019.

Dampier, William. 1729. A voyage to Terra Australia *in A voyage to New Holland etc.* by Captain William Dampier. Third edition.1729. Project Gutenberg Australia. gutenberg.net.au/ebooks/e00046.html. Downloaded 18/06/2019.

Dalziel, H. 1879? *British Dogs: their varieties, history, characteristics, breeding, management, and exhibition. The Bazaar* Office. London. archive.org/details/britishdogstheir00dalzrich/ Downloaded 18/09/2019.

Edwards, C. A. 1995. *Australian Cattle Dogs: Old Timers.* YFP Publications.

Edwards, S. T. 1800. *Cynographia Britannica: consisting of coloured engravings of the various breeds of dogs existing in Great Britain.* London, 1800. books.google.com.au/books? Read online 8/08/2019.

Flynn, M. 1993. *The Second Fleet: Britain's grim convict armada of 1790.* Library of Australian History, Sydney.

Frost, A. 2012. *The First Fleet: the real story.* Black Inc., Collingwood, Vic.

Grant, K. & Finlayson, A. A. 1977. *The roads around Sydney: past present and future.* University of New South Wales.

Hancock, D. 2014. *Dogs of the Shepherds: a review of pastoral breeds.* Crowood Press, Ramsbury, Marlborough, Wilts.

Hubbard, C. L. B. 1949. *An Introduction to the Literature of British Dogs.* Published by the author at Ponterwyd, Wales.

Hunter, J. 1793. *An Historical Journal of the Transactions at Port Jackson and Norfolk Island.* With the Discoveries which have been made in New South Wales and in the Southern Ocean, since the publication of Phillip's Voyage, compiled from the Official Papers; Including the Journals of Governor Phillip and King, and of Lieut. Ball; and the Voyages of the first Sailing of the Sirius in 1787, to the Return of that Ship's Company to England in 1792. A digital text sponsored by University of Sydney Library, Sydney, 2003. Prepared from the print edition published by John Stockdale. London. purl.library.usyd.edu.au/setis/id/huntran. Downloaded 19/07/2019.

JaneDogs. Australia's 150 years of DogRegistration. https://janedogs.com/australias- 150-years-of-dog-registration/

JaneDogs. Australian Cattle and Australian Stumpy Tail Cattle Dog. https://janedogs.com/australian-cattle-and-australian-stumpy-tail-cattle-dog/

Kaleski, R. L. 1903. Cattle Dogs. *Agricultural Gazette of New South Wales.* August 1903.

Kaleski, R. L. 1910. Cattle Dogs and Sheep Dogs. *Farmers Bulletin* 38. New South Wales Department of Agriculture.

Kaleski. R. L. 1911. The Working Dogs of Australia, p. 201-209 *in RAS Annual* 1911.

Kaleski, R. L. 1933. *Australian Barkers and Biters*, new ed. Endeavour Press, Sydney.

Kaleski, R. L. 1947? *Dogs of the World: showing the origin of the canine and feline species from the Australian marsupial lion about three million years ago, the most notable dogs springing from it, and illustrations therewith.* William Brooks, Sydney.

Little, C. C. 1957. *The Inheritance of Coat Colour in Dogs.* Howell, NY.

Macintyre, S. 2004. *A Concise History of Australia.* 2nd ed. Cambridge University Press, Cambridge.

Parsonson, I. M. 1998. *The Australian Ark: a history of domesticated animals in Australia.* CSIRO Publishing, Collingwood, Vic.

Perry, T. M. 1957. *The spread of settlement in the original nineteen counties of New South Wales 1788-1829: an historical geography*. PhD thesis, Australian National Uiversity.

Roberts, I., Carlton, R. & Rushworth, A. 2010. *Drove Roads of Northumberland*. The History Press, Stroud, Glos., 2010.

Robinson, R. 1990. *Genetics for Dog Breeders*. 2nd ed. Pergamon Press, Oxford,

Royal Agricultural Society of New South Wales and Royal National Agricultural and Industrial Association of Queensland show catalogues.

Shaw, V. 1881. *The Illustrated Book of the Dog*. Cassell, Petter, Galpin, London. archive.org/details/illustratedbooko00shawrich. Downloaded 1/08/2019.

Spira, H. R. (ed.) 1988. *An Historical record of Australian Kennel Controls*. ANKC, Melbourne.

Stonehenge (pseud. of J. H. Walsh). 1882. *The Dogs of the British Islands*, being a series of articles on the points of their various breeds, and the treatment of the diseases to which they are subject. 4 th ed. Horace Cox, London. Archive.org/details/dogsofbritishisl00walsrich/

Taplin, W. 1804. *The Sportsman's Cabinet*, or A correct delineation of the various dogs used in the sports of the field: including the canine race in general. London, 1804. archive.org/details/sportsmanscabine02inlond. Downloaded 01/08/2019.

Tench, W. 1793. *Complete Account of the Settlement at Port Jackson* Including An Accurate Description of the Situation of the Colony; of the Natives; and Of Its Natural Productions, Prepared from the print edition published by G. Nicol and J. Sewell. London 1793. University of Sydney Library, Sydney, 1998. setis.library.usyd.edu.au/ozlit. Downloaded 18/07/2019.

Warner, R. M. (ed.). 1990. *Over-Halling the Colony*: George Hall, Pioneer. Australian Documents Library, Sydney.

Warner, R. M. (ed.) 1995. *The Colony Over-Halled*: a family tree of the descendants of pioneers George and Mary Smith Hall, 1995. Australian Documents Library, Sydney.

White, John n.d. *Journal of a Voyage to New South Wales*. Web edition published by eBooks@Adelaide. Downloaded 25/04/2019. ebooks. adelaide.edu.au/w/white/john/journal/

Willis, M. B. 1989. *Genetics of the Dog*. Gollancz Witherby, London.

ENDNOTES

Preface

1. Australian Cattle Dog Society of NSW 1978. *Notes from the breed seminar*. ACDS of NSW, Sydney.
2. Sanderson, A. 1981. *The Complete Book of Australian Dogs*. 1981. Frenchs Forest, Currawong Press.

Introduction

1. Hancock, D. 2014. *Dogs of the Shepherds*, p. 67.
2. Dalziel, H. 1888. *British Dogs*, *in* Hancock, D. 2014. *Dogs of the Shepherds*, p. 25.
3. Pickard, J. 1999 The first fences: fencing the colony of New South Wales 1788-1823. *Agricultural History* 73(1) Winter, 1999).
4. Frost, A. 2012. *The First Fleet*, p. 29.
5. Collins, D. 1798. *An Account of the English Colony of New South Wales*, v.1.
6. First Fleet Fellowship, Vic. Inc.'The Eleven Ships'. firstfleetfellowship. org.au/ships/eleven-ships/. Read online 12/08/2019.
7. Parsonson, I. M. 1998. *The Australian Ark*, p. 5.
8. Parsonson, I. M. 1998. *The Australian Ark*, p. 93.
9. Free Settler or Felon? 'Third Fleet Convicts 1791'. https://www.jenwilletts.com/5_november_1791.htm. Read online 23/08/2019.
10. Warner, R. M. (ed.). 1990. *Over-Halling the Colony*, p. 27.
11. Howard, A. J. 1990. The *Coromandel*, pp. 35-66 *in* Warner, R.M. (ed.) 1990. *Over-Halling the Colony*.
12. Bowd, D. G. 1990. Settling in. Warner, R. M. (ed.) 1990. *Over-Halling the Colony* p. 368.
13. Kennel News. *Sydney Mail* 15 May 1897.
14. Sir Bedivere. The Australian Cattle Dog. *The Town and Country Journal* 9 September 1903 pp. 34-35.
15. Kaleski, R. L. 1903. Cattle Dogs. *Agricultural Gazette of New South Wales*. August 1903, pp. 34-35.
16. *Sydney Mail*. 26 April 1933, p. 38.

1. The Australian dingo

1. Dorey, F (2021). Origins of the First Australians. https://australian.museum/learn/science/human-evolution/the-spread-of-people-to-austr alia/ Read online 23 May 2021.

2. Cairns, K. M. & Wilton, A. N. 2016. New insights on the history of canids in Oceania based on mitochondrial and nuclear data. *Genetica*. Published online 17 September 2016.

3. Dayton, L. 2016. How did the dingo get to Australia? sciencemag.org/news/2016/04/how-did-dingo-get-australia. Downloaded 19/07/2019.

4. Fillios, M. and Taçon, P. 2016. Who let the dogs in? A review of the recent genetic evidence for the introduction of the dingo to Australia and implications for the movement of people. *Journal of Archaeological Science: Reports*. 10.1016/j.jasrep.2016.03.001.

5. Fillios, M. *et al*. 2012.The impact of the dingo on the thylacine in Holocene Australia. *World Archaeology*, 44:1, 118-134.

6. Dampier, William. 1729. *A Voyage to Terra Australia*.

7. Cook, J. 1893. *Captain Cook's Journal During His First Voyage Round the World*.

8. Banks, Sir Joseph. [n.d.]. *The Endeavour Journal*, p. 118.

9. Banks, Sir Joseph. [n.d.]. *The Endeavour Journal*, p. 126.

10. The midshipman may have been thinking of a Carolina dog.

11. Banks, Sir Joseph. [n.d.]. *The Endeavour Journal*, p. 126.

12. White, J. [n.d.]. *Journal of a Voyage to New South Wales*.

13. Balme, J. and O'Connor, S. 2016. Dingoes and Aboriginal social organization in Holocene Australia. *Journal of Archaeological Science: Reports* 7 (2016) p. 778.

14. Koungoulos, L. & Fillios, M. 2020. Hunting dogs down under? On the aboriginal use of tame dingoes in dietary game acquisition and its relevance to Australian prehistory. *Journal of Anthropological Archaeology* 58 (2020) 101146. Downloaded 15/04/2020.

15. Hunter, J. 1793. *An Historical Journal of the Transactions at Port Jackson and Norfolk Island*, pp. 63-64.

2. New South Wales colonial dogs

1. *Sydney Gazette*. Sunday 15 February 1807 p. 1. NLA: Trove, downloaded 18/07/2019.

2. *Sydney Gazette*. Saturday 15 August 1812 p. 1. NLA: Trove, downloaded 8/07/2019.

3. "HMS Sirius" 1788 (Navy Escort) First Fleet (England to NSW, Australia.) geni.com/projects/HMS-Sirius-1788-Navy-Escort-First-Fleet-England-to-NSW-Australia/45977. Downloaded 21/09/2019.

4. Early European settlement 1788-1810. https://www.parliament.nsw.gov.au/about/Pages/1788-to-1810-Early-European-Settlement.aspx

5. Tench, W. 1793. *A Complete Account of the Settlement at Port Jackson*, p. 116.

6. *Sydney Gazette*. Sunday 21 July 1805 p. 2. NLA: Trove, downloaded 8/07/2019.

7. Hancock, D. 2014. *Dogs of the Shepherds*, p. 103.

8. Bewick, T. 1790. *A General History of the Quadrupeds*, p. 325.

9. Bewick, T. 1790. *A General History of the Quadrupeds*, p. iv.

10. Bewick, T. 1790. *A General History of the Quadrupeds*, pp. 327-328.

11. Bewick, T. 1790. *A General History of the Quadrupeds*, p. 329.

12. coally: probably a reference to colour. Compact edition. Oxford English Dictionary, Clarendon Press, 1971.

13. Sinmez, C. C. *et al.* 2017. Tail docking and ear cropping in dogs: a short review of laws and welfare aspects in Europe and Turkey. *Italian Journal of Animal Science.* 16(3). Read online 1/07/2020.

14. Bewick, T. 1790. *A General History of the Quadrupeds*, p. 330.

15. Edwards, S.T. 1800. *Cynographia Britannica.*

16. Taplin, W. 1804. *The Sportsman's Cabinet*, pp. 123-124.

17. Beilby, W. 1897. *The Dog in Australasia*, p. 290.

18. Beilby, W. 1897. *The Dog in Australasia*, p. 303-306.

19. Beilby, W. 1897. *The Dog in Australasia*, p. 430.

3. The Tasmanian Smithfield

1. Beilby, W. 1897. *The Dog in Australasia*, pp. 304-309.

2. Hancock, D. 2014. *Dogs of the Shepherds*, p. 128.

3. Hancock, D. 2014. *Dogs of the Shepherds*, p. 128.

4. Edwards, C. A. 1995. *Australian Cattle Dogs*, p. 180.

5. Kaleski, R. L. 1907. The Australian Cattle Dog. *The Bookfellow* 1(1): 10-11.

6. *Sydney Gazette*. Sunday 3 November 1805 p. 2. NLA: Trove. Downloaded 8/07/2019.

4. Robert Lucian Stanislaus Kaleski (1877-1961)

1. assayer (metallurgy): one who analyses an ore, alloy, etc., in order to determine the quantity of gold, silver, or other metal in it.

2. Peter Kaleski was a grand nephew of John Kaleski. Peter's father used to tell of holidays spent on "Uncle Bob's farm" near Liverpool. "They enjoyed their holidays with Uncle Bob," Peter remembered, "but didn't care much for Uncle Bob's dogs".

3. Kaleski, R. L. 1933. *Australian Barkers and Biters*, new ed, p. 9.

4. *Sydney Mail*. Wednesday 16 March 1921 p. 26. NLA: Trove. Read online 5/07/2019.

5. *Sydney Mail*. 29 November 1922 p. 30.

6. Parsons, A. D. 1992. *The Australian Kelpie*. Viking O'Neill/Penguin Books, Ringwood, Vic.

5. Kaleksi's "burrowing"

1. Stonehenge (pseud. of J.H. Walsh). 1882. *The Dogs of the British Islands*, pp. 195-197.
2. Dalziel, H. 1879? *British Dogs*, p. 207.
3. Shaw, V. 1881. *The Illustrated Book of the Dog*, p. 77.

6. George Hall (1764-1840)

4. Hall, K. 1990. The Hall Clan, p. 21 *in* Warner, R. M. (ed.). 1990. *Over-Halling the Colony.*
5. Warner, R. M. (ed.). 1990. *Over-Halling the Colony*, p. 27.
6. Hall, K. 1990. The Hall Clan, p. 34 *in* Warner, R. M. (ed.). 1990. *Over-Halling the Colony.* The following embarked on the *Coromandel* with George and Mary Hall and their four children: James and Jane Davison and their two sons, John and Frances Howe and their two daughters, Andrew and Mary Johnston and their five sons, John Johnston (unmarried), James and Susannah Mein, Andrew Mein (unmarried), William and Sarah Stubbs and three children, John and Ann Turnbull and four children.
7. Howard, A. J. 1990. The *Coromandel*. Warner, R. M. (ed.). 1990. *Over-Halling the Colony*, pp. 65-66.
8. McClymont, J. and Kass, T. 'Old Toongabbie and Toongabbie'. Dictionary of Sydney, 2010. dictionaryofsydney.org/entry/old_ toongabbie_and_toongabbie. Downloaded 29/07/2019.
9. Bowd, D. G. 1990. Settling in. Warner, R. M. (ed.). 1990. *Over-Halling the Colony*, p. 67.

7. The Hall Empire c.1810-c.1840

1. *Sydney Gazette*. Saturday 11 April 1812 p. 1. NLA: Trove. Downloaded 18/07/2019.
2. HRN vol. 7 (1809, 1810, 1811) p. 566. NLA: Trove. Read online 30/08/2019.
3. Macquarie to Liverpool 18/10/1811. HRN vol. 7 (1809,1810, 1811) p. 602. NLA: Trove. Read online 30/08/2019.
4. *Sydney Gazette*. 26 September 1812 p. 1. NLA: Trove. Downloaded 18/07/2019.
5. Howes Track was known as the Bulga Road. During the 1890s the name Putty Road came into use.
6. *The Australian*. Thursday 23 December 1824 p. 2. NLA: Trove. Downloaded 18/07/2019.
7. Archives Office of New South Wales. Colonial Secretary re Land. Reel1079. p. 199 *in* Brenan, R. 1990. They Hitched their Wagon to a Star. Warner, R. M. (ed.) 1990. *Over-Halling the Colony.*

8. Brenan, R. 1990. They Hitched their Wagon to a Star. Warner, R. M. (ed.) 1990. *Over-Halling the Colony*, p. 138.

9. Scott, J. 1990. The Hall Estate or "Firm", Warner, R. M. (ed.) 1990. *Over-Halling the Colony*, p. 83.

10. Kaleski, R. L. 1907. The Australian Cattle Dog. *The Bookfellow* 1(1): 10-11.

11. Kaleski, R. L. 1903. Cattle Dogs. *Agricultural Gazette of New South Wales*. August 1903, pp. 34-35.

12. Kaleski, R. L. 1910. Cattle dogs and sheep dogs. New South Wales Department of Agriculture. *Farmers Bulletin* 38.

13. Kaleski, R. L. 1907. The Australian Cattle-dog. *The Bookfellow* 1(1):10-11.

14. Bowd, D. G. 1990. Settling in. Warner, R. M. (ed.) 1990. *Over-Halling the Colony*, p.69.

15. Scott, J. 1990. The Hall Estate or "Firm". Warner, R. M. (ed.) 1990. *Over-Halling the Colony*, p. 97.

16. Australian Agricultural Company First Annual Report 26 May 1824. Parsonson, I. *The Australian Ark*, pp. 55-56.

17. Parsonson, I. *The Australian Ark*, p. 56.

18. The Beef Shorthorn Society of Australia. beefshorthorn.org.au/origins/. Read online 1/09/2019.

19. Scott, J. C. 1990. The Hall Estate or "Firm". Warner, R. M. (ed.) 1990. *Over-Halling the Colony*, p. 91.

20. RDP 2001-07: A History of Last-Resort Lending and Other Support for Troubled Financial Institutions in Australia 4. The 1840s Depression Bryan Fitz-Gibbon and Marianne Gizycki. October 2001. rba.gov.au/publications/rdp/2001/2001-07/1840s-depression.html. Downloaded 8/02/2019.

21. Eureka! The rush for gold. sl.nsw.gov.au/stories/eureka-rush-gold. Read online 5/10/2019.

8. The Halls and the Halls Heeler after 1840

1. run: In Australia, the term "run" refers to any large area of grazing land. The term "station" refers to grazing property. The distinction is one of land title but the two terms are commonly used interchangeably. A "farm" is smaller.

2. Scott, J. C. 1990. The Hall Estate or "Firm". Warner, R. M. (ed.). 1990. *Over-Halling the Colony*, pp. 94-96.

3. selection: "free selection before survey" of crown land in some Australian colonies under land legislation introduced in the 1860s. The Acts concerned were intended to encourage closer settlement and allow those with limited means to acquire land.

4. Yarco 1931. Dogleg Fences. *The Queenslander*, Thursday 15 January 1931, p. 15. NLA: Trove. Downloaded 12/02/2021. Though hardly ever seen nowadays, the old "dogleg" fences are still a good proposition for small jobs where saplings are plentiful and wire is scarce. Short forks are set in the ground at the required height, the bottom rails are placed in these, and then a pair of strong stakes are sunk six inches in the ground, one on either side of each fork, and leaned across the bottom rail, thus forming another fork to hold the top rail. If these are cut double length, it adds greatly to the strength of the fence, when heavy timber is used, and three rails are put up, the result is a yard that will give satisfactory use for years, as well as being far the quickest to build.

5. *The Sydney Morning Herald*. Saturday 29 March 1873 p. 5. NLA: Trove. Downloaded 4/05/2019.

6. Kaleski, R. L. 1911. The Working Dogs of Australia. *RAS Annual* 1911, pp. 201-209.

7. Kaleski, R. L. 1907. The Australian Cattle Dog. *The Bookfellow* 1(1): 10-11.

8. Kaleski, R. L. 1903. Cattle Dogs. *Agricultural Gazette of N.S.W.* August 1903, p. 756.

9. Kaleski, R. L. 1910. Cattle Dogs and Sheep Dogs. *Farmers Bulletin* 38. New South Wales Department of Agriculture, 1910.

10. Australia Post. History. en.wikipedia.org/wiki/Australia_Post#History. Read online 15/09/2519.

11. New South Wales Government Archives. Shipping records 1820-1840. Searched 1998.

12. Hancock, D. 2014. *Dogs of the Shepherds*, pp. 26.

13. Hancock, D. 2014. *Dogs of the Shepherds*, pp. 101-102.

14. As late as the 1990s some ACDs were registered as merle coloured and some breeders referred to dogs with no black head markings as merle.

15. Kaleski, R. L. 1903. Cattle Dogs. *Agricultural Gazette of N.S.W.* August 1903, p. 756.

16. Kaleski, R. L.1910. Cattle Dogs and Sheep Dogs. *Farmers Bulletin* 38. New South Wales Department of Agriculture, 1910.

17. Kaleski. R. L. 1911. The Working Dogs of Australia. *RAS Annual* 1911, p. 201-209.

18. Kaleski, R. L. 1930. Whence came Australian dogs? *American Kennel Gazette*, 1 September 1930 p. 26-28.

19. *The Town and Country Journal* would have appeared close to its stated date of issue. Government publications commonly appeared later than their imprint date.

20. Sir Bedivere. 1903. The Australian Cattle Dog, p. 34. *The Town and Country Journal*. 9 September 1903.

21. Illustration missing from the copy of *The Sportsman's Cabinet* referred to in Endnote above .

22. Sir Bedivere. 1903.The Australian Cattle Dog, p. 34. *The Town and Country Journal*. 9 September 1903.

23. Rose, J. 1908. The Australian Cattle Dog. *RAS Annual 1908*, pp. 233-237.

24. Atoa, 1930. Australia's Cattle Dog. *Our Dogs of Australia*, 21 November 1930, p. 14.

25. Barratt, R. E. 1941. Australian Blue Cattle Dogs are without a peer. *American Kennel Gazette* January 1941.

26. Barratt, R. E.1941. Australian Blue Cattle Dogs are without a peer. *American Kennel Gazette* January 1941.

27. Kaleski, R. L. 1903. Cattle Dogs. *Agricultural Gazette of N.S.W.* August 1903, p. 756.

28. Kaleski, R. L.1910. Cattle Dogs and Sheep Dogs. *Farmers Bulletin* 38. New South Wales Department of Agriculture, 1910.

29. Edwards, C. A. 1995. *Australian Cattle Dogs: old timers*, pp. 48-55. YFP Publications.

30. Hancock, D. 2014. *Dogs of the Shepherds*, pp. 125-126.

11. Kaleski on Cattle Dogs

1. Kaleski, R. L. 1903. Cattle Dogs. *Agricultural Gazette of New South Wales*. August 1903, p. 34-35.

2. Kaleski, R. L. 1910. Cattle dogs and sheep dogs. New South Wales Department of Agriculture. *Farmers Bulletin* 38, p. 6.

3. Beilby, Walter 1897. *The Dog in Australasia*, pp. 304-307. George Robertson, Melbourne.

4. Kaleski, R. L. 1911. The Working Dogs of Australia. *RAS Annual 1911* p. 201-209.

5. Kaleski, R. L. 1907. The Australian Cattle Dog. *The Bookfellow* 1(1): 10-11.

6. Edwards, C. A. 1995. *Australian Cattle Dogs: old timers*, pp. 10-13. YFP Publications.

7. Perry, T. M. 1957. The spread of settlement in the original nineteen counties of New South Wales 1788-1829: an historical geography, p. 76.

8. Walters, B. J. 1974. Letter to Gary Somerville, obedience judge, dated 1 May 1974.

9. Alan F. Forbes, sometime Australian Cattle Dog Breeder (*Pacific kennels*, 1950s), All Breeds judge, and author of the "Interpretation of the Breed" for the ANKC's Judges Training Scheme, c. 1966,

10. Robinson, R. 1999. *Genetics for Dog Breeders*. 2nd ed., p. 133, 160-161. Butterworth-Heinemann, London.
11. Little, C. C. 1957. *The Inheritance of Coat Colour in Dogs*. Howell, New York.
12. Schaible, R. H. 1976. Linkage of a pigmentary trait with a high level of uric excretion in the Dalmatian dog. *Genetics* 68.
13. Schiable, R. H. 1981. A Dalmatian study. *American Kennel Club Gazette* 98(4):48-52.

12. Breed standards

1. *Sydney Mail*. 5 July 1922 p. 2.
2. *Sydney Mail*. 26 July 1922 p. 46.
3. *Sydney Mail*. 13 September 1922 p. 29.
4. *Sydney Mail*. 20 September 1922 p. 2.
5. *Sydney Mail*. 1 November 1922 p. 42.
6. *Sydney Mail*. 29 November 1922 p. 30.
7. Seymour, A. 1978. Apparent faults in the Australian Cattle Dog today, pp. 45-48. *Notes from the breed seminar*. ACDS of NSW, Sydney.
8. Crowley, W. D. 1986. Australian Cattle Dogs – do they deserve to win more BIS? *National Dog Magazine*, July 1986, p. 10.
9. Hewson-Fruend, H. J. 2003. Changes in Australian Cattle Dog Breed Standards. Clark, N. R. 2003. *A Dog Called Blue*, p. 117.

13. Dogs, Shows and Breeders to 1950

1. Clark, N. R. 2003. *A Dog Called Blue*, p. 32.
2. The Kennel. *Brisbane Courier*. 116 March 1918 p. 13.
3. Barrat, C. and Latchford, L.A. c.1934. *The Sun Dog Book*.
4. Kaleski, R. L. 1921. Cattle & Sheep Dogs at the Show. *Sydney Mail* 13 July 1921 p. 28.
5. Kaleski, R. L. 1922. Decline of Cattle and Sheep Dogs in Australia. *Sydney Mail* 5 July 1922 p. 2.
6. Dodd. E. E. 1934. Open letter to B. C. George. *Dog World of Australasia* 7(8)6, 15 October 1934.
7. George, C. B. 1934. [Reply to E. E. Dodd]. *Dog World of Australasia* 7(10)9. 15 December 1934.
8. Moore, D. 1936. [Sydney Royal Results, 1936]. *Dog World of Australasia* 9(25)5-6. 30 April 1936.
9. Moore, D. 1936. Points for the Sydney 'Royal' Selectors. *Dog World of Australasia* 9(3)4. 30 May 1936.

10. Stibbard, T. A. 1936. Open letter to C.D. Lawrence Esq., Cattle Dog and Kelpie Judge, RAS Show. *Dog World of Australasia* 9(4)10. 31 July 1936.

11. *Brisbane Courier Mail*. 8 September 1906, p. 15.

12. Court-Rice, C. 1911+. *The Dog Book for Australasia*. George G. Philip & Son, Sydney. Various editions 1911+

13. *Brisbane Courier Mail* 30 June 1923, p, 20.

14. Lawrence, C. D. & Blakeney, A. A. 1925. Standards of Sheep and Cattle Dogs. *Agricultural Gazette of NSW*, 1 October 1925, pp.745-746,

15. Edwards, C. A. 1995. *Australian Cattle Dogs: old timers*. YFP Publications.

16. Cattle Dog Standard. 1931. *Our Dogs of Australia*, p. 3, 22 December 1931,

17. Kennel Control Council (Vic.) 1950. *Standards of the Breeds*, adopted 18 July 1950. KCC, Melbourne.

18. Clark, N. R. 2003. *A Dog Called Blue*, pp. 72-81.

19. *Our Dogs and Feathers* 30 April 1925, p. 11.

20. *Queensland Kennel Club Yearbook*. Brisbane 1946.

21. Silent Chief for England. *Our Dogs of Australia*. 31 March 1930 p. 15.

22. *Dog World of Australasia*. 5(4)8 29 April 1933.

23. Standard Stock Dog Association. *Our Dogs of Australia* 30 April 1931 p. 20.

24. *The Sydney Stock and Station Journal* Tuesday 10 September 1918 p. 2.

25. From an Irish street ballad of the 1790s, "The wearing of the Green".

14. The Australian Cattle Dog since World War II

1. *Truth* Sunday 13 July 1947 p. 13. NLA: Trove. Downloaded 17/11/2019.

2. *Queensland Times* Wednesday 13 April 1949 p 2. Downloaded 17/11/2019.

3. Bevis, A. 196-. Letter relating to *Little Logic, Logic Return* and *Hillview Brighton Boy*, fig. 55 *in* Clark, N. R. 2003. *A Dog Called Blue*, p. 57.

4. McGorien, T. 1953. Dogs took best dog and bitch awards at Royal show. *The Land* 10 April 1953 p. 30.

5. Clark, N. R. 2003. *A Dog Called Blue*, pp. 36-40.

6. Forbes, A. F. c1966. The Australian Cattle Dog. Lecture no. 41. RASKC., Sydney.

7. Southall, B. 1992. What have we done to the Australian Cattle Dog? *Queensland Dog World* pp. 18-19, 24. August 1992.

8. Hewson-Fruend, H. J. 2003. Changes Australian Cattle Dog breed standards and type, *in* Clark, N. R. 2003. *A Dog Called Blue*, p. 117.

15. Betty Southall (1914-2008)

1.   stampede (American)

16. The Australian Stumpy Tail Cattle Dog

1.   The publications that document Margaret Davis's recollections are in the CCCQ library collection. The entire collection is in storage containers and is inaccessible. Ms Davis is an Internationally accredited All Breeds judge and a long term researcher into canine history.
2.   ANKC, 1988. Preserving the Stumpy-tail Cattle Dog. *KCC Kennel Gazette* December 1988, p. 3.
3.   Hewson-Fruend, H. J. 2003. Tail-length Inheritance in the Australian Stumpy Tail Cattle Dog, *in* Clark, N. R. 2003. *A Dog Called Blue*, pp. 145-147.
4.   Collis, J. H. 1999. *Australia's First Working Dog*. Yepoon, FASB Trading.
5.   Merchant, B. M. and Kennedy, L. c.2002. *Application to FCI for recognition of the Australian Stumpy Tail Cattle Dog*. [unpublished].
6.   Collis, J. H. 1999. *Australia's First Working Dog*. Yepoon, FASB Trading, p. 6.
7.   Clark, N. R. 2003. *A Dog Called Blue*, p. 29.
8.   Robinson, R. 1990. *Genetics for Dog Breeders*.
9.   Willis, M. B. 1989. *Genetics of the Dog*.
10. Hewson-Fruend, H. J. 2003. Tail-length Inheritance in the Australian Stumpy Tail Cattle Dog, *in* Clark, N. R. 2003. *A Dog Called Blue*, pp. 145-147.
11. Haworth, K. *et al.* 2001. Canine homolog of the T-box transcription factor T; failure of the protein to bind to its DNA target leads to a short-tail phenotype. *Mammalian Genome* 12:212-218.
12. Hytonen, M. *et al.* 2009. Ancestral T-Box mutation is present in many, but not all, short-tailed dog breeds. *Journal of Heredity* 100(2)236-240.
13. Indrebø, A, *et al.* 2007. A study of inherited short tail and taillessness in Pembroke Welsh Corgi. *Journal of Small Animal Practice*. doi: 10.1111/j.1748-5827.2007.00435.
14. Hytonen, M. *et al.* 2009. Ancestral T-Box mutation is present in many, but not all, short-tailed dog breeds. *Journal of Heredity* 100(2)236-240.
15. Hancock, D. 2014. *Dogs of the Shepherds*, p. 101.
16. Hancock, D. 2014. *Dogs of the Shepherds*, p. 100.

17. Gathering the threads

1. Holloway, G. 1978. The origin and history of the Australian Cattle Dog. *Notes from the breed seminar*. ACDS of NSW, pp. 6-10.
2. Sanderson, A. 1981. The Complete Book of Australian Dogs. 1981. Frenchs Forest, Currawong Press.
3. Australian National Kennel Council, 2009. Breed Standard Extension adopted by the Club and ANKC 1998. Produced by Australian Cattle Dog Club of NSW Inc. in collaboration with Australian National Kennel Council Breed Standard Extension. Reconfirmed with amendments 2009. Produced by Australian Cattle Dog Club of NSW Inc. in collaboration with Australian National Kennel Council.
4. Forbes, A. F. c1966. The Australian Cattle Dog. Lecture no. 41. RASKC., Sydney.
5. Kaleski, R. L. 1911. The Working Dogs of Australia. *RAS Annual* 1911 pp. 201-209.
6. Clark, N. R. 2003. *A Dog Called Blue*, pp. 36-40.
7. A Country Dog Judge. 1935. The pastoral dogs of Australia. *Sydney Mail* 12 June 1935, p. 41.
8. Anon. 1934. Dog Man and Agriculturist. *The World's News*. 1 Aug 1934 p. 5. NLA: Trove. Downloaded 24/08/2020.
9. Paterson, A. B. "Clancy, of 'The Overflow'".

INDEX